A LETTER TO THE WOMEN OF ENGLAND

and

THE NATURAL DAUGHTER

A LETTER TO THE WOMEN OF ENGLAND

and

THE NATURAL DAUGHTER

Mary Robinson

edited by Sharon M. Setzer

broadview literary texts

National Library of Canada Cataloguing in Publication

Robinson, Mary, 1758–1800
    Letter to the women of England on the injustice of mental subordination; and, The natural Daughter/Mary Robinson; edited by Sharon M. Setzer

(Broadview literary texts)
Originally published: London : Longmans, 1799.
Includes bibliographical references.
ISBN 1-55111-236-1

1. Robinson, Mary, 1758–1800. 2. Women's rights—Great Britain—History. 3. Women—Great Britain—Social conditions. 4. Sex discrimination against women—Great Britain—History.
I. Setzer, Sharon M. II. Title. III. Title: Natural Daughter. IV. Series.

HQ1236.5.G7R62 2002   828'.609   C2002-903731-X

Broadview Press Ltd. is an independent, international publishing house, incorporated in 1985. Broadview believes in shared ownership, both with its employees and with the general public; since the year 2000 Broadview shares have traded publicly on the Toronto Venture Exchange under the symbol BDP.

We welcome comments and suggestions regarding any aspect of our publications—please feel free to contact us at the addresses below or at broadview@broadviewpress.com.

North America
PO Box 1243, Peterborough, Ontario, Canada K9J 7H5
3576 California Road, Orchard Park, NY, USA 14127
Tel: (705) 743-8990; Fax: (705) 743-8353
email: customerservice@broadviewpress.com

UK, Ireland, and continental Europe
Thomas Lyster Ltd., Units 3 & 4a, Old Boundary Way
Burscough Road, Ormskirk
Lancashire, L39 2YW
Tel: (01695) 575112; Fax: (01695) 570120
email: books@tlyster.co.uk

Australia and New Zealand
UNIREPS, University of New South Wales
Sydney, NSW, 2052
Tel: 61 2 9664 0999; Fax: 61 2 9664 5420
email: info.press@unsw.edu.au
www.broadviewpress.com

Broadview Press Ltd. gratefully acknowledges the financial support of the Government of Canada through the Book Publishing Industry Development Program for our publishing activities.

This book is printed on acid-free paper containing 30% post-consumer fibre.

Series editor: Professor L.W. Conolly
Advisory editor for this volume: Colleen Franklin

PRINTED IN CANADA

Eco-Logo Certified
30 % Post.

Contents

Acknowledgments

This project never would have come to fruition without the support of my family and many colleagues at North Carolina State University. I am particularly indebted to the late Mike Reynolds, who first encouraged me to pursue my interest in Robinson and vetted my proposals for summer grants to work at the British Library. Barbara Baines, Tony Harrison, Leila May, Elaine Orr, Don Palmer, Maria Pramaggiore, Jon Thompson, and many others listened, read drafts, and offered useful suggestions and welcome bits of encouragement along the way. Gary Wilson and other members of the Interlibrary Loan Department of the D.H. Hill Library at NCSU responded to my numerous requests for books and microfilm with extraordinary courtesy and dispatch.

I also wish to acknowledge the contributions of many others beyond the community of NCSU. Donna Landry and Anne Mellor read drafts of my first publication on *The Natural Daughter* and offered many useful suggestions; Julie Shaffer shared her copy of *The Natural Daughter*; Alexander Gourlay called my attention to the headless woman in Hogarth's engraving *Noon*; Fiona Easton and Lt. Commander Andrew David of the Hakluyt Society answered my questions about the islands of Oreehoua and Tahoora; Lee Sorensen helped me to track down visual images; Elizabeth Dunn and other members of the staff of Duke University's Rare Book, Manuscripts, and Special Collections Library often went far beyond the call of duty in helping me to find elusive pieces of information.

In many places too numerous to cite separately, I am deeply indebted to Judith Pascoe. Her published work on Mary Robinson led me to *The Morning Post* and various other sources that I probably would not have discovered on my own. More importantly perhaps, her unfailing generosity in sharing unpublished findings, responding to e-mail inquiries, and reading drafts exemplified a spirit of scholarly collaboration that fostered new insights and relieved many lonely hours in my attic. With admiration and gratitude, I dedicate this edition to Judith.

George Dance, Portrait of Mary Robinson, 1793.
By permission of the Folger Shakespeare Library.

Introduction

Mary Robinson's *Letter to the Women of England, on the Injustice of Mental Subordination*, and her last novel, *The Natural Daughter*, were published separately in 1799, amid wide-spread controversy over the abilities, duties, and rights of women. While both works may be read as partial apologias for Robinson's own life, their spirited interrogation of oppressive gender laws reveals the mind of an author who was able to look beyond herself and to envisage a future in which women "speak and write their opinions freely" and "become citizens of the world." Robinson's particular emphasis on the achievements of women writers not only challenges degrading stereotypes of the so-called "weaker sex" but also foregrounds the historical significance of the pen as an instrument of female empowerment. Although many of Robinson's poems speak to the same issues, the voice of feminist protest is often buried beneath the more conventional voice of feminine complaint and the highly polished, decorative surface of her verse.

In her *Letter to the Women of England*, Robinson deliberately adopts "the strongest, but most undecorated language" to challenge the tyrannical laws of custom that render women the disempowered, "defenceless sex." As she champions their claims to "the participation of power, both mentally and corporeally," Robinson boldly advances the feminist agenda of Mary Wollstonecraft's *Vindication of the Rights of Woman* (1792). Explicitly identifying her *Letter* as an argument on the "same subject" by an author of the "same school," Robinson asserts that it would take "*a legion of Wollstonecrafts*" to combat the "prejudice and malevolence" perpetuating the subjugation of women. Robinson's bold declarations of equality and her persistent interrogation of the sexual double standard in *A Letter to the Women of England* help to clarify the ideological bases of her plot in *The Natural Daughter*. Indeed, one might almost call the novel a female revenge fantasy in which Robinson herself plots the death of tyrannical husbands and fathers and the vindication of a heroine who is wrongfully accused of bearing an illegitimate child.

Although affinities with Wollstonecraft constitute one of the strongest possible recommendations of Robinson's pamphlet and novel today, the atmosphere was very different in 1799. In the previous year, Wollstonecraft's husband, William Godwin, had unwittingly sabotaged her reputation by publishing *Memoirs of the Author of A Vindication of the Rights of Woman*.[1] Readers were scandalized to learn of Wollstonecraft's previous liaison with Gilbert Imlay, her suicide attempts, and her illegitimate daughter, Frances (Fanny) Imlay, born in France in 1794. With its disclosure of these and other details, the *Memoirs* provoked a storm of ridicule and condemnation, which quickly spread to Robinson and other women writers who had voiced sympathy for the initial goals of the French Revolution.[2] In the most scurrilous attacks, such as Richard Polwhele's satiric poem *The Unsex'd Females* (see Appendix C), the alliance of anti-feminist sentiment with anti-Jacobin politics served to popularize the damning association of women writers with prostitution and revolution.

Robinson's Life and Writing

On January 14, 1798, only days after the publication of Wollstonecraft's *Memoirs*, Robinson started the autobiographical narrative that became the centerpiece of her own posthumously published memoirs.[3] Claiming narrative authority over a life that was in many respects far more scandalous than Wollstonecraft's, Robinson represents herself as a gothic heroine victimized by the duplicity of others and the "progressive evils" of her own "too acute sensibility"

---

[1] Wollstonecraft died on September 10, 1797, ten days after giving birth to a daughter, Mary Wollstonecraft Godwin (later Shelley), who would write *Frankenstein* (1818) and other novels.

[2] Robinson's place on the anti-Jacobin hit list of 1798 had been secured by the revolutionary sentiments expressed in her novel *Walsingham; or, The Pupil of Nature* (1797). It appeared along with Wollstonecraft's *Memoirs* amid the deluge of stigmatized books and pamphlets in James Gillray's reactionary cartoon "New Morality," published in *The Anti-Jacobin Review and Magazine* 1 (1798).

[3] *The Memoirs of the Late Mrs. Robinson, Written by Herself. With Some Posthumous Pieces.* 4 vols. (London: R. Phillips, 1801). Hereafter cited in text as *Memoirs*. Although the narrative of Robinson's life was completed by someone else (probably her daughter, Maria Elizabeth), the title implicitly advertises the memoirs "Written by Herself" as a corrective to unauthorized memoirs, such as the anonymously published *Memoirs of Perdita* (London: G. Lister, 1784), a highly salacious account of Robinson's love affairs with the Prince of Wales and others.

(*Memoirs* 1: 12). Born in Bristol on November 27, 1756, Mary was, by her own account, something of an anomaly in the prosperous merchant family of Nicholas and Hetty Darby.[1] As the only surviving daughter in a household of three lively boys, Mary evinced the most "romantic" and "melancholy" tendencies even as a young child. She played "mournful melodies" on her harpsichord and took "great delight learning epitaphs and monumental inscriptions" (*Memoirs* 1: 14). By the age of seven, she was able to recite Pope's "Elegy to the Memory of an Unfortunate Lady." "Flattered and praised into a belief that [she] was a being of a superior order," Mary slept in a bed of the "richest crimson damask," wore clothes of the "finest cambric," and began to compose verses of her own (*Memoirs* 1: 22–23).

Like many other details in Robinson's *Memoirs*, those pertaining to her lineage and early life tend to obscure the boundaries between hard fact, psychologically revealing fantasy, and fictional convention. This is particularly true of the self-portrait emphasizing the difference between Mary and her three "uncommonly handsome" brothers. While they were all "fair and lusty," Mary was, by her own account, much less favored "in point of personal beauty." Her complexion was "swarthy," and her eyes "were singularly large in proportion to [her] face, which was small and round, exhibiting features peculiarly marked with the most pensive and melancholy cast" (*Memoirs* 1: 11). Read against portraits by Reynolds, Gainsborough, and other artists who captured her legendary beauty as an adult,[2] this verbal portrait of the artist as a young girl evokes the story of the ugly duckling who was, in fact, a swan. The underlying suggestions of a Freudian family romance gather force as Robinson's subsequent references to her godfather, Lord Northington, include tantalizing hints that she was his natural daughter.[3]

---

[1] The birth date given in Robinson's *Memoirs* (November 27, 1758) is exactly two years later than the date recorded in the Register of Baptisms at the church of St. Augustin the Less in Bristol. I am indebted to Alix Nathan for bringing this discrepancy to my attention.

[2] Many contempoary portraits are reproduced in John Ingamell's *Mrs. Robinson and Her Portraits* (London: Trustees of the Wallace Collection, 1978).

[3] Freud uses the term "family romance" to describe a wish-fulfillment fantasy: "the child's imagination becomes engaged in the task of getting free from the parents of whom he now has a low opinion and of replacing them by others, who, as a rule, are of higher social standing," "Family Romances," *The Standard Edition of the Complete Psychological Works of Sigmund Freud*, trans. and ed. James Stratchey (London: Hogarth Press, 1959), 9: 238–39.

In the absence of any solid evidence, Robinson's hints of her blood relation to Lord Northington invite speculation about her imaginative investment in the archetypal fantasy of discovering a secret aristocratic lineage. The fantasy may have held a particular appeal for Mary after her father's ill-fated speculation in a whaling venture left him encumbered with debts and bound, by a "fatal fascination," to an American mistress. With the collapse of the family fortune and the separation of her parents, Mary's privileged, almost fairy-tale existence came to an end.

A new phase of Mary's life began with her enrollment in the London boarding school of Meribah Lorrington, a most "extraordinary woman" who had received a "masculine education" from her father. Winning Mary's admiration as well as her "sincere affection," Mrs. Lorrington apparently exerted an influence which was far more powerful than that of the strait-laced sisters of Hannah More, governesses of the Bristol academy where Mary had passed some time as a day student. Although she probably did not acquire very much in the way of classical knowledge during her brief time with Mrs. Lorrington, Mary was, by her own account, an attentive, hard-working student. She developed "a taste for books," and she received high praise for her own early poetic endeavors. She also saw the devastating effects of alcohol as Mrs. Lorrington's "superior acquirements ... yielded to the intemperance of her ruling infatuation" (*Memoirs* 1: 33). The subsequent closure of Mrs. Lorrington's school necessitated Mary's removal to another, where she remained until financial worries prompted her mother to open a boarding school of her own in Chelsea. Eager to assist in the venture, Mary took responsibility for the younger pupils' reading and wardrobes. Just as the school seemed to promise an "honourable independence," however, Captain Darby suddenly returned from America and commanded his wife to give up an enterprise that wounded his sense of pride.

While receiving the "finishing points" of her education at Oxford House, Mary was introduced to several influential members of London's theatrical world. Mr. Hull, the manager of Covent Garden Theatre, "seemed delighted" by her recitation of passages from the script of Nicholas Rowe's tragic heroine Jane

Shore.[1] Shortly thereafter, the renowned David Garrick of Drury Lane Theatre conceived a plan for Mary to make her stage debut playing Cordelia to his King Lear. As the date approached, however, Mrs. Darby became increasingly anxious about her daughter's exposure to the "perils" and "temptations" of a profession that would make her an object of public display and consumer interest. Understandably enough, Mrs. Darby's anxieties were heightened by the "stern injunction" of her estranged husband: "Take care that no dishonour falls upon my daughter. If she is not safe at my return I will annihilate you" (*Memoirs* 1: 48).

According to Robinson's *Memoirs*, these threatening words contributed to the pressure that sealed her unfortunate union with Thomas Robinson. The handsome young law clerk had won his way into Mrs. Darby's good graces through his "indefatigable" attentions to her son George after he came down with smallpox. When Mary succumbed to the disease just as George was recovering, Thomas "exerted all his assiduity to win [her] affections," and Mrs. Darby apparently exerted all her influence to advance his suit. "Repeatedly urged and hourly reminded of [her] father's vow," Mary finally acquiesced to her mother's wishes and promised Thomas her hand in marriage (*Memoirs* 1: 61–62). With no fanfare and no "sensation of any sentiment beyond that of esteem," Mary exchanged vows with Thomas in a private ceremony at the church of St. Martin-in-the-Fields on April 12, 1773.

Soon after their inauspicious "clandestine" wedding, Robinson, at the age of sixteen, discovered that her husband's character and financial prospects were considerably below the expectations he had raised. Although he had presented himself as the nephew and heir of a wealthy Mr. Harris in Wales, Thomas was, in fact, his illegitimate son. Worse still, Robinson learned that Thomas was already deeply in debt and virtually enslaved by propensities for

---

[1] Based on the life of Edward IV's mistress, *The Tragedy of Jane Shore* was first performed in 1714 and remained popular throughout the century. Within the context of Robinson's *Memoirs*, references to her oral performances of *Jane Shore* and Pope's "Elegy to the Memory of an Unfortunate Lady" seem to foreshadow her real misfortunes as an abandoned mistress of the Prince of Wales. Robinson's identification with the wrongs suffered by Rowe's heroine is suggested by additional references to *Jane Shore* in *A Letter to the Women of England* (43) and *The Natural Daughter* (106).

gambling and womanizing. In 1775, scarcely six months after the birth of their daughter, Maria Elizabeth, Thomas was committed to debtor's prison, where he entertained prostitutes and stubbornly refused to accept the work offered him. Sharing his confinement for the better part of a year, Robinson cared for their infant daughter, wrote poetry, and won the patronage of Georgiana, Duchess of Devonshire, one of the most dazzling lights in the aristocratic Whig circle.[1]

After her husband was released from prison in August 1776, Robinson turned her thoughts once again to the acting career that she had started to pursue before her marriage. On December 10, 1776, Robinson made her debut at Drury Lane Theatre in the role of Shakespeare's Juliet. Comparing her to "a diamond in the rough," one reviewer observed that she needed only the "polish of time" and experience to become "a considerable ornament to the stage."[2] As Robinson became increasingly popular and prosperous in her theatrical career during the next three years, her husband became increasingly profligate. Their marriage was evidently beyond repair long before Robinson made her legendary appearance as Perdita in a command performance of Shakespeare's *The Winter's Tale* on December 3, 1779.

Cast in the role of a lovely shepherdess who discovers her lost identity as a princess, Robinson no doubt performed her part with all the conviction of an actress who is granted theatrical license to enact a hyperbolic version of her own secret fantasy. The effect, in

---

[1] Robinson pays tribute to the Duchess of Devonshire in the highly flattering passages describing the Duchess of Chatsworth in *The Natural Daughter*. The identification would have been immediately apparent to contemporary readers who knew that "Chatsworth" was the country estate of the Devonshire family. In *The Natural Daughter*, as well as in other tributes to the Duchess included in Appendix A, Robinson glosses over Georgiana's penchant for gambling and other unsaintly aspects of her character. The very title of Robinson's novel, however, gestures obliquely towards Georgiana's own natural daughter, Eliza Courtney, born February 20, 1791. According to Amanda Foreman, "Georgiana was never allowed to acknowledge Eliza, although her existence eventually became an open secret." See *Georgiana: Duchess of Devonshire* (New York: Random House, 1998), 260.

[2] *Town and Country Magazine* 8 (1776): 660. For a more detailed account of Robinson's stage career, see Philip H. Highfill, Jr, et al, *A Biographical Dictionary of Actors, Actresses, Musicians, Dancers, Managers and Other Stage Personnel in London, 1660–1800* (Carbondale: Southern Illinois UP, 1973–93), 13: 31–47.

any event, played directly into the fantasies of the seventeen-year-old Prince of Wales, who had considerable dramatic propensities of his own. Adopting the name of Shakespeare's rebellious Prince Florizel (Perdita's lover in the play), the Prince initiated a passionate "epistolary intercourse" with the enchanting "Perdita" (*Memoirs* 1: 50). Before long, they were involved in conspicuous public flirtations and secret rendezvous. After receiving numerous promises of his eternal devotion and financial support, Robinson, at the age of twenty-three, left her dissolute husband and became the Prince's mistress. As his request, she also resigned her position at Drury Lane Theatre after closing the 1780 season with a triumphant performance in Lady Craven's *The Miniature Picture*.[1]

Approximately one year after it began, the Shakespearean romance of Robinson and the Prince broke off amid a flurry of gossip about their mutual infidelities. Newspaper columnists began to exercise their theatrical wit by aligning Robinson with Rowe's Jane Shore and other dramatic characters who exemplified the degradation of an abandoned royal mistress. Robinson, however, continued to be known as "The Perdita," and her identity as a "lost" or "fallen" woman was repeatedly reinscribed by cartoons, unauthorized memoirs, spurious editions of her letters, and a steady stream of newspaper gossip about her affairs with the Prince and his close friend Lord Malden.[2]

After spending several months on the continent in the fall of 1781, Robinson returned to London with the latest Parisian fashions and first-hand accounts of the flattering attentions she had received from Marie Antoinette and a number of aristocratic male

---

1   On May 26, *The Morning Chronicle* published the following congratulatory notice: "A theatrical correspondent remarks, that nothing could have saved the Miniature Picture but Mrs. Robinson's well-timed performance of Sir Harry Bevel; when the audience found the *sprightly coxcomb* transformed into the *sentimental lady* in the last act, they expressed their discontent, and wished rather to see Mrs. Robinson in her breeches to the end of the piece. Too much praise cannot be given to Mrs. Robinson for her performance of the character, and the evident pains she took to assist the dramatick efforts of her own sex." Robinson's particular celebrity as a "breeches actress" began on May 10, 1779, when she played Jacintha in *The Suspicious Husband*. Her subsequent breeches roles included Shakespeare's Viola, Rosalind, and Imogen.

2   For an illuminating account of narratives spawned by the popular press, see Anne Mellor, "Making an Exhibition of Her Self: Mary 'Perdita' Robinson and Nineteenth-Century Scripts of Female Sexuality," *Nineteenth-Century Contexts* 22 (2000): 271–304.

admirers. Back in London, Robinson kept reporters busy charting the varying course of her intrigues with Lord Malden, Charles James Fox, and Banastre Tarleton, a dashing lieutenant colonel who had fought with Cornwallis's army in America. By the end of 1782, Tarleton and Robinson were confirmed lovers, and their liaison continued, with some interruptions, for approximately fifteen years.

Although Robinson was shunned in some circles until the very end of her life, she gradually gained a more respectable reputation during her extended liaison with Tarleton. The changing perception no doubt owed something to the onset of "*a violent rheumatism, which progressively deprived her of the use of her limbs*" (*Memoirs* 2: 96). Even though gossip sometimes attributed the lingering paralysis to complications brought on by a miscarriage, images of Robinson as a brazen prostitute gradually faded as newspapers circulated reports about her precarious health and her medical treatments at Bath and various other spas which figure prominently in *The Natural Daughter*.

By the late 1780s, Robinson's infamy as former mistress of the Prince of Wales and others was almost overshadowed by her burgeoning fame as the author of pseudonymous poems that appeared in the daily newspapers under the signatures of "Laura" and "Laura Maria." As Judith Pascoe has argued, these pseudonyms and others helped Robinson to shed her identity as "The Perdita" and "to reinvent herself" as a circumspect woman of genius and sensibility.[1] Noted particularly for her plaintive, melodious strains, Robinson's "Laura" elicited highly sympathetic and complimentary responses from a number of men, including Robert Merry, a phenomenally popular poet who wrote under the names of "Della Crusca" and "Leonardo."

By 1791, however, Robinson's poetic identities as "Laura" and "Laura Maria" made her, once again, the target of vicious attacks. Having shared the acclaim of the so-called "Della Cruscan School," Robinson was swept up in the rising tide of abuse as critics became increasingly hostile to the emotional and stylistic extravagance of Della Cruscan verse. The ridicule and stinging

---

[1]   *Romantic Theatricality: Gender, Poetry, and Spectatorship* (Ithaca and London: Cornell UP, 1997), 173.

invectives hurled by the Tory satirist William Gifford and others, however, did not arise from purely disinterested aesthetic judgments. Rather, they were inextricably bound up with a political agenda to discredit everyone and everything suspected of fostering revolutionary sympathies.[1]

As enthusiasm for the Della Cruscan School followed roughly the same downward curve as English sympathy for the French Revolution, Robinson continued to reinvent herself as a poet while also establishing her reputation as a novelist. According to her *Memoirs*, Robinson's first novel, *Vancenza; or the Dangers of Credulity* (1792), "*sold in one day*," thanks largely to "the celebrity of the author's name, and the favourable impression of her talents given to the public by her poetical compositions" (*Memoirs* 2: 128). Running to a fourth edition by 1793, *Vancenza* was followed by *The Widow, or a Picture of Modern Times* (1794), *Angelina; a Novel* (1796), *Hubert de Sevrac; a Romance of the Eighteenth Century* (1796), *Walsingham; or, the Pupil of Nature* (1797), *The False Friend: A Domestic Story* (1799), and *The Natural Daughter. With Portraits of the Leadenhead Family* (1799).

Like her poetic personae, Robinson's fictional heroines are typically somewhat whitewashed versions of herself—extraordinarily beautiful and refined women suffering from unrequited love, domestic tyranny, class prejudice, malicious rumor, and libertine assaults upon their virtue. Although reviews were mixed, the most enthusiastic endorsements of Robinson's fiction often adopted the same terms that critics had used to applaud her poetic performances as "Laura" and "Laura Maria." In one particularly glowing review attributed to Wollstonecraft, for example, appreciative assessments of Robinson's melancholy Della Cruscan poses resonate in the praise bestowed on the eponymous heroine of her novel *Angelina*:

> In the portrait of Angelina we behold an assemblage of almost every excellence which can adorn the female mind,

---

[1]   For more extensive discussions of Della Cruscan verse and its reception history, see Jerome J. McGann, *The Poetics of Sensibility: A Revolution in Literary Style* (Oxford: Clarendon, 1996), 74–96, and Judith Pascoe, *Romantic Theatricality*, 68–94.

beaming mildly through clouds of affliction and melancholy. Her situation will interest the feelings of the reader, and the disclosure of her history and character form an agreeable and important scene in the catastrophe. The sentiments contained in these volumes are just, animated, and rational. They breathe a spirit of independence, and a dignified superiority to whatever is unessential to the true respectability and genuine excellence of human beings.[1]

Published in February 1796, the same month that Robinson was introduced to William Godwin, Wollstonecraft's expression of such liberal sentiments carried an implicit vindication of Robinson's own character and almost certainly raised her expectations of a close friendship with Wollstonecraft.

Wollstonecraft, however, apparently found Robinson herself considerably less appealing than the title character of *Angelina*.[2] Indeed, Wollstonecraft is generally assumed to be the author of the exceedingly harsh judgment which the *Analytical Review* passed on Robinson's next novel, *Hubert de Sevrac*, the story of an aristocratic French émigré who eventually becomes "the convert of liberty." Making only passing reference to Robinson's "moral, that the vices of the rich produce the crimes of the poor," the review focuses on one overriding complaint:

> Mrs. Robinson writes so rapidly, that she scarcely gives herself time to digest her story into a plot.... She certainly possesses considerable abilities; but she seems to have fallen into an

---

[1] Originally published in the *Analytical Review* (Feb. 1796), this review of *Angelina* is reprinted in *The Works of Mary Wollstonecraft*, ed. Janet Todd and Marilyn Butler (London: William Pickering, 1989), 7: 461–62.

[2] There is some evidence of a few congenial meetings between the two women in *Collected Letters of Mary Wollstonecraft*, ed. Ralph Wardle (Ithaca: Cornell UP, 1979), 370, 376. One may detect a note of jealousy, however, in the letter Wollstonecraft addressed to Godwin on December 13, 1796, the day after they had dined with Robinson: "I was even vext with myself for staying to supper with Mrs. R. But there is a manner of leaving a person free to follow their own will, that looks so like indifference, I do not like it. Your *tone* would have decided me—But, to tell you the truth, I thought, by your voice and manner, that you wished to remain in society—and pride made me *wish* to gratify you," (367).

errour, common to people of lively fancy, and to think herself
so happily gifted by nature, that her first thoughts will answer
her purpose. The consequence is obvious; her sentences are
often confused, entangled with superfluous words, half-
expressed sentiments, and false ornaments.[1]

With its emphasis on the effects of hasty composition, this review
echoes the charges brought against Robinson's Della Cruscan
verse. Any serious consideration of Robinson's political statement
in the novel is put aside as the review hastens to the dismissive
conclusion that Robinson "could write better, were she once
convinced, that the writing of a good book is no easy task."

Although Robinson herself later acknowledged that most of her
work "had been composed in too much haste" (*Memoirs* 2: 161),
Wollstonecraft's criticism seems to be inflected with at least a touch
of jealousy for a woman who probably could have spent more time
writing if she had spent less time entertaining William Godwin. As
entries in Godwin's diary indicate, he became a frequent visitor at
Robinson's home after they were introduced by Robert Merry in
February 1796. The visits came to an end, however, shortly after
Godwin's marriage to Wollstonecraft in March 1797, and they did
not resume until January 1798, some four months after her death.[2]
The most obvious inference is that Godwin broke off his association with Robinson at Wollstonecraft's request. With her advancing pregnancy and increasing concern for respectability,
Wollstonecraft was no doubt wary of her husband's association with
"the celebrated Mrs. Robinson," "a most accomplished and delightful woman."[3]

For all her so-called celebrity, however, Robinson died in
obscurity at her daughter's cottage near Windsor Forest on

---

[1] This review is reprinted in *The Works of Mary Wollstonecraft*, 7: 486.

[2] The manuscripts of Godwin's unpublished diary and some of Robinson's letters to
him are part of the Abinger deposit at The Bodleian Library, University of Oxford.
These items are on microfilm at The Perkins Library, Duke University, Durham, NC.
One of the letters from Robinson to Godwin, dated August 24, 1800, is included in
Appendix A of Pascoe's *Mary Robinson: Selected Poems*, 367–70.

[3] Godwin included this assessment of Robinson in an autobiographical fragment,
quoted in C. Kegan Paul, *William Godwin: His Friends and Contemporaries* (Boston:
Roberts Brothers, 1876), 1: 154.

December 26, 1800. As Robinson's last letters to Godwin and others reveal, the theme of neglected genius running throughout her published work found a poignant coda in the final months of her own life. In addition to her painful consciousness of neglect, Robinson also suffered from poverty, illness, and the mental exhaustion of trying to earn a living by her pen. Despite the enormous productivity of her last years and a number of favorable reviews, her "funeral was attended only by two literary friends ... whose friendship and benevolence had cheered her while living and followed her to the Grave" (*Memoirs* 2: 164). One of those friends was William Godwin.

A Letter to the Women of England

The heavy anti-feminist atmosphere of 1799 may help to explain why Robinson first published her *Letter to the Women of England, on the Injustice of Mental Subordination* under the pseudonym of Anne Francis Randall. By writing under the signature of a fictitious woman who had no past, Robinson no doubt hoped to shield her argument from vicious *ad feminam* attacks.[1] As the response to Wollstonecraft's *Memoirs* vividly illustrated, many critics were adept at using salacious details of a woman's private life to undermine the credibility of her public voice. If Robinson evaded this most unscrupulous form of biographical criticism, however, she left herself wide open to charges of guilt by association. As one hostile

---

[1]   Robinson, nevertheless, may have wished to excite some speculation about her authorship of the pamphlet. On March 28, 1799, *The Morning Post* published an extract from her epistolary novel *The False Friend* which seems calculated to do just that. The puff is reproduced in Appendix B, 301–02, to illustrate the relationship, and difference, between the public voice of Robinson's Anne Francis Randall and the private voice of her epistolary heroine Gertrude St. Ledger. Gertrude's *potential* to become a full-fledged disciple of Wollstonecraft is suggested by her villainous tutor's jeering prophecy: "I make no doubt but you will shortly become a *he-she* philosopher; that you will pretend to inculcate new doctrines, on the potency of feminine understanding, and the absurdity of sexual subordination. You will preach on the sublimity of intellectual gratification, and oppose the majesty of mind against the supremacy of the senses. You will become an advocate for universal toleration: you will hope to equalize the authority of the sexes, and to prove that woman was formed to think, and to become the rational companion of man; though we all know that she was merely created for our amusement" (2: 77).

reviewer observed, "Mrs. R. avows herself of the school of Wollstencroft [sic]; and that is enough for all who have any regard to decency, order, or prudence, to avoid her company."[1]

While the first pages of Robinson's *Letter* boldly declare her alliance with Wollstonecraft, they also signal her departure from Wollstonecraft's mode of "philosophical reasoning." Observing that "the same subject may be argued in a variety of ways," Robinson announces that she will not follow Wollstonecraft in criticizing "the doctrines of certain philosophical sensualists," most notably Rousseau. Instead, Robinson argues more directly from her own experience, translated into ostensibly hypothetical cases. Robinson's own sense of alienation, for example, almost throbs beneath the thin hypothetical veil as she asks her readers to "imagine" a woman "driven from society; deserted by her kindred; scoffed at by the world; exposed to poverty; assailed by malice; and consigned to scorn ..." (43). At such moments, Robinson seems to be pleading her own case more than the general injustice of mental subordination.

At other moments, Robinson enlarges upon a theme that Wollstonecraft squeezed into a footnote that cited examples of heroic women who defied the general rule of mental subordination. Wollstonecraft's express wish to see women as "neither heroines nor brutes," but simply as "reasonable creatures," no doubt explains her decision "not [to] lay any great stress on the example of a few women who ... acquired courage and resolution" from a "masculine education."[2] Robinson, however, devotes much of her *Letter* to examples of such heroic women from antiquity to her own day. And as some of her examples illustrate, female courage and resolution are not entirely dependent upon the benefits of a masculine education.

---

1 *The Gentleman's Magazine* 69 (1799): 311. For a full text of this review and others, see Appendix G.

2 *A Vindication of the Rights of Woman*, in *The Works of Mary Wollstonecraft*, 5: 145–46. As Alice Brown suggests, Wollstonecraft was probably also aware of obvious anti-feminist rebuttals to arguments that did stress the achievements of extraordinary women: i.e. they could easily be dismissed as exceptions to the general rule, or they could be cited as proof that women already had ample opportunities. *The Eighteenth-Century Feminist Mind* (Detroit: Wayne State UP, 1987), 108–09.

One might conclude that Robinson, suffering from the anxiety of influence, seized upon some old heroic theme that Wollstonecraft had left unsung. Robinson's emphasis on examples of heroic women, however, is probably more closely related to her sense of audience, specifically the women of England. Although Wollstonecraft had addressed some of her remarks directly to women, her moderate tone and general mode of philosophical reasoning were undoubtedly calculated to make a particularly favorable impression upon men. As the letter of dedication prefacing her *Vindication* implied, Wollstonecraft's most privileged audience was, in fact, a French man, Charles Maurice de Talleyrand-Périgord, author of a report advocating educational reform.[1]

While Robinson's title clearly signals a generic elevation and redirection of the letter to the women of England, it also marks a particularly significant departure from what Katharine Jensen has called the paradigm of "Epistolary Woman." As Jensen explains, Epistolary Woman was essentially a "male creation," confining women to the highly emotional genre of the love letter.[2] Glaringly apparent in spurious editions of Robinson's letters to the Prince of Wales, the paradigm also informed her Della Cruscan verse epistles and her epistolary novels. Breaking away from the feminine tradition of private letters to advance a public feminist argument, Robinson's *Letter to the Women of England* includes a direct attack on the supposition that "women are only worthy of receiving *billet doux*, because the extent of their own literary requirements is that of writing them" (56, n.2).

More subtle, but no less telling, is Robinson's departure from the bluestocking tradition of instructional letters prescribing the proper conduct for "ladies." To varying degrees, this tradition informed Hester Chapone's *Letters on the Improvement of the Mind* (1773), Catharine Macaulay's *Letters on Education* (1790), Laetitia Matilda Hawkins' *Letters on the Female Mind* (1793), Maria Edgeworth's *Letters for Literary Ladies* (1795), and a number of other

---

[1] Mary Hays took Wollstonecraft's efforts to win over a male audience a step further in her *Appeal to the Men of Great Britain in Behalf of Women* (1798).

[2] *Writing Love: Letters, Women, and the Novel in France, 1605–1776* (Carbondale: Southern Illinois UP, 1995), 2.

works that used an epistolary format to advance proposals for the development of women's intellectual abilities. Although Robinson advocates a few specific innovations, including a university for women, her *Letter to the Women of England* is finally not so much a polite call for educational reform as it is a polemical attack on the sexual double standard. The comparatively militant tone of Robinson's *Letter* is underscored by her much belated announcement of its "prominent subject"—"that woman is denied the first privilege of nature, the power of SELF-DEFENCE" (74).[1]

Somewhat paradoxically, Robinson's departure from the forms adopted by her female contemporaries ultimately underscores her dependence upon the writing of men. Robinson, in fact, frequently abandons her own voice or consigns it to marginal commentary while she appeals to the authority of female histories compiled by men. Of the ninety-seven pages that constitute the first edition of Robinson's *Letter*, for example, fourteen are devoted primarily to quotations of passages translated from the Latin *De Philologia*, by the Dutch scholar Gerhardi Joannis Vossius. Although she does not cite more contemporary collections of exemplary women's lives, such as George Ballard's *Memoirs of British Ladies* (1775), William Alexander's *The History of Women* (1779), or the anonymously published *Biographium Faemineum* (1766), their additional testimonies to the mental equality of women make Robinson's argument appear even less extraordinary.

What distinguishes Robinson's *Letter*, however, is not so much her argument *per se* but the wide range of her examples, which openly challenged the exclusionary practices of earlier biographers. The *Biographium Faemineum*, for example, not only pointedly excluded "infamous courtesans" but also silently passed over a number of worthy women from the lower ranks of society. Although Ballard was more "democratic," Ruth Perry observes that all of his "learned ladies were respectable and pious." Few of them wrote novels or plays, and "none were self-supporting writers in

---

1   Robinson is invoking an idea that had considerable cultural currency. Cf. Dryden's *Absalom and Achitophel*, 2: 148 ("Self-defence is Nature's eldest law"); Samuel Butler's *Remains*, 2: 27 ("Self-preservation is the first law of nature"); and Wollstonecraft's *A Vindication of the Rights of Woman*, 110 ("the care necessary for self-preservation is the first natural exercise of the understanding").

the Grub Street marketplace."[1] Significantly, these marginalized or excluded groups are well represented both in the text of Robinson's *Letter* and in her appended "List of British Female Literary Characters Living in the Eighteenth Century." In the text of her letter Robinson even went so far as to acknowledge the heroic spirit of women who were better known simply as mistresses, lunatics, transvestites, or murderers. According to the damning review published in *The Gentleman's Magazine*, Robinson was guilty not only by association with Wollstonecraft but also by association with "the motley list of heroines" appended to her *Letter* and "the anecdotes of female characters of all descriptions, interspersed in it." As the reviewer's language here suggests, Robinson's *Letter* was threatening precisely because it mixed together women of presumed virtue with those of ill repute.

Robinson had provoked similar outrage in the fall of 1780 when she had had the audacity to take a side box at the theater. In a letter to the editor of *The Morning Post* on September 27, an offended "Dramaticus" urged the theater managers "to preserve the side-boxes for the modest and reputable part of the other sex; or at least ... to refuse them to actresses, swindlers, [and] wantons in high keeping." Adding another voice to the outcry on October 9, "No Flatterer" suggested that even if Robinson had "every virtue under the canopy of heaven, ... her past theatrical life exempted her from that title she might otherwise claim to a place in the side boxes, which have ever been considered as appropriated to persons of rank, fortune, and character only." Written almost twenty years after this fracas over side boxes, Robinson's *Letter* simultaneously evokes both her own tainted past and a stage tradition of heroines who not only violated the laws of chastity but also spoke out against the forces that contributed to their undoing. The epigraph on the title page of Robinson's *Letter* aligns her own voice most directly with that of Calista, the heroine of Nicholas Rowe's "she-tragedy" *The Fair Penitent* (1703):

---

[1]   Ruth Perry, ed. *Memoirs of Several Ladies of Great Britain Who Have Been Celebrated for their Writings or Skill in the Learned Languages, Arts and Sciences.* By George Ballard. 1752 (Detroit: Wayne State UP, 1984), 12.

How hard is the condition of our sex,
Through ev'ry state of life the slaves of man!
In all the dear, delightful days of youth
A rigid father dictates to our wills,
And deals out pleasure with a scanty hand;
To his, the tyrant husband's reign succeeds;
Proud with opinion of superior reason,
He holds domestic business and devotion
All we are capable to know, and shuts us,
Like cloistered idiots, from the world's acquaintance
And all the joys of freedom; wherefore are we
Born with high souls but to assert ourselves,
Shake off this vile obedience they exact,
And claim an equal empire o'er the world?
(3. 39–52)[1]

Robinson's epigraph ("Wherefore are we / Born with high Souls, but to *assert ourselves?*") clearly signals her intention to pick up Calista's interrogation of the patriarchal law and her role as a spokeswoman for her sex.[2]

In addressing the women of England as a group, Robinson no doubt hoped to foster a spirit of female solidarity that would cut across boundaries of economic and social standing. As Robinson later observed, however, there was little evidence of this spirit even among the ranks of "enlightened" women writers:

… even among themselves there appears no sympathetic association of soul; no genuine impulse of affection, originating in

---

[1] *The Fair Penitent*, ed. Malcolm Goldstein (Lincoln: U of Nebraska P, 1969), 34.

[2] Robinson was probably well aware that the first two lines of Calista's speech and her closing question had appeared as the epigraph on the title page of an earlier pamphlet, *Woman Not Inferior to Man: Or, A Short and Modest Vindication of the Natural Right of the Fair-Sex to a Perfect Equality of Power, Dignity, and Esteem with the Men* (London: John Hawkins, 1739). This pamphlet, published as the work of a pseudonymous "Sophia, a Person of Quality," often seems much closer to the spirit and tone of Robinson's *Letter* than Wollstonecraft's *Vindication* does. According to Marie Mulvey Roberts, "Sophia" was, in fact, a man, François Poullain de la Barre. See *The Pioneers: Early Feminists*, ed. Marie Mulvey Roberts and Tamae Mizuto. 2nd ed. (London: Routledge / Thoemmes, 1995), xii.

congeniality of mind. Each is ardent in the pursuit of fame; and every new honour which is bestowed on a sister votary, is deemed a partial privation of what she considers as her birth-right.[1]

Robinson's effort to combat such self-defeating rivalry with liberal praise for her female contemporaries evinces a spirit of generosity striving to overcome the resentment she felt for being shunned by Wollstonecraft and others.[2] Although Robinson herself was an expert at self-promotion, *A Letter to the Women of England* exhibits a strong commitment to the feminist principle that women need to promote each other.

The Natural Daughter[3]

The first sentence of *The Natural Daughter* situates the opening scene in April, 1792, a year in which "the great topic of conversation" was the French Revolution.[4] Momentous events in France, however, would seem to be the last thing on the mind of Robinson's Mr. Alderman Bradford as he sets out for the fashionable resort of Bath with his long-suffering wife and their two daughters, Martha and Julia. While Robinson's heroine, Martha, is a sensible young woman of twenty-one, the other members of the Bradford family bear a striking resemblance to the stereotypical creatures ridiculed by Tobias Smollett's Matthew Bramble in one of his letters from Bath:

---

[1] "Present State of the Manners, Society, &c. &c. of the Metropolis of England," *The Monthly Magazine* 10 (1800): 220. Judith Pascoe confirms Robinson's authorship of this anonymously published work in the introduction to *Mary Robinson: Selected Poems*, 30, n. 18.

[2] In her *Memoirs*, Robinson wrote, "I have almost uniformly found my own sex my most inveterate enemies; I have experienced little kindness from them; though my bosom has often ached with the pang inflicted by their envy, slander, and malevolence" (1: 176).

[3] The following discussion includes excerpts from my longer essay "Romancing the Reign of Terror: Sexual Politics in Mary Robinson's *Natural Daughter*," *Criticism* 39 (1997): 531–55.

[4] *The Annual Register, or a View of the History, Politics, and Literature, for the Year 1792* (London: 1799), 126.

Every upstart of fortune, harnessed in the trappings of the mode, presents himself at Bath, as in the very focus of observation.... Knowing no other criterion of greatness, but the ostentation of wealth, they discharge their affluence without taste or conduct, through every channel of the most absurd extravagance; and all of them hurry to Bath, because, here, without any further qualification, they can mingle with the princes and nobles of the land.[1]

Had she wished to follow fictional conventions of her day, Robinson might have introduced a series of suitors to complicate a plot leading to the engagement or marriage of both daughters in the last chapter. Instead, Robinson marries off her heroine very early in the novel to a man with "an unblemished reputation," "a comfortable and spacious family mansion," and an enviable income of four thousand pounds a year (117). As Martha soon discovers, however, Mr. Morley's "good qualities" are attended by "some peculiarities," not the least of which is a determination to exercise his authority as a husband. From this point on, *The Natural Daughter* becomes a fictional extension of Robinson's argument in *A Letter to the Women of England*.

As Eleanor Ty has recently argued, Robinson deserves particular credit for her efforts to displace "traditional [i.e. sentimental] scripts for women" with "new narratives that empower the feminine subject."[2] Central to this project is the creation of a heroine who is, in many respects, Robinson's own fictional double—an abandoned wife pressed by financial necessity to pursue careers as an actress, novelist, and poet.[3] The adventures of Martha Morley

---

[1] *The Expedition of Humphrey Clinker* (1771), ed. James L. Thorson (New York: Norton, 1983), 34. Robinson's Mr. Alderman Bradford has apparently made his money through stocks and trade, the typical sources of wealth for men elected to the Board of Aldermen governing the City of London, an area of roughly one square mile on the north bank of the River Thames. His neighborhood, "Crutched-Friars," is among the unfashionable ones scornfully mentioned by Smollett's Matt Bramble.

[2] *Empowering the Feminine: The Narratives of Mary Robinson, Jane West, and Amelia Opie, 1796–1812* (Toronto: U of Toronto P, 1998), 72.

[3] It is instructive to read the employment histories of Robinson and her heroine Martha Morley against contemporary works such as Priscilla Wakefield's *Reflections on the Present Condition of the Female Sex* (1798). As the excerpts included in Appendix D suggest, Martha is not simply a double of Robinson, but a more broadly representative character, exemplifying the plight of the genteel woman with very limited employment options.

offer a good bit of wry commentary on Robinson's own quest for empowerment in the competitive literary marketplace of the 1790s. More importantly, perhaps, they call for a rewriting of the literary history that has ensconced Elizabeth Barrett Browning's *Aurora Leigh* (1857) as "the first work in English by a woman writer in which the heroine herself is an author."[1] Although it is a less polished work than *Aurora Leigh*, Robinson's *Natural Daughter* is arguably just as daring in its exploration of new possibilities for women and new directions for the novel as a genre.

Viewed within the historical context of the 1790s, *The Natural Daughter* assumes far more social and literary significance than traditional narratives about the novel have allowed. In his joint biography of Robinson and Tarleton, for example, Robert Bass claims that Robinson composed "a thin, novelized autobiography" almost by default, after abandoning her original plan to write a fictional exposé of Susan Priscilla Bertie, the natural daughter of the Duke of Ancaster and the recent bride of Tarleton. The plan miscarried, Bass conjectures, because Robinson was unable to find any hint of scandal in Susan's past beyond the accident of her birth.[2] In looking for an illegitimate daughter outside the text, however, Bass fails to say anything about the illegitimate daughter within the text, the infant Frances, who was conceived in a Paris prison some five months before the assassination of Jean-Paul Marat, on July 13, 1793. Insofar as Robinson's heroine sacrifices her reputation to befriend this infant and her birth-mother, there is certainly reason to question why the textual genesis of the novel should be traced to a rivalry with Susan Priscilla Bertie rather than to a sympathetic identification with women like Mary Wollstonecraft, the mother of another illegitimate Frances conceived in revolutionary France.

Depending on how one defines the term "natural daughter," the potential referents within the text include not only the illegitimate infant Frances but the heroine, Martha, especially if she is compared to her sister, Julia. Although Julia is the favored

---

1   *The Norton Anthology of English Literature*, ed. M.H. Abrams et al., 7th ed. (New York: Norton, 2000), 2: 1174.
2   *The Green Dragoon. The Lives of Banastre Tarleton and Mary Robinson* (1957; rpt. Columbia SC: Sandlapper Press, 1973), 392–93.

daughter, noted for her docile temperament and conspicuous sensibility, she imprisons their mother in a mad house, poisons her own illegitimate child, and eventually ends her infamous career by committing suicide in the bed of Robespierre. By constructing a narrative that repeatedly defines Martha in opposition to her "unnatural" sister and Frances in opposition to her "unnatural" father, Robinson complicates the easy equation between "natural" and "illegitimate" as well as the identification of her title character. Insofar as the title may be understood to name the novel itself, Robinson also undermines the easy assumption that her narrative is the illegitimate offspring of a prostitute muse trafficking in the demand for scandal.

Robinson calls attention to the disparate resonances of her own title through her satiric portrait of Martha's "dashing" publisher, Mr. Index.[1] Although he buys her first novel, a sentimental tale, for ten pounds, Mr. Index encourages Martha to capitalize on the demands for topical satire and scandal. Above all else, however, he admonishes her to "mind a title":

A title is the thing above all others. It pleases every order of the high world, and charms into admiration every species of the low: it will cover a multitude of faults: a kind of compendious errata, which sets to rights all the errors of a work, and makes it popular, however incorrect and illiterate it may appear to the eyes of fastidious critisers.... Do not forget that a title is a wonderful harmonizer of things, in all ranks and all opinions of men, both morally and politically. (210)

This advice certainly highlights the commodity status of Robinson's own title, *The Natural Daughter. With Portraits of the Leadenhead Family.* Insofar as it appeals to a prurient interest in the scandal of illegitimate birth and a demand for satiric character sketches drawn from "real life," the title undoubtedly answers to

---

[1] For an illuminating account of Robinson's relations with her publishers, see Jan Fergus and Janice Farrar Thaddeus, "Women, Publishers, and Money, 1790–1820," *Studies in Eighteenth-Century Culture* 17 (1987): 191–207. According to their findings, Robinson received £60 for *The Natural Daughter.*

Mr. Index's jaded perception of what "will sell." As a number of squibs in *The Morning Post* suggest, Robinson herself was not above courting the fashionable, gossip-loving audience that Mr. Index seems to have in mind.[1] Throughout the novel, however, Robinson punningly subverts his solemn injunction to "mind a title" by routinely failing to capitalize the titles of nobility except at the beginning of sentences. This symbolic rejection of aristocratic privilege plays directly into a tradition of sensibility popularized by Diderot's *Le fils naturel* (1757), Restif de la Bretonne's *La fille naturelle* (1767), and other works that extended Rousseau's valorization of the "natural man" to the illegitimate or "natural" child.[2]

This tradition flourished in the literary marketplace of the late 1790s, even in the midst of widespread Francophobia. Early in 1799, before Robinson's *Natural Daughter* appeared, her publishers, Longman and Rees, brought out an English translation of Diderot's novel, entitled *The Natural Son*. In the previous year, Anne Plumptre and Stephen Porter had both used the same title for their separate translations of an enormously popular play by the German poet and playwright Augustus von Kotzebue.[3] While Robinson's *Natural Daughter* capitalized on the popularity of these highly sympathetic representations of illegitimate sons, it also put in an implicit bid for sexual equality.[4]

As it repeatedly criticizes the social distinctions that foster scandal, *The Natural Daughter* clearly moves beyond the realm of local gossip to participate in a revolutionary debate on the rights of women and illegitimate children. On November 2, 1793, the French Convention passed what Lynn Hunt has called "one of

---

[1]   On July 30, 1799, for example, the newspaper announced, "Expectation is on tip-toe to know whom Mrs. Robinson means to pourtray as the Leadenhead Family, in her forth-coming novel of *"The Natural Daughter."*

[2]   Marie Maclean discusses this tradition in *The Name of the Mother: Writing Illegitimacy* (London and New York: Routledge, 1994), 59.

[3]   Another translation, entitled *Lover's Vows*, was published by Elizabeth Inchbald in 1797. This version of the play, enacted numerous times at Covent Garden Theatre, later became a hot topic of moral controversy in Jane Austen's *Mansfield Park* (1814).

[4]   Speaking before the House of Lords in 1800, Lord Mulgrave observed that illegitimate daughters had "to struggle with every disadvantage from their rank in life" while their male counterparts usually suffered "little comparative consequence." Quoted in Lawrence Stone, *The Family, Sex and Marriage in England, 1500–1800* (New York: Harper & Row, 1977), 534.

its most controversial laws" when it gave illegitimate children "equal rights of inheritance."[1] In the wake of strong opposition, however, the law was officially suspended in 1795 with the decree that "Legal actions concerning paternity are forbidden."[2] Insofar as it legalized a sexual double standard, leaving the burden of illegitimacy to rest with unwed mothers, the decree was part of a larger project to reinscribe gender boundaries as well as the gendered boundaries between public and private life.

As the Revolution became increasingly bloody and abandoned its early commitment to the rights of women as well as men, Robinson and other women writers continued to support the original democratic goals even as they denounced the excesses of the Jacobin leaders Marat and Robespierre.[3] Robinson's mixed response to the Revolution finds particularly telling antecedents in Helen Maria Williams's *Letters from France*. (See Appendix E.) As Gary Kelly indicates, Williams frequently "distinguishes a 'good' Revolution, with feminine traits, from the 'bad' (Jacobin) Revolution, with masculine traits."[4] Robinson herself figures the separation by polarizing her characters, pitting the radical innocence of the infant Frances against the corruption of the "sanguinary monster" Marat. Although the Revolution had already been identified with monstrosity by Edmund Burke and other conservatives, Robinson blatantly subverts their distinctions between French monstrosity and English morality. Indeed, as the climactic scene revealing the identity of Frances's "monstrous father" suggests, Jacobin terrorism was not the antithesis of English law and order but rather, in some instances, its own dark double.

Taking exception to the subversive tendencies of Robinson's narrative voice, contemporary reviewers found little to praise in

---

1   *The Family Romance of the French Revolution* (Berkeley: U of California P, 1992), 66.

2   Jenny Teichman, *Illegitimacy: An Examination of Bastardy* (Ithaca: Cornell UP, 1982), 155.

3   See Robinson's poetic account of the Reign of Terror in *The Progress of Liberty* (Appendix E) and Helen Maria Williams's sketches of the Jacobin terrorists in *Letters from France* (Appendix F).

4   "Revolution and Romantic Feminism: Women, Writing, and Cultural Revolution," in *Revolution and English Romanticism: Politics and Rhetoric*, ed. Keith Hanley and Raman Selden (New York: St. Martin's, 1990), 119.

The Natural Daughter apart from the occasional "pieces of truly elegant poetry."[1] *The European Magazine* expressed sorrow that a woman of Robinson's "genius, capable of soaring to the sublimest subjects in Poetry," had stooped to a "vitiated taste for the marvelous and improbable." Moving on to more substantive issues, the reviewer complained, "every characteristic of a moral Novel is wanting....[E]very page of the work demonstrates that it ought to have been [called] The *Unnatural* Wife, Daughter, and Sister."[2] The hostile *British Critic* made much the same point when it characterized Robinson's heroine as a "decidedly flippant female, apparently of the Wollstonecraft school." As the concluding sentence of the review suggests, Robinson's Martha was nothing less than a pernicious embodiment of "the morals and manners which tended to produce" the French Revolution.[3] Ironically enough, the searing indictments of *The Natural Daughter* issued by Robinson's contemporaries underscore the very features of the novel that are most likely to interest readers today.

---

[1] *The Monthly Magazine* 9 (1800): 640. For more extensive excerpts from contemporary reviews, see Appendix H.

[2] *The European Magazine* 37 (1800): 138–39.

[3] *The British Critic* 16 (1800): 320–21.

Mary Robinson: A Brief Chronology

1756   Born in Bristol on November 27 to Hester and
        Nicholas Darby
1768   Moves to London with her mother and youngest
        brother, George, after forced sale of the family
        property in Bristol
1769   Attends boarding school in Chelsea
1773   Prepares for her stage debut under the tutelage of
        David Garrick
        Marries Thomas Robinson at St. Martin-in-the-
        Fields on April 12
1774   Gives birth to a daughter, Maria Elizabeth
        Robinson, on October 18
1775   Goes to debtor's prison with husband and infant
        daughter
        Publishes first volume, *Poems by Mrs. Robinson*
        Meets Georgiana, Duchess of Devonshire
1776   Meets Richard Brinsley Sheridan, the new manager
        of Drury Lane Theatre
        Makes debut at Drury Lane Theatre as
        Shakespeare's Juliet on December 10
1777   Gives birth to a second daughter, Sophia, who dies
        in infancy
        Publishes *Captivity; a Poem. And Celadon and Lydia;
        a Tale*
1779   Plays Perdita in a command performance of
        Shakespeare's *The Winter's Tale* on December 3; soon
        afterwards receives the first of many ardent epistles
        from the Prince of Wales, writing under the name
        of "Florizel" (Perdita's lover in the play)
1780   Resigns position at Drury Lane Theatre after
        triumphant performance as Eliza in Lady Craven's
        The Miniature Picture on May 24
        Separates from her husband shortly thereafter and
        lives as mistress of the Prince of Wales. Their affair
        apparently ended in December.

1781   Receives £5,000 from George III in exchange for the letters written by his son

Visits France; meets Marie Antoinette in Paris

1782   Begins long liaison with Banastre Tarleton

1783   Robinson's supposed pregnancy and indisposition after a miscarriage are topics of newspaper gossip throughout the summer. By the fall, she is suffering from the painful and debilitating rheumatism that plagued her for the rest of her life.

1784   Goes to the continent with Tarleton after the claims of creditors force the sale of her personal belongings

1785–87   Newspapers carry reports of Robinson's visits to various spas on the continent, including Aix-la-Chapelle and St. Amand in Flanders. Her father dies on December 5, 1785.

1788   Returns to London in January

Begins publishing poems in *The World*, a daily newspaper, under the signature of "Laura" and soon becomes associated with the poetic "school" of "Della Crusca" (Robert Merry)

1789   Begins publishing poems in *The Oracle*, a rival of *The World*

(Storming of the Bastille in Paris on July 14)

1790   Publishes *Ainsi va le Monde*, a poem that openly declared her revolutionary sympathies

1791   Publishes *Poems* and a prose pamphlet, *Impartial Reflections on the Present Situation of the Queen of France*

1792   Publishes first novel, *Vancenza; or the Dangers of Credulity*

Visits France; leaves Calais on September 2, barely escaping an order for the arrest of British subjects in France

(France declares war against Austria and Hungary on April 20)

1793   Publishes a verse satire, *Modern Manners*; *A Monody to the Memory of the Late Queen of France*; and a slim volume of poems, *Sight, the Cavern of Woe; and Solitude*. Her mother dies in August.

(Louis XVI is executed on January 21; France declares war on England on February 1; Jacobins take control of the National Convention on June 2; Charlotte Corday assassinates Jean-Paul Marat on July 13; Marie Antoinette is executed on October 16.)

1794   Publishes second novel, *The Widow*
First performance of Robinson's *Nobody*, a farce on female gamblers, is disrupted by a hostile audience at Drury Lane
(Wollstonecraft's daughter, Fanny Imlay, is born on May 14; Robespierre is executed on July 28.)

1796   Publishes two novels, *Angelina* and *Hubert de Sevrac*; a tragedy, *The Sicilian Lover*; and a sonnet series, *Sappho and Phaon*
Meets William Godwin in early February and Mary Wollstonecraft shortly thereafter

1797   Publishes *Walsingham; or, the Pupil of Nature*
(Wollstonecraft dies on September 10.)

1798   Begins writing her memoirs on January 14; resumes social intercourse with Godwin
(Godwin publishes *Memoirs of the Author of A Vindication of the Rights of Woman* in early January; Banastre Tarleton marries Susan Priscilla Bertie on December 17.)

1799   Engaged as poetry editor for *The Morning Post*; meets Coleridge, who is also writing for the newspaper
Publishes her last two novels, *The False Friend* and *The Natural Daughter*; and a prose pamphlet, *A Letter to the Women of England, on the Injustice of Mental Subordination* (reissued later in the year as *Thoughts on the Condition of Women, and on the Injustice of Mental Subordination*)

1800   Arrested for a debt of £63 in May
Publishes a translation of Joseph Hagar's *A Picture of Palermo* and her last volume of poems, *Lyrical Tales*
Dies at Englefield Cottage, Old Windsor, on December 26

Buried in the cemetery at Old Windsor on
December 31

1801   Posthumous publication of *The Memoirs of Mrs.
Robinson, Written by Herself. With Some Posthumous Pieces*

A Note on the Texts

The text of *A Letter to the Women of England* is based on the first edition, published under the pseudonym of Anne Frances Randall in March, 1799, by the London firm of T.N. Longman and O. Rees. The pamphlet was reissued later the same year under Robinson's own name as *Thoughts on the Condition of Women, and on the Injustice of Mental Subordination*. This so-called "second edition" is like the first except for alterations on the title page and the inclusion of a brief "Advertisement":

> FINDING that a Work on a subject similar to the following, has lately been published at Paris, Mrs. Robinson is induced to avow herself the Author of this Pamphlet. The first Edition was published in February last, under the fictitious Signature of *Anne Frances Randall*; and the mention of Mrs. Robinson's works was merely inserted with a view to mislead the reader respecting the REAL AUTHOR of the Pamphlet.

As two pieces of evidence in *The Morning Post* suggest, Robinson altered her title to echo that of Charles-Guillaume Theremin's seventy-six page pamphlet *De la condition des femmes dans les Républiques* (Paris, 1799). Robinson herself may have written a misleading puff that characterized Theremin's pamphlet as "little more than a translation" of her own.[1]

The text of *The Natural Daughter* is based on the first edition in the holdings of The Lilly Library, Indiana University. Published by T. N. Longman and O. Rees in August of 1799, the first edition of 1000 copies apparently sold well enough to justify a second edition in 1799, printed in Dublin by Brett Smith for Wogan, Burnet, Porter, Moore, Jones, Fitzpatrick, Rice, Dornin, Folingsby, and Burnside. In all probability, the slight variations in punctuation and spelling were introduced by

---

[1] This puff, published in *The Morning Post* on August 31, 1799, appeared the day after a brief account of Theremin's pamphlet. For a full text of both items in *The Morning Post*, see Appendix B, 302–03.

the printer without any specific authorization from Robinson herself.

In both texts, I have eliminated running quotation marks, standardized the usage of double and single quotations, modernized the long "s," and silently corrected a few obvious printer's errors. I have also regularized some inconsistent spellings and punctuation (i.e. sooth / soothe, Plummet-Castle / Plummet Castle). Otherwise, I have endeavored to retain the characteristic features of Robinson's style, including her idiosyncratic spellings and her penchants for italics, semi-colons, and hyphenated words. Her footnotes, which I have numbered along with my own, are all followed by the designation "M.R.'s note" in brackets. Many of the editorial notes presuppose that some readers will have a particular interest in Robinson's writing and its cultural contexts. Others are intended primarily for the convenience of general readers who are relatively unfamiliar with eighteenth-century life and literature.

A

LETTER

TO THE

WOMEN OF ENGLAND,

ON THE INJUSTICE OF

MENTAL SUBORDINATION.

WITH

ANECDOTES.

BY ANNE FRANCES RANDALL.

alias M.rs Robinson.

" Wherefore are we
" Born with high Souls, but *to assert ourselves?*"
ROWE.

London:

PRINTED FOR T. N. LONGMAN, AND O. REES, NO. 39,
PATERNOSTER ROW.

1799.

Facsimile title page. Rare Books Division. Department of Rare Books
and Special Collections. Princeton University Library.

A LETTER TO THE WOMEN OF ENGLAND

CUSTOM, from the earliest periods of antiquity, has endeavoured to place the female mind in the subordinate ranks of intellectual sociability. WOMAN has ever been considered as a lovely and fascinating part of the creation, but her claims to mental equality have not only been questioned, by envious and interested sceptics; but, by a barbarous policy in the other sex, considerably depressed, for want of liberal and classical cultivation. I will not expatiate largely on the doctrines of certain philosophical sensualists, who have aided in this destructive oppression, because an illustrious British female, (whose death has not been sufficiently lamented, but to whose genius posterity will render justice) has already written volumes in vindication of "*The Rights of Woman.*"[1] But I shall endeavour to prove that, under the present state of mental subordination, universal knowledge is not only benumbed and blighted, but true happiness, originating in enlightened manners, retarded in its progress. Let WOMAN once assert her proper sphere, unshackled by prejudice, and unsophisticated by vanity; and pride, (the noblest species of pride,) will establish her claims to the participation of power, both mentally and corporeally.

In order that this letter may be clearly understood, I shall proceed to prove my assertion in the strongest, but most undecorated language. I shall remind my enlightened country-women that they are not the mere appendages of domestic life, but the partners, the equal associates of man: and, where they excel in intellectual powers, they are no less capable of all that prejudice and custom have united in attributing, exclusively, to the thinking faculties of man. I argue thus, and my assertions are incontrovertible.

---

[1] The writer of this letter, though avowedly of the same school, disdains the drudgery of servile imitation. The same subject may be argued in a variety of ways; and though this letter may not display the philosophical reasoning with which "*The Rights of Woman*" abounded; it is not less suited to the purpose. For it requires a *legion of Wollstonecrafts* to undermine the poisons of prejudice and malevolence [M.R.'s note]. In the second chapter of her *Vindications of the Rights of Woman*, Wollstonecraft includes an extended critique of Rousseau's *Émile* to illustrate her claim that "the Sensualist ... has been the most dangerous of tyrants," *The Works of Mary Wollstonecraft*, 5:93.

Supposing that destiny, or interest, or chance, or what you will, has united a man, confessedly of a weak understanding, and corporeal debility, to a woman strong in all the powers of intellect, and capable of bearing the fatigues of busy life: is it not degrading to humanity that such a woman should be the passive, the obedient slave, of such an husband? Is it not repugnant to all the laws of nature, that her feelings, actions, and opinions, should be controuled, perverted, and debased, by such an help-mate? Can she look for protection to a being, whom she was formed by the all wise CREATOR, to protect? Impossible, yet, if from prudence, or from pity, if for the security of worldly interest, or worldly happiness, she presumes to take a lead in domestic arrangements, or to screen her wedded shadow from obloquy or ruin, what is she considered by the imperious sex? but an usurper of her husband's rights; a domestic tyrant; a vindictive shrew; a petticoat philosopher; and a disgrace to that race of mortals, known by the degrading appellation of the *defenceless sex*.

The barbarity of custom's law in this *enlightened* country, has long been exercised to the prejudice of woman:[1] and even the laws of honour have been perverted to oppress her. If a man receive an insult, he is justified in seeking retribution. He may chastise, challenge, and even destroy his adversary. Such a proceeding in MAN is termed honourable; his character is exonerated from the stigma which calumny attached to it; and his courage rises in estimation, in proportion as it exemplifies his revenge. But were a WOMAN to attempt such an expedient, however strong her sense of injury, however invincible her fortitude, or important the preservation of character, she would be deemed a murderess. Thus, custom says, you must be free from error; you must possess an unsullied fame: yet, if a slanderer, or a libertine, even by the most unpardonable falshoods, deprive you of either reputation or repose, you have no remedy. He is received in the most fastidious societies, in the cabinets of nobles, at the toilettes of coquets and prudes, while you must bear your load of obloquy, and sink beneath the uniting efforts of calumny, ridicule, and malevolence. Indeed we have

---

[1] The ancient Romans were more liberal, even during the reigns of their most atrocious tyrants: and it is to be presumed that the intellectual powers of British women, were they properly expanded, are, at least, equal to those of the Roman ladies [M.R.'s note].

scarcely seen a single instance where a professed libertine has been either shunned by women, or reprobated by men, for having acted either unfeelingly or dishonourably towards what is denominated the *defenceless sex*. Females, by this mis-judging lenity, while they give proofs of a degrading triumph, cherish for themselves that anguish, which, in their turn, they will, unpitied, experience.

Man is able to bear the temptations of human existence better than woman, because he is more liberally educated, and more universally acquainted with society. Yet, if he has the temerity to annihilate the bonds of moral and domestic life, he is acquitted; and his enormities are placed to the account of *human frailty*. But if WOMAN advance beyond the boundaries of decorum,

Ruin ensues, reproach, and endless shame,
And one false step, entirely damns her fame.[1]

Such partial discriminations seem to violate all laws, divine and human! If WOMAN be the weaker creature, her frailty should be the more readily forgiven. She is exposed by her personal attractions, to more perils, and yet she is not permitted to bear that shield, which man assumes; she is not allowed the exercise of *courage* to repulse the enemies of her fame and happiness; though, if she is wounded,—she is *lost for ever*!

Supposing that a WOMAN has experienced every insult, every injury, that her vain-boasting, high-bearing associate, man, can inflict: imagine her, driven from society; deserted by her kindred; scoffed at by the world; exposed to poverty; assailed by malice; and consigned to scorn: with no companion but sorrow, no prospect but disgrace; she has no remedy. She appeals to the feeling and reflecting part of mankind; they pity, but they do not seek to redress her: she flies to her own sex, they not only condemn, but they avoid her. She talks of punishing the villain who has destroyed her: he smiles at the menace, and tells her, *she is*, a WOMAN.

Let me ask this plain and rational question,—is not woman a human being, gifted with all the feelings that inhabit the bosom

---

[1] These lines, spoken by the heroine of Nicholas Rowe's *The Tragedy of Jane Shore* (1. 2. 189–90), are part of a larger speech attacking the sexual double standard.

of man? Has not woman affections, susceptibility, fortitude, and an acute sense of injuries received? Does she not shrink at the touch of persecution? Does not her bosom melt with sympathy, throb with pity, glow with resentment, ache with sensibility, and burn with indignation?[1] Why then is she denied the exercise of the nobler feelings, an high consciousness of honour, a lively sense of what is due to dignity of character? Why may not woman resent and punish? Because the long established laws of custom, have decreed her *passive*! Because she is by nature organized to feel every wrong more acutely, and yet, by a barbarous policy, denied the power to assert the first of Nature's rights, self-preservation.[2]

How many vices are there that men perpetually indulge in, to which women are rarely addicted. Drinking, in man, is reckoned a proof of good fellowship; and the *bon vivant* is considered as the best and most desirable of companions. Wine, as far as it is pleasant to the sense of tasting, is as agreeable to woman as to man; but its use to excess will render either brutal. Yet man *yields* to its influence, because he is the *stronger-minded* creature; and woman *resists* its power over the senses, because she is the *weaker*. How will the *superiorly* organized sex defend this contradiction? Man will say his passions are stronger than those of women; yet we see women rush not only to ruin, but to death, for objects they love; while men exult in an unmeaning display of caprice, intrigue, and seduction, frequently, without even a zest for the vices they exhibit. The fact is simply this: the passions of men originate in sensuality; those of women, in sentiment: man loves corporeally, woman mentally: which is the nobler creature?

Gaming is termed, in the modern vocabulary, a masculine vice. Has vice then a *sex*? Till the passions of the mind in man and woman are separate and distinct, till the sex of vital animation, denominated soul, be ascertained, on what pretext is woman deprived of those amusements which man is permitted to enjoy? If gaming be a vice (though every species of commerce

---

[1] Robinson's questions here recall those of Shylock in Shakespeare's *The Merchant of Venice*: "Hath not a Jew hands, organs, dimensions, senses, affections, passions.... If you prick us, do we not bleed? ... if you wrong us, shall we not revenge?" (3. 1. 59–67).

[2] See Introduction, 23, n. 1.

is nearly allied to it), why not condemn it wholly?[1] why suffer man to persevere in the practice of it; and yet in woman execrate its propensity? Man may enjoy the convivial board, indulge the caprices of his nature; he may desert his home, violate his marriage vows, scoff at the moral laws that unite society, and set even religion at defiance, by oppressing the defenceless; while woman is condemned to bear the drudgery of domestic life, to vegetate in obscurity, to *love* where she abhors, to *honour* where she dispises, and to *obey*, while she shudders at subordination. Why? Let the most cunning sophist, answer me, WHY?

If women sometimes, indeed too frequently, exhibit a frivolous species of character, we should examine the evil in which it originates, and endeavour to find a cure. If the younger branches of some of our nobility are superficially polished, and wholly excluded from essential knowledge, while they are regularly initiated in the mysteries of a gaming table, and the mazes of intrigue, can we feel surprized at their soon discovering an aptitude to evince their hereditary follies? We know that women, like princes, are strangers to the admonitions of truth; and yet we are astonished when we behold them emulous of displaying every thing puerile and unessential; and aiming perpetually at arbitrary power, without one mental qualification to authorize dominion. From such women, the majority of mankind draw their opinions of sexual imbecility; and, in order that their convenient plea may be sanctioned by example, they continue to debilitate the female mind, for the sole purpose of enforcing subordination.

Yet, the present era has given indisputable proofs, that WOMAN is a thinking and an enlightened being! We have seen a Wollstonecraft, a Macaulay, a Sévigné;[2] and many others, now living, who embelish the sphere of literary splendour, with genius of the first order. The aristocracy of kingdoms will say, that it is

---

[1] Robinson herself had launched an attack on female gamesters in *Nobody* (1794), a two-act comedy that ran for only three nights at Drury Lane Theatre.

[2] In Wollstonecraft's estimate, Catharine Macaulay (1731–1791) was the supreme English "example of intellectual acquirements supposed to be incompatible with the weakness of her sex." Her works included an eight-volume *History of England* (1763–1783) and *Letters on Education* (1790). Marie de Rabutin-Chantal, Marquise de Séveigné (1626–1696), often regarded as the most influential woman writer of France, was best known for her posthumously published letters to her daughter.

absolutely necessary to extort obedience: if all were masters, who then would stoop to serve? By the same rule, man exclaims, If we allow the softer sex to participate in the intellectual rights and privileges we enjoy, who will arrange our domestic drudgery? who will reign (as Stephano[1] says, while we are vice-roys over them) in our household establishments? who will rear our progeny; obey our commands; be our affianced vassals; the creatures of our pleasures? I answer, women, but they will not be your slaves; they will be your associates, your equals in the extensive scale of civilized society; and in the indisputable rights of nature.[2]

In the common occurrences and occupations of life, what in man is denominated high-spirit, is in WOMAN termed vindictive. If a man be insulted and inflicts a blow upon his assailant, he is called a brave and noble-minded creature! If WOMAN acts upon the same principle of resistance, she is branded as a Zantippe,[3] though in such a situation she would scarcely meet with a Socrates, even if, in the scale of comparison, she possessed stronger corporeal, as well as mental, powers, than the object of her resentment.

How comes it, that in this age of reason we do not see statesmen and orators selecting women of superior mental acquirements as their associates? Men allow that women are absolutely necessary to their happiness, and that they "had been brutes" without them.[4]

---

[1]   Robinson is apparently recalling lines from Shakespeare's *The Tempest*, in which Stephano, the drunken butler, tells Caliban of his plot to kill Prospero: "His daughter and I will be king and queen—'save our Graces! And Trinculo and thyself shall be viceroys" (3. 2. 106–108).

[2]   The Mahometans are said to be of the opinion that WOMEN have no souls! Some British husbands would wish to evince that they have no SENSES, or at least not the privilege of using them: for a modern wife, I mean to say that which is denominated a *good one*, should neither hear, see, speak, nor feel, if she would wish to enjoy any tolerable portion of tranquillity [M.R.'s note]. Robinson's association of "Mahometan" (i.e. Islamic or Turkish) customs with the degradation of women has antecedents in Wollstonecraft and many other eighteenth-century authors. One notable exception is Lady Mary Wortley Montagu (1689–1762). In one of her letters from Turkey, she remarks, "Our Vulgar Notion that they [the Turks] do not own Women to have any Souls is a mistake." See *The Complete Letters of Lady Mary Wortley Montagu*, 1: 363.

[3]   Zantippe, wife of Socrates, was a proverbial example of female shrewishness.

[4]   Cf. Thomas Otway's *Venice Preserv'd*: "Oh Woman! lovely Woman! Nature made thee / To temper Man: we had been brutes without you" (1. 336–37). The unidentified quotation in Robinson's next sentence may be a conventional poeticism rather than a deliberate echo of one particular source.

But the poet did not insinuate that none but silly or ignorant women were to be allowed the *supreme honour* of unbrutifying man, of rendering his life desirable, and of "smoothing the rugged path of care" with their endearments. The ancients were emulous of patronizing, and even of cultivating the friendship of enlightened women. But a British Demosthenes, a Pythagoras, a Leontius, a Eustathius, or a Brutus, would rather pass his hours in dalliance with an unlettered courtezan, than in the conversation of a Theano, a Themiste, a Cornelia, a Sosipatra, or a Portia.[1] What is this display of mental aristocracy? what but the most inveterate jealousy; the most pernicious and refined species of envy and malevolence?

Let me ask the rational and thinking mortal, why the graces of feminine beauty are to be constituted emblems of a debilitated mind? Does the finest symmetry of form, or the most delicate tint of circulation, exemplify a tame submission to insult or oppression? Is the strength of intellect, in woman, bestowed in vain? Has the SUPREME DISPOSER OF EVENTS given to the female soul a distinguished portion of energy and feeling, that the one may remain inactive, and the other be the source of her destruction? Let the moralist think otherwise. Let the contemplative philosopher examine the proportions of human intellect; and let us hope that the immortality of the soul springs from causes that are not merely *sexual.*

Cicero says, "There was, from the beginning such a thing as Reason; a direct emanation from nature itself, which prompted to good, and averted from evil." Reason may be considered as a part of soul; for, by its powers, we are taught intuitively to hope for a future state. Cicero did not confine the attribute of Reason to sex; such doctrine would have been completely Mahometan!

---

[1] Demosthenes was a famous Greek orator of the fourth century B.C. Pythagoras, a Greek philosopher and mathematician of the fifth century B.C., was the instructor, and perhaps the husband, of Theano, mentioned on p. 54, below. Leontious, an Aristotelian philosopher of the sixth century B.C., was the husband of Themiste, mentioned on p. 54, below. Eustathius, a classical scholar of the twelfth century, was the husband of Sosipatra, mentioned on p. 55, below. Marcus Brutus, a Roman statesman who participated in the conspiracy to assassinate Julius Caesar, was the husband of Portia. Following Brutus's "honorable" suicide, Portia reputedly ended her own life by swallowing live coals.

The most celebrated painters have uniformly represented angels as of no sex. Whether this idea originates in theology, or imagination, I will not pretend to determine; but I will boldly assert that there is something peculiarly unjust in condemning woman to suffer every earthly insult, while she is allowed a sex; and only permitting her to be happy, when she is divested of it. There is also something profane in the opinion, because it implies that an all-wise Creator sends a creature into the world, with a sexual distinction, which shall authorise the very extent of mortal persecution. If men would be completely happy by obtaining the confidence of women, let them unite in confessing that mental equality, which evinces itself by indubitable proofs that the soul has no sex. If, then, the cause of action be the same, the effects cannot be dissimilar.

In what is woman inferior to man? In some instances, but not always, in corporeal strength: in activity of mind, she is his equal. Then, by this rule, if she is to endure oppression in proportion as she is deficient in muscular power, *only*, through all the stages of animation the weaker should give precedence to the stronger. Yet we should find a Lord of the Creation with a puny frame, reluctant to confess the superiority of a lusty peasant girl, whom nature had endowed with that bodily strength of which luxury had bereaved him.

The question is simply this: Is woman persecuted and oppressed because she is the *weaker* creature? Supposing that to be the order of Nature; let me ask these human despots, whether a woman, of strong mental and corporeal powers, is born to yield obedience, merely because *she is a woman*, to those shadows of mankind who exhibit the effeminacy of women, united with the mischievous foolery of monkies? I remember once, to have heard one of those modern Hannibals[1] confess, that he had changed his regiments three times, because the regimentals were *unbecoming*!

If woman be the *weaker* creature, why is she employed in laborious avocations? why compelled to endure the fatigue of household drudgery; to scrub, to scower, to labour, both late and early, while the powdered lacquey only waits at the chair, or behind

---

[1] Hannibal was a Carthaginian general of the second century B.C.

the carriage of his employer?[1] Why are women, in many parts of the kingdom, permitted to follow the plough; to perform the laborious business of the dairy; to work in our manufactories; to wash, to brew, and to bake, while men are employed in measuring lace and ribands; folding gauzes; composing artificial bouquets; fancying feathers, and mixing cosmetics for the preservation of beauty? I have seen, and every inhabitant of the metropolis may, during the summer season, behold strong Welsh girls carrying on their heads strawberries, and other fruits from the vicinity of London to Covent-Garden market, in heavy loads which they repeat three, four, and five times, daily, for a very small pittance; while the *male* domesticks of our nobility are revelling in luxury, to which even their lords are strangers. Are women thus compelled to labour, because they are of the WEAKER SEX?

In my travels some years since through France and Germany, I often remember having seen stout girls, from the age of seventeen to twenty-five, employed in the most fatiguing and laborious avocations; such as husbandry, watering horses, and sweeping the public streets. Were they so devoted to toil, because they were the *weaker* creatures? and would not a modern *petit maître* have fainted beneath the powerful grasp of one of these rustic or domestic amazons?

Man is said to possess more personal courage than woman. How comes it, then, that he boldly dares insult the *helpless* sex, whenever he finds an object unprotected? I here beg leave to present a true story, which is related by a polished and impartial traveller.——[2]

---

[1] As Priscilla Wakefield observed, the inequity was compounded by a serious discrepancy in pay: "A footman, especially of the higher kind, whose most laborious task is to wait at table gains ... at least £50 per annum, whilst a cook-maid, who is mistress of her profession, does not obtain £20, though her office is laborious, unwholesome, and requires a much greater degree of skill than that of a valet." Advocating more employment opportunities for women in the manufacture and sale of female finery, Wakefield urged "women of rank" to patronize "their humbler sisters," rather than the "brood of effeminate beings in the garb of men" who were displacing them. See *Reflections on the Present Condition of the Female Sex* (London: J. Johnson, 1798), 151, 153. The first part of Mary Ann Radcliffe's *The Female Advocate; Or, an Attempt to Recover the Rights of Women from Male Usurpation* (1799) is also specifically concerned with "The Fatal Consequences of Men Traders Engrossing Women's Occupations."

[2] The source of this story has not been identified.

"A foreign lady of great distinction, of a family to whom I had the honour to be well known, was appointed to be married to a young gentleman of equal rank: the settlements were all made, the families agreed, and the day was come for the union. The morning of the same day, the ceremony of the marriage being fixed for the same evening, the lover being young, thoughtless, and lost with passion, when alone with the bride, insinuated, in the softest and most endearing terms, that he was her husband in every sense but a few trifling words, which were to pass that night from the mouth of the priest; and, that if she loved him, as he presumed she did, she certainly would not keep him one moment in anxiety; much less ten or twelve hours, which must be the case, if she waited for the ceremony of the church. The lady, astonished at what she had heard, discovered in her looks not only the warmest resentment, but resolved in her heart to be amply revenged; and having had an excellent education, was well acquainted with the world, and no stranger to the artifices of designing men in affairs of love; after recovering a little her surprise, determined to keep her temper, and promised with a smile, obedience to her lover's will, and begged him to name the place proper for such a design; which, being mutually agreed on for four in the afternoon, the indiscreet lover, ravished at his expectation, met, agreeable to appointment, the lady, in a garden leading to the house, where they proposed the interview. When walking together, with all seeming tenderness on both sides, the lady, on a sudden, started from her lover, and threw him a pistol, holding another in her right hand, and spoke to him to this effect: 'Remember for what infamous purpose you invited me here: you shall never be a husband of mine; and such vengeance do I seek for the offence, that, on my very soul, I vow, you or I shall die this hour. Take instantly up the pistol, I'll give you leave to defend yourself; though you have no right to deserve it. In this, you see, *I* have honour; though *you* have none.'

"The lover, amazed at this unforeseen change, took up the pistol, in obedience to her commands, directing it towards the earth, threw himself at her feet, and was going to say a thousand things in favour of his passion; the lady gave attention a few minutes, pointing the pistol to his breast; while the lover, with a voice confused, and every other appearance of despair, begged her pity and her pardon; declared his love for her was such, that he was deprived of all power of reflection; that he had no views of offending; that all he said was for want of thought, that his reason was absent, and that her beauty was the cause of all.—'Beauty!' says the lady, interrupting him, 'Thou art a villain! I'll hear no more, for one of us must die this moment.'—The lover perceiving her violent anger, and finding that all his soft phrases had no effect on her, in his distraction raised the pistol then in his hand a little higher; thinking, by its appearance in that situation, to affect his admired lady with some terror, while he continued to pursue his defence; but alas! no sooner did the angry fair perceive the pistol of her lover raised breast high, but, that instant being the crisis of her resentment, she fired upon him, and shot him through the heart. He fell; and in falling, being deprived of both speech and reason, his pistol went off, and the consequence was, her collar bone was broke, and much blood followed. She clapped her handkerchief to the wound, ran to her coach, which was waiting at the garden door, ordered her servant to take care of the dead body, and directed some others to conduct her with the utmost expedition to her father's house; to whom she related the whole affair. Proper assistance was instantly sent for; and I being that day at table with the physician of the Court, who was also of this family, went with him; saw the wound, and was well instructed in the particulars of this adventure. The lady was never so much as called to a trial for the death of her lover; because all the circumstances proved the truth of what she had related: her promising to marry him that night, was so powerful an argument of her love for the deceased, that no other motive could have produced so dreadful an event. The lady was cured of her wound, threw herself into a convent; and, from despair for the loss of her lover, languished a few weeks, and then followed him, as she hoped, to the other world. The brother of the lover, according to the custom of the country, fought the brother of the lady, and killed his antagonist. He flew to Spain for refuge, where I afterwards saw him a colonel in a regiment of that nation."

This short story will prove that the mind of WOMAN, when she feels a correct sense of honour, even though it is blended with the very excess of sensibility, can rise to the most intrepid defence of it. Yet had such a circumstance taken place in Britain, the perpetrator of this heroic act of indignant and insulted virtue, would probably have suffered an ignominious death, or been shut up during the remainder of her days as a confirmed *maniac*;[1] for HERE woman is placed in the very front of peril, without being allowed the means of self-preservation, and that very resistance which would secure her from dishonour, would stigmatize her in the world's opinion.

What then is WOMAN to do? Where is she to hope for justice? Man who *professes* himself her champion, her protector, is the most subtle and unrelenting enemy she has to encounter: yet, if she determines on a life of celibacy and secludes herself wholly from his society, she becomes an object of universal ridicule.

It has lately been the fashion of the time, to laugh at the encreasing consequence of women, in the great scale of human intellect. Why? Because, by their superior lustre, the overweening and ostentatious splendour of some men, is placed in a more obscure point of view. The women of France have been by some popular, though evidently prejudiced writers, denominated little better than she-devils![2] And yet we have scarcely heard of one instance, excepting in the person of the vain and trifling Madame Du Barry, in which the females of that country have not displayed almost a Spartan fortitude even at the moment when they ascended the scaffold. If there are political sceptics, who affect to place the genuine strength of soul to a bold but desperate temerity, rather than to a sublime effort of heroism, let them contemplate the last moments of Marie Antoinette; this extraordinary WOMAN, whose days had passed in luxurious splendour; whose

---

[1] The fate of Miss Broderick is still recent in the memory of those who either condemned her rashness, or commiserated her misfortunes [M.R.'s note]. Brought to trial in 1794 for shooting a lover who deserted her, Ann Broderick was judged not guilty by reason of insanity. Her story is related in *The Trial of Miss Broderick, for the Willful Murder of George Errington* (Edinburgh, 1795).

[2] Robespierre, for example, denounced Théroigne de Méricourt as a "She-devil in ruffles" when she attempted to organize a Republican women's club. Quoted in Candice E. Proctor's *Women, Equality, and the French Revolution* (New York: Greenwood Press, 1990), 143.

will had been little less than law! Behold her hurled from the most towering altitude of power and vanity; insulted, mocked, derided, stigmatized, yet *unappalled* even at the instant when she was compelled to endure an ignominious death! Let the strength of her mind, the intrepidity of her soul, put to shame the vaunted superiority of man; and at the same time place the female character in a point of view, at once favourable to nature, and worthy of example.[1] France has, amidst its recent tumultuous scenes, exhibited WOMEN whose names will be the glory of posterity. Women who have not only faced the very front of war,[2] but thereby sustained the heroic energies of their countrymen, by the force of *example* and the effect of *emulation*. Even the rash enthusiast, CORDAY, whose poniard annihilated the most sanguinary and atrocious monster that ever disgraced humanity, claimed our pity, (even while religion and nature shuddered), as she ascended the fatal scaffold, to expiate the deed she had accomplished.[3]

Let us take a brief retrospect of events in British history, and let the liberal mind dwell with rapture on the heroic affection evinced by the illustrious Eleonora, consort of Edward the First.[4] Tradition may then point out the learned Elizabeth, (with all her *sexual* failings) and then judge whether England ever boasted a more wise or more fortunate sovereign: one, more revered in

---

[1] Robinson offered more extensive tributes to Marie Antoinette in an anonymously published pamphlet, *Impartial Reflections on the Present Situation of the Queen of France* (1791), and *A Monody to the Memory of the Late Queen of France* (1793).

[2] The *Demoiselles* FERNIG, who followed, and shared the perils of Dumourier's army [M.R.'s note]. According to a report in *The Monthly Magazine*, the two sisters "headed the French troops, in 1791, with the same boldness" that Joan of Arc had demonstrated two hundred years before. Unlike Joan, however, they wore "female attire, and pretended neither to prophecy nor revelation," 1 (1796): 400.

[3] Charlotte Corday (1768–1793), often described as a modern Joan of Arc, stabbed the Jacobin leader Jean-Paul Marat in his bathtub on July 13, 1793. He immediately became a martyr, and she was sent to the guillotine on July 17. For Helen Maria Williams's account of Corday's death, see Appendix F, 320.

[4] According to one contemporary source, Queen Eleanor epitomized the good wife whose "tongue is always employ'd in kind and healing offices." After an assassin wounded her husband with a poisoned knife, "she daily licked his wrinkling Wounds with her Tongue, whilst he was asleep, and thereby extracted all the Poyson out." See *Look E're You Leap: Or, a History of the Lives and Intrigues of Women.* 10th ed. (London: Edw. Midwinter, 1720), 108.

council; more obeyed in power; or more successful in enterprize. And yet Elizabeth was but a woman! A woman with *all* her sex's frailties.[1]

"The glories of a part of the reign of Anne, rise thick as the beauties of a constellation; this, the plain of Blenheim, and the field of Ramilies can witness."[2]

It may not be amiss, for the advantage of my unlettered readers, here to introduce an extract from the learned VOSSIUS, in his treatise *de philologia*, concerning illustrious WOMEN who had excelled in polite literature. It consists chiefly of such female names as he had not before celebrated, among his poets and historians: and the list might have been very much enlarged, since the time that Vossius wrote.[3]

"It is wrong," says this learned and *liberal* author, "to deny that the fair sex are capable of literature; all the old philosophers thought better of them.[4] Pythagoras instructed not men only, but WOMEN; and among them Theano, whom Laertius makes to be his wife, and St. Clement calls the first of women; declaring that she both *philosophized* and wrote *poems*. The Stoics, Epicureans, and even the Academicks, delivered their lessons freely to both sexes, and all conditions. Themiste, the wife of Leontius, to whom there is extant, an epistle of Epicurus, was a disciple of this philosopher.

"Atossa queen of Persia, is said to be the *first* who taught the art of writing epistles.

"In the time of Alexander the Great, flourished Hipparchia, the sister of Metroples the Cynic, and wife of Crates. She wrote

---

1   An historical writer in his account of Russia, speaking of the *Czarina* Elizabeth, says "her reign was most uncommonly glorious. She abolished all capital punishments, and introduced a species of lenity in the operations of government, before *unknown* in Russia" [M.R.'s note].

2   The battles of Blenheim (1704) and Ramillies (1706) marked two significant victories for the English in the War of Spanish Succession (1701–14). The source of Robinson's quotation has not been identified.

3   About a century and a half ago [M.R.'s note]. Gerardus Joannes Vossius (1577–1649) was a distinguished Dutch scholar and author of many works, including the posthumously published *De quatuor artibus popularibus, de philologia et scientiis mathematicis litri tres* (1650). The passages that Robinson quotes appear in the second chapter of the second book.

4   It was reserved for modern Englishmen to question their capability [M.R.'s note].

of philosophical arguments, essays and questions to Theodorus, surnamed the Deist.

"Pamphila, the Egyptian, who lived in the time of Nero, wrote eight books of Historical Miscellanies.

"Agallis, of Corcyra, is celebrated for her skill in grammar. She ascribes the invention of the play at ball, to her countrywoman Nausicaa; who is the only one, of all his heroines, which Homer introduces at this diversion.

"Quintilian, celebrated three Roman WOMEN, in words to this effect. Cornelia the mother of the Gracchi, contributed much to the eloquence of her sons; and her learned stile is handed down to posterity in her letters. The daughter of Lælius expressed in her conversation the eloquence of her father. There is an oration of the daughter of Quintus Hortensius, delivered before Triumvirs, which will ever be read to the honour of her sex. Quintilian has omitted the learned wife of Varus, and Cornisicia the poetess, who left behind her most exquisite epigrams. This WOMAN, who flourished in the reign of Octavius Caesar, used to say that *learning alone was free, as being entirely out of the reach of fortune.*[1]

"Catherine of Alexandria was a learned WOMAN; she is said to have disputed with fifty philosophers, at the age of eighteen, and so far to have overcome them by the subtlety of her discourse, as to have converted them to the christian religion.

"Who was more learned than Zenobia, queen of Palmyra, by religion a Jew? We have the testimony of her conqueror himself, the emperor Aurelian, to her character in his letters to the Roman senate. Trebellius Pollio says, 'she spoke Egyptian, read Latin into Greek, and wrote an abridgement both of Alexandrine and Oriental history. Her master, in the Greek, was Dionysius Longinus, who was called a living library, and a walking museum.'

"Sosipatra, wife of the famous Eustathius remembered all the finest passages, of all the poets, philosophers, and orators; and had an almost inimitable talent of explaining them. Though her husband was a man of high celebrity in learning, yet she so far

---

[1] Cornisicia, happily, did not live in Britain, where learning, and even moderate *mental* expansion, are not thought necessary to female education; at least in the eighteenth century! [M.R.'s note].

out-shone him, as to *obscure his glory;*[1] and after his death she took upon her the education of youth.

"What shall we say of Eustochium, daughter of Paulla the Roman, who was learned in Latin, Greek, and Hebrew; and most assiduous in the study of the sacred scriptures? St. Jerom speaks many things in her praise; there are epistles of the same father, extant, to several illustrious WOMEN, as Paulla, Læta, Fabrilla, Marcella, Furia, Demetrias Salvia and Gerontia. Why should we mention others to whom we have letters extant of Ambrose, Augustin, and Fulgentius? The compliments of the fathers are testimonies of their learning.[2]

"Hypatia was the daughter of that Theon of Alexandria, whose writings now remain. She was a vast proficient in astronomy. This woman was murdered, through religious frenzy, by the Alexandrine mob; because she made frequent visits to Orestes, the philosopher.

"At the same time flourished Eudocia, whose name before was Athenais, daughter of Leontius the philosopher, and wife of the emperor Theodosius the younger. She was deep read both in Greek and Latin learning; skilled in poetry, mathematics, and all the philosophical sciences.

"About the year of Christ, 500, Amalasuenta, the daughter of Theodoric king of the Goths, and wife of Eutharic who was made consul by the emperor Justin, was celebrated both for her learning and her wisdom. PRINCES are said to come and advise with her, and admire her understanding.[3] She took upon her the administration of affairs, in the name of her son, Athalaric, who

---

1   The fear that emulation may, in some instances, produce superiority, probably occasions that illiberal neglect of female genius, and that perseverance in affording British women the contracted and trivial educations which stigmatize the present era. Yet were the youth of the eighteenth century committed to the care of some living females, both manners and morals would greatly be benefited [M.R.'s note].

2   Men of modern education suppose that women are only worthy of receiving *billet doux*, because the extent of their own literary acquirements is that of writing them. And it is to be lamented, that our classical scholars, and men of extensive observation, scarcely condescend to acknowledge that there can be such a thing as a WOMAN of genius [M.R.'s note].

3   If the great men of the present day paid more attention to the genius and good sense of some British women, they would be considerable gainers by the experiment [M.R.'s note].

was left king, at eight years of age; and whom she instructed in all the polite learning *before unknown to the Goths.*[1]

"Helpis, the learned wife of the learned Boethius, flourished in 530. She left behind her hymns to the apostles.

"Bandonia, the scholar of St. Radegundis, wrote the life of her holy mistress. She died in 530.

"About 650 lived Hilda, an ENGLISH abbess, celebrated by Pits[2] among English writers, and Bede in his ecclesiastical history. She was daughter of Hereric, prince of Deira, and aunt of Aldulph, king of the East Saxons.[3]

"About 770 Rictrude, a noble virgin, made great proficiency in literature under her master Alcuin; after whose departure out of England, she shut herself up to her studies in the monastery of Saint Bennet at Canterbury, where she produced many writings.

"About two centuries lower down, under the emperors Otho I. and II. lived the nun Rhosoitar, skilled both in the Latin and Greek languages. She wrote a panegyrick upon the deeds of the Othos; six comedies, the praises of the Blessed Virgin, and St. Dennis in elegiac verse, with other works.

"In the year of Christ 1140, flourished Anna Comnena, daughter of Alexius Comnenus, emperor of Constantinople. This WOMAN, in the fifteen books of her Alexiad, which she wrote upon the deeds of her father, displayed equally her eloquence and her learning.

"St. Hildegard of Mentz, was famous about eight years after, and at the same time flourished St. Elizabeth of Schonua, sister of king Ecbert. The monkish writers celebrate them for their visions, which received the sanction of pope Eugenius III. But *we* mention them for their historical, didactical and epistolary writings, a collection of which has been published. St. Catherine Senensis also wrote epistles, and various treatises in the dialogue manner, which

---

[1] Query. Might not the society of *some* living *English women,* if properly appreciated, tend to the reformation of certain *gothic* eccentricities; as well as, by comparison, produce more masculine energies? Men would be shamed out of their *effeminate* foibles, when they beheld the masculine virtues dignifying the mind of woman [M.R.'s note].

[2] John Pits (1560–1616) was an English scholar, priest, and biographer.

[3] This was at a period when English women, (excepting those devoted to celibacy), were rarely taught either to read or write. It cannot be therefore a matter of surprize, that their minds were enervated by monkish superstition; the origin of those idle tales respecting ghosts, witches, &c. [M.R.'s note].

are now extant, as well as her life, written by Raimund her confessor, a Dominican friar. Whatever was the sanctity of these women, of their learning we have certain monuments.

"In the year 1484, under Charles VIII. king of France, flourished Gabriele de Bourbon, princess Trimouille. Catalogues of her various writings are preserved in French authors. About three years after, Cassandra Fidele, a Venetian girl, acquired great applause, by an excellent oration delivered publicly, in the UNIVERSITIES of PADUA,[1] in behalf of Betruri Lamberti, her relation. She won the SUPREME CROWN in PHILOSOPHY! This oration was afterwards printed at Modena.

"Alike for her own learning, and her patronage of the learned, Margaret of Valois queen of Navarre, merited of mankind. Joan, the daughter of this princess, had by Anthony of Bourbon, Henry the Fourth, king of France, founder of the family now reigning.

"Bologna boasts several learned WOMEN; among which were Joanna Blanchetta, and Novella Andrea, and the learned Catherina Landa, we read of in Bambo's epistles.

"What shall we say of Joanna married to Philip archduke of Austria, duke of Burgundy, and, by his wife, king of Spain. She answered extempore, in Latin, the orations made to her through the several towns and cities, after her accession.[2]

"Sir Thomas More, chancellor of England, had three daughters, Margaret, Elizabeth, and Cæcilia; of whom their father took care that they were not only very chaste but very learned. Because he rightly judged that their chastity would be, by this means, the more secure.[3]

"The learning of Fulvia Olympia Morata, daughter of Perigrine Moratus, is evident from writings she has left: and that Hippolita Taurellas was equal, appears from her writings, collected together with those of Morata.

---

[1] A Cassandra in the universities of England, at the *present period*, would be considered as one of those literary bugbears, a *female philosopher*, and would consequently be treated with ridicule and contempt [M.R.'s note].

[2] Our English sovereign Elizabeth, gave similar proofs of learning on several occasions [M.R.'s note].

[3] Read this, ye English fathers and husbands, and retract your erroneous opinions, respecting female education [M.R.'s note].

"It is needless, in England, to quote Queen Elizabeth, or the lady Jane Grey, as eminent instances of the kind; because our historians are full of their praises upon the subject."

Vossius mentions farther only Anne Schurman, a noble WOMAN, whose Latin poetry recommends her to this day.[1] He thinks, that if this catalogue were added to those he had given separately, of the FEMALE POETS and HISTORIANS, sufficient examples would appear in behalf of women, that they were *equally capable of fine literature with the other sex.*

We might add to these, says another author "the two Le Fevres, among the French: one of them married to Monsieur Dacier; and the other to the famous Le Clerc: and among ourselves, Mrs. Catherine Philips, Mrs. Cenlivre, Mrs. Behn, and Mrs. Elizabeth Singer, (afterwards Mrs. Rowe), as in no degree, according to their *several walks of literature*, inferior to any that have been mentioned."[2]

The name of the Grecian poetess, Sappho, is probably known to almost every reader. Some anecdotes of this celebrated WOMAN, who lived near 600 years before Christ, may be found in the Abbé Barthelimi's Travels of Anacharsis the Younger: and in the account of this poetess, preceding Mrs. Robinson's legitimate sonnets.[3]

---

[1] Vossius does, in fact, mention three other women between Queen Elizabeth and Anne Schurman. Although the *English Short-Title Catalogue* lists no English translation, these omissions and others suggest that Robinson was quoting from a text that had been translated and edited by someone else, possibly the unidentified author mentioned in the paragraph below.

[2] Anne Dacier (1654–1720), wife of the classical scholar André Dacier, translated many works, including *The Iliad* (1711) and *The Odyssey* (1716). Katherine Philips (1631–64) won celebrity as a coterie poet writing under the signature of "Orinda." Her collected *Poems*, including an unfinished translation of Corneille's *Horace*, were posthumously published in 1667. Susanna Centlivre (1667–1723), an actress known for her daring exploits, later became one of the most successful playwrights of her day. Aphra Behn (1640–1689), a prolific dramatist of the Restoration period, is best known today as the author of *Oroonoko; or, The Royal Slave* (1688), a narrative that exposes the horrors of the slave trade. Elizabeth Singer Rowe (1674–1737), a poet and prose writer, was noted both for her piety and her mastery of foreign languages. Her most popular work was *Friendship in Death: In Twenty Letters from the Dead to the Living* (1728).

[3] Robinson is referring to her own volume *Sappho and Phaon. In a Series of Legitimate Sonnets, with Thoughts on Poetical Subjects, and Anecdotes of the Grecian Poetess* (1796). Publishing a number of poems before and after under the signature of "Sappho," Robinson was sometimes dubbed "the British Sappho."

Since the beginning of the present century, we have seen many examples, not only of natural genius, but of enthusiastic resolution, even in unlearned women; prompted by the purest and most feminine passion of the human soul.[1] We have known WOMEN desert their peaceful homes, the indolence of obscure retirement, and the indulgence of feminine amusements, to brave the very heat of battle, stand to their gun, amidst the smoak and din of a naval engagement;[2] conceal the anguish of their wounds; and, from the very heroism of love, repeatedly hazard their existence. How few men have we seen so nobly uniting the softest passion of the soul, with the enthusiasm of valour. When man exposes his person in the front of battle, he is actuated either by interest or ambition: woman, with neither to impel her, has braved the cannon's thunder; stood firmly glorious amidst the din of desolation; "begrimed and sooted in the smoak of war;"[3] and yet she is, by the undiscriminating or prejudiced part of mankind, denominated the *weaker* creature.

As another striking example of female excellence, of invincible resolution, of attachment, marking a sublimity of character which will put to shame those puerile cavillers who attempt to depreciate the mental strength of woman, even where it is blended with the most exquisite sensibility, I transcribe the following events, in the words of a brave and liberal British officer; whose feelings and manners, enlightened by philanthropy and polished by learning, will be long remembered with regret and admiration.[4]

"Lady Harriet Ackland had accompanied her husband to

---

[1] A memorable instance of genuine and invincible attachment appeared in the conduct of the misguided and unfortunate Sophia Pringle: and though justice condemned her crime, pity will never refuse a sigh to the memory of her heroic affection [M.R.'s note]. Pringle was convicted of forgery and executed in 1787 after she refused to accept a pardon offered on the condition that she identify her accomplice/lover. Her story is related in William Cole's *Exalted Affection; or Sophia Pringle, a Poem* (Salisbury, 1789).

[2] Hannah Snell, and several others, equally brave and romantic [M.R.'s note]. Snell assumed a male disguise and went to sea in 1745 with the hopes of finding her husband, a Dutch sailor who had deserted her. Her extraordinary adventures were related in an anonymously published biography *The Female Soldier* (1750), and she was later described as "the famous Mademoiselle D'Eon of lower life." (See p. 73, n. 1, below.) She died in Bethlehem Hospital for the insane in 1792.

[3] Shakespeare [M.R.'s note]. Cf. *Twelfth Night*, 5. 1. 52–53.

[4] The late General Burgoyne [M.R.'s note]. John Burgoyne (1722–1792) included the narrative of Lady Harriet in *A State of the Expedition from Canada, as Laid Before the*

Canada, in the beginning of the year 1776. In the course of the campaign, she traversed a vast space of country, in different extremities of season, and with difficulties that an European traveller will not easily conceive, to attend in a poor hut at Chamblee upon his sick bed.

"In the opening of the campaign of 1777, she was restrained from offering herself to a share of the fatigue and hazard expected before Ticonderago, by the positive injunctions of her husband. The day after the conquest of that place, he was badly wounded, and she crossed the Lake Champlain to join him.

"As soon as he recovered, Lady Harriet proceeded to follow his fortunes through the campaign; and at Fort Edward, or at the next camp, she acquired a two-wheeled tumbrel, which had been constructed by the artificers of artillery, something similar to the carriage used for the mail in the great roads of England. Major Ackland commanded the British grenadiers which were attached to Frazer's corps; and consequently were always the most advanced post of the army; their situations were often so alert, that no person slept out of their clothes.

"In one of these situations, a tent, in which the Major and Lady Harriet were asleep, suddenly took fire. An orderly serjeant of grenadiers, with great hazard of suffocation, dragged out the first person he caught hold of; it proved the Major. It happened in the same instant, that Lady Harriet had, unknowing what she did, and perhaps not perfectly awake, providentially made her escape, by creeping under the walls of the back part of the tent. The first object she saw, on the recovery of her senses, was the Major, on the other side; and, in the same instant, again in the fire, in search of her. The serjeant again saved him; but not without the Major being very severely burned in the face, and different parts of the body: every thing they had with them in the tent was consumed.

House of Commons (London: J. Almon, 1780), 127–29. According to Charles Neilson, Burgoyne added "touching and romantic" details to an incident that "was not so very extraordinary that it might not have been enacted by any other pretty woman, under the same circumstances, who loved her husband." See *An Original, Compiled, and Corrected Account of Burgoyne's Campaign* (1844; Port Washington, NY: Kennikat Press, 1970), 173. Many readers have noted similar embellishments in Burgoyne's highly flattering verses "To Mrs. Robinson," reprinted in her *Memoirs*, 4: 99–101.

"This accident happened a little before the army passed Hudson's river. It neither altered the RESOLUTION nor the chearfulness of Lady Harriet; and she continued her progress, a partaker of the fatigues of the advanced corps.

"The next call upon her FORTITUDE was of a different nature; and more distressing, as of longer suspense. On the march of the 19th of September, the grenadiers being liable to action every step, she had been directed by the Major to follow the route of the artillery and baggage, which was not exposed. At the time the action began, she found herself near a small uninhabited hut, where she alighted.

"When it was found that the action was becoming general and bloody, the surgeons of the hospital took possession of the same place, as the most convenient for the care of the wounded. Thus was this lady, in hearing of one continued fire of cannon and musketry for four hours together, with the presumption, from the post of her husband at the head of the grenadiers, that he was in the most exposed part of the action. She had three FEMALE companions; the Baroness of Reidesel, and the wives of two British officers, Major Harnage, and Lieutenant Reynell: but in the event, their presence served but little for comfort. Major Harnage was soon brought to the surgeons, very badly wounded; and a little after came intelligence, that Lieutenant Reynell was shot, dead. Imagination will want no help to figure the state of the whole group.

"From the date of that action, to the 7th of October, Lady Harriet, with her usual serenity, stood prepared for new trials! And it was her lot, that their severity increased with their numbers. She was again exposed to the hearing of the whole action; and at last received the shock of her individual misfortune, mixed with the intelligence of the general calamity, that the troops were defeated, and that Major Ackland, desperately wounded, was a prisoner.

"The day of the 8th was passed by Lady Harriet and her companions in inexpressible anxiety: not a tent, not a shed was standing, except what belonged to the hospital: their refuge was among the wounded and the dying. The night of the 8th the army retreated; and at day-break on the 9th, reached very advantageous ground. A halt was necessary to refresh the troops, and to give time to the batteaux loaded with provisions, to come a-breast.

"When the army was upon the point of moving after the halt, I received a message from Lady Harriet, submitting to my decision a proposal of passing to the camp of the enemy, and requesting General Gates's permission to *attend her husband*! Lady Harriet expressed an earnest solicitude to execute her intentions, if not interfering with my designs.

"Though I was ready to believe, for I had experienced, *that patience and fortitude, in a supreme degree, were to be found, as well as every other virtue*, under the most tender forms, I was astonished at the proposal, after so long an agitation of spirits; exhausted not only for want of rest, but absolutely for want of food; drenched by rains for twelve hours together; that a woman should be capable of such an undertaking as delivering herself to the enemy, probably in the night, and uncertain of what hands she might fall into, appeared an effort, *above human nature*!

"The assistance I was enabled to give, was small indeed. I had not even a cup of wine to offer her; but I was told she had found, from some kind and fortunate hand, a little rum and dirty water. All I could furnish to her was an open boat, and a few lines, written upon dirty and wet paper, to General Gates, recommending her to his protection.

"Mr. Brudenell, the chaplain to the artillery, the same gentleman that had officiated so signally at General Frazer's funeral, readily undertook to accompany her; and with one *female* servant and the Major's *valet de chambre*, who had a ball, which he had received in the late action, then in his shoulder, she moved down the river, to meet the enemy! But her distresses were not yet at an end.

"The night was advanced before the boat reached the enemy's outposts; and the centinel would not let it pass, nor even come on shore. In vain Mr. Brudenell offered the flag of truce; and represented the state of the extraordinary passenger. The guard, apprehensive of treachery, and punctilious to his orders, threatened to fire into the boat, if she stirred before day-light. Her anxiety and suffering were thus protracted through seven or eight dark and cold hours, and her reflections upon that first reception could not give her very encouraging ideas of the treatment she was afterwards to expect. But it is due to justice, at the close of this adventure, to say, that she was received and accommodated by General Gates with all the humanity and respect that her rank, her merits, and her fortunes deserved.[1]

"Let such as are affected by these circumstances of alarm, hardship, and danger, recollect that the subject of them was A WOMAN! of the most tender and delicate frame; of the gentlest manners; habituated to all the soft elegancies and refined enjoyments that attend high birth and fortune; and far advanced in a state in which the tender cares, always due to the sex, become indispensably necessary. Her mind, alone, was formed for such trials."[2]

The most argumentative theorists cannot pretend to estimate mental by corporeal powers. If strength or weakness are not allowed to originate in the faculty of thought, Charles Fox, or William Pitt, labouring under the debilitating ravages of a fever, is a weaker animal than the thrice-essenced poppinjay, who mounts his feathered helmet, when he should be learning his Greek alphabet.[3] If strength of body is to take the lead of strength of mind, the pugilist is greater than the most experienced patriot; the uncultivated plough-boy surpasses the man of letters; and the felicity of kingdoms would be as safe in the hands of a savage Patagonian ruler, as under the stronger faculties of the most accomplished Statesman. By this rule, monarchs should select their

---

1   The writer of this letter once knew General Gates, and believes him capable of every thing liberal and humane, which General Burgoyne's statement attributes to his character [M.R.'s note]. After settling near Bristol in 1766, Horatio Gates (1728–1806) and his family moved close to London in 1768, the same year that the Darby family relocated. The paths of the two families may have crossed before Gates left England for the last time in 1772 and joined the American army. Gates was eventually defeated by Cornwallis and Tarleton in the battle of Camden, SC, in 1780. See Paul David Nelson's *General Horatio Gates: A Biography* (Baton Rouge: Louisiana State UP, 1976).

2   The enlightened and liberal writer of this pathetic story, confesses, that the subject of it was not *masculinely* educated. Yet she displayed the glorious energy of Roman constancy, mingled with affections the most pure, and sentiments the most exalted! An ARRIA or a PORTIA could have done no more [M.R.'s note]. Arria and Portia were Roman women who demonstrated their constancy by committing suicide. See p. 47, n. 1, above, and p. 82, n. 2, below.

3   William Pitt (1759–1806) served as prime minister from 1783–1801 and again from 1804–1806. Charles James Fox (1749–1806) was a leader of the political opposition. According to some sources, he was also Robinson's lover for a brief period after her affair with the Prince of Wales.

cabinets by the standard of measurement; and while the first minister could say with Sir Andrew Ague-cheek, "I am as tall a man as any in Illyria," he may laugh to scorn the most gigantic talents.[1] This question does not admit of argument; it is self-evident.

And yet, though it be readily allowed that the primary requisites for the ruling powers of man, are strong *mental* faculties; woman is to be denied the exercise of that intuitive privilege, and to remain inactive, as though she were the least enlightened of rational and thinking beings. What first established, and then ratified this oppressive, this inhuman law? The tyranny of man; who saw the necessity of subjugating a being, whose natural gifts were equal, if not superior, to his own. Let these mental despots recollect, that education cannot *unsex* a woman; that tenderness of soul, and a love of social intercourse, will still be hers; even though she become a rational friend, and an intellectual companion. She will not, by education, be less tenacious of an husband's honour; though she may be rendered more capable of defending her own.

A man would be greatly shocked, as well as offended, were he told that his son was an idiot; and yet he would care but little, if every action proved that his wife were one. Tell a modern husband that his son has a strong understanding, and he will feel gratified. Say that his wife has a masculine mind, and he will feel the information as rather humbling than pleasing to his self-love. There are but three classes of women desirable associates in the eyes of men: handsome women; licentious women; and good sort of women.—The first for his vanity; the second for his amusement; and the last for the arrangement of his domestic drudgery. A thinking woman does not entertain him; a learned woman does not flatter his self-love, by confessing inferiority; and a woman of real genius, eclipses him by her brilliancy.

Not many centuries past, the use of books was wholly unknown to the commonality of females; and scarcely any but superior nuns, then denominated "*learned women*" could either read or write. Wives were then considered as household idols,

---

[1]   In Shakespeare's *Twelfth Night*, Sir Andrew Aguecheek boasts, "I think I have the back-trick simply as strong as any man in Illyria" (1. 3. 123–24). The lines echo the description given by his companion, Sir Toby Belch, earlier in the same scene: "He's as tall a man as any's in Illyria."

created for the labour of domestic life, and born to yield obedience. To brew, to bake, and to spin, were then deemed indispensably necessary qualifications: but to think, to acquire knowledge, or to interfere either in theological or political opinions, would have been the very climax of presumption! Hence arose the evils of bigotry and religious imposition. The reign of credulity, respecting supernatural warnings and appearances, was then in its full vigour. The idle tales of ghosts and goblins, and the no less degrading and inhuman persecutions of age and infirmity, under the idea of witchcraft, were not only countenanced, but daily put in practice. We do not read in history of any act of cruelty practised towards a *male bewitcher*; though we have authentic records to prove, that many a weak and defenceless woman has been tortured, and even murdered by a people professing Christianity, merely because a pampered priest, or a superstitious idiot, sanctioned such oppression.[1] The *witcheries* of mankind will ever be tolerated, though the frenzy of fanaticism and the blindness of bigotry sink into oblivion.

In or about the year 1759, were published some excellent lines, from the pen of a British woman,[2] addressed to Mr. Pope, whose cynical asperity towards the enlightened sex was not one of his least imperfections. I shall only give an extract:

> In education all the difference lies,
> WOMEN, if taught, would be as brave, as wise,
> As haughty man, improv'd by arts and rules;
> Where GOD makes one, *neglect* makes twenty fools.
> Can women, left to weaker women's care,

---

[1] Although some men were, in fact, persecuted for witchcraft, Mary Daly argues that the "prime targets [of witch-hunts] were women living outside the control of the patriarchal family." See *Gyn/Ecology: The Metaethics of Radical Feminism* (Boston: Beacon, 1978), 186.

[2] I believe Lady Mary Wortley Montague, the same WOMAN, whose name should be immortalized, for having first introduced to Europe the blessing of INOCULATION [M.R.'s note]. The lines come from a poem entitled "An Epistle to Mr. Pope, Occasioned by his *Characters of Women*," published in *The Gentleman's Magazine* 6 (1736): 745. Robinson may have seen a reprint or later version of the poem, which was actually written by one of Montagu's friends, Anne Ingram (neé Howard), Viscountess Irwin (1696–1764).

Mislead by CUSTOM, Folly's fruitful heir,
Told that their charms a monarch may enslave,
That beauty, like the gods, can kill and save;
And taught the wily and mysterious arts,
By ambush'd dress, to catch unwary hearts;
If wealthy born, taught to lisp French, and dance,
Their morals left, Lucretius like, to chance;
Strangers to Reason and Reflection made;
Left to their passions, and by them betray'd;
Untaught the noble end of glorious Truth,
Bred to deceive, e'en from their earliest youth;
Unus'd to books, nor Virtue taught to prize,
Whose mind, a savage waste, all desart lies;
Can these, with aught but trifles, fill the void,
Still idly busy, to no end employ'd:
Can these, from such a school, with virtue glow,
Or tempting vice, treat like a dang'rous foe?
Can these resist when soothing Pleasure woos,
Preserve their virtue, when their fame they lose?
Can these, on other themes, converse or write,
Than what they hear all day, and dream all night?
Not so the Roman female fame was spread,
Not so was CLELIA or LUCRETIA bred!
Not so such heroines true glory sought,
Not so was PORTIA or CORNELIA taught.
PORTIA, the glory of the female race;
PORTIA, more lovely in her *mind* than face;
Early inform'd by *Truth's* unerring beam,
What to reject, what justly to esteem.
Taught by *Philosophy*, all *moral good*;
How to repel, in youth, th' impetuous blood:
How ev'ry darling passion to subdue;
And Fame, through *Reason's* avenues, pursue.
Of Cato born; to noble Brutus join'd;
Supreme in beauty, with a ROMAN MIND!

The women, the Sévignés, the Daciers, the Rolands, and the
Genlis's of France, were the first, of modern times, to shake off the

yoke of sexual tyranny.[1] The widow of Scarron, (afterwards Madame de Maintenon,) was an ornament to her sex, till she became the dupe of a profligate monarch, and the instrument of bigot persecution.[2] The freezing restraint which custom placed on the manners of other nations, and which is as far removed from true delicacy as the earth is from the heavens, in France, threw no chilling impediment on the progress of intellect. Men soon found by experience, that society was embellished, conversation enlivened, and emulation excited, by an intercourse of ideas. The younger branches of male nobility in France, were given to the care of female preceptors; and the rising generations of women, by habit, were considered as the rational associates of man. Both reason and society benefited by the change; for though the monasteries had less living victims, though monks had fewer proselytes, the republic of letters had more ornaments of genius and imagination.

Women soon became the idols of a polished people. They were admitted into the councils of statesmen, the cabinets of princes. The influence they obtained contributed greatly towards that urbanity of manners which marked the reign of Louis the Sixteenth. The tyrants of France, at the toilettes of enlightened WOMEN, were taught to shudder at the horrors of a Bastille: which was never more crowded with victims, than when bigotry and priestcraft were in their most exulting zenith. I will not attempt to philosophize how far the influence of reason actuated on more recent events. That hypothesis can only be defined by posterity.

It is an indisputable fact that a *woman*, (excepting in some cases of supposed witchcraft) if thrown into the water, has, as Falstaff

---

[1] Marie-Jeanne Philipon, Madame Roland (1754–1793), one of the most influential women in revolutionary France, was arrested and later executed during the Reign of Terror. While in prison, she wrote her *Memoirs*. Stéphanie-Félicité Ducrest de Saint-Aubin, Comtesse de Genlis (1746–1830), wife of a Girondin leader beheaded in 1793 and mistress of the Duke of Orleans, escaped from France during the Reign of Terror. Her prolific output as a writer included *Adelaide and Theodore; Or, Letters on Education* (1782) and a series of letters on literature and politics commissioned by Napoleon.

[2] Françoise d'Aubigné, Marquise de Maintenon (1635–1719) was the governess of Louis XIV's illegitimate children and later became his second wife. Although she won considerable acclaim for her patronage of the arts and her efforts to improve female education, she was also accused of encouraging the king's campaign against the Huguenots.

says, "a strange alacrity at sinking."[1] And yet a woman must not be taught to swim; it is not feminine! though it is perfectly masculine to let a woman drown merely because she is a woman, and denied the knowledge of preserving her existence. In this art the savages of Oreehoua and Tahoora are initiated from their infancy; the females of those islands are early taught the necessary faculty of self-defence.[2] They are familiarized to the limpid element at so early a period that a child of four years old, dropped into the sea, not only betrays no symptoms of fear, but seems to enjoy its situation. The women consider swimming as one of their favourite diversions; in which they amuse themselves when the impetuosity of the dreadful surf that breaks upon their coast, is encreased to its utmost fury, in a manner equally perilous and extraordinary. And yet these courageous females are denominated of the *weaker* sex.

A celebrated geographer[3] remarks, that "the best test of civilization, is the respect that is shewn to women."

The little regard shewn to the talents of women in this country, strongly characterizes the manners of the people. The Areopagites, once put a boy to death for putting out the eyes of a bird: and they argued thus, says an elegant writer, *il ne s'agit point là d'une condamnation pour crime, mais d'un jugement de moeurs, dans une republique fondée sur les moeurs.*[4]

Heaven forbid that the criterion of this national and necessary good, should be drawn from the conduct of mankind towards British women. There is no country, at this epoch, on the habitable globe, which can produce so many exalted and illustrious

---

1 In Shakespeare's *The Merry Wives of Windsor*, Falstaff remarks, "you may know by my size that I have a kind of alacrity in sinking" (3. 5. 12–13).

2 Oreehoua and Tahoora, now called Lehua and Kaula, are two small islands close to Naiihau in the Hawaiian islands.

3 Salmon [M.R.'s note]. Thomas Salmon (1679–1767) wrote many geographical and historical works, including a three-volume *Modern History, or the Present State of all Nations* (1739). According to the *Dictionary of National Biography*, it was later continued under a variety of fictitious names.

4 The Areopagites were members of the Areopagus, the high council in ancient Athens. The quotation, from an unidentified source, may be translated to read: "it is not a question of punishment for a crime, but a judgment of morals, in a republic founded on morals."

women (I mean mentally) as England. And yet we see many of them living in obscurity; known only by their writings; neither at the tables of women of rank; nor in the studies of men of genius; we hear of no national honours, no public marks of popular applause, no rank, no title, no liberal and splendid recompense bestowed on British literary women! They must fly to foreign countries for celebrity, where talents are admitted to be of no SEX, where genius, whether it be concealed beneath the form of a Grecian Venus,[1] or that of a Farnese Hercules,[2] is still honoured *as* GENIUS, one of the best and noblest gifts of THE CREATOR.

Here, the arts and the sciences have exhibited their accomplished female votaries. We have seen the graces of poetry, painting, and sculpture, rising to unperishable fame from the pen, the pencil, and the chissel of our women. History has lent her classic lore to adorn the annals of female literature; while the manners of the age have been refined and polished by the wit, and fancy of dramatic writers. I remember hearing a man of education, an orator, a legislator, and a superficial admirer of the persecuted sex, declare, that "the greatest plague which society could meet with, was a *literary woman!*"

I agree that, according to the long established rule of custom, domestic occupations, such as household management, the education of children, the exercise of rational affection, should devolve on woman. But let the partner of her cares consider her zeal as the effect of reason, temporizing sensibility, and prompting the exertions of mutual interest; not as the constrained obse-

---

[1]   Lady Hamilton, and Helen Maria Williams, are existing proofs, that an English woman, like a prophet, is never valued in her own country. In Britain they were neglected, and scarcely *known*; on the continent, they have been nearly IDOLIZED! [M.R.'s note]. Lady Emma Hamilton (1761?–1815) was the beautiful and charming wife of Sir William Hamilton, the English ambassador to Naples. Owing to her humble birth and former position as Hamilton's mistress, Emma was shunned by the Queen of England. In Naples, however, she became a leading member of high society and an intimate friend of Queen Maria Carolina. Although Williams was certainly known in England as the author of *Letters from France*, her reputation was tarnished by the anti-Jacobin press, which denounced her politics as well as her extra-marital liaison with John Hurford Stone. Cf. Richard Polwhele's disparaging commentary on Williams in *The Unsex'd Females*, Appendix C, 308, n.3.

[2]   A famous marble statue attributed to the Greek sculptor Glykon. It was one of the most celebrated pieces in the art collection of the wealthy Farnese family of Italy.

quiousness of inferior organization. Let man confess that a wife, (I do not mean an *idiot*), is a thinking and a discriminating helpmate; not a bondswoman, whom custom subjects to his power, and subdues to his convenience. A wife is bound, by the laws of nature and religion, to participate in all the various vicissitudes of fortune, which her husband may, through life, be compelled to experience. She is to combat all the storms of an adverse destiny; to share the sorrows of adversity, imprisonment, sickness, and disgrace. She is obliged to labour for their mutual support, to watch in the chamber of contagious disease; to endure patiently, the peevish inquietude of a weary spirit; to bear, with tacit resignation, reproach, neglect, and scorn; or, by resisting, to be stigmatized as a violator of domestic peace, an enemy to decorum, an *undutiful* wife, and an unworthy member of society. Hapless woman! Why is she condemned to bear this load of persecution, this Herculean mental toil, this labour of Syssiphus; this more than Ixion's sufferings, as fabled by heathen mythologists?[1] Because she is of the *weaker* sex.

Tradition tell us that the Laura of Petrarch, whose name was immortalized by the Genius of her lover during twenty years of unabating fondness, could neither *read* nor *write!*[2] Petrarch was a poet and a scholar; I will not so far stigmatize his memory, as to attribute his excessive idolatry to the intellectual obscurity of his idol. Yet from the conduct of some learned modern philosophers, (in every thing but love), the spirit of cynical observation might trace something like jealousy and envy, or a dread of rivalry in mental acquirements. We have seen living husbands, as well as lovers, who will agree with the author of some whimsical stanzas, printed in the year 1739, of which I remember the following lines,[3]

---

[1] In Greek mythology, Hercules gained immortality by performing twelve seemingly impossible feats; Sisyphus was doomed to perform the futile task of rolling a large stone uphill, only to have it roll back down; and Ixion suffered the torments of being bound to a wheel of fire.

[2] Publishing poems under the pseudonym of "Laura," Robinson wrote herself into the Petrarchan tradition even as she wrote against it. Her most deliberate intervention was a long verse epistle "Petrarch to Laura" (1790), modeled after Pope's "Eloisa to Abelard."

[3] Robinson's source has not been identified.

Now all philosophers agree
That WOMEN should not LEARNED be;[1]
For fear that, as they wiser grow,
More than their husbands they should know.
For if we look we soon shall find,
Women are of a tyrant kind;
They love to govern and controul,
Their bodies lodge *a mighty soul!*
The sex, like horses, could they tell
Their equal strength, would soon rebel;
They would usurp and ne'er submit,
To bear the yoke, and champ the bit.

Constrained obedience is the poison of domestic joy: hence we may date the disgust and hatred which too frequently embitter the scenes of wedded life. And I should not be surprized, if the present system of mental subordination continues to gain strength, if, in a few years, European husbands were to imitate those beyond the Ganges. There, wives are to be purchased like slaves, and every man has as many as he pleases. The husbands and even fathers are so far from being jealous, that they frequently offer their wives and daughters to foreigners.[2]

However contradictory it may seem, to contracted minds, I firmly believe that the strongest spell which can be placed upon the human affections, is a consciousness of freedom. Let the husband assume the complacency of the friend, and he will, if his wife be not naturally depraved, possess not only her faith but her

---

[1] Should modern preceptors object to the classics through fear that the minds of English women would be corrupted by the writings of an Ovid, a Martial, or a Tibullus: let them recollect, that there lived also a Virgil, a Terence, a Lucan, and a Propertius. They should also remember that their native language presents the works of Wycherly, Vanbrugg, Prior, and Rochester; and that they cannot so contaminate, as those of Shakespeare, Denham, Steel, Cowley, Waller, Addison, Shenstone, and many more, can *purify* [M.R.'s note].

[2] We have some British *sposos* who already advance *half way* in this liberal system of participation, stepping somewhat beyond the polished tract of Italian *cecisbeos*: it may be said of such husbands as it was of Cataline, that he was *alieni appetens, sui profusus*: greedy after the goods of others, and lavish of his own [M.R.'s note]. *Spòsos* are husbands; and *cicisbèos* are married women's gallants.

affection. There is a resisting nerve in the heart of both man and woman, which repels compulsion. Constraint and attachment, are incompatible: the mind of woman is not more softened by sensibility than sustained by pride; and every violation of moral propriety, every instance of domestic infidelity, every divorce which puts asunder "those whom God has joined," is a proof of that maxim being a false, I may say a ludicrous one, which declares that MAN was born to *command*, and WOMAN to *obey*! excepting in proportion as the intellectual power devolves on the husband.

If a woman receives an insult, she has no tribunal of *honour* to which she can appeal; and by which she would be sanctioned in punishing her enemy. What in man, is laudable; in woman is deemed reprehensible, if not preposterous.[1] What in man is noble daring, in woman is considered as the most vindictive persecution. Supposing a woman is calumniated, robbed at a gaming table, falsely accused of mean or dishonourable actions, if she appeals to a stranger; "it is no business of his! such things happen every day! the world has nothing to do with the quarrels of individuals!" If she involves a dear friend, or a relation in her defence; she is "a dangerous person; a promoter of mischief; a revengeful fury." She has therefore no remedy but that of exposing the infamy of her enemy; (for sexual prejudices will not allow her to fight him *honourably*), even then, all that she asserts, however disgraceful to her opponent, is placed to the account of womanish revenge. The dastardly offender triumphs with impunity, because he is the noble creature man, and she a *defenceless*, persecuted woman.

Prejudice (or policy) has endeavoured, and indeed too successfully, to cast an odium on what is called a *masculine* woman; or, to

---

[1] We have a living proof of this observation in the person of Madame D'Eon. When this extraordinary female filled the arduous occupations of a soldier and an embassador, her talents, enterprize, and resolution, procured for her distinguished honours. But alas! when she was discovered to be a WOMAN, the highest terms of praise were converted into, "eccentricity, absurd and masculine temerity, at once ridiculous and disgusting" [M.R.'s note]. Wollstonecraft included "Madame d'Eon" among her list of "heroines" who "acquired courage and resolution" from a "masculine education." As an autopsy report revealed in 1810, however, D'Eon was, in fact, a male. For a full account of his extraordinary life, see Gary Kates's biography, *Monsieur D'Eon is a Woman: A Tale of Political Intrigue and Sexual Masquerade* (1995).

explain the meaning of the word, a woman of enlightened understanding. Such a being is too formidable in the circle of society to be endured, much less sanctioned. Man is a despot by nature; he can bear no equal, he dreads the power of woman; because he knows that already half the felicities of life depend on her; and that if she be permitted to demand an equal share in the regulations of social order, she will become omnipotent.

I again recur to the prominent subject of my letter, viz. that woman is denied the first privilege of nature, the power of SELF-DEFENCE. There are lords of the creation, who would not hesitate to rob a credulous woman of fortune, happiness, and reputation, yet they would deem themselves justified in punishing a petty thief, who took from them a watch or a pocket handkerchief. *Man* is not to be deprived of *his* property; *he* is not to be pilfered of the most trifling article, which custom has told him is necessary to *his* ideas of luxury. But WOMAN is to be robbed of that peace of mind which depended on the purity of her character; *she* is to be duped out of all the proud consolations of independence; defrauded of her repose, wounded in the sensibilities of her heart; and, because she is of the *weaker* sex, she is to bear her injuries with *fortitude*.

If a man is stopped on the highway, he may shoot the depredator: and he will receive the thanks of society. If a WOMAN were to act upon the same principle, respecting the more atrocious robber who has deprived her of all that rendered life desirable, she would be punished as a *murderer*. Because the highwayman only takes that which the traveller can afford to lose, and the loss of which he will scarcely feel; and the WOMAN is rendered a complete bankrupt of all that rendered life supportable. The swindler and the cheat are shut out from society; but the avowed libertine, the very worst of defrauders, is tolerated and countenanced by our most fastidious British females. This is one of the causes why the manners of the age are so unblushingly licentious: *men* will be profligate, as long as *women* uphold them in the practice of seduction.

If, in the common affairs of life, a man be guilty of perjury, on conviction he is sentenced to undergo the penalty of his crime, even though the motive for committing it, were unimportant to the community at large, and only acting against the plea of individual interest. But if a man takes an oath, knowing and premeditatedly resolved to break it, at the altar of the Divinity, his crime is tolerated, and he pleads the force of example, in extenuation of his apostacy. Man swears to love and to cherish his wife, never to forsake her in sickness, or in health, in poverty or wealth, and to keep to her *alone* so long as they both shall live. Let me ask these law makers, and these law *breakers*, these sacriligious oath takers, whether nine out of ten, are not conscious of committing perjury at the moment when they make a vow so universally broken? But man is permitted to *forswear* himself, even at the altar dedicated to the SUPREME BEING! He is allowed, even *there*, to consider the *most* sacred of ceremonies as merely a political institution, of which he may exclusively avail himself as far as it tends to the promotion of his interest, while neither the publicity, nor the number of his infidelities, attach the badge of worldly censure to his conduct. He is still the lordly reveller; the master of his pleasures; the tolerated breaker of his oath: he pleads the frailty of human nature, though he, as the stronger creature, is supposed to possess an omnipotent source of mental power; he urges the sovereignty of the passions, the dominion of the senses, the sanction of long established custom. He is a man of universal gallantry; he is consequently courted and idolized by the generality of women, though all his days and all his actions prove, that woman is the victim of his falsehood.

Now examine the destiny of the *weaker* sex, under similar circumstances. WOMAN is to endure neglect, infidelity, and scorn: she is to endure them patiently. She is not allowed to plead the frailty of human nature; she is to have no passions, no affections; and if she chance to overstep the boundaries of chastity, (whatever witcheries and machinations are employed to mislead her;) if she violates that oath, which, perhaps the pride of her kindred, family interest, ambition, or compulsion, extorted from her, CUSTOM, that pliant and convenient friend to man, declares her infamous. While women, who are accessaries to her disgrace, by countenancing her husband's infidelities, condemn the wife with all the vehemence of indignation; because woman is the weaker creature, and most subjected to temptation! because man errs voluntarily; and woman is seduced, by art and by persecution, from the paths of Virtue.

There is scarcely an event in human existence, in which the

oppression of woman is not tolerated. The laws are made by man; and self-preservation is, *by them*, deemed the primary law of nature. Hence, woman is destined to be the passive creature: she is to yield obedience, and to depend for support upon a being who is perpetually authorised to deceive her. If a woman be married, her property becomes her husband's;[1] and yet she is amenable to the laws, if she contracts debts beyond what that husband and those laws pronounce the necessaries of existence. If the comforts, or even the conveniences of woman's life rest on the mercy of her ruler, they will be limited indeed. We have seen innumerable instances, in cases of divorce, where the weaker, the defenceless partner is allotted a scanty pittance, upon which she is expected to live *honourably*; while the husband, the lord of the creation, in the very plenitude of wealth, in the very zenith of splendour, is permitted openly to indulge in every *dishonourable* propensity. Yet, he is commiserated as the injured party; and she is branded with the name of infamous: though he is deemed the *stronger*, and she the *weaker* creature.

Frailty, through all the stages of social intercourse, appears to be most enormous in those who are supposed to have least fortitude to sustain the powers of self-resistance. Yet, such is the force of prejudice, the law of custom, against woman, that she is expected to *act* like a philosopher, though she is not allowed to *think* like one. If she pleads the weakness of her sex, her plea is not admitted; if she professes an equal portion of mental strength with man, she is condemned for arrogance. Yet, if a General be sent into the field of battle with a force inferior to that of the enemy, and is vanquished, the plea of inequality in resisting powers is admitted, and *his* honour is exonerated from every imputation: WOMAN encounters an all-commanding enemy; *she* is subdued;—and *she* is eternally dishonoured!

The laws of man have long since decreed, that the jewel, Chastity, and the purity of uncontaminated morals, are the brightest ornaments of the female sex. Yet, the framers of those laws are indefatigable in promoting their violation. Man says to

---

[1] The Married Women's Property Act of 1870 allowed wives to keep up to £200 of their earnings. The passage of a new act in 1884 allowed them to keep all property they acquired before and during marriage.

woman, without chastity you are declared infamous; and at the same moment, by a subtle and gradual process, he undermines the purity of her heart, by a bold defiance of all that tends to the support of religion and morality. Man thus commits a kind of mental suicide; while he levels that image to the lowest debasement, which he has ostentatiously set up for universal idolatry.

It is not by precept, but by example, that conviction strikes deeply into the thinking mind. Man is supposed to be the more wise and more rational creature; his faculties are more liberally expanded by classical education: he is supposed to be more enlightened by an unlimited intercourse with society. He is permitted to assert the dignity of his character; to punish those who assail his reputation; and to assume a superiority over all his fellow creatures. He is not accountable to any mortal for the actions of his life; he may revel in the follies, indulge the vices of his *superior* nature. He pursues the pleasures or the eccentricities of his imagination, with an avidity insatiable: and he perpetually *proves* that human passions subjugate *him* to the degradations of human frailty; while woman, the *weaker* animal, she whose enjoyments are limited, whose education, knowledge, and actions are circumscribed by the potent rule of prejudice, she is expected to *resist* temptation; to be invincible in fortitude; strong in prescient and reflecting powers; subtle in the defence of her own honour; and forbearing under all the conflicts of the passions. Man first degrades, and then deserts her. Yet, if driven by famine, insult, shame, and persecution, she rushes forth like the wolf for prey; if, like Milwood, she finds it "necessary to be rich" in this sordid, selfish world, she is shunned, abhorred, condemned to the very lowest scenes of vile debasement; to exist in misery, or to perish unlamented.[1] No kindred breast will pity her misfortunes; no pious tear embalm her ashes: she rushes into

---

[1] George Lillo's tragedy *The London Merchant: Or, the History of George Barnwell* (1731) was revived in 1796, with Mrs. Siddons playing the role of Millwood. After seducing the innocent young hero and convincing him to kill his rich uncle, Millwood explains that she was merely following the example set by men: "My soul disdained, and yet disdains, dependence and contempt. Riches, no matter by what means obtained, I saw secured the worst of men from both. I found it, therefore, necessary to be rich, and to that end I summoned all my arts" (4. 18). Cf. Robinson's less sympathetic allusion to Millwood in *The Natural Daughter*, 276.

the arms of death, as her last, her only asylum from the monsters who have destroyed her.

Woman is destined to pursue no path in which she does not find an enemy. If she is liberal, generous, careless of wealth, friendly to the unfortunate, and bountiful to persecuted merit, she is deemed prodigal, and over-much profuse; all the good she does, every tear she steals from the downcast eye of modest worth, every sigh she converts into a throb of joy, in grateful bosoms, is, by the world, forgotten; while the ingenuous liberality of her soul excites the imputation of folly and extravagance. If, on the contrary, she is wary, shrewd, thrifty, economical, and eager to procure and to preserve the advantages of independence; she is condemned as narrow-minded, mean, unfeeling, artful, mercenary, and base: in either case she is exposed to censure. If liberal, unpitied; if sordid, execrated! In a few words, a generous woman is termed a *fool*; a prudent one, a *prodigal*.[1]

If WOMAN is not permitted to assert a majesty of mind, why fatigue her faculties with the labours of any species of education? why give her books, if she is not to profit by the wisdom they inculcate? The parent, or the preceptress, who enlightened her understanding, like the dark lantern,[2] to spread its rays internally only, puts into her grasp a weapon of defence against the perils of existence; and at the same moment commands her not to use it. Man says you *may* read, and you *will* think; but you shall not evince your knowledge, or employ your thoughts, beyond the boundaries which we have set up around you. Then wherefore burthen the young mind with a gaudy outline which man darkens with shades indelible? why expand the female heart, merely to render it more conscious that it is, by the tyranny of custom, rendered vulnerable? Let man remember, that

A little learning is a dangerous thing.[3]

---

1 Robinson probably meant *miser* rather than *prodigal*. This emendation is suggested by a handwritten correction in the copy of Robinson's *Letter* at the Princeton University Library.

2 A lantern with a shutter or sliding panel that can be closed to keep the light from spreading.

3 From Alexander Pope's *An Essay on Criticism*, I. 215.

Let him not hope for a luxurious mental harvest, where the sun of cultivation is obscured by impenetrable prejudice; that cloud which has too long spread over the mind of woman a desolating darkness. So situated, woman is taught to discriminate just sufficiently to know her own unhappiness. She, like Tantalus, is placed in a situation where the intellectual blessing she sighs for is within her view;[1] but she is not permitted to attain it: she is conscious of possessing equally strong mental powers; but she is obliged to yield, as the weaker creature. Man says, "you shall be initiated in all the arts of pleasing; but you shall, in vain, hope that we will contribute to your happiness one iota beyond the principle which constitutes our own." Sensual Egotists! woman is absolutely necessary to your felicity; nay, even to your existence: yet she must not arrogate to herself the power to interest your actions. You idolize her personal attractions, as long as they influence your senses; when they begin to pall, the magick is dissolved; and prejudice is ever eager to condemn what passion has degraded.

A French author,[2] who wrote in the early part of the present century, says, "The empire we exercise over the fair sex is usurped; and that which they obtain over us is by nature. Our submission very often costs them no more than a glance of the eye; the most stern and fierce of mankind grow gentle at the sight of them.[3] What a whimsical conduct it is to dispute with women

---

1 Tantalus, in *The Odyssey*, is condemned to a pool in Hades where he is tormented by the water and fruits that always evade his grasp. An anti-feminist response could certainly make much of the reason why the gods put him there: he betrayed the favoritism they had shown by allowing him to eat at their table when he invited them to a feast, and served up the body of his son.

2 Monsieur Tourriel, author of an Examination whether it was wisely done to abolish that law of the Romans, by which women were kept under the power of guardianship all their lives [M.R.'s note]. Although Jacques de Tourreil (1656–1715) was known primarily for his translations of Demosthenes, an English translation of the work from which Robinson is quoting appeared in *Common Sense; or, the Englishman's Journal* on Sept 1 and 8, 1739. The first installment argued the case against women and provoked spirited response from the anonymous "Sophia" and other feminist writers. The second installment, arguing in favor of women, included the passages that Robinson quotes and various commonplaces of eighteenth-century feminist discourse (i.e. "the soul has no Sex").

3 If this remark *were* true, it is to be lamented that they do not grow liberal and *unprejudiced* also [M.R.'s note].

the right of managing their own estates, while we give up our liberties at so cheap a rate."

The same author, in the same work, says, "It rarely happens, that we share with women the shame of their errors, though we are either the authors, or the accomplices of them. On the other hand, how many follies have we, that are peculiar to ourselves; how many occasions are there where *their* modesty conceals more merit, than *we* can shew, with all our vanity!"

Supposing women were to act upon the same principle of egotism, consulting their own inclinations, interest, and amusement only, (and there is no law of Nature which forbids them; none of any species but that which is framed by man;) what would be the consequences? The annihilation of all moral and religious order. So that every good which cements the bonds of civilized society, originates wholly in the forbearance, and conscientiousness of woman.

I wish not to advise the sex against cultivating what modern writers term, the GRACES.[1] I would have woman highly, eminently polished; she should dance, if her form be well proportioned; she should sing, if nature has endowed her with the power of conveying that harmony so soothing to the senses. She should draw, paint, and perform fanciful tasks with her needle; particularly if her frame be delicate, her *intellects* feminine. But if nature has given her strong mental powers, half her hours of study should be devoted to more important acquirements. She should likewise, if strong and active, be indulged in minor sports; such as swimming, the use of the ball, and foot racing, &c. We should then see British Atalantas, as well as female Nimrods.[2]

However singular it may appear to a reflecting mind, hunting, certainly one of the most barbarous of masculine sports is,

---

[1] The mind of woman, in proportion as it is expanded by education, will become refined. Mental emulation would be the best safeguard against the vanity of sensual conquest [M.R.'s note].

[2] Atalanta, in Greek myth, was particularly noted for her fleetness of foot. Refusing to marry unless a suitor could outrace her, Atlanta was finally overcome by Melanion because she stopped to pick up the three golden apples that Venus had instructed him to drop along the way. Nimrod, in the Old Testament, is described as "a mighty hunter before the Lord" (Genesis 10: 9).

in Europe, tolerated as an amusement for the *softer* sex! There again, *weakness* is, by the humane ordinance of man, devoted to persecution. The harmless stag and timid hare are hunted to destruction, even by women!—Why, in this single instance, does man agree in the propriety of masculine pursuits? Why does the husband, without apprehension or disgust, permit the *tender, weak*, and *delicate* partner of his cares to leap a quarry or a five-barred gate, at the same time that he would deem it the excess of arrogance, to offer an opinion, on any subject which MAN considers as exclusively adapted to his discussion. I can only conclude that a wife has full permission to break her neck; though she is forbid to think or speak like a rational creature.[1]

Why are women excluded from the auditory part of the British senate? The welfare of their country, cannot fail to interest their feelings; and eloquence both exalts and refines the understanding.[2] Man makes woman a frivolous creature, and then condemns her for the folly he inculcates. He tells her, that beauty is her first and most powerful attraction; her second complacency of temper, and softness of manners. She therefore dedicates half her hours to the embellishment of her person; and the other half to the practice of soft, languishing, sentimental insipidity. She disdains to be strong minded, because she fears being accounted masculine; she trembles at every breeze, faints at every peril, and yields to every assailant, because it would be unwomanly to defend herself. She sees no resemblance of her own character in the Portias and Cornelias of antiquity; she is

---

[1] A husband infers from this conduct, that he permits his wife to act like a *mad-woman*, but he does not allow her to think like a *wise one* [M.R.'s note].

[2] Many of the American tribes admit women into their public councils, and allow them the privileges of giving their opinions, *first*, on every subject of deliberation. The ancient Britons allowed the female sex the same right: but in modern Britain women are scarcely allowed to express any opinions at all! [M.R.'s note]. Although some women had been allowed to observe proceedings in the House of Commons earlier in the eighteenth century, they were banned in 1778. According to Norman Wilding and Philip Laundy, the ban was "so rigorous ... that Mrs. Sheridan had to wear male attire in order to hear her husband's speeches." The ban remained in effect until a separate "Ladies' Gallery" was created after the fire of 1834. See *An Encyclopædia of Parliament*, 3rd ed. (New York: F.A. Praeger, 1968), 416.

content to be the epitome of her celebrated archetype, the *good woman* of St. Giles's.[1]

The embargo upon words, the enforcement of tacit submission, has been productive of consequences highly honourable to the women of the present age. Since the sex have been condemned for exercising the powers of speech, they have successfully taken up the pen: and their writings exemplify both energy of mind, and capability of acquiring the most extensive knowledge. The press will be the monuments from which the genius of British women will rise to immortal celebrity: their works will, in proportion as their educations are liberal, from year to year, challenge an equal portion of fame, with the labours of their classical *male* contemporaries.

In proportion as women are acquainted with the languages they will become citizens of the world. The laws, customs and inhabitants of different nations will be their kindred in the propinquity of nature. Prejudice will be palsied, if not receive its death blow, by the expansion of intellect: and woman being permitted to feel her own importance in the scale of society, will be tenacious of maintaining it. She will know that she was created for something beyond the mere amusement of man; that she is capable of mental energies, and worthy of the most unbounded confidence. Such a system of mental equality, would, while it stigmatized the trifling vain and pernicious race of high fashioned Messalinas, produce such British women, as would equal the Portias and Arrias of antiquity.[2]

---

1   This elegant and estimable female, is represented headless;—and I believe *almost* the only female in the kingdom *universally* allowed to be a *good woman* [M.R.'s note]. Robinson may be alluding to the shop sign of "The Good Woman" in the London parish of St. Giles, as represented in William Hogarth's engraving "Noon." As Ronald Paulson explains, the sign depicts "a headless woman, one who has no tongue and is no longer the conventional 'scolding woman' or shrew." See *Hogarth; High Art and Low* (New Brunswick, NJ: Rutgers UP, 1992), 2: 146.

2   Pætus being commanded by the emperor Nero, to die by his own hands, his wife [Arria], an illustrious Roman woman, was permitted to take leave of him. She felt the impossibility of surviving him, and plunging the poniard into her bosom, exclaimed "*Pætus it is not much*," and instantly expired. This anecdote I relate for the information of my unlearned readers [M.R.'s note]. Robinson probably thought it was unnecessary to elaborate on the negative example provided by Valerie Messalina, the notoriously unfaithful wife of the Roman Emperor Claudius I. She committed suicide to escape execution for her crimes.

Had fortune enabled me, I would build an UNIVERSITY FOR WOMEN; where they should be politely, and at the same time classically educated; the depth of their studies, should be proportioned to their mental powers; and those who were *incompetent to the labours of knowledge*, should be dismissed after a fair trial of their capabilities, and allotted to the more humble paths of life; such as *domestic and useful occupations*. The wealthy part of the community who neglected to educate their female offspring, at this seminary of learning, should pay a fine, which should be appropriated to the maintenance of the unportioned scholars. In half a century there would be a sufficient number of learned women to fill all the departments of the university, and those who excelled in an eminent degree should receive honorary medals, which they should wear as an ORDER of LITERARY MERIT.

O! my unenlightened country-women! read, and profit, by the admonition of Reason. Shake off the trifling, glittering shackles, which debase you. Resist those fascinating spells, which, like the petrifying torpedo, fasten on your mental faculties.[1] Be less the slaves of vanity, and more the converts of Reflection. Nature has endowed you with personal attractions: she has also given you the mind capable of expansion. Seek not the visionary triumph of universal conquest; know yourselves equal to greater, nobler, acquirements: and by prudence, temperance, firmness, and reflection, subdue that prejudice which has, for ages past, been your inveterate enemy. Let your daughters be liberally, classically, philosophically,[2] and usefully educated; let them speak and write their opinions freely; let them read and think like rational creatures; adapt their studies to their strength of intellect; expand their minds, and purify their hearts, by teaching them to feel their mental equality with their imperious rulers. By such laudable exertions, you will excite the noblest emulation; you will explode the super-

---

[1] A torpedo is a kind of fish, now more commonly known as the cramp-ray, numb-ray, or electric-ray.

[2] By Philosophy, the writer of this Letter means rational wisdom; neither the flimsy cobwebs of pretended metaphysical and logical mysteries; nor the unbridled liberty which would lead to the boldness of licentious usurpation. A truly enlightened woman never will forget that conscious dignity of character which ennobles and sustains, but never can DEBASE her [M.R.'s note]. Robinson may be responding to Polwhele's charges in *The Unsex'd Females*. See Appendix C, 305, n. 2; 308, n. 1.

stitious tenets of bigotry and fanaticism; confirm the intuitive immortality of the soul, and give them that genuine glow of conscious virtue which will grace them to posterity.

There are men who affect, to think lightly of the literary productions of women: and yet no works of the present day are so universally read as theirs. The best novels that have been written, since those of Smollet, Richardson, and Fielding, have been produced by women: and their pages have not only been embellished with the interesting events of domestic life, portrayed with all the elegance of phraseology, and all the refinement of sentiment, but with forcible and eloquent, political, theological, and philosophical reasoning. To the genius and labours of some enlightened British women posterity will also be indebted for the purest and best translations from the French and German languages. I need not mention Mrs. Dobson, Mrs. Inchbald, Miss Plumptree, &c. &c.[1] Of the more profound researches in the dead languages, we have many female classicks of the first celebrity: Mrs. Carter, Mrs. Thomas (late Miss Parkhurst), Mrs. Francis, the Hon. Mrs. Damer, &c.&c.[2]

Of the Drama, the wreath of fame has crowned the brows of Mrs. Cowley, Mrs. Inchbald, Miss Lee, Miss Hannah More, and others of less celebrity.[3] Of Biography, Mrs. Dobson, Mrs.

---

[1] Susannah Dobson (?–1795) translated many works, including Jacques de Sade's *Life of Petrarch*. Elizabeth Inchbald (1753–1821) and Ann Plumptre both won considerable acclaim for their translations of plays by the German playwright August von Kotzebue. See Introduction, 30, n. 3.

[2] Elizabeth Carter (1717–1806) was best known for her translation of the works of Epictetus from the Greek. Anne Francis established her reputation as a poet and scholar with *A Poetical Translation of the Song of Solomon, from the Original Hebrew, with a Preliminary Discourse, and Notes, Historical, Critical, and Explanatory* (1781). Although Anne Seyour Damer (1748–1828) was widely regarded as a woman of learning, she was better know for her sculpture.

[3] Hannah Cowley (1743–1809) wrote over a dozen plays, including *The Runaway*. When it was produced at Drury Lane Theatre in 1778, Robinson played the leading role of Emily Morley. Cowley and Robinson later became bitter rivals in their exchange of Della Cruscan verse epistles published under the respective signatures of "Anna Matilda" and "Laura." Sophia Lee (1750–1824) and her sister Harriet (1757–1851) both wrote fiction and plays. The proceeds from Sophia's comedy *The Chapter of Accidents* (1780) enabled the sisters to establish a school for girls at Bath. Hannah More (1745–1833) established her reputation as a dramatist in the late 1770s with *Percy* and *The Fatal Falsehood*. By the end of the century, however, she was better known as the author of moralizing works, such as *Cheap Repository Tracts* (1795–98) and *Strictures on the Modern System of Female Education* (1799).

Thickness, Mrs. Piozzi, Mrs. Montagu, Miss Helen Williams, have given specimens highly honourable to their talents.[1] Poetry has unquestionably risen high in British literature from the productions of female pens; for many English women have produced such original and beautiful compositions, that the first critics and scholars of the age have wondered, while they applauded. But in order to direct the attention of my fair and liberal countrywomen to the natural genius and mental acquirements of their illustrious contemporaries, I conclude my Letter with a list of names, which, while they silence the tongue of prejudice, will not fail TO EXCITE EMULATION.

P.S. Should this Letter be the means of influencing the minds of those to whom it is addressed, so far as to benefit the rising generation, my end and aim will be accomplished. I am well assured, that it will meet with little serious attention from the MALE disciples of MODERN PHILOSOPHY. The critics, though they have liberally patronized the works of British women, will perhaps condemn that doctrine which inculcates mental equality; lest, by the intellectual labours of the sex, they should claim an equal portion of power in the TRIBUNAL of BRITISH LITERATURE. By the profound scholar, and the unprejudiced critic, this Letter will be read with candour; while, I trust, *its purpose* will be deemed beneficial to society.

Exeter, Nov. 7, 1798.

---

[1] Ann Ford Thicknesse (1737–1824) wrote *Sketches of the Lives and Writings of the Ladies of France* (1778), a work that may have informed Robinson's appreciative assessment of French women on pp. 67–68, above. Hester Lynch Thrale Piozzi (1741–1821) was best known for her *Anecdotes of the Late Samuel Johnson* (1786). Elizabeth Montagu (1720–1800), dubbed "Queen of the Blues" (i.e. Bluestockings) by Samuel Johnson, published *An Essay on the Writings and Genius of Shakespeare* (1769).

LIST
of British
FEMALE LITERARY CHARACTERS
Living in the Eighteenth Century.[1]

A.

Anspach, Margravine of——Tour to the Crimea, and Dramatic Pieces.

B.

Barbauld, Mrs.——Poems and Moral Writings.
Brooke, Mrs.——Novels and Dramatic Pieces.
Bennet, Mrs.——Novelist.

C.

Carter, Mrs.——Greek and Hebrew Classic, Poetess, &c. &c.
Cowley, Mrs.——Poems, Comedies, Tragedies, &c. &c. &c. &c.
Crespigny, Mrs.——Novelist.
Cosway, Mrs.——Paintress.

D.

Dobson, Mrs.——Life of Petrarch, from the Italian.
D'Arblæy, Mrs.——Novels, Edwy and Elgiva, a Tragedy, &c. &c. &c.
Damer, Hon. Mrs.——Sculptor, and Greek Classic.

F.

Francis, Mrs.——Greek and Latin Classic.

G.

Gunning, Mrs.——Novelist.
Gunning, Miss——Novelist, and Translator from the French.

H.

Hayes, Miss——Novels, Philosophical and Metaphysical Disquisitions.
Hanway, Mrs.——Novelist.

I.

Inchbald, Mrs.——Novels, Comedies, and Translations from the French and German.

---

[1]   In order to escape the imputation of partiality, the names are arranged alphabetically [M.R.'s note].

L.

Linwood, Miss——Artist.

Lee, Misses——Romances, Comedies, Canterbury Tales, A
Tragedy, &c. &c.

Lennox, Mrs.——Novelist.

M.

Macauley Graham, Mrs.——History of England, and other works.

Montagu, Mrs.——Essay on the Writings and Genius of
Shakespeare; being a Defence of him from
the Slander of Voltaire.

More, Miss Hannah.——Poems, Sacred Dramas, a Tragedy, and
other moral pieces.

P.

Piozzi, Mrs.——Biography, Poetry, British Synonymy, Travels,
&c. &c. &c.

Plumptree, Miss——Translations from the German, a Novel, &c.

Parsons, Mrs.——Novelist.

R.

Ratcliffe, Mrs.——Romances, Travels, &c. &c.

Robinson, Mrs.——Poems, Romances, Novels, a Tragedy,
Satires, &c. &c.

Reeve, Miss——Romances and Novels.

Robinson, Miss——Novelist.

S.

Seward, Miss——Poems, a Poetical Novel, and various other
works.

Smith, Mrs. Charlotte——Novels, Sonnets, Moral Pieces, for the
Instruction of Youth; and other works.

Sheridan, late Mrs.——Sidney Biddulph, a Novel.

T.

Thomas, Mrs. late Miss Parkhurst——Greek and Hebrew Classic.

Thickness, Mrs.——Biography, Letters, &c.

W.

Wolstonecraft, Mrs.——A Vindication of the Rights of Woman,
Novels, Philosophical Disquisitions,
Travels, &c.

Williams, Miss Helen Maria——Poems, Travels, a Novel, and
other miscellaneous pieces.

West, Mrs.——Novels, Poetry, &c. &c.

Y.

Yearsley, Mrs.——Poems, a Novel, a Tragedy, &c. &c.

There are *various degrees of merit* in the compositions of the female writers mentioned in the preceding list. Of their several claims to the wreath of Fame, the Public and the critics are left to decide. Most of them have been highly distinguished at the tribunal of literature.

THE

NATURAL DAUGHTER.

WITH

PORTRAITS OF

THE LEADENHEAD FAMILY.

A NOVEL.

By Mrs. ROBINSON,

AUTHOR OF POEMS, WALSINGHAM, THE FALSE FRIEND, &c. &c. &c.

——— Can fuch things be,
Without our fpecial wonder ?   SHAKESPEARE.

IN TWO VOLUMES.

· VOL. I.

LONDON:

PRINTED FOR T. N. LONGMAN AND O. REES, PATERNOSTER-ROW.

1799.

CHAPTER I

On a bright April morning in the year one thousand seven hundred and ninety-two, Mr. Alderman Bradford, with his wife and daughters, Martha and Julia, set out from Crutched-Friars for the benefit of the Bath waters.[1] In our journey through life we are destined to meet with travellers of every denomination; but the most disgusting of all the various species we are created to encounter, is the opulent and ostentatious traveller. Without any motive but that of exciting attention, such a being measures the path of thorns and roses, sickening with satiety, and eternally extorting either our wonder or our pity: we wonder at the blind prodigality of Fortune, and we pity the wretch who, though revelling in her favours, seems incapable of enjoying even the shadow of felicity.

Such a traveller was Peregrine Bradford. A new coach splendidly emblazoned with richly fancied heraldry; four coal-black steeds, which might have graced the triumphal car of an Hector or an Alexander;[2] and two gaudy-liveried attendants, who wore upon their jackets glowing samples of their master's store of wealth and love of ostentation, composed the outward characteristics of the pompous invalid: whose luxurious life had been the bane of his constitution, and whose enormous fortune had deprived him of almost every felicity.

Those who have too much power to gratify their inclinations, are no less wretched than those who have too little. Satiety is a more uneasy sensation than necessity: and the greatest blessings of life, when fairly appreciated, tend most effectually to shorten our existence.—Wealth produces indolence; indolence is the parent of lassitude, and lassitude incapacitates the mind for every human enjoyment. Mr. Bradford was wealthy without being happy; he was weary, though not laborious; he was sad without cause for sorrow; irritable without being crossed in his inclinations; ostentatious without being generous; haughty, though not

---

[1]   See Introduction, 27, n. 1.
[2]   Alexander the Great; and Hector, valiant leader of the Trojans in Homer's *The Iliad*. Throughout the novel, Robinson often invokes such heroic names to underscore the ridiculous pretensions of decidedly unheroic characters.

dignified; indefatigable in the toil of disobliging; and, though he lived only for the world, he followed every propensity of his perverse nature, in defiance of the world's opinion.

Peregrine was verging on his fifty-seventh year, when he first began to recollect that he was mortal. His temper was not softened by the indulgence he experienced. His person was corpulent and unwieldy by the excess of luxurious living: his enemies laughed at him; his friends pitied him; and his family, could they have forgotten the bonds of propinquity, would have despised him.

Within the gaudy vehicle were placed the breathing appendages of his domestic establishment who were honoured with the name of the family; a wife, whose fair round face displayed both health and plenty; whose brow was settled into a tacit placidity, by that softener of human sorrows, Resignation; while a smile adorned her lip: but whether it was a smile of conscious pleasure, or of half-subdued contempt, I will leave the physiognomist to determine.

Opposite to Mrs. Bradford sat her youngest born, her favourite Julia. While Martha, the eldest and least beloved, occupied the place *vis-à-vis* to her papa, whose gouty foot, enveloped tenfold in flannel, rested on her knee, while his tongue every moment uttered the complainings of a discontented spirit.[1]

Julia was small in stature; fair, delicately formed, humble, obedient, complacent, and accommodating. Her face was pretty, her features being regular, and her eyes soft and languishing. The romantic tendency of her mind seemed to influence it even in the choice of her habiliments: the most delicate colours added to the transparency of her complexion; and she seemed, like the snow-drop, to droop at every breeze that the soft breath of April wafted through the carriage.

Martha, wrapped in a convenient travelling-coat of scarlet cloth, with a beaver hat, and a face full of dimples, talked gaily, laughed heartily, though sometimes, by suddenly darting forward to make shrewd and lively observations, discomposing the dignified countenance of the suffering Mr. Bradford.

---

[1] Gout, one of the most ubiquitous male ailments in eighteenth-century literature, is characterized by severe swelling in the joints of the hands and feet. Although it is exacerbated by excessive food and drink, gout is now attributed to an hereditary metabolic disorder.

Martha had just attained her twenty-second year; Julia was three years younger: Martha was giddy, wild, buxom, good-natured, and bluntly sincere in the tenor of her conversation. They had been separated ever since their infancy. The eldest was sent to a country boarding-school for education, because she was gay, robust, and noisy; while Julia passed her hours of study under the care of a French governess in the splendid mansion of Crutched-Friars. Thus prepared for the great world, the sisters started upon society: the gentle Julia, admired as a model of feminine excellence; and the unsophisticated Martha considered as a mere masculine hoyden.

As soon as the coach passed the barrier of Hyde Park,[1] Mr. Bradford for the first time since their embarkation, addressed his companions: "You see, girls," said he with a look of more pomposity than wisdom; "you see that I am going to Bath, with all this expence, merely with a view to make your fortunes."

"I thought that they were already made, sir, and that you went to Bath for the benefit of your health," said Martha.

"You had no business to think," said Mr. Bradford; "it was your duty to listen."

"You wish me then to be thoughtless, sir?" cried Martha.

"Be quiet, child," said Mrs. Bradford, with a tone of reprehension; "you know that your father will not bear contradiction; and, in his state of suffering, it is natural to be peevish."

"There now!" exclaimed Mr. Bradford; "peevish! I wish you had my gout, and we should then see whose temper is the most fretful."

"I did but speak, my love——"

"You have no business ever to speak; cannot you be content to ride in your own coach-and-four, but you must pick quarrels for nothing. You know as well as I do, that I am impatient to marry the girls off. Juley deserves a good husband, and Patty wants one to keep her in order; for she is beyond my management."

"You never tried me, sir," said Martha; "for I don't believe that since I was three years old, I have passed six months in your presence."

---

[1]   Coaches traveling west from London to Bath passed a toll gate at Hyde Park Corner. From there, the road to Bath was approximately 106 miles. Hounslow and Colnbrook, mentioned below, were usually the first stops along the way.

"There again! eternal reproaches! always grumbling; never satisfied; can nothing teach you good manners? Mrs. Bradford, why don't you speak; are you dumb?"

"I did not suppose that it would be agreeable. You are so out of humour that it is difficult to know how to please you."

"We'll return to Crutched-Friars," said Mr. Bradford; "I won't throw away my money, and hear abuse into the bargain. Since I set foot in the carriage you have done nothing but fret and contradict me." The coachman was ordered to turn back, and Julia bursting into tears, conjured her father to consider his own health beyond all other things; and to compose his nerves, which were so cruelly agitated by her sister's unaccountable behaviour. Mrs. Bradford was silently acquiescent, when a sudden jolt of the carriage threw Mr. Bradford on his knees; he roared aloud with agony; Mrs. Bradford shrieked; Julia fainted;—and, terrible to relate, Martha could not refrain from laughing.

The group was now thrown into such complete confusion, that to proceed or to return seemed alike impracticable: the coach was stopped, the invalid, with some difficulty, was re-seated; Julia's sensibility dissolved in tears; and Martha sincerely felt for the pain which her father suffered.

"If this is travelling in style, God keep me from elegance!" cried Mr. Bradford; "this comes of vanity, and obliging a pack of whimsical women, who do not know their own minds five minutes together:—then they will go, and then they won't."

"Who ordered the coach to return?" inquired Martha.

"Who bought the coach, and who has a right to burn the coach, if he pleases?" interrupted Mr. Bradford: "Coachman, go back to the city:—I have changed my mind; I won't stir an inch with these troublesome women."—The coachman obeyed, and the cavalcade accordingly moved back towards Crutched-Friars.

CHAPTER II

Reader, have you ever seen a coquet struggling betwixt the conflicts of pride and inclination? Have you ever seen a restive horse spurred onward, and yet persevering in a retrograde motion, which marked the obstinate temper of the animal? Have you observed a skiff in a storm, borne at the will of the surge, and labouring to put to sea, though contrary gales retarded its progress? If thou hast seen such things, imagine the situation of Peregrine Bradford, while he reflected that the new coach, the new horses, and the new liveries, had been purchased to no purpose!

As they returned through Kensington, Mrs. Bradford, thinking to soothe her suffering partner, ventured once more to utter her opinion. "Indeed, my love," said she, taking his hand and smiling; "I have no great opinion of the Bath waters. I hear various accounts of them; they are of an inflammatory quality, and you are already a little irritable; besides Bath is a very expensive place, and we sober citizens are always better in our own sphere."——Mr. Bradford bit his lip and looked angry.——"Not but you have a right to do what you please with your fortune," continued Mrs. Bradford. "Heaven knows you worked hard enough to get it; toiled late and early; and rose your name from nothing, by your own merit. Perhaps all the great folks we should meet with cannot say as much."

"The wise ones would say less," cried Martha.

"Dear mama! how you talk!" said Julia; "greatness consists in worth."

"And who is worth more than I?" cried Mr. Bradford.

"But your worth is not of the kind which Julia means," said Martha.

"Who wanted your interpretation?" cried Mr. Bradford; "you were glad enough to go jaunting to Bath; you were glad enough to snap at a husband; but if you do not mind your temper, you will not keep him long."

"Sweetness of temper will not always make an husband amiable," said Mrs. Bradford sighing.

"But it is a very necessary qualification for those who are in want of one," cried the invalid. "If you had not been good tempered, I never should have thought of marrying you; for God knows, you had no other recommendation."

"Some virtues at least, sir, are evident in my mother's character," said Martha; "and I think you may name patience among the number."

"What should make her otherwise than patient?" inquired Mr. Bradford. "Has she not every thing that can render a woman happy? Is she not envied by all her acquaintance; and shall I not leave her the richest widow on the east side of St. Paul's?"[1]

"What signifies flattering one with hopes," said Mrs. Bradford. "God knows! I do not look forward to such good fortune."

"I warrant you would not remain a widow six months," said Mr. Bradford; "you would be looking out for some blockhead or other, to torment you for the remainder of your days."

"Never!" interrupted Mrs. Bradford; "the memory of my first husband would always prevent the possibility of my taking a second."

"That's very fine talking," cried the invalid; "but I wish I could only put you to the trial."

"I wish you could, with all my soul!" sighed Mrs. Bradford; "the world should then see how I would lament you. My sorrow should not last while my weeds[2] were worn, as some widows do, I promise you."

"The time will come when you will have an opportunity of proving your words," said Mr. Bradford, sighing.

"Pray Heaven it may, my love! and the sooner the better," replied his wife.

"Martha would not act so by a husband," cried the invalid. "She would forget him before her mourning was threadbare."

"That would depend upon his value, sir," interrupted Martha; "in all human probability my feelings would not resemble those of my mother, for the chance is a million to one that I should not have such a husband to lament."

"God forbid!" sighed Mrs. Bradford. Martha could not help smiling.

---

[1] St. Paul's Cathedral, the primary church of the City of London, was a convenient point of reference for distinctions between the commercial district to the east and the more fashionable residential and shopping areas in the West End.

[2] Mourning clothes.

"Well, I am glad that we are going back," added Mrs. Bradford, after a short pause. "I hate the thoughts of making new acquaintances; and I really think that none but people of consequence ought to travel."

"And who is of more consequence than myself?" inquired the invalid peevishly.

"My mother means persons of rank and title," said Martha.

"I can buy a title," cried Mr. Bradford; "but a title cannot always buy a citizen."[1]

They now passed a chaise and four, with royal liveries. Mr. Bradford instantly recollected his new coach and its well appointed appurtenances; and with the hope of exciting the attention of the illustrious traveller stopped to make inquiries who it was. The carriage, to his inexpressible chagrin, passed on: but one of the servants who followed, civilly informed the invalid that it was the Duke of York on his journey to Bath for the benefit of the waters.[2]

"Blessings on him!" cried Mrs. Bradford; "for he is an honour to the nation!"

"You see," interrupted her husband, "that every body who has understanding, or a proper sense of their own dignity of character, goes to Bath: you also find that princes as well as citizens are subject to infirmities."

"Indeed, my dear, we are better at home," said Mrs. Bradford: "you are but weak and will only expose yourself."

"Who wanted your advice? Keep it for your daughter Martha, Mrs. Bradford," interrupted her husband; "I don't desire to hear it; and since you are so forward in giving counsel I have a great mind to go to Bath after all, merely because I will not submit to be governed by your opinion. The first people in the land follow their own inclination, and why should not I? John, turn back towards Hounslow." Thither they went, and there I leave them.

---

[1] Cf. the second definition of *citizen* in Samuel Johnson's *A Dictionary of the English Language* (1755): "a townsman; a man of trade; not a gentleman."

[2] Frederick, the Duke of York, was the second son of George III. Robinson became acquainted with him during her affair with the Prince of Wales.

CHAPTER III

By the time that they stopped, Mr. Bradford's gout became so painful, that all thoughts of proceeding on their journey that day were laid aside. On their arrival at the inn, dinner was ordered, while the young travellers set out to walk on the heath; and Mrs. Bradford sat down to a game at cribbage with the invalid.

"Try, for once, if you can amuse me," said Mr. Bradford. "I am sure I have been plagued enough to-day with your caprices and ill-humours. A man had better be hanged than married; for in both cases he has a string of misfortunes."

"You are never *satisfied!*"

"Pardon me, Mrs. Bradford, I have had *enough* of wedlock," retorted her husband. While they were quarrelling over their cribbage-board, another kind of scene was acting on the heath: Julia and her sister had not strolled an hundred yards when they were overtaken by a fashionable youth in a curricle with four horses;[1] he was handsome, and displayed an air of distinction both by his dress and conduct: for he looked like any thing but a man: and he drove like nothing but a maniac.—After staring the fair pedestrians into confusion, he stopped near the foot-path and inquired whither they were going.

"Pursue your way, sir," said Martha gravely.

"This is my way, nothing like it," said the baronet. "I am going to lady Pen Pryer's; the dowager waits dinner; but if you have a mind for a frolic, here is room enough for us all."

"Pray give yourself no trouble on our account," said Julia, blushing and turning from him.

"Trouble! that's well enough! no, no, trouble is out of our vocabulary: we men of rank seek nothing but amusement. So come along; lady Pen will be glad to see you, I dare swear; and if she sulks and looks stiff, why we'll take leave of the dowager and be off, that's all.—I'm for sport,—catch me who can! nothing like it."

"Do you mean to insult us?" said Julia.

---

[1] A curricle was a light, two-wheeled carriage, typically drawn by two horses rather than four.

"By Jupiter I mean nothing; nobody can accuse me of such a thing.—I have been upon town ever since I was fourteen; and I know how to enjoy life as well as any man."

"You seem strangely ignorant"——

"Ignorant!" interrupted sir Lionel, looking earnestly in Martha's face: "who the devil wants to be wise? I have all the pleasure of life without giving myself any trouble; and what should a man of fashion learn but to amuse himself?"

A servant at this moment overtook the young truants, to inform them that dinner was nearly ready. Sir Lionel, wishing them much sport, ascended his curricle and drove full speed towards Colnbrook.

"What a strange mortal!" said Martha, smiling.

"What a ridiculous coxcomb!" added Julia. "The woman who could admire such a being must be, indeed, wretched.—Did you observe how he drove his poor horses; I thought I should faint; what an unfeeling savage!"

"It will be fortunate if his horses are the only sufferers he will meet with in his journey through life," said Martha. As she spoke she looked back just in time to behold the curricle overset, and the volatile Baronet precipitated to some distance. Julia shrieked and leant upon the servant's arm, while Martha flew with hasty steps towards the scene of calamity.

The baronet was more alarmed than hurt. His nose had met the ground rather abruptly, and the fine tints of his complexion were deepened by an unseemly stream, that flowed from it. Martha inquired eagerly how the baronet felt; offered her hand-kerchief; ran to the brook by the road side, and dipped it in the cold spring, then applied it to his bleeding nose, and refreshed the almost sinking object of her attentions. Julia stood at a distance, overwhelmed with terror. For the sight of blood would have been too severe a trial for her sensibility.

The baronet no sooner recovered from his alarm than he exclaimed, "Curse the frisky animals! I cannot dine with the dowager this figure." Then turning to his groom, he added, "Go on to lady Penelope Pryer's, and say, that I have met a lady on the road, whom I have not seen for some time, and that we are gone to dine together at Hounslow. Now, my gay ones," added he, addressing Martha and her sister, "you are in luck; I am yours for the day:—where shall we amuse ourselves?"

Julia informed sir Lionel, that her father expected her at Hounslow; that he was mistaken in the objects of his attention, and that her sister's affected humanity was always involving her in difficulties. They proceeded towards the inn, and the baronet walked beside them.

On entering the town a chaise passed with a female of fashion. Sir Lionel hailed it. The post-boys stopped. It was lady Pen Pryer; and the baronet was speedily borne off in triumph.

Before the chapter closes, the reader shall have a brief outline of the character last introduced. Sir Lionel Beacon was born to the inheritance of a splendid fortune; but having been an only son, and his father dying while he was an infant, he had been left wholly to the care of his mother—a woman of contracted mental acquirements, though of inordinate personal vanity. Lionel, even from his infancy, presented a model of symmetry and feature scarcely to be equalled. He also possessed a liberal, open, and generous heart; but he was thoughtless, dissipated, wild, and devoted to pleasure. He was resolved to *live all his days*, and therefore he determined not to protract them beyond that period when health, youth, and a fervid flow of spirits should enable him to fulfil his purpose. Such is the personage who will make a conspicuous figure in the following pages.

CHAPTER IV

Mr. Bradford had dined and was wrapped in the arms of Morpheus;[1] and Mrs. Bradford was twisting her thumbs before the fire, when the sisters entered the inn. They stole unto another apartment, ate a short dinner, and were talking of their morning adventure, when they heard a shriek in the room where they had left their father. The good man had fallen into a fit of apoplexy,

---

[1] The god of sleep and dreams.

and his wife concluding that he was dead, vociferated loudly for assistance. Julia, on seeing the situation of her father, sunk upon the carpet: while Martha, more judicious in her feelings, loosened his neck-cloth, opened his waistcoat, rubbed his temples, and bathed his face with volatile spirit.

The invalid did not recover for some time, and as soon as he found the use of his tongue he inquired who had made him in such a confounded pickle. "I warrant that busy jade Patty!" exclaimed Mr. Bradford. Julia hung about her father in tears, and was honoured with his thanks and his caresses. Little more passed that day, and early on the next morning they set forward on their journey.

To the rational traveller the day would have appeared fine, clear, and bracing: But Mr. Bradford thought it cold and comfortless. He sat in the corner of his emblazoned vehicle wrapped in fur and fleecy hosiery, growling and shivering; while the peasant passed by, whistling and glowing with health and exercise. "Confound luxury!" exclaimed Mr. Bradford; "it only puts one out of humour with the whole world. Why is that poor vagabond more happy than myself?"

"Because he is satisfied, sir," said Martha; "the poor have little to trouble them, except the provision for their day's subsistence."

"A little is sufficient for the laborious," said Mr. Bradford.

"How commendable are those who make a virtue of necessity," replied Martha. "The laborious live scantily, but they are always contented."

"Because they have no feelings," said Julia.

"Or rather feelings of the right sort," interrupted Martha. "For though below luxury, they are above its fascinations."

"I give away many hundreds every year," said Mr. Bradford, "and all the world knows it."

"The merit is therefore diminished," said Martha.

"The proudest gratification that the heart can experience," said Julia, "is that of relieving the unfortunate."

"From the sense of obligations," again interrupted her sister.

"How can we bestow favours without their being felt?" said Julia.

"By evincing that conscious pleasure which renders the obligation ours," replied Martha. The coach now ascended a hill, and a lame soldier addressed the travellers. He uncovered his right arm, which had been withered in the service of his country. Julia shuddered, and closed her eyes. Martha threw a shilling into his hat, and Mr. Bradford loudly exclaimed against the insolence of vagrants.

"He did but beg," said Martha.

"What else could he do?" cried her father.

"He might have robbed."

"He would have been hanged," added Mr. Bradford.

"Or he would perhaps have starved," said Martha.

"No matter! of what use is a lame soldier?" said Mr. Bradford.

"Of infinite use, if only to remind the wealthy of their obligations," said Martha.

"What do we owe to them?"

"All we possess that is truly valuable—private safety and national honour."

"We pay the vagabonds," said Mrs. Bradford.

"You cannot ensure their lives."

"Nor they our property," said the invalid.

"But they defend it, while in return we expose them to peril," said Martha.

"What are their lives in comparison with the wealth of kingdoms?"

"Very little, according to the distributions of fortune," said Martha. "But the poor wounded soldier, with his rags and mendicity, has still one badge which gold cannot purchase—honour."

"O! that may be bought," said Mr. Bradford.

"Pardon me, sir," replied Martha; "It may be hired; but being lent to every fool, that species of honour is grown so common, it is scarcely worth possessing."

The soldier still walked slowly beside the carriage. Mr. Bradford let down the glass, and asked him if he had no home.

"None but my country, your honour," said he; "and that proves but a comfortless one."

"You are an impostor, I believe, and ought to be sent to jail," cried Mr. Bradford.

"His wound is not fictitious," said Martha.

"Who cares for his wound?" cried Mr. Bradford.

"In truth, but few," replied his daughter; "or it would not be exposed as a stigma on humanity."

"What made him shew it?"

"Necessity, the most pressing of all stimulators," replied Martha.

"The knave is happier than his betters," said Mr. Bradford: "he has every privilege that I possess."

"Sir, you forget that of upbraiding his misfortunes," retorted Martha.

"He has health and liberty; as much money as he knows how to use; and more impudence than he ought to display," said Mr. Bradford.

"His health is the effect of temperance; his liberty the work of his own valour; his scanty fortune is the source of his effrontery:—for the human mind rises in energy in proportion as it is stung by persecution." Mr. Bradford fell into a lethargic doze, and a profound silence followed.

At supper, Julia could not eat for thinking of the soldier's wounded arm; while he, by the private order of Martha, had been lodged near the inn, and provided with a comfortable meal.

Julia, in the morning, recounted her dreams, and declared they dwelt entirely on the soldier's distress. Martha had no vision to repeat; she had passed the night in wakeful rumination; but the precarious state of her father's health, and the oblivion which would more than darken his tomb, mingled with the remembrance of the wounded beggar.

They rose early; and Martha, not knowing how to employ her time till breakfast, wrote the following stanzas:

o PITY! if thy holy tear
   Immortal decks the wing of Time,
'Tis when the SOLDIER's honour'd bier
   Demands the glittering drop sublime!
For who, from busy life remov'd,
Such glorious, dang'rous toil has prov'd,
As HE, who on the embattled plain
   Lies, nobly slain!

HE, who forsakes his native shore
   To meet the whizzing ball of death;
Who, mid the battle's fateful roar,

Resigns his ling'ring, parting breath;
Who, when the deafening din is done,
So well deserves as Valour's son,
The proud, the lasting wreath of fame,
    To grace his name?

Hard is his fate, the sultry day
    To wander o'er the burning plain;
All night to waste the hours away,
    Mid howling winds and beating rain.
To talk, O vision sadly sweet!
With her his eyes will never meet,
And find at morn's returning gleam
    'Twas but a dream!

To mark the haughty brow severe;
    To hear th' imperious, stern command:
To heave the sigh, to drop the tear,
    While mem'ry paints his native land.
To know, the laurel he has won
Twines round the brow of FORTUNE's son
While HE, when strength and youth are flown,
    Shall die UNKNOWN.[1]

CHAPTER V

Mr. Bradford made a voluptuous breakfast on cold turkey and
madeira.[2] The poor soldier was sitting on the door-bench, with a
crust of bread and a small mug of smaller beer. "There's a guzzling
vagrant!" said Mr. Bradford: "I knew he wanted for nothing."

---

[1] This poem was published as "The Old Soldier" in *The Morning Post* on August 31,
    1799. Cf. Wordsworth's poem "The Discharged Soldier," incorporated into *The
    Prelude* (1805), 4. 400–504.

[2] A sweet fortified wine produced on Madeira, an island off the northwest coast of
    Africa.

"It would be hard that he should," said Martha, "since so scanty a pittance can supply his necessities."

"He likes that sort of living. He would not feel the advantages of luxury."

"Suffer me to make the trial," said Martha, disjointing a wing of turkey, and filling a bumper of madeira.

"You would not dare to expose yourself, would you?" said the invalid.—"The vagabond is presuming: he follows us, and encroaches on your kindness!"

"Kindness is to him so rare, that he makes its possession a holiday," said Martha.

"Then it should be a fast-day," said Mr. Bradford.

"To those he is probably accustomed," replied Martha; "therefore this day he shall feast." So saying, she opened the window, and made the heart bound with gratitude that had long throbbed with unmerited suffering.

The coach being ordered to the inn-door, the party again set forward; Mr. Bradford complaining of short breath and a laboured circulation, which abated nothing in its difficulty till they reached the scene of destination.

On entering Bath they found a spacious house in the Upper Crescent ready for their reception; and the invalid not being gifted with patience under mortal suffering, immediately dispatched his servant for the best physician. The son of Esculapius arrived.[1] The invalid poured forth his long catalogue of maladies, which was answered briefly in four emphatic words: "You must live temperately."

"And pray, doctor, what do you call temperance?"

"Eating sparingly and of plain diet." Mr. Bradford was silent.

"Going to bed and rising early; avoiding supper, wine, and strong soups." The invalid hemmed.

"Sleeping only as long as Nature demands for refreshment, but never after eating heartily." Mr. Bradford sighed.

"Keeping your mind easy, your temper placid; never permitting the trifles of existence to ruffle or disturb you." The citizen groaned. The physician prescribed, received his fee, and departed.

---

[1] Asclepius, or Aesculapius, was the Greek god of medicine.

"Let me see what I am to have for my guinea," said Mr. Bradford, reading the prescription. "Only one line! Little enough for the money, God knows! Martha, ring the bell, and send this scrawl to the apothecary's, and order me a pint of mulled madeira against I wake: I am wondrous sleepy."

"Sir, remember the doctor——"

"D—n the doctor; I shall follow my own inclinations. I had rather be my own master in Crutched-Friars than any doctor's fool in the universe." The servant now entered with a bill of fare—turtle soup, game, poultry, fish: "An excellent catalogue!" said Mr. Bradford. "Order me specimens of each."

"Sir, remember the doctor!" repeated Martha.

"What has he to do with my business?" said Mr. Bradford, adding a round oath.

"Sir, he declares that such food is poison."

"And am I not going to swallow his drugs by way of antidote? Do, Mrs. Bradford, order this girl to be quiet."

"Patty, why will you contradict your father?" said her mother.

"My father will kill himself——"

"No matter; you must not contradict him," said Mrs. Bradford.

"Indeed, Patty, your conduct afflicts me," cried Julia. "Pray let our father do what he pleases." Martha sighed as she bowed assent; and while dinner was preparing, the invalid indulged in his usual custom of sleeping for an appetite.

In the evening the whole party went to the play. It was the tragedy of Jane Shore,[1] for the benefit of an unknown lady. Mr. Bradford snored through the five acts, Julia wept incessantly, and Martha, as the curtain dropped, stole out of the box to dispatch a short note she had written with a pencil during the performance. In the lobby she found a messenger, to whom she gave it, requesting him, at the same time, to inform the person for whom it was intended, that a letter would be left, with farther communication, at the library in the Orange-Grove[2] on the following morning.

As she spoke, an observer looked earnestly in her face. The inquiry which she had made, and of which the reader will know

---

[1]   See Introduction, 13, n. 1.
[2]   A small park planted with elms, named after William of Orange.

more hereafter, convinced him of her future intentions. He followed her to the box, and taking his seat on the last bench, never ceased gazing at her during the remainder of the evening. Julia was exhausted with weeping. The scenes of Shore's progressive sufferings were too affecting for her sensibility. But Martha, whose feelings were of a very different species, enjoyed the cheerful hour which followed, and smiled and even laughed repeatedly. "Unfeeling girl!" exclaimed Julia. The box observer shook his head. The play being ended, they returned home to supper; and at two in the morning Mr. Bradford was carried to his chamber with his usual quantum of two bottles of madeira, and his cooling draught from the repository of Galen.[1]

As Mrs. Bradford was rolling the alderman's limbs in fleecy hosiery, her accustomed nightly occupation, he informed her that he was determined, since he had travelled so far and at such an expence, to make some figure before he returned to London. "I have," cried he, with an emphatic tone, "hitherto been nobody!"

"True, my love!" said Mrs. Bradford.

"I shall not let the world remain any longer in ignorance: I shall shew mankind that a rich citizen is as great a man as the first lord in the land, and as proud too."

"Many of them are prouder," interrupted Mrs. Bradford.

"Now, my dear wife," said the invalid, "I must caution you not to let down our consequence by forgetting yourself."

"That will be the only way to feel that I have any," replied the simple Mrs. Bradford.

"But above all I charge you not to think of thwarting my opinions. I have never known or felt my value."

"Nor I neither, Mr. Bradford."

"I have always demeaned myself by my own folly, and have been a fool, as one may say."

"Very true, my love!" cried Mrs. Bradford.

"Therefore, my dear wife, we will turn over a new leaf. From this day you must remember that money makes the mare to go."

"My dear, you know you are only alderman," said Mrs. Bradford.

---

[1]   A Greek anatomist and physician of the second century.

"Gold will buy every thing; and who knows but I may soon die and leave you a title?"

"That would be charming, indeed!" said Mrs. Bradford.

"All in good time. But you must not suppose that I will patiently endure being contradicted. I came to Bath to prove my consequence; and if I am to be snapped, and snubbed, and governed like a baby, I shall go back more ridiculous than I came."

"That is impossible, my love," said Mrs. Bradford. "But you are always foreseeing misfortunes; you know that you told me, when you came first to court me, that we were destined to live thirty years together."

"Was that a misfortune, Mrs. Bradford?"

"No, my love: but you added that you should then die, and leave me a disconsolate widow. Though I trust in God that your prediction will not be verified, for I should not be a widow long." Mrs. Bradford's tears interrupted her.

"I believe you, my dear—I believe you, upon my soul!" said the invalid. "I know your disposition too well to suppose such a thing possible. If all women were like you, my love, there would not be a bachelor in existence." As he spoke, Mrs. Bradford, whose attention was absorbed by what she thought her husband's flattering eulogium, pressed his gouty hand in assurance of her gratitude. The pain which her emotion occasioned, by a sympathetic tenderness in both parties, turned the tide of panegyric with almost a magical velocity; while the invalid exclaimed, "Zounds, Mrs. Bradford, you have no more feeling than a stone! A man had better be dead than plagued with such a mortal! I wish I had never married you; you are not capable of nursing a bear!"

"I am sure, my dear, I have had practice enough," replied Mrs. Bradford; "for I have nursed you at least these ten years."

"And you shall nurse me ten more; for I will live to plague you."

"God forbid!" exclaimed Mrs. Bradford, again bursting into a flood of tears, which for that night ended the conversation.

CHAPTER VI

Early in the morning Mr. Bradford's servant entered his chamber with a glass of water steaming from the pump. "Sir," said he, opening the curtains hastily, "the doctor says you must drink this the moment you awake."

"But he did not tell you that I must be awakened to drink it."

"He ordered that you should take three glasses."

"He ordered! and pray what right has any man to order me?" said Mr. Bradford. "You know that I will not be commanded; and since the doctor chooses to insist upon the business, you may tell him from me that I will act as I think proper."

"Sir, there is no good in cheating the doctor."

"That's a fine joke, truly!" exclaimed Mr. Bradford. "I gave the doctor one-pound-one; he sends me a dose of hot water that costs him nothing. I should like to know which has most reason to complain of being cheated!"

"You cannot live without his advice, sir."

"Nor can he live without my guinea; so the obligation is mutual."

"But, sir, every body submits——"

"Therefore I am determined to resist," interrupted Mr. Bradford.

"Then, sir, you have no business at Bath."

"Business is out of the question: I came here to forget business, to enjoy life, to shew the world that I have as much money as my neighbours; and who that can purchase wine will ever think of drinking water?"

"Think of your gout, sir!"

"I came here to forget my gout; for I have thought of it till I fear I shall never get it out of my head again," said Mr. Bradford.

"Indeed, sir, you must obey your physician."

"Why must I? Do you not know that I will not submit to be governed? Have I not convinced all my family, long since, that I am the most obstinate man in the universe?"

"True, sir: but your life is at stake."

"And what is that to you? You will get nothing by my living."

The servant sighed, and Mr. Bradford ordered his usual breakfast of cold meat and madeira.

At noon he sallied forth in his rolling-chair. Julia and Martha walked beside him, two servants followed the wheels, while with slow and pompous solemnity they proceeded to the Orange-Grove, where they entered the library.

Martha took up a London newspaper, but Julia never read diurnal prints, because the accounts of casualties were too distressing for her excessive sensibility. The appearance of the groupe excited universal attention, and curiosity was on tiptoe, when the invalid demanded to see the various subscription-books then open for the season.[1] "You may set down Mr. Alderman Bradford in them all," said the invalid; "I suppose money is the thing wanted, and, thank God! I have plenty to give." As he spoke, a lady entered the library. She was veiled, and evidently avoided the inquiring eyes of those whose attention was attracted by the elegance of her figure. She approached Martha, and thanked her for five guineas which she had that morning received for a benefit ticket. The lady held a handkerchief to her face, and spoke in a low voice. Martha blushed, and stole out of the library. At the door they parted. After taking a turn on the Parade, Martha re-entered the shop, where the first person she saw was the lobby observer, who had the preceding evening watched her so inquisitively. His eyes oppressed her. She endeavoured, but in vain, to avoid them: her confusion only tended to augment his interest; and during several minutes she was the exclusive object of his attention.

The arrival of a new visitor relieved Martha from her embarrassment. The stranger was a female, whose appearance and manners bespoke the altitude of fashion. She was not young, but she had once been handsome. She was eager to know whose names were on the Bath list; declared that she had not seen a single mortal since her arrival that looked like any thing human. Then turning suddenly round, gazed stedfastly at the sisters, and inquired, "Who are they? Where do they come from? What are they doing at Bath? I never saw them before! What rank do they hold in society?"

Nobody knew any thing about them. The strange lady fixing her eyes on Julia continued,

---

[1]   Upon coming to Bath, visitors of any consequence signed a guest register and added their names to subscription lists for plays, concerts, balls, libraries, etc.

"I like the fair one; she is an elegant girl. I suppose that big man is the father," glancing at Mr. Bradford. "He looks like an alderman that has eaten a turtle, and then crept into the shell. I wonder what could bring such comical people to Bath! I shall inquire at the pump-room who they are: somebody must know them, they are so completely ridiculous." Her attention was now drawn by another object. "Heavens! Morley, where did you come from?" exclaimed she, addressing Martha's lobby observer. "What amusement can a man of your serious turn of mind possibly receive among the gay and the dissipated? I always thought you liked melancholy scenes, feasted on the tears of suffering virtue, and breathed responsively to the sighs of sorrowing bosoms!" Mr. Morley bowed slightly, and quitted the library.

"What a pedantic creature!" was the comment that followed. "I would give any thing to know what brought him to Bath! He neither games nor intrigues: he is neither sick nor fanciful. He can have no business here."

"He came to procure a benefit-play for an amiable but unfortunate lady," said an astonished listener.

"How gothic! There must be some unknown reason for such laborious benevolence! Is the woman young or handsome?"

"Both, madam."

"I thought so! Of what species is she?"

"Human," was the laconic answer.

"I mean, of what character?"

"Her distress is the best voucher for her reputation," replied the person addressed.

The lady, silenced by this remark, sauntered towards the pump-room; and the sisters, having selected books for their entertainment, were quitting the shop, when they perceived their hero of the *haut ton*,[1] sir Lionel Beacon.

---

[1]   High fashion, or high society.

CHAPTER VII

After looking round, and yawning till he infected the whole circle, he exclaimed, "Bath is a bore!"

"A bore!" repeated Mr. Bradford with astonishment. Sir Lionel continued—

"Nothing but dipping dowagers and splenetic spinsters! Not a soul that a man of fashion knows! I only arrived this morning, and I am tired of it already. No chance of a frolic! Nothing human to be seen, go where one will!" Then looking round, he added, "A book-shop! I'm off! I hate books amazingly. Never read! And if I had the arrangement of things, all the volumes in the kingdom should be burnt, excepting the Racing Calendar. Reading only makes men stupid and women insolent. Besides, why should a man of rank ever have the trouble to think, while he can hire poor vagabonds to take that labour off his hands? When I was on my travels I enjoyed life astonishingly. I lived as an Englishman ought. I knew every opera-dancer on the continent, drank the best wine, wore the handsomest coats, supported the most fashionable girls, and was thought the most famous judge of what was pleasant of any Englishman that had ever travelled before me; while my tutor passed his time in hunting antiquities, poring over books, and, whenever he had an opportunity, which scarcely happened once a month, in lecturing me on my prodigality."[1]

As the baronet concluded his soliloquy, he turned towards Julia, who stood rapt in amazement. "Where shall we go?" said he. "How shall we pass our time till dinner? Cannot you take me home with you? I know nobody!——O! by Jove, here comes a famous fellow! an astonishing good figure!" So saying, he placed Julia's arm within his, and dashed toward the threshold, where Mr. Bradford had halted lest some unlucky movement of the boisterous baronet should dislodge him from his rolling vehicle. Sir Lionel, unappalled by the frowns of the citizen, continued——

---

[1]   Sir Lionel Beacon gives a fairly stereotypical account of the privileged young Englishman's Grand Tour of the continent. See Jeremy Black's *The British Abroad: The Grand Tour in the Eighteenth Century* (New York: St. Martin's, 1992).

"Why, my knight of the fleece! what could induce you to wander so far from home? It was only two days since that I heard of you at Hounslow! What brings you to Bath? You are too wary to gamble, except in the stocks. Pray are you a bull or a bear? I should suppose you too unfashionable to be the former; though, by your shaggy appearance, you have an amazing resemblance of the latter."

"What a fortunate thing it is to be born honourable!" said Mr. Bradford; "it saves so much trouble."

"I wish we could exchange our honour for your gold," replied sir Lionel.

"That would never do," said Mr. Bradford; "we should lose too much by the discount. We speculate on interest in proportion as we possess principal."

"We have interest as well as you," replied sir Lionel: "but as to principle, we care little about it. You toil, we sport; you sow, and we reap the harvest."

"It is well you have an opportunity," retorted Mr. Bradford; "for your high stations are sometimes barren."

"You are amazingly witty," said sir Lionel, "and I shall certainly be better acquainted with you." The inquisitive lady now passed the door. "There goes old Pen Pryer! I must make my bow, and rally her into good-humour. She looks astonishingly sulky, because she caught me making love to the chambermaid at Devizes.[1] I thought to vex the old girl: but she took it in high dudgeon,[2] and left me to pay the reckoning. I won't say a civil thing to her these six months, and that will make her amazingly miserable." As he spoke, Lady Pen beckoned him; while Mr. Bradford, with his family, returned to the Crescent, little pleased with the adventures of the morning.

---

[1] A town approximately fifteen miles east of Bath.
[2] Anger or ill humor.

CHAPTER VIII

At night they visited the rooms, more dressed and more looked at than any persons in the circle. Mr. Bradford was a tolerable whist-player,[1] and Julia danced like a sylph. Sir Lionel was her partner; not because he liked the trouble of dancing, or the fatigue of saying civil things, but for a more important reason—he excited the jealousy and mortified the vanity of lady Penelope Pryer.

Mr. Bradford had won two rubbers, when Mr. Morley, in a low whisper, informed him that he was playing with a practised sharper. "And what is that to you?" cried the citizen. "Mind your own affairs, and I warrant I will take care of mine." Contradiction, even in the form of friendly counsel, was ever obnoxious to this son of Mammon;[2] for this reason he doubled his stake on the succeeding rubbers, betted largely on the honours, and at three in the morning rose a loser of one thousand guineas.[3] His gouty spasms increased with his ill-fortune; and his mental agony was, on arriving at the Crescent, only to be equalled by his corporeal suffering. Again a servant was dispatched for a physician.

Martha ventured to utter her regrets that interest should be a plea for the destruction of health: but her remonstrances proved unfortunate; for on the following day she was commanded, with her mother, to set out for London. "Julia shall stay with me," said Mr. Bradford; "she neither advises nor contradicts me." They departed.

Martha was quitting Bath, when the chaise was stopped by Mr. Morley, who presented her a letter, and immediately departed.

---

[1] Whist was a popular eighteenth-century card game, similar to bridge. A "rubber," mentioned below, is a series of games; "honours" is a collective term for the four or five highest cards in the trump suit.

[2] The name *Mammon*, which means "riches," is commonly used to personify a lust for worldly wealth. In *Paradise Lost*, Milton describes Mammon as "the least erected Spirit that fell / From Heav'n, for ev'n in heav'n his looks and thoughts / Were always downward bent, admiring more / The riches of heav'n's pavement, trodden gold, / Than aught divine or holy" (1. 679–83).

[3] A guinea was a gold coin worth one pound and five pence. Mr. Bradford's loss in one evening, then, came to £1050, approximately ten times the average yearly income of shopkeepers and tradesmen, and more than one hundred times the sum his daughter Martha later earns from the sale of her first novel.

She broke the seal, and read the contents aloud to her mother. They were as follows:

> You appear to be sensible, humane, and amiable: I possess an independent fortune, and am a bachelor. I offer you my heart, because I think you worthy of possessing it. I have made inquiries respecting your sudden departure, and in a few hours after your arrival in London I shall call at your house for an answer. I want no fortune with you; I only wish you to be the partner of mine. Decide speedily and candidly.

Mr. Morley kept his word, and on the evening of their return to Crutched-Friars made them a visit. His conduct was liberal and sincere, his language frank and affectionate, his family and character unexceptionable, his person manly and pleasing. Martha requested three days to consider the question, and at the termination of that period Mr. Morley obtained her leave to write to Bath for the consent of her father.

Reader, Martha was not in haste for an husband: but she, like her father, was weary of perpetual contradiction. The evident partiality which had been shewn to her sister made her sigh for similar attentions. There is no pang equal to the throbbing of an unattached heart; for without an object to interest and to please, life is but a dream of visionary enjoyment. Yet Martha was not one of those romantic females who are led from the paths of rationality by the phantoms of vanity and caprice: she knew that love, which is not founded in esteem, cannot be of long duration. The reader may draw his opinion of her sentiments from her own pen, in the following stanzas:

LOVE said to REASON, "Know my pow'r,
    Nor vaunt thy pedant rules;
I can the sweetest natures sour,
    And make the wisest fools!

"I bid Philosophy submit,
    I make the dullest gay;

To idiots lend a gleam of wit,
    And darken wisdom's ray.

"I can teach proud and freezing scorn
    To feel my potent skill;
The sternest face with smiles adorn,
    The cold with rapture fill."

"'Tis true," indignant REASON said,
    "Too much of pow'r's thy own;
Yet 'tis where *I* refuse my aid,
    And only THOU art known.

"But Time, that conquers e'en thy art,
    Bids REASON's altar burn;
And as he calms the feverish heart,
    I triumph in my turn."

CHAPTER IX

While Martha was preparing what hope represented as a path of
roses, Julia was by her gentle acquiescence hurrying her father
towards the margin of the grave. Never contradicted, he indulged
in every luxury, ate immoderately, played deeply, fretted incessantly, drank inordinately, and slept three times during the
twenty-four hours. His malady increased, his form became every
hour more corpulent; his temper more irritable; his pocket more
light; and his expences more heavy. Julia had formed many fashionable acquaintances, for she knew the art of being all things to
all people; among others she was honoured with the particular
attentions of lady Pen Pryer: not because Julia had accomplishments and beauty; but because she was almost perpetually
followed by sir Lionel Beacon: and lady Pen wisely thought the
surest method of knowing what passed, was that of never losing
sight of the objects who awakened her curiosity.

Sir Lionel imperceptibly became a favourite with Mr. Bradford. He was pleasant, lively, and good humoured: he would drink with him, and bet with him; for the baronet was an adept in making himself at home in all societies. Besides, Julia thought him entertaining and amiable; and Julia's opinion was omnipotent, because it never opposed that of her father. Mr. Bradford already anticipated the honour of calling his daughter "my lady," while the baronet only looked forwards to the plain and more common appellation of *mistress.*

Mr. Morley having obtained the father's consent, found little difficulty in adding to it the fair hand of Martha. They were married with decent privacy—they did not publish to the world by pomp and idle parade, that their affections were brought to a climax. From the church they set out for Derbyshire, where Mr. Morley, possessing a clear estate of four thousand pounds per annum, with a comfortable and spacious family mansion, was considered as a man of unblemished reputation.

Mr. Morley, with some good qualities, had also some peculiarities. He was rigidly tenacious of an husband's authority; extremely correct in religious duties; a jealous admirer of subordination; and a most decided enemy to every thing that could possibly degrade the dignity of his ancestry: for Mr. Morley, in the female line, had descended from nobility; and though by his indefatigable labour to obtain the character of a philanthropist and a christian he had exalted his name, he would have felt no repugnance in knowing that it was also embellished by a title.

Morley House was pleasantly situated on the skirts of a valley; overshadowed by a mountain, and at half a mile's distance from a village, whose thinly scattered cottages were the abodes of poverty and labour. Mr. Morley seldom roved beyond the boundaries of his own manor; and though he evinced his benevolence twice a year by public donations, he seldom met his indigent neighbours, excepting at church, where his devout and unremitting attention to sacred doctrines rendered him an example worthy of imitation.

Mr. Morley was one of those prejudiced mortals who consider women as beings created for the conveniences of domestic life. He married because his manor house was lonely; and he chose a girl of Martha's open and ingenuous temper, because he imagined that he might govern her with facility; believing that the sense of obligations for her removal from parental tyranny, would render her passive when he asserted the authority of an husband. A few months after their arrival in Derbyshire Mr. Morley was called to a distant part of England, to transact business of an important nature. One morning, during his absence, Martha, to whom constraint had given a zest for roving, resolved on visiting the neighbouring hamlet, to explore the habitations of the poor and the laborious. She had strolled farther than she intended, when on passing a small thatched cottage at the end of the village, she heard a deep groan, which arrested her footsteps. She listened; it was repeated. She knocked at the door, but no one answered: she tried the latch, opened it, and entered.

She found a female, young and pretty, with an infant lying beside her, on a poor pallet, and with every appearance of poverty and pain. Mrs. Morley approached the bed: the child was only a few hours old. The mother placing her hands before her eyes, would have concealed her tears, but they rolled down her pale cheek involuntarily. The scene was penetrating, and Martha's heart was tender. A tattered curtain, which was fastened before the casement, rendered the apartment gloomy. Mrs. Morley took the infant in her arms towards the door; it was asleep and tranquil. Over a chair which stood near the threshold was thrown a muslin morning dress:—the fashion of it struck Mrs. Morley's eyes, and, from that single circumstance, she concluded that the mother of the new-born villager was more than what her miseries bespoke her. The child was again placed in its mother's arms. It already seemed to enjoy the warmth of a maternal bosom. She sighed as she pressed it still closer to her heart; and with a feeble voice entreated Mrs. Morley to leave her.

Martha kneeling by the side of the bed, took the sufferer's hand, which was white and beautiful, while with tenderness and sympathy she inquired why she uttered such piercing tones. "Have you no medical aid? Do you want the comforts necessary to your situation?" said she.

"Alas! earthly consolation has long been an alien to my heart," sighed the young woman. "But we cannot quit this state of suffering when we grow weary of its trials."

"It will be hard indeed if, at your time of life, the world becomes a tedious scene. You are scarcely authorized in wishing for death, while you have the powers of rendering life supportable to yourself or beneficial to others."

"Yours is the language of religious resignation," replied the young woman; "but despair will sometimes vanquish even that last resource. I am too wretched to reason on the chimeras of hope,—they have so long deceived me." She could not proceed—tears which evidently flowed from a full heart suppressed the powers of utterance. Mrs. Morley caught the contagious sorrow, and in silent sympathy presented such relief as she thought necessary for the stranger's present situation. It was modestly rejected.

"Will you endeavour to be more tranquil?" said Mrs. Morley. The sufferer sighed and shook her head impressively.

"What can I do to serve you?" inquired Martha. "I cannot leave you so distressed in mind without some hope of rendering you more happy."

"Advise me how to conceal my infant."

"To conceal it!" repeated Mrs. Morley, with an emotion of surprize. "Why should it be concealed?"

"Because I am not what my miseries bespeak me. Born to expect an happier destiny, my proud heart withers in concealment of those wrongs, which a less delicately organized mind would quickly find redressed."—Mrs. Morley's bosom shuddered.

"But," added the young woman, "thank Heaven! I still can live by mental exertion."

"There is no harder labour," interrupted Mrs. Morley with a sigh. "Yet little do the dull and proud imagine how dearly the children of genius earn even the highest patronage which ostentation offers. The toils of intellect are more severe than even the miseries of adversity."

"Having borne the pressure of conscious reproof, I shall not sink beneath the most laudable and honourable of occupations; my fortitude will be invincible."

"And yet I heard you groaning deeply."

"It was for my sleeping infant," replied the unknown, "the innocent object who is unconscious of its fate. A stranger, setting out on a journey through an unfeeling world,—exposed to poverty,—unprotected, unacknowledged—the offspring of a mysterious destiny—" She paused a few moments, then with an agonized tone exclaimed, "O God! there is no rest for feeling bosoms, but in the grave!"

Mrs. Morley took the child in her arms and kissed it.—"Ah! madam," continued its mother, "the noblest blood circulates in the beating heart of that sweet infant. But it is born to sorrow."

"And could you part with it?" said Mrs. Morley, taking its dimpled hand, and pressing it to her lips. "Could you bear to leave the little innocent——?"

"I cannot bear to witness the sorrow which I shall heap upon it. Better were it that the child should never know its mother, than know her to reproach her." She spoke feebly and seemed near fainting.

"You exhaust your strength; compose your mind, I conjure you," said Mrs. Morley; "and I will see you again to-morrow. Have you no attendant?"

"Yes, a good old woman. She is gone to the other end of the village to fetch me some nourishment. She will soon return. Pray, oh! pray, do not expose my situation. I can bear any thing but public shame——."

"To-morrow I will see you again," said Mrs. Morley, proceeding towards the door where she met the old woman:—they passed each other, but not a word was uttered.—

Mrs. Morley on her return home ruminated on the situation of the young unknown. The rain began to pour, and she was ill prepared to resist it. On her arrival at the manor-house she employed the housekeeper in selecting a variety of articles for the comfort and subsistence of the sufferer; and without attending to her own safety again immediately set out with a basket of provisions for the cottage. She did not mention the situation of the object who excited her interest; because secrecy was the delight of her charitable propensities.

She found the mother and her infant sleeping. The balm of sympathy was the opiate which lulled the aching heart; and the idea of being noticed by one feeling mortal, seemed to compensate for the whole world's unkindness. She had not slept soundly during many months;—she had longed, ardently longed, for sleep eternal! Mrs. Morley did not wake her; but placing the basket on a chair near her bed, stole away unheard and unseen by all, excepting the recording eye of an Omniscient approver!

CHAPTER X

The rain which had penetrated Mrs. Morley's dress, though her heart was warm, chilled its circulation. She was on the following day seized with feverish shiverings, and confined to her bed. Her only anxiety was for the young mother's safety, and her only ruminations were those of devising means to obtain intelligence how she had passed the night. During the day, she received a letter from Mr. Morley, informing her that new business of the utmost importance, no less than the death of an uncle, who had left him a large addition to his fortune, obliged him to set off without delay for Brussels. He requested that she would reconcile her mind to the separation which would not be of many weeks, and that she would not fail to write by every opportunity. Mrs. Morley's union with her husband owed its source to sentiment more than to passion; she could therefore exist out of his presence. She felt the value of fortune by the indulgence of her benignant propensities, and the augmentation of those powers reconciled her to the absence of her husband.

Her fever increased, and during several days she was confined to her bed. At the end of a week she sent for her old house-keeper, who had lived many years in the family, and desired her to take a fresh basket of provisions, some linen, and a letter to the last cottage in the village. "Leave them, but say nothing," cried Mrs. Morley, "if you love me, or value my friendship."

Mrs. Grimwood obeyed as far as the first part of her commission went: but to *say nothing* was too severe an injunction. She made more than ordinary haste, because she went on the wing of curiosity. On approaching the door she entered abruptly, where she saw the old nurse with the infant on her knee. The mother had removed to an inner chamber.

Mrs. Grimwood stood silent and meditating. The child was dressed in fine muslin and lace, the emblems of a fond mother's harmless vanity.

"Whose child is this?" said Mrs. Grimwood.

"A lady's," answered the nurse.

"What lady's?"

"I am not permitted to tell."

"Why?"

"Because I do not know."

"Where is the mother?"

"Not far off," said the nurse.

"I believe you," cried Mrs. Grimwood, "I believe you; though he who ought to be the father is at some distance."

"Alack!" was the sighed reply. The sagacious housekeeper pondered.

"Well, here is provision, both of food and raiment: but it is the last that I will bring," said Mrs. Grimwood. She threw the basket on the ground, glanced at the unoffending object of suspicion, and with majestic precision measured back her steps towards home.

The old nurse brought daily intelligence from the cottage; and at the end of a fortnight Mrs. Morley was well enough to make another visit to the invalid. She found her considerably recovered; and the question was again started, "How shall I conceal my infant?" It was a fine girl; and many a noble parent would have been glad to have owned it: but the want of a few words from a priest had condemned it to shame and to oblivion.

Mrs. Morley played with the infant, and it smiled. She wished it were her own, and at the same moment it pressed her finger with its little hand. "I shall be sorry to part with the pretty creature," said she. The child seemed to look with an imploring eye. Mrs. Morley, bursting into tears, kissed and caressed it. At this moment Mrs. Grimwood passed the cottage door. It was open; so were her eyes. The infant was satisfied; so was Mrs. Grimwood.

"Will you trust the child with me for a few hours?" said Mrs. Morley.

"Most willingly," replied the mother.

"Our housekeeper is a good sort of woman, and she may assist us in finding an asylum for the pretty angel." The mother sighed deeply, but said nothing.

The child was carefully wrapped in a flannel mantle, and Mrs. Morley tripped lightly with her charge along the village; little foreseeing that her steps would lead to a labyrinth of adventures.

CHAPTER XI

The evening sun shed its last beams on the no less ruddy cheek of the infant stranger, when Mrs. Morley was returning with it towards the cottage. She had loitered till it was near twilight in shewing her little treasure to the whole family, and the event furnished many themes for conjecture and suspicion. Mrs. Morley's lonely rambles, her recent confinement, her husband's absence, the provisions and the clothes sent to the cottage, the old nurse's ambiguous answers to Mrs. Grimwood's questions, and the fine dress of the infant, were subjects of mysterious and ambiguous animadversion.

On Mrs. Morley's return to the birthplace of the fugitive she found the doors shut and the windows closed. The inhabitants had departed. Her amazement and chagrin were not to be described. She stood mute and wonder-struck. She removed the flannel from the infant's face: it was sleeping sweetly. A dimpled smile played round its mouth: its hands were placed upon its breast. The soft breath ascended fragrantly to her lip as she kissed its cheek. It had the aspect of a cherub. It was deserted—by whom? By its mother! The offspring of frailty! the heir to shame! the friendless, helpless, guiltless child, probably, of an illicit passion!

"These are the fatal effects of barbarous and prejudiced opinions!" said Mrs. Morley. "This innocent creature is left to the mercy of a stranger, because its parents have erred against the laws of moral rectitude! It is left even without a name! A female, thrown upon an unfeeling world, abandoned by the bosom which Nature has stored with nourishment to save it!" She could not proceed: she wept abundantly; and the infant was once more conveyed to Morley-house, as a full confirmation of all that had been shrewdly conjectured.

CHAPTER XII

While Mrs. Morley was occupied in the offices of philanthropy, her sister Julia was employed in the senseless pursuits of modern dissipation. Lady Pen Pryer was still her constant companion, and the volatile baronet their divided inamorato;[1] while Mr. Bradford hourly augmented his store of complaints in proportion as he diminished the sources of his enjoyment.

The season for drinking the Bath waters being over, lady Pen proposed a trip to Weymouth.[2] "All the world will be there," said she; "and it will be ten to one that Julia returns at least with a title." Mr. Bradford's ear caught the flattering sound; Julia heaved a languishing sigh, and sir Lionel requested permission to be of their party.

On a burning summer morning the four black steeds were again put in motion; lady Pen and sir Lionel leading the way in the baronet's curricle, and the wealthy invalid anticipating the renovation of health from the salubrious effects of aquatic breezes.

Julia had considerably improved under the auspices of a woman of fashion. She now *rouged* highly, talked boldly, gazed steadfastly, laughed sarcastically, and sighed significantly. Her dress was less after the vestal *costume*: she knew how to fold her drapery after the manner of a Grecian Venus or a Roman Messalina: she could smile like Lais, and make love like Sappho:[3] she was

---

[1] A male intimate or lover.

[2] The spring season at Bath ended in June. During the warmer months of July and August, many tourists flocked to Weymouth, a town on the Dorset coast, which became a popular resort after George III's first visit in the summer of 1789.

[3] According to Lemprière's *Classical Dictionary*, Venus, the Greek goddess of beauty, was also "patroness of courtesans"; Valeria Messalina was the notoriously unfaithful wife of the Roman emperor Claudius I; and Lais was a "celebrated courtesan" in Greece during the fourth century B.C. One of Robinson's contemporaries, "Peter Pindar" (John Walcott), referred to Lais as "the Mrs. Robinson of Greece."

the perpetual retailer of anecdote for the amusement of lady Pen; and she professed an abhorrence of every thing serious or literary, in compliment to the taste of the dissipated baronet.

Mr. Bradford's relish for the good things of this world was not diminished by his intercourse with the bad ones. He could swallow the most insipid flattery as well as the most savoury viands. He drank the intoxicating streams of the grape with a new set of noble associates, till they produced the same effect on his mind as the waters of Lethe.[1] The world was to him newly created. He for the first time knew how to live, at the moment when reflection should have taught him how to die. But the rankest weeds are those of oldest growth. Mr. Bradford had long panted for the society of nobility as he had panted for breath, and both equally promised his approaching destruction.

A few weeks put a period to his enjoyments. Death judiciously made a full stop; for the citizen expired immediately after eating a voracious dinner given by sir Lionel on the birth-day of Julia. The consternation which this sudden event occasioned is not to be described. Lady Pen wrote an extempore epigram on the catastrophe; and Julia fainting in the arms of sir Lionel, was conveyed senseless from the scene of calamity.

Reader, lament not the death of Peregrine Bradford, but lend your ready tears to the tide of Julia's sorrows. Sir Lionel for a moment forgot his lovely lady Pen, and Julia, from the day of her birth, will ever remember sir Lionel.

In twelve hours after the death of Mr. Bradford, the corpse set out for London. The baronet had a horse to run at York, and also took his departure, accompanied by lady Pen Pryer, who was not acquainted with all that had passed during her poetical reverie. Julia's consternation was only to be equalled by her grief: she had lost her dear, her indulgent father; she had also lost both her peace of mind and honour. The four black steeds conveyed her back to London in every sense of the word a modern girl of fashion.

Mrs. Bradford was not wholly inconsolable. She did all that a wife is expected to do on similar occasions—she wore weeds,

---

[1] Drinking water from Lethe, a mythological river in Hades, made the dead forget their previous existence.

placed an armorial lozenge over the door, thereby kindly informing the public that a rich widow was to be disposed of to the highest bidder; and after weeping the usual and decent time, she set out, with her disconsolate Julia, on a visit to Mrs. Morley in Derbyshire.

In all the towns through which they passed Julia distributed small money to the poor who flocked round the carriage. The rich widow Bradford disdained, like some of our nobility, to travel unknown: she did not fly through towns and villages without a single blessing from the poor and the unhappy. She knew the value of wealth, by making a little benevolence go a great way in the scale of popularity; and she considered a name as of some use besides embellishing the pages of an emblazoned calendar. Twenty pounds, bestowed in the purchase of pious ejaculations, rendered Mrs. Bradford of more importance in her journey to Derbyshire than as many thousands have made as many nobles during the expensive travels of their minority. So cheap is a good name; and yet how few will take the pains to become purchasers!

On their approaching Morley-house, they found its mistress walking on the lawn, with the little fugitive in her arms. It had been made a Christian, and its name was Frances. Mrs. Morley hastened to meet her relations, and led them into the parlour followed by Mrs. Grimwood, to whose care she had consigned the infant. After the usual ceremonies of friendly meeting—

"Dear, Martha, whose child is this?" cried Julia, looking earnestly at Frances.

"Is it not extremely pretty?" inquired Mrs. Morley.

"It is very like you," said Julia. Mrs. Grimwood's mouth was curved at the corner while she looked vacantly towards the window.

"Pray tell me who are its parents?" continued Julia.

"That nobody knows," replied Mrs. Grimwood officiously, at the same time elevating her eye-brows, and half smiling.

Mrs. Bradford now took the child in her arms. "Well!" exclaimed she, "I protest I have seen somebody as like this baby as two peas!"

"It has Martha's mouth," added Julia.

"I am sure it has my mistress's nose," cried Mrs. Grimwood.

"There is something like Patty about the chin," said Mrs.

Bradford; "and if she had been married long enough, I should have sworn it was my grandchild.—What think you, my good woman?" Mrs. Grimwood sighed, but said nothing.

CHAPTER XIII

Frances, who had been placed at nurse in a neighbouring farm-house, grew daily in strength as she increased in beauty. Mrs. Morley frequently visited the fugitive, but heard nothing from its mother. Mr. Morley, at the expiration of four months, returned; and Morley-house presented a scene of the most promising domestic happiness.

Julia dedicated all her hours to elegant acquirements. She drew with taste and skill; she sang correctly and pleasingly; she had made a considerable progress in the polite languages; and her memory being retentive, she could repeat most of the best passages in the English poets. Her mind was tinctured with romantic propensities, which appeared, at times, more extraordinary than natural; while her person improved in delicacy, and her temper seemed soft even to the excess of sensibility.

On the Sunday after Mr. Morley's return, Julia and Mrs. Bradford attended him to church. Mrs. Morley had strolled out immediately after breakfast, and did not come back till near the hour of dinner. She had been to visit her little *élève*,[1] who was sickening for the measles. Mr. Morley, on seeing her, remarked that he was astonished at her forgetting the duties of religion, when so fashionable a girl as her sister thought them worthy of attention.

"Perhaps Martha has been to see her little favourite," said Julia: "it seems to engross all her affections."

"What favourite?" inquired Mr. Morley hastily.

Julia reddened. "I hope I have not said any thing which I ought not to have uttered!" cried she, hesitating. "I thought you knew, of course, that my sister had a little *protegée*!"

---

[1] A pupil, or charge.

"What does it mean?" said Mr. Morley: "To whom does Julia allude?"

Mrs. Morley was addressed so abruptly, that she knew not what answer to make: but after some confused and faltering attempts to speak, she replied, "She means my little girl, at farmer Oldham's."

"*Your* little girl!" cried Mr. Morley.

"My little adopted——" added Martha, again hesitating.

"You might have requested my permission before you adopted any *protegée*," said Mr. Morley. "An husband's acquiescence is, I think, necessary on occasions of such importance."

"It is a poor little helpless, forsaken creature," said Mrs. Morley; "and were you to see it, you would not, you could not blame me."

"Indeed," added Julia, "you would love the infant; it is so astonishingly like my sister."

"I wish it were my own!" sighed Mrs. Morley.—Mr. Morley's face reddened.

"You could not idolize it more," said Julia; "for it seems the pride and pleasure of your existence. You are devoted to it, almost exclusively."

"Indeed!" muttered Mr. Morley. "And pray where did you find this fascinating object?" Martha was preparing a reply, when Mrs. Grimwood entered the parlour to say that Frances was in convulsions, and that the wife of farmer Oldham was come to tell her mistress she feared that she was dying. Mrs. Morley rose from the table, and darted out of the room; while her astonished husband and Julia gazed earnestly at each other.

"What means all this?" inquired Mr. Morley.—Mrs. Grimwood replied, "Indeed, sir, nobody knows what it means."

"Do not judge hastily," said Julia, addressing Mr. Morley. "You know my sister has been ill, and perhaps she will not bear interrogation. The poor baby cannot help it."

"Help what?" cried Mr. Morley, with evident inquietude.

"You are so hasty!" said Mrs. Bradford. "I dare say that Martha will acquit herself."

"Who has accused her?" inquired the husband.

"Not I," said Julia. "Heaven knows I believe the story, even with all its improbabilities!"

"What story? You will make me seriously uneasy," said Mr. Morley.

"Nay, ask Martha," replied Julia; "I do not choose to meddle with such an ambiguous matter. The infant is really a sweet creature, and evidently of no mean extraction. Perhaps my sister loves it for its strong resemblance to herself."

"Who is its father?" said Mr. Morley.

"That she never mentions."

"Its mother?"

"She will not tell."

"By heavens, this has more meaning than discretion!" said Mr. Morley. "I will see the infant."

He hastened to farmer Oldham's; he saw the infant. It was on Martha's bosom, bathed with her tears. Mr. Morley desired his wife to return with him.

"Not while my little darling is in this precarious state," said she. "I am not destitute of feeling."

"Nor am I of discernment," interrupted Mr. Morley. "I *command* you to obey me!" Martha had never heard such words spoken with such an emphasis. Her colour came and went. She looked a refusal, and hugged the child still closer to her bosom.

"It is some beggar's offspring," said Mr. Morley. "Some artful, low-born jade has imposed on your mistaken sensibility."

"That it is a beggar renders it more dear to me," replied Mrs. Morley.

"There are times and places for all things."

"Blest was the time, though sad the dwelling, where I found poor Frances," said Mrs. Morley, bursting into tears. As she spoke, Mrs. Bradford and Julia entered the room.

"Heavens! Martha, why are you in tears?" said Julia, taking her hand, and at the same time glancing at the infant.

"My poor little Frances!" said Mrs. Morley, when her words were arrested by her distress.

Julia looked a tacit reproof. "You are wrong, indeed," cried she, in an audible whisper. "Were the child your own, you could not feel more afflicted."

"Perhaps I should feel less," replied Mrs. Morley; "for in that case the little darling would not be deemed an object of charity. It is its helpless, its unacknowledged state that makes me sympathize in its sufferings."

Mr. Morley again desired his wife to return home. "Do not refuse," said Julia: "remember that it is your husband who commands, and I conjure you to obey."

Martha gave the child to Mrs. Oldham, and attended her family.

The evening at Morley-house was neither social nor happy. Mr. Morley was more than thoughtful: his wife little less than despairing for the fate of Fanny. Mrs. Bradford said nothing: but Julia looked an infinity of things. She lamented that her sister did not seem so happy as she expected to find her; and hoped that when she married, she should be able to assimilate her ideas with those of her husband. There could be no domestic harmony where hearts did not beat in unison. Sympathy, she continued, was the soul of sentiment; and it was the duty of every wife to consider her husband's will as the foundation of her felicity.

"Then women, from the moment that they marry, do not submit to personal captivity only?" said Martha. "Marriage, in that case, is little better than slavery. I detest the thought of enforced subordination!" Mr. Morley rose from his seat and walked about the room.

"You were not at church, Martha!" said he, with a tone of ill-humour.

"I was quite as well employed," replied Mrs. Morley.—Julia shook her head. Her husband again addressed her.

"Religious duties should never be neglected. The most exalted situation is embellished by the exercise of piety."

"And the most wretched solaced by the assiduities of benevolence."

"Another day might have been devoted to your purpose," said Mr. Morley.

"And have risen to shew me the corpse of Fanny!" replied Martha.

"You might have sent the child every aid; you had no occasion to disgrace yourself by personal attendance. Familiarity is the source of humiliation."

"I acknowledge no distinction but that which originates in virtue." Mr. Morley grew uneasy.

"When I married you, Martha, I did not suppose that those were your opinions."

"If it was your intention to present me a new set, my dear Mr. Morley, it was of little importance what were the old ones."

"Pray, Martha, do not speak so decidedly to your husband," said Julia. "Remember how often you used to vex our good father by contradicting him!"

"Your father was a peevish, vulgar man," cried Mr. Morley. "I *pitied* your sister, and therefore married her——"

"That all the world may follow your *example*," said Mrs. Morley.

"I released you from parental authority——"

"To teach me that of an husband."

Julia observed the increasing altercation, and in tears quitted the room. What passed on the following morning the reader shall know in the next chapter.

CHAPTER XIV

Mr. Morley rose early, and summoned Mrs. Grimwood to the breakfast-room. "Grimwood," said he, "you have been a faithful servant in the family during many years. You have always proved yourself diligent and honest. I have no reason to suppose that you would utter a falsehood—and I therefore question you with confidence. How long is it since my wife first took this infant under her protection?"

"Just about the time that my mistress was ill, and confined to her bed."

"Ill! and confined to her bed! when——? I never heard that she had been ill; what was her malady?" inquired Mr. Morley.

"I do not know, sir."

"Whom did she see? who attended her?"

"She saw nobody but an old woman, who lived a short time in the village," replied Mrs. Grimwood, with some hesitation.

"Find her!—produce her!" cried Mr. Morley rapidly:— "There is some mystery in this strange adoption.—What think you of this child?" continued he, after a short pause.

"I think it very like my mistress, sir."

"She loves it excessively," said Mr. Morley.

"As if it were her own," rejoined Mrs. Grimwood.

"How did my wife pass her time during my absence?"

"In rambling about near the manor-house," replied the house-keeper.

"Did she go to church?"

"Not often.—She used to visit all the little cottages, and talk as familiarly with the poor people in them, as though they had been her equals."

"She is very condescending!" interrupted Mr. Morley, peevishly.

"O very, sir. She had no pride."

"Not an atom!" said he, biting his lip.

"She is not at all like Miss Julia."

"As unlike as day and night," replied Mr. Morley. "But hasten to the village, and find the old convenient jade who was the keeper of my wife's confidence. We will hear what account she gives of the infant."

Mrs. Grimwood set out on her important embassy. Crossing the meadows she overtook Mrs. Morley, who was going to inquire how Fanny had passed the night.—They parted at farmer Oldham's, after the following brief conversation:

"Heaven grant that I may find my little darling living.—I feel that I love the poor innocent, in proportion as it is persecuted."

"My master seems very much displeased at your attentions.—He thinks that you demean yourself by taking notice of a child whom nobody knows—and who ought to be sent to the parish."

"I would rather toil to support it," said Mrs. Morley. Mrs. Grimwood made no comments; she was too busily employed in making conjectures. She hastened to the village, and her inquiries proved nearly fruitless. For all she learnt was, that the old woman was a Welsh midwife, and only a few weeks resident at the cottage.

She returned towards home. Mr. Morley met her more than half way. She made her report; and he made up his mind, that his wife was the mother of little Fanny.

A few days after this event a letter arrived at Morley-house. It came from lady Pen Pryer, informing the family that she should, on her way to Buxton,[1] make them a visit. Lady Pen was volatile

---

[1] A popular spa town developed in the late eighteenth century by the fifth Duke of Devonshire, the husband of Robinson's patroness Georgiana.

and dissipated; but she was a woman of rank, and Mr. Morley felt infinite delight in associating with people of distinction. Mrs. Morley's opinions were in this instance also different from those of her husband: she expressed some discontent at the visit proposed; and wished lady Pen had totally forgotten that there was such a family in existence.

"That would be rather a difficult task," said Mr. Morley. "The name is as old as Alfred's."[1]

"Were it contemporary with Adam's it were of little importance," replied Martha.

"Well!" sighed Julia, "of all things upon earth I should like to marry a man of an illustrious ancestry."

"And I wish you *had* married one," interrupted Mrs. Morley; "for, in my opinion, existing worth is far more estimable than hereditary honours." At this moment lady Pen's chaise stopped at the lawn, and Mr. Morley requested that Julia would hasten to welcome her. "*You* are accustomed to persons of fashion, and will not feel embarrassed," said he.

Lady Pen had, before Julia tripped over the lawn, been handed from her chaise by sir Lionel Beacon. Julia's colour changed, and an evident distress marked her demeanour, while she faintly articulated the joy she felt at so flattering a visit. Sir Lionel scarcely noticed Julia; while lady Pen, with a sorrowful tone remarked, that she was astonishingly altered!

"Amazingly thin and pale!" added sir Lionel. "I hope you have been gay and full of fun since I saw you? Nothing like it! I beg you to be in spirits, for I shall not stay here long. I am going to see a famous fellow who is doing penance near Derby."

"A highwayman?" inquired Mr. Morley.

"No, by Jupiter! a nobleman. An amazing good fellow, but astonishingly run out."

"By gaming?" said Mr. Morley.

"By all sorts of sport. A capital dasher. Has debauched more wives and daughters than any man of his age in the three kingdoms."

"And what is he doing in Derbyshire?" said Mr. Morley.

"That is more than I know, and if I did, I would not tell,"

---

[1] Alfred the Great, king of the West Saxons from 871 to 899.

replied sir Lionel. "Some snug intrigue; a 'squire's wife or a farmer's daughter. He has more things at nurse than his estate, I'll warrant him.—An amazing fine fellow, only five-and-twenty, and astonishingly knowing."

"I never heard of a young nobleman so sequestered in this part of the country," cried Mr. Morley, reddening.

"Perhaps Martha has," said Julia.

"Never," replied Mrs. Morley.

"How should you?" inquired sir Lionel. "He had changed his name, and passes for a country gentleman."

"A young nobleman passing for a gentleman; impossible!" said Martha.

"Pray, how does he call himself?" said Mr. Morley.

"His real name is lord Francis Sherville."

"Francis!" repeated Mr. Morley.

"His travelling title is Mr. Wickham," added the baronet.

Here the conversation took another topic, and, at the conclusion of it a walk was proposed by sir Lionel, to make sport in the village. "I want to reconnoitre; perhaps there is some game worth starting, and I am amazingly fond of rural amusements," said the baronet.

In the evening sir Lionel's scheme was put in practice, and the whole group set out on foot; some to torment, and others to be tormented.

CHAPTER XV

On passing the door of farmer Oldham's mansion, Mrs. Oldham, sitting by the roadside, was playing with little Fanny. Mrs. Morley stopped for a moment to embrace her *protegée*, when Julia informed Lady Penelope, that there was a secret history attending the infant.

"A secret!" said her ladyship; "Heavens let me hear it; perhaps we may find it out."

"The child is a fugitive, adopted by my sister, during her husband's journey on the continent."

"Perhaps it is her own," cried lady Pen.

Julia smiled.

Lady Pen communicated the intelligence she had just heard to sir Lionel: and he, without further ceremony, inquired of Mrs. Oldham to whom the child belonged.

"Nobody knows, sir, excepting Mrs. Morley," replied Mrs. Oldham.

"That is amazingly astonishing!" cried the baronet. "There is something wonderfully famous in belonging to nobody:—and who is to provide for it?"

"Heaven knows!" said Julia; "I am certain that Mr. Morley will not."

"Then I will," interrupted sir Lionel. "By Jove, the little vagabond shan't die for want of a parent. If every child were abandoned by its father, what would become of inheritance?"

"You mean if every father owned his own children," said lady Pen.

"Well, this may be mine for aught I know; and why should not I adopt it? It is not the first that has been at a loss where to claim its father: and it does not follow that, by being legitimate, it would do honour to its family."

"You would not be so frantic!" said lady Pen.

"'Tis better to be mad than inhuman," replied the baronet: "one disease is curable; but the other, being born with us, is beyond the reach of medicine."

"The whole world will condemn you," said lady Penelope.

"So will they poor little Nobody,"[1] replied sir Lionel; "and there are two reasons why I am the fittest to bear the world's severity; first, because I am a man; and secondly, because I defy its opinion. I have made many a woman wretched; and I think it is time that I should, at least, endeavour to make *one* happy.—It is a famous fine girl,—and astonishingly in luck. How do you call it?"

"Frances, sir," said Mrs. Oldham.

"Sherville's, by Jupiter!" exclaimed the baronet; "this accounts for his seclusion. I thought the hermit had his idol: he is too clever a fellow to lose his time for nothing." Mr. Morley's eyes seemed bent on vacancy; his brow was contracted; his arms were folded. Julia inquired emphatically what made him so thoughtful; and sir

---

[1] A possible allusion to Robinson's *Nobody*. See *A Letter to the Women of England*, 45, n. 1.

Lionel remarked that "it was a wise child who knew its own father."[1]

They returned to Morley-house; the evening passed merrily, but Mr. Morley was not present. His mind was too unquiet to be occupied or amused by trivial conversation. The name of Frances, the resemblance which every body discovered between his wife and the infant; her ready acquiescence to accept his proposals of marriage; her illness during his absence, and all the concurring circumstances already related, established conviction in his mind, that he had been duped, and his wife dishonoured. "Why," said he, "did I select a girl of Martha's unpolished manners? because I thought that she possessed also a simplicity of character which would render her the domestic companion, the artless friend. She makes my house the rendezvous for intrigue. She adopts a bastard to dissipate my fortune. She avows opinions hostile to the authority of an husband; and she openly associates with the very dregs of the creation! It is now time to act decidedly."

Mr. Morley was walking on the lawn before the house, while he uttered this soliloquy. Julia was at her chamber window, and overheard it; she descended; she approached him; she inquired tenderly why he had quitted the company; conjured him to rouse his spirits, and to banish every suspicion from his bosom.—"It is not, it cannot be possible that my sister, even for a moment, would deceive so amiable, so indulgent an husband; one who selected her when he might have chosen a wife from the whole race of women."

Mr. Morley sighed and listened. Julia's motive was not that of tranquillizing a perturbed imagination; it was not that of harmonizing the chords of domestic unison. She had another motive. She wished to pique sir Lionel, who was at the same moment whispering soft nonsense to lady Pen at the parlour window. Mr. Morley, not knowing nor observing this circumstance, placed on Julia's conduct another interpretation.

Early on the following day sir Lionel set out on horseback, to find his friend lord Francis Sherville; who, as was before mentioned, from mysterious motives had assumed the name of Mr. Wickham. Mr. Morley, during his absence, employed the

---

[1] A proverbial expression dating back to ancient Greece.

whole morning in making inquiries in the village—but to no purpose; nobody knew to whom Fanny belonged, or where she came from; though everybody spoke of Mrs. Morley's unbounded goodness towards her. While he was conversing with Mrs. Oldham upon the subject, his pulse beating quick with the fever of anxiety, sir Lionel and lord Frances passed them on horseback. Mr. Morley felt a sensation of mortified pride, at what he thought would look like jealously, and a too familiar condescension. Sir Lionel observed his embarrassment, and riding up to the door of the farm-house presented lord Francis; whose youth, handsome person, and easy elegance of manners, in no degree tended to soothe Mr. Morley's inquietude.

They returned to Morley-house; lord Francis and the baronet on horseback; Mr. Morley on foot; consequently the two former (taking the high road, and the latter proceeding across the meadows) reached the lawn some time before him. On his approach he observed sir Lionel and lady Pen walking together; while lord Francis and Mrs. Morley were seated on a bench at the upper end of the lawn. Julia was standing at her chamber window, alone.

Mr. Morley's sensations were too poignant for the resistance of human fortitude. He therefore stopped short; took a circuitous path round the back of the house, and with a heart throbbing for revenge, hastened to communicate his feelings to the sympathizing Julia.

He entered her chamber pale and agitated. She flew towards him. "Heavens!" exclaimed the tender-hearted girl, "why are you thus distressed? who is that stranger that is walking with my sister?"

"Lord Francis Sherville."

"I thought so!" cried Julia; "yet I conjure you to do nothing rashly. He is a man much given to impetuosity."

"You know him then?"

"I saw him frequently when I was at Bath with my father."

"Did Martha see him too?"

"Unquestionably, she cannot but remember him," replied Julia.

"Why?" inquired Mr. Morley earnestly.

"Because he is so singularly handsome."

"Is he generally thought so?"

"By women invariably," replied Julia. "But he is less dangerous than handsome."

"Why?"

"Because he is a professed libertine—a practiced seducer."

"He shall not remain under my roof; he shall not, by Heavens!"

"Have patience," interrupted Julia. "I still hope that Martha is innocent."

"Did you ever doubt it?"

Julia after some hesitation replied,—"How unkindly do you question me.—I love my sister dearer than my life.—I wish to think her worthy of such an heart as yours.—Let me therefore see you tranquil.—I cannot bear to witness your chagrin, your wretchedness." She was interrupted by her tears.

Martha now entered the house, to inquire whether Mr. Morley had returned. Mrs. Grimwood replied in the affirmative, at the same time adding:"My master is talking with Miss Julia in her bedchamber." Mrs. Morley was not more than woman; her dressing-room was adjoining to Julia's apartment; she felt herself drawn imperceptibly towards the key-hole, that mischievous aperture which Vulcan invented to annoy the daughters of his frail partner.[1] Her head was bowed by chagrin, and her ear unfortunately met the chasm of communication, just as Mr. Morley's lips pressed the fair hand of Julia. She had heard enough to pique her pride, and to authorize her resentment. She returned to the garden.

Lord Francis was still pensively seated on the bench where Mrs. Morley had left him, sir Lionel and lady Pen having strolled to an alcove in an adjacent wilderness.—Mrs. Morley and lord Francis continued in close conversation; and among other things the fugitive infant became the subject of their discourse. The young nobleman was not without feeling, though dissipated and high-bred. The fate of little Fanny interested his heart; and when Mrs. Morley concluded her story, he involuntarily took her by the hand and pressed it.

---

[1] Vulcan, the deformed son of Jupiter and Juno, was identified with Hephaestus, the Greek god of fire and metalworking. His "frail" wife, Venus, had a number of lovers, including Mars, the god of war.

Mrs. Morley's eyes were full of tears; she rose and, with lord Francis, entered the wilderness. The hour was yet early, and he proposed strolling to the farm-house to see little Fanny. Mrs. Morley's bosom was shielded by conscious innocence, and she agreed to accompany him. Julia saw them pass the garden-gate; she watched them across the first meadow; she fell in tears into the arms of Mr. Morley, exclaiming, "Oh Heavens! is it possible?"

CHAPTER XVI

On their arrival at Mrs. Oldham's they found little Fanny sleeping in her cradle. Lord Francis gazed earnestly at its features; they were flushed with the glow of noon, and she looked more beautiful than ever. Over her head was thrown a Cambric handkerchief. It was marked with the letter S, and a coronet.[1] He enquired of Mrs. Morley what sort of woman the mother appeared to be. She described her minutely.—"Have you any of her hand-writing?" Mrs. Morley produced a short note, which she had received from her during her illness. Lord Francis changed colour as he read it; but made no comment. They returned to Morley-house; but on entering the garden-gate a letter was presented to Mrs. Morley by Mrs. Grimwood, requesting that she would no longer insult the honour of her husband, but remain at farmer Oldham's till her conduct could be explained to his satisfaction. The letter also informed her, that her mother and Julia, unable to witness her imprudence, had during her absence set out for London.

Mrs. Morley's consternation was undescribable; but her pride was equal to her amazement. She turned from the gate, and in tears proceeded towards the farm-house. Lord Francis walked beside her, and conjured her to acquaint him with the cause of her distress. She could only articulate, "Little Fanny!"

---

[1] A coronet, or small crown, was an emblem reserved, by social convention, for members of nobility.

"That cause shall be removed," said he; "a few hours shall place Fanny in a new asylum. I will adopt her." Mrs. Morley's heart bounded with joy.—Her every wish seemed now accomplished.—How generous, how benevolently noble did such conduct appear, when contrasted with the jealous and suspicious pride of Mr. Morley. Her tears flowed in torrents, but they were tears of rapture; an helpless, unknown, innocent, and forsaken infant had found a liberal friend, a voluntary patron, at a moment when it was exposed to vulgar persecution. Mrs. Morley forgot her own forlorn and unprotected situation, in the good fortune of her little favourite.

Reader, you may remember that Mr. Morley offered to marry Martha without a dowry; and you may also conclude that Mr. Bradford accepted the proposal. In consequence of this prudent arrangement, the ceremony of making a marriage-settlement was omitted; and Martha was now driven from her husband's home, without the means of future subsistence. She was young and handsome. Lord Francis was discerning and persuasive.—But Mrs. Morley's virtue had one invulnerable safeguard—Pride: not the little vanity of birth or fortune; the variegated bubble, Fame, blown from the trumpet of frothy adulation; it was the pride of a feeling mind, the dignity of self-approbation. She did not, like Julia, sigh or weep with ostentatious sensibility. Her feelings were not the effects of habit; they were the energies of nature.

As soon as they entered the farm-yard, a countryman was dispatched for a chaise, and lord Francis informed Mrs. Oldham of his purpose.

"By whose authority, sir, do you remove the child?" was Mrs. Oldham's question.

"By Mrs. Morley's."

"I grieve to part with it," said Mrs. Oldham.

"So should I," cried Mrs. Morley; "but that I know it will be kindly treated. Lord Francis will love it tenderly; I am sure he will; his heart is all feeling and generosity. He is not like Mr. Morley." She now recollected her recent insult; she shuddered. Lord Francis whispered, "Dear, amiable woman——why are you thus unhappy? I will provide for your little Fanny. I would, if you allowed me, be your protector also."—Mrs. Oldham departed to pack up Fanny's clothes, and Mrs. Morley was left in the parlour with lord Francis.

"Tell your unfeeling husband," said his lordship, "that this infant shall never more offend him.—Say that it is mine; that I will give it even my name." Mrs. Morley's heart glowed with admiration; but she had not courage to avow that she had been driven from her home; and thrown upon his mercy: there again her pride became her safeguard.

"How shall I contrive to see Fanny in future?" said Mrs. Morley.

"I shall place her with a friend near London, and you shall be informed of every thing I purpose."

The chaise arrived. Fanny's small bundle was put into it. Mrs. Oldham kissed the little fugitive. Mrs. Morley pressed it to her heart.—"I give thee, sweet infant," said she, "to a warm and generous bosom, that will foster thee. I would, at the peril of any thing less than reputation, toil to support thee. Go to the arms of thy noble, thy benevolent protector."—Again she kissed the cheek on which a tear from her eyes had fallen while she spoke. It looked like a rose, sprinkled with the dews of morning.—Lord Francis now took the infant in his arms; again Mrs. Morley kissed it. "I am but an aukward nurse," said he, smiling.

"You are an angel!" cried Mrs. Morley.—Lord Francis had placed his foot upon the step of the carriage, but such words, from such a woman, drew him back with something like magnetic influence. Mrs. Morley coloured.—Lord Francis took her hand.— "Did I hear you rightly?" said he.

"The expression was involuntary," replied Mrs. Morley.

"And therefore beyond all value," said lord Francis.

Mrs. Morley trembled.—She felt her danger; she was alarmed; her voice was inarticulate; he led her back to the parlour, and not knowing the magnitude of her distress at that moment, self-love interpreted its effects in his own favour! Mrs. Morley, fearful of his error, was now compelled to be explicit. "I am of all human beings the most unhappy," said she. "I am abandoned by my family, and deserted by my husband; I can return to Morley-house no more."

"Then go with little Fanny," said lord Francis; "be her protec-tress.—See she smiles upon you; she implores you; can you resist the eloquence of nature!" Mrs. Morley leant on the arm of lord Francis; her eyes were bent upon the ground.

"Perhaps by my aukward nursing the little forlorn one will die," said lord Francis. "I only wish to get it safe to London.— Perhaps your mother will relent when I explain the business. Let me conduct you to her."

Mrs. Morley had given Mrs. Oldham's servant all the money she had about her, as a gratuity for her care of Fanny; and a thought now struck her, that she would be the best companion for lord Francis. The girl was called, she did not know the strange gentleman, and would not trust herself alone with him to London.

"Will you go with *me*?" said Mrs. Morley.

The girl consented, and in a quarter of an hour, they all set out together.

CHAPTER XVII

Mr. Morley had taken three hours to ruminate on his conduct, when he ordered Mrs. Grimwood to go in search of his wife. "I have been rash," said he, "I have been hasty; she may yet be innocent." Lady Pen had not been idle during the morning; she had set a servant to watch lord Francis and Mrs. Morley, and she consequently knew all that had passed at farmer Oldham's.

"My wife is a foolish impetuous woman," said Mr. Morley.

"She will trouble you no more," cried lady Pen; "for she is far enough off by this time. Lord Francis will not relinquish her without some resistance."

"Lord Francis!" cried Mr. Morley.

"Do you not know they are gone together?" said lady Pen.

"Whither?"

"That is an amazingly comical question!" said sir Lionel.

"A very natural one," replied Mr. Morley.

"The whole affair is perfectly natural," said lady Pen; "a young wife, who has a suspicious husband and an irresistible lover, can do nothing more natural than to plague the one, and make the other happy."

"For my part, I think the plan famous," said sir Lionel. "Sherville is an amazing fellow, and I honour his ingenuity. The thing has succeeded astonishingly, and Mrs. Morley has proved herself a woman of genius."

"Curse on her genius!" said Mr. Morley; "it was an evil one."

"A very liberal one notwithstanding," interrupted sir Lionel; "and a very popular one too."

"Are they gone alone?"

"A family party," said lady Pen.

"O! if she is with her mother I am satisfied," said Mr. Morley. Lady Pen laughed—sir Lionel hummed a tune. Lady Pen continued:

"Lord Francis will travel in a new character."

"It is the first time he has had any character at all," said sir Lionel.

"Your language is inexplicable," said Mr. Morley.

"As Sherville's conduct," interrupted the baronet.

"Is lord Francis gone with Mrs. Bradford and my wife?" inquired Mr. Morley. Mrs. Grimwood now entered the room, and with a countenance that bespoke the nature of her intelligence. Lady Pen, wishing still to protract time for the purpose of favouring the escape of the runaway,[1] abruptly stopped the housekeeper just as she was arranging her words and features for the solemn disclosure, by saying, "Mr. Morley knows all that you have to tell him. You may therefore spare yourself the trouble."

"I wish I could spare my master his heart ache," said Mrs. Grimwood; "but I knew how it would be from the first moment that I saw the infant."

"What infant, my wife's adopted fugitive?"

"My lord's acknowledged——"

Here Mrs. Grimwood stopped. The word which should have followed was too indelicate for the chaste lips of a venerable spinster.

---

[1] As a "runaway," Robinson's Martha Morley may be, at least in part, a reinvention of Emily Morley, the heroine of Hannah Cowley's comedy *The Runaway*. Robinson herself played the role a number of times between 1778 and 1780.

"They are all gone together," resumed Mrs. Grimwood, "set off in a post chaise and four for London."

"Famous, by Jupiter!" exclaimed sir Lionel.

"Infamous!" retorted Mr. Morley.

"I knew it all," cried the baronet. "We settled the thing astonishingly. I saw that you wanted to get rid of your wife, and your obligations to me are amazing."

"They *are* amazing indeed!" said Mr. Morley.

"There we differ in opinion," cried lady Penelope. "Nothing can be more common. I suspected the affair last year at Bath; and my suspicions were confirmed by Mrs. Morley's sudden marriage. I came hither merely to know what lord Francis was doing; and the moment that I found him secluded, with an assumed name, I guessed how things were. Having seen the end of the comedy, I shall bid you farewel." Her ladyship's chaise now drew up to the lawn, and Mr. Morley was again left to ruminate on his rash conduct.

CHAPTER XVIII

Lord Francis and Mrs. Morley pursued their way towards London: the former, at times thoughtful, and at others impressively attentive; the latter, deeply penetrated by the unkindness of her husband, and almost fearful of presenting herself before her family.

On her arrival in Crutched-Friars, she found the doors closed against her; the servant at the same time informing her messenger that Miss Julia was confined to her bed with grief for her sister's conduct, and that Mrs. Bradford was then on the eve of a second marriage. It was in vain that Mrs. Morley sent frequent messages, intreating to be heard. It was equally useless that she wrote to explain her conduct. Her letters were returned unopened; and without one guinea in her pocket, she found herself in the metropolis with no friend to succour, no home to shelter her.

Lord Francis, who had waited the event with impatience, again renewed his offer of protection: but Mrs. Morley's pride prevented her accepting it. She did not fear so much the pain of future want as the pressure of immediate necessity. After various and urgent applications to her mother, she received a donation of five guineas. The servant who delivered them informed her that they were the last she must expect, her mother and sister being determined never again to acknowledge her.

With this small pittance she hired a single apartment in a small house near Lincoln's-Inn Fields,[1] wrote a letter to thank lord Francis for his kindness and protection, and assured him that if at any future period he should repent his purpose respecting little Fanny, she would receive and support her by every exertion of industry and affection.

Lord Francis, on reading Mrs. Morley's letter, became almost frantic. Her mental and personal graces had made an indelible impression on his mind: but it was without success that he adopted every probable method of tracing her to the obscurity she had chosen; it was in vain that he employed various persons to make inquiries. Mrs. Morley's high spirit rendered her virtue more secure in her mean habitation, surrounded with poverty and wounded by neglect, than it would have been under the roof of an imperious father or of a suspicious husband.

Mrs. Morley, finding every hope of family aid delusive, and seeing in a daily paper a pompous account of her mother's second marriage at the family seat in Kent, where oxen were roasted whole, rural diversions exhibited, and a large concourse of visitors invited, among others, lady Penelope Pryer and sir Lionel Beacon; and conscious that ostentation was the bane of true philanthropy, determined on employing her last guinea in advertising for an asylum as companion to a single lady. How was she to succeed without a character? Thence arose a difficulty which seemed insurmountable. At this important moment she recollected an old friend of her father's, a wealthy merchant, who resided in the city. She without reserve by letter unfolded her situation, obtained an

---

[1] A residential area developed on the site of common fields in close proximity to Lincoln's Inn, one of the four Inns of Court established to provide training in the English law. As a newlywed, Robinson had lived with her mother in a "large old-fashioned mansion" in the Fields while her husband, Thomas, was serving out his apprenticeship at Lincoln's Inn (*Memoirs* 1: 74–75).

interview, pleaded her innocence and her distress, and was promised both present pecuniary aid and future protection. Mr. Dodson was far advanced in years, a widower, and the father of a numerous progeny: his moral character was unblemished, and his connections, by his deceased wife's relationship to persons of fashion, were extended to the western circles of the metropolis.

A respectable situation was shortly after found; Mr. Dodson first requesting that Mrs. Morley would change her name, and carefully avoid every thing that might discover what had passed in her family. With reluctance she acquiesced; and under the assumed title of Mrs. Denison she became the humble dependent of lady Louisa Franklin.

The day after her entering on her new scene of trial lady Louisa set out for Tunbridge.[1] She was a young widow, a few months before returned from the continent, where she had buried her husband; and nearly, by her assiduities during his long illness, reduced herself to be the partner of his grave. Lady Louisa had resided several weeks at Tunbridge previous to Mrs. Morley's becoming an inmate of her family, and had only made a short visit to the metropolis for the purpose of arranging her late husband's affairs.

On Mrs. Morley's arrival at her new home she found every flattering prospect of felicity. Lady Louisa was gentle and amiable, strictly discreet, and, though handsome, liberal even to her own sex, in whatever situation Fortune had placed them.

It was late in the evening when they reached Tunbridge. Lady Louisa retired to rest; and Mrs. Morley, fatigued by the journey, and weary with rumination, also hastened to her chamber. Lady Louisa was of a pensive turn of mind. Sorrow for the loss of her husband had thrown a gloom over her soul which dissipation could not gladden. She read much, visited but seldom, never gamed, and rarely smiled, except when she had an opportunity of relieving the unhappy.

---

[1] Tunbridge Wells was an inland spa in Kent, less than forty miles from London. According to Phyllis Hembry, the population of Tunbridge started to rise significantly in 1793, owing to the wartime influx of military officers, French *emigrés*, and English aristocrats who could no longer safely travel on the continent. *The English Spa 1560–1815* (London: Athlone, 1990), 240.

A month passed, and Mrs. Morley's mind became reconciled to her situation. She almost entirely secluded herself, lest by being seen she should meet with some of her city friends, who might recollect her, even in her altered situation. Lady Louisa's retired mode of living favoured Mrs. Morley's concealment, and she had no cause for inquietude, excepting that which originated in her anxiety for the safety and health of little Fanny.

Mrs. Morley frequently found lady Louisa in tears. They passed many hours every day in reading, and the books which they selected were of the most romantic and melancholy kind. In the evening lady Louisa walked alone till the close of twilight. Her health required exercise, and her sincere regrets shunned the broad glare of day, as well as the inquisitive gaze of those insects that flutter in the meridian of fashionable splendour. Mrs. Morley, conceiving that lady Louisa exposed herself to some danger in her solitary twilight rambles, once ventured to propose accompanying her. Lady Louisa paused. "Alas! my dear Denison!" said she, sighing, "you little imagine that, by making you my companion, I should place a reputation in your hands!"

"A reputation!" repeated Mrs. Morley.

"I have a load of sorrow on my heart: by participation it might be lightened," said lady Louisa, bursting into tears.

The amiable qualities which characterised the speaker's mind interested her hearer with more than common sympathy. "You may trust me," said Mrs. Morley.

"Oh! could you pity a woman who, with the splendours of the world around her, with fortune, youth, and the affections of her family, forgot them all, and yielded herself up to misery and dishonour?" Mrs. Morley started.

"Heavens! lady Louisa!"

"Unless you can feel for such a woman, you must not hope for confidence."

"I can," said Mrs. Morley; "I *have* felt for such a woman." Here they were interrupted, and the conversation ended.

CHAPTER XIX

Mrs. Morley had no farther opportunity, that day, of speaking to lady Louisa alone. In the evening the lovely widow received a visit from sir Lionel Beacon, who had that morning arrived at Tunbridge, and who had been, during many months, the admirer of lady Louisa. Mrs. Morley's fears were awakened by the danger of detection; and she even meditated a disclosure of all that had passed, rather than live in a state of perpetual inquietude.

Several days elapsed, and sir Lionel was always eager to attend on lady Louisa. Her spirits became more cheerful, and she talked more gaily; her countenance wore a more animated appearance, and her weeds, which she had worn near twelve months, were changed to a slighter mourning, as a signal that the storm of grief had abated; and nothing but an experienced pilot was now wanting to guide her course once more towards the port of matrimony.

Sir Lionel's motives were of a less moral tendency. He considered lady Louisa as fair game. She was young, handsome, tender-hearted, and a widow. The world considered her as immaculate; and that single opinion, even had she possessed less powerful attractions than those of mind and person, would have been sufficient to establish his plan of regular seduction.

Every day and every hour sir Lionel displayed his idolatry of the fascinating widow. The extraordinary graces of his figure rendered him a dangerous votary. He was pleasant and lively, but so misguided in his opinions of women, that he only estimated their worth in proportion as they evinced a partiality for his person. Mind, was to the fascinating baronet wholly unimportant, excepting where the fair possessor displayed a mind to render him happy. Yet sir Lionel had an excellent heart in every thing which did not appertain to women. He was good-tempered and thoughtless, yet liberal and brave. He was by nature formed "to love and to persuade:" but his education had been neglected. He had been finely, exquisitely molded, but spoiled in polishing.

His attachment to lady Penelope Pryer had destroyed him; for judging of every woman by the sample she presented, he scarcely believed that the sex was capable of any thing noble, generous, or estimable. He was destined to discover his error in the society of lady Louisa Franklin.

The attentions of such a man naturally excited universal envy; envy gave birth to conjecture, and conjecture naturally fostered the slanders of the malevolent. Sir Lionel was rather flattered than vexed by the buz of calumny: he sought for *eclat*;[1] he delighted in notoriety. He knew that there were many fascinating women, but he wished to prove that there was but one sir Lionel Beacon.

Mrs. Morley was not one of the many who suspected lady Louisa, but she was one of the few who pitied her approaching disgrace. Her name was already mentioned ambiguously, and her change of mourning was, by some good-natured observers, deemed a proof that single blessedness was no longer the widow's portion. She was too young to vegetate in a state of insensibility; she was too handsome to escape the discerning eyes of sir Lionel Beacon; she was too rich to want a friend, and too sentimental to pass a life of inanity. Such were the comments of the discerning and the malignant.

The baronet now always attended lady Louisa in her evening walks. They were frequently seen wandering along the fields and lanes in the vicinity of Tunbridge. At length it was rumoured that a red house, at about a mile distant, was the scene of rendezvous; and every person in the fashionable world considered the affair as a decided attachment.

Mrs. Morley entertained a sincere regard for lady Louisa, and was considerably chagrined by the reports which were circulated to her disadvantage. The spot of assignation had been confidently mentioned; and under the firm persuasion that she should prove the report erroneous, Mrs. Morley resolved to make inquiries on the subject. For this purpose, one evening, when she knew that lady Louisa was engaged with sir Lionel, she set out on foot for the Red-house, fully convinced in her own mind that her friend had been slandered; and as firmly determined, in case she should be right in her conjecture, to inform lady Louisa of all that was reported.

The house had been minutely described, and she found no difficulty in obtaining admittance. She entered the parlour, and

---

[1] Public acclaim or applause.

in a cradle, fast asleep, she discovered little Fanny! The joy which she experienced was not to be described. She fell upon her knees, snatched the infant to her bosom, kissed it a thousand times, and was just preparing to make further inquiries, when lady Louisa and sir Lionel stopped at the door.

Mrs. Morley precipitately retreated through a back garden, and fortunately reached home without farther observation.

Lady Louisa made no scruple to avow her partiality for sir Lionel, and he was by the world considered as her acknowledged lover, when Mrs. Morley was informed that the baronet was not exclusively devoted to lady Louisa; for that he passed those hours which were not dedicated to her, with another female in the vicinity of Tunbridge. Love is blind; and every observer, excepting one, plainly discovered that sir Lionel's motives were not those of an honourable union. Mrs. Morley lamented the credulity of lady Louisa, at the same time that she trembled for her safety.

On a moonlight evening, returning from a visit to little Fanny, she heard voices at a short distance before her. She discovered two persons walking slowly, and she knew the accent of one of them. It was the baronet. Concluding that his companion was lady Louisa, she walked slowly till she came to a garden-gate. There he embraced her, and they parted. She returned home, and to her infinite surprise found lady Louisa alone. She had not been out of the house during the evening. Shortly after, while lady Louisa was undressing, Mrs. Morley, with brief sincerity, informed her of what had happened. The intelligence seemed to affect her, and to distress her extremely. She nevertheless thanked Mrs. Morley for her information, and assured her that she should consider it as a farther proof of friendship if she would make more inquiries that might release her mind from the excess of anxiety. "In a few days," said lady Louisa, "I should have given my hand to sir Lionel. My present chagrin and future happiness depend on the truth or falsehood of your assertions."

The concluding words called a momentary blush into the cheek of Mrs. Morley. Her soul was too ingenuous to bear suspicion; and she resolved, even at the peril of discovering her own situation, to ascertain the extent of the baronet's apostasy.

Sir Lionel dined with lady Louisa the following day, but made excuses to depart early, saying he had business to transact of the utmost importance. It was in vain that lady Louisa requested him to attend her to the Rooms: he was decided; and his obstinate refusal more than half confirmed her apprehensions.

Mrs. Morley, whose regard for lady Louisa had more weight than any selfish consideration, followed the baronet at some distance till he again reached the garden-gate. Three gentle taps were the signals for rendezvous, and again a female obeyed the summons. Mrs. Morley's zeal in the cause of friendship induced her to advance within hearing of the lovers. Sir Lionel's watchful eyes observed her in her ambush, and she was instantly made a prisoner. But the baronet was too accomplished an adept in the mysteries of gallantry to let a spy escape with intelligence. The garden-gate was open, and Mrs. Morley was led, unwillingly, to the house where, on entering the first room, she discovered, pale and trembling, her own sister.

CHAPTER XX

Julia shrieked, the baronet looked aghast, and Mrs. Morley nearly shrunk to the ground with confusion. "This is amazingly astonishing!" exclaimed sir Lionel. "Where the devil did you come from? and what is become of that famous fellow whom you left to console himself with old mother Grimbald? Why, you look as fresh as a daisy! and if you behave yourself, and don't blab, I will fall in love with you myself, to make you the fashion." Julia was near fainting.

"This is no house for a frolic!" continued the baronet: "old Crutched-Friars will soon spoil sport! Let us be off! Let us set the dowagers in an uproar! You are amazingly handsome, and astonishingly in luck, and I am a famous fellow for protecting young heroines! Besides, I want to break with the widow, and this will be an amazing opportunity! What say you, Mrs. Morley? Answer me quickly: catch me while you can! Nothing like it!"

"Sister," said Julia, erecting her head, and endeavouring to suppress the emotions of jealous indignation, "you will act wisely in avoiding the presence of our mother. Your indiscretion has nearly broken the hearts of all your relatives; and after what has happened, you must be sensible that we can no longer acknowledge you." Martha's proud mind could not stoop to a further explanation: she quitted the room, and with a full heart returned home to lady Louisa.

Mrs. Morley had frequently endeavoured to discover by what means little Fanny became the *protegée* of lady Louisa Franklin, and all she could learn was, that a particular friend had placed the infant under her protection. "His name, and motive for so doing, are and must be a profound secret." Mrs. Morley dared not be too pressing in her interrogatories, lest it should lead to a suspicion that she had some knowledge of the infant.

On her return to lady Louisa's, she flew to her dressing-room, where she was waiting to prepare for the Rooms, when, on abruptly entering, she discovered lord Francis Sherville. She faintly shrieked, and would have retreated, but lord Francis, seeing a female, young and nearly overwhelmed with surprise, rushed after her. She would have concealed her face, but her hands seemed to lose their power; and she was, without strength to resist, led back to lady Louisa's apartment.

"Heavens!" exclaimed lord Francis, lifting her veil, and pressing her hand to his lips, "do I behold Mrs. Morley?"

"Come, come, Frank," said lady Louisa, "this species of gallantry will not suit the manners of Mrs. Denison. I conjure you to make an apology for your rudeness, and to let her retire."

"Part with her!" exclaimed lord Francis; "no, no Louisa; I know too well her value. She shall never go unless she condescends to take me with her. I have been the cause of her disgrace, and I will henceforth be her protector."

"Her disgrace!" repeated lady Louisa. While she was speaking, lady Pen Pryer was announced.

"Then I am indeed discovered!" said Mrs. Morley, sighing. Lord Francis led her to an adjoining room, while lady Pen was ushered into that of lady Louisa.

Mrs. Morley frankly unfolded all that had happened since she had seen lord Francis in London. She conjured him to extricate her from the embarrassment which would inevitably follow a discovery of her real name and situation: she expressed the most grateful sentiments of esteem and affection for lady Louisa, and declared that she should feel the most poignant affliction in losing her friendship and good opinion.

Though Mrs. Morley and lord Francis had precipitately retreated, they had not failed to excite the curiosity of lady Pen Pryer. She heard a door suddenly closed, and she found in lady Louisa's dressing-room a man's hat, which lord Francis had in his haste forgotten. These signs of still something more than met the eye, determined her to satisfy her ruling propensity, even at the expence of friendship and good manners. There had been some busy tongues, which, though lady Pen had not arrived two hours, conveyed the popular topic to her ear; and the almost incessant attentions of sir Lionel to lady Louisa, produced her present unseasonable visit.

Concluding that the baronet was the person concealed, and thinking to enjoy the doubtful gratification of exposing her lover, and destroying the reputation of her friend, she resolved on waiting till midnight, rather than relinquish her post of security. Mrs. Morley and lord Francis, knowing the mania of lady Pen, and dreading the result of her inquiries, concerted a plan to defeat her. The room where they were concealed opened to a long balcony-gallery, from which lord Francis descended, not without some peril, to the highroad:—determining to wait near the door till lady Pen's departure, and then to inform lady Louisa that he had been mistaken in the person of Mrs. Morley, for which he would readily make an apology in any manner, in which she would condescend to accept one.

While lady Pen was sitting at the toilette of her friend, her cheek glowing with rage, and her eyes darting the lightnings of jealous vengeance, sir Lionel entered the room. He did not expect to find lady Penelope; and for a moment he seemed embarrassed: but recovering his *nonchalance*, he inquired, "Well, my dowager, what mischief are you plotting? You seem astonishingly busy, no doubt in some famous conspiracy; for women are amazingly fond of mystery."

"We leave that to your sex," said lady Pen; "you are wonderfully sagacious."

"Nothing like it," replied the baronet. "I have been frolicking with a brace of city dames, astonishingly handsome."

Lady Louisa smiled with proud contempt.

"This will not do," cried lady Penelope; "I heard you."

"So much the worse for you," said the baronet; "for I have been making love ever since sun-set."

"And making fools," said lady Pen.

"That I leave to the women," replied sir Lionel; "but if I do not tell truth may I be scouted for a blockhead. I have been amused famously. An astonishing good frolic, by Jupiter!"

"You may call it a frolic to be detected with a woman who pretends to character; you may call it famous, but I call it profligate in the extreme!" said lady Penelope.

"What! are you going to preach me a sermon?" interrupted sir Lionel; "but since you seem to know all, I need not take the trouble to deny it."

Lady Penelope now rose and departed; and in less than an hour nothing was heard in the Rooms but that sir Lionel Beacon had been detected concealed in lady Louisa's bed-chamber.

CHAPTER XXI

One of the first persons whose ear met this unpleasing intelligence, was Miss Julia Bradford. It was communicated by lady Pen, with all appropriate embellishments; and the credulous fair one was carried to her lodgings in violent hysterics. While the buz was going round with all its vehemence, sir Lionel and lady Louisa entered the Rooms; and shortly after them Mrs. Popkins (late Mrs. Bradford,) who informed the whisperers, one by one, that sir Lionel had been seen by one of her footmen descending from the balcony of lady Louisa's apartment. This was indubitable confirmation; and the supposed guilty parties were by the whole circle sent to Coventry.[1]

---

[1]   To be "sent to Coventry" was to be ostracized or consigned to disgrace. The proverbial phrase dates back to the English Civil War, when Puritans doomed royalist sympathizers to imprisonment in the town of Coventry.

Sir Lionel, who was little accustomed to neglect, soon discovered that some mystery was on foot, inimical to his fame and popularity. Mrs. Popkins and lady Pen were prominent figures on the theater of scandal; and the baronet was the theme of public animadversion, when lord Francis entered the circle; his leg had been grazed in descending from the balcony, and he wore his handkerchief wrapped round it. The singularity of this circumstance diverted the torrent of malevolence; and lord Francis's accident was for a moment thought more interesting than even sir Lionel's gallantry.

"Good Heavens! my lord," exclaimed Mrs. Popkins, "how did you come by that leg?"

"I was born with it, madam," said lord Francis gravely.

Mrs. Popkins was struck dumb, when lady Penelope inquired how long lord Francis had been at Tunbridge.

"From the moment that I arrived," said his lordship.

The baronet now exclaimed, "What brought you here, lord Francis?"

"Four horses," was the laconic answer.

The inquisitive circle, now finding that their motives were defeated, recurred to the popular topic of the evening, but the presence of lord Francis reduced the eloquence of embellishment to little more than monosyllables, accompanied by shrugs, smiles, sighs, hems, ha's, and nods of confirmation.

Lady Louisa finding herself eyed askance by the fastidious, shunned by the correct, and familiarly addressed by the profligate, thought it time to elucidate the mystery of her brother's concealment, by asking him aloud, "how he could rashly hazard his life, by descending from such a dangerous eminence!"

This brief question opened all eyes with astonishment. Lady Louisa shortly after quitted the scandalous committee; and lady Penelope's indefatigable mind was once more employed in the labour of conjecture.

Mrs. Popkins, on her return home, found her daughter Julia seriously indisposed; the shock which she had received, she attributed to her unexpected interview with her sister, of which circumstance she now availed herself in order to disguise the real cause of her agitation. Mrs. Popkins was overwhelmed with chagrin. What! all her honours, all her consequence to be blighted in its full bloom, by the presence of an imprudent, outcast daughter! The idea was not to be borne. Julia wept abundantly. "Ah, my love!" exclaimed Mrs. Popkins, "your delicate sensibility cannot bear to witness the folly of our graceless Martha; we will therefore quit this scene of humiliation, and endeavour to forget her."

The carriage was ordered to be at the door on the following morning; Mrs. Popkins sent cards of *congé* [1] to all the fashionable water-drinkers; and at nine o'clock they were ready for their departure.

CHAPTER XXII

It so happened that Mrs. Morley had been to the Red-house to see little Fanny, and was returning along the lane near the garden-gate of her mother's habitation, when the carriage drew up for their departure. The throbbings of filial affection had not been subdued by the chilling unkindness or austere pride of Mrs. Popkins; and Martha, the scorned, neglected, and outcast Martha, stood near the coach-door when her mother sallied forth to enter it. Her countenance was dejected; but her cheek was flushed with perturbation; she heard the sound of her mother's voice, and the deep colour in a moment became pale as ashes.

Mrs. Popkins appeared, leading her favourite Julia. Martha stepped forward.—"Oh madam!" exclaimed she, "can you, will you refuse to own me?" Julia placed her hand before her eyes and trembled; while Mrs. Popkins, with dignified apathy, ascended the carriage.—Mrs. Morley's heart was almost bursting with distress; conscious of unmerited disdain, and yet glowing with the pride of virtuous indignation. The coach drew on, and Mrs. Morley stood watching its progress till it turned a corner, and she lost sight of it.

While she remained in her reverie, sir Lionel arrived to take leave of Julia. Mrs. Morley was little pleased by the interruption of such a visitor, and would have departed; but the baronet was

---

[1] Cards announcing departure.

not easily discarded; he rejoiced in the absence of Julia, because it afforded him an opportunity of addressing a new object. Mrs. Morley knew not how to act. She dared not return to lady Louisa's lodgings, knowing that sir Lionel would follow her; and that the plan she had concerted with lord Francis would by that means be frustrated. She continued walking along the lane, when turning an angle suddenly, she met lady Penelope on horseback, attended by lord Francis Sherville.

Mrs. Morley's consternation was visible; she could scarcely support herself: lady Pen's indignation was no less marked; but the most evident astonishment, blended with regret, expressed itself in every feature of lord Francis. They passed each other without any comment, excepting from sir Lionel, who remarked that, "Old Pen would be amazingly jealous, and astonishingly unhappy."

The baronet seeing little prospect of *eclat* in his lonely walk with Mrs. Morley, and knowing that at that hour the public *promenades* were thronged with visitors, took his leave, and set out in search of lady Louisa. But she was otherwise engaged, in listening to the morning discovery which had been made by lady Penelope Pryer. While they were deeply engaged in conversation, Mrs. Morley unexpectedly entered the room. "By Heavens! the very woman!" exclaimed lady Pen; "the runaway wife of Mr. Morley, and the avowed mistress of lord Francis Sherville!"

Mrs. Morley's distress was now brought to its climax. Lady Penelope's words confirmed all that had passed on her meeting lord Francis the preceding evening; and she was requested by lady Louisa to quit the apartment. She obeyed; and dreading the unpleasant embarrassment that would attend an elucidation of events, resolved without further delay to escape from the scene of persecution.

With this determination she engaged a place in the stage-coach; and having some hours to spare, resolved once more to take her leave of Fanny. The carriage was obliged to pass the door of the Red-House, and the driver had promised to call there for her.

Mrs. Morley had wept and sighed over her little favourite, till twilight had some time closed, when the stage-coach stopped at the door. Again she kissed the rosy cheek of Fanny; again she fervently recommended her to the protection of that Being, who guards the innocent and sustains the feeble. The coachman was in haste; and Mrs. Morley, depressed almost to despondency, again set out for London.

CHAPTER XXIII

Before day-light Mrs. Morley reached the place of her destination. She had not uttered one syllable since she quitted Tunbridge, and the night being imperviously dark, the journey had seemed tediously long. When they stopped at the inn door in Holborn,[1] a passenger descending, put forth his hand to assist her; she accepted his aid, and thanked him. It was lord Francis.

Her astonishment was infinite. She had not power to speak; lord Francis conjured her not to be offended; declared that his motive was merely that of protecting her; and requested permission to render himself useful, in whatever was requisite for her honour and tranquility.

Mrs. Morley's situation was perplexing in the extreme. She had neither friends nor home to receive her. The attention, of lord Francis at such a moment made her tremble; but the magnitude of her peril again served to awaken the energy of her soul. She knew that she could only by stratagem escape the spell that surrounded her, and she therefore for the present accepted his offers of attention.

They entered the inn. A waiter was dispatched to provide a convenient lodging for Mrs. Morley, who still assumed the name of Denison. A second-floor in the vicinity of Bloomsbury-square was speedily hired; and, in the evening, she repaired thither, accompanied by lord Francis.

The first-floor was occupied; Mrs. Morley and her protector passed the remainder of the day together. His conduct was respectfully attentive; and her spirits sunk into the deepest melancholy. During several days lord Francis repeated his visits; till one morning, on entering her apartment, she observed his countenance as

---

[1]   An area in central London.

pale as death: he attempted to speak, but his voice faltered; and he threw himself into a chair without uttering a syllable.

Mrs. Morley was alarmed; her heart at that moment first told her, that it owned lord Francis as its sovereign. She was afflicted even to agony. He appeared to her a new creature; and she could not conceal the interest his situation excited. Lord Francis being somewhat recovered, thanked Mrs. Morley, and departed. Four days passed and she neither heard from nor saw him. Her fears interpreted his silence, to the most dreadful calamity that could now befal her. All the pangs which persecution, poverty, and scorn had hitherto inflicted on her bosom, seemed trivial in comparison with its anxiety for the safety of lord Francis.

During this period of suspence, a new gleam of hope opened to her view. She was informed by the mistress of the house where she lodged, that the lady in her first-floor was a provincial actress of the most promising talents. Mrs. Morley had often meditated a dramatic trial; and in her present forlorn and unprotected situation, the attempt seemed irresistible. Without ceremony she introduced herself to the stranger; and to her utter astonishment instantly recognized, in her altered situation, the mother of little Fanny.

The meeting cannot be described;—joy, shame, gratitude, hope, fear, and astonishment succeeded each other:—while the agitated mother, falling on Mrs. Morley's neck inquired, "Is my child still living?"

The cause of lord Francis's sudden distress, and the motive for his having discontinued his visits, now appeared evident. Mrs. Morley had long suspected that he was the father of Fanny, and her suspicions were by his absence confirmed indubitably. She therefore without hesitation informed Mrs. Sedgley, (for such she learnt was the name of Fanny's mother,) of all that had happened. When she came to that part of her story which mentioned lord Francis having taken the infant under his protection, Mrs. Sedgley exclaimed, "Oh heavens!" and fainted.

The consequence of this disclosure was a determination on the part of Mrs. Sedgley to quit London. On the following morning Mrs. Morley proposed being the companion of her journey, which was to join a company of comedians then performing at a provincial theater. Mrs. Morley felt a strong inclination to adopt a profession which promised both fame and independence. An arrangement was immediately made, and at seven o'clock they commenced their journey together. The stage-coach having no other passengers, the dramatic heroines soon became perfectly acquainted; and, as ingenuous minds are naturally communicative, Mrs. Sedgley, with little hesitation, began to unfold the history of her own misfortunes.

CHAPTER XXIV

There is a degree of innate vanity which possesses enlightened minds, whether they are raised and refined by nature or by education, which renders the pain of suppressing their prouder feelings more intolerable than even the humiliations of poverty or neglect. Mrs. Sedgley felt this intuitive pride. She had been accustomed to respect, esteem, and attention, and she could not bear the idea of being treated as one divested of those claims which expansion of intellect entitled her to feel. Conscious that fortune was her foe, and labouring under a stigma, of which she knew herself undeserving, she resolved to lose no time in exciting an interest in Mrs. Morley's bosom, by that candour which is the sure basis of friendship and affection.

As soon as the wheels of their carriage ceased to roll over the pavement of the metropolis, Mrs. Sedgley addressed her companion. "I feel myself bound by all the laws of gratitude and sincerity," said she, "to unfold, in some measure, the origin of my past and present vicissitudes. You have taken a liberal and noble interest in my destiny. You once preserved that which was dearer to me than life; but which pride and the dread of exposure would have tempted me to abandon.

"Early in infancy I lost my mother; my father was of a temper sternly and haughtily reserved; he was proud even to imperious tyranny. Born to a situation of life which invested him with power over his inferiors, he acknowledged no distinctions but those of rank and birth. It was my misfortune to be of a disposition rash and impetuous.—I loved my father tenderly; but I could not wear the trammels of severe restraint without repining—even in his presence. When I was eighteen years of age, my father proposed retiring to his estate in Scotland, where a Gothic castle, which had been uninhabited ever since his minority, was preparing for his reception. It was situated on a craggy steep which over-shadowed a valley. The ramparts were covered with ivy, and the turrets just peeped above the trees that had, for ages, darkened the acclivity.

"The domestics who had been to Scotland for the purpose of rendering this spacious castle habitable, returned with accounts so melancholy, with legends so terrific, that I felt my soul shudder at the thought of becoming the inmate of a dwelling so solitary, and so calculated to inspire the mind with all the horrors of romance. My father paid little attention to my feelings on this subject; he hinted that if he could bear seclusion so gloomy, and content himself in abjuring the busy scenes of social intercourse, no other part of the family had a right to form the least objection.—The day was fixed for our departure.

"Just at this period a woman of rank and education, a particular friend of the family, was on the point of setting out for Italy. She had wearied herself by fashionable pleasures, was going for the benefit of her health, and informed my father that she should be happy in having me as a companion. The thought delighted me. My entreaties were united with tears; and my parent, never having been fond of me, was soon persuaded to consent. We set out together. I thought myself the happiest of mortals.

"Two years elapsed, and we continued in Italy: we passed our winters at Naples; our summers at Pisa. Time flew on pinions of delight, and no melancholy thought ever interrupted my felicity, excepting when memory brought to my view, aided by the strong powers of Fancy, the gloomy turrets and the ivied ramparts of the old Scottish castle. Never did the declining possessor of an hereditary palace feel a more acute sense of horror in contemplating the mausoleum of his ancestors, where he should end his vain career of splendour, than that which I experienced when I reflected that I should suddenly be transported from the enchanting, the ecstatic scenes of Italian luxury, to the thorny, mouldering, noiseless solitudes of Drumbender Castle.

"The tumults attending the continental war, alarmed my travelling protectress; and to my inexpressible chagrin, I was informed of her sudden determination to revisit her native country. During my absence from England I had frequently written to my father; but though by other channels I knew that he was in health, I never received the smallest proof of notice or solicitude from him. The last letter which mentioned his name, informed me that he was become a perfect misanthrope, more cynical than Timon,[1] more solitary than an anchoret: that he excluded every thing human from his society; passed his whole time in abstruse studies; and had resolved, on my return to England, to make me the sole companion of his perpetual sequestration.

"The volatile spirit of my heart nearly caused it to burst at receiving this intelligence. I beheld all the visionary horrors of Drumbender Castle. I saw, in imagination, all the mystic wonders which adorn the pages of the most popular romances: I felt as though I were destined to develope mysteries, to traverse midnight glooms and subterraneous caverns. I beheld, amidst the moonlight avenues of haunted forests, pale and ghastly spectres, bearing their airy poniards drenched in blood.—I heard their groans, their thrice echoed warnings; and I even anticipated the hour when I should wander a pale ghost upon the mountain-side, while the castle bell should toll me to my hidden grave.—I was almost frantic.

"We set out for England: on our arrival on the French frontiers we found some difficulty in procuring horses; and still more in obtaining provisions, during our short sojourn at a miserable post-house by a wood-side. I proposed proceeding without taking any refreshment; but our host of *le bonnet rouge*[2] informed us, that we should encounter no small peril in departing after sun-set:—'For,' said he, 'all soldiers are men of gallantry, and pretty women are fair plunder in times of hostility.' My friend smiled and replied, that she did not fear any thing they might attempt; 'For,' added she, 'courage and humanity are uniformly allied, whatever warfare there may be among kings and kingdoms.'

---

[1]   A wealthy citizen of Athens in the fifth century B.C., notorious for his hatred of mankind.

[2]   The red "cap of liberty" worn as an expression of revolutionary politics.

"This compliment produced the desired effect: the landlord thanked my companion for the good opinion she entertained of his nation; and the carriage was ordered to the door without further interruption. But just as we were stepping into it, a courier approached the step. We demanded to know his business.—'I belong,' said he, 'to an English gentleman, whose horses have been taken from his chaise by the French soldiery; and who, finding it impossible to proceed for want of a fresh supply, requests as a particular favour, if you have room in your carriage, that you will convey him as far as the next post-house.' My companion, as well as myself, was delighted at the idea of finding not only a countryman, but a protector. In a few minutes the traveller approached on foot; recounted his misfortunes without the smallest deviation from the courier's story, and after a short interview at the carriage-door, we agreed to accept him as a companion.

"His conversation was enlightened, his manners polished, and his person handsome; we travelled not only safely but merrily; each heart silently congratulating itself for the good fortune and security which had attended our hazardous expedition.

"On our arrival at Paris, we found every thing wild and licentious. Order and subordination were trampled beneath the footsteps of anarchy: the streets were filled with terrifying *spectacles*; and the people seemed nearly frantic with the plentitude of dominion; while the excess of horror was strongly and strikingly contrasted by the vaunted display of boundless sensuality.

"I passed a few days in Paris, two years before, in my *route* to Italy: the change was awful and impressive. I sighed when I recollected the causes of the metamorphosis, and I shuddered while I contemplated the effects.

"We hired a *suite* of rooms at the *Hotel de la Revolution*; for our departure was no longer optional. We were informed that we must give a full and circumstantial account of ourselves; whence we came; whither we were going; what were our occupations, names, ages, places of birth, motives for travelling, political sentiments, rank, fortune, and connections, before we could possibly be permitted to pass through the land of universal liberty.

"On the evening of our arrival, while I was undressing, an

elegant girl, about seventeen years of age, came tiptoe into my chamber. She pressed her finger on her lip, and at the same time presented me the key of the Hotel.——I was at first at a loss to comprehend her meaning, but she sighed and shook her head, while she inarticulately whispered, 'Be away so soon as possible;——you are no safe in the Hotel of mine father.'

"I hastened to the apartments of my companions,—gave the alarm with as much caution as possible, and after presenting the amiable girl a gold locket with a Venetian chain, which I wore round my neck, (for she refused to accept money as a reward for her kindness,) we all stole down the stair-case into the garden of the *Palais Royale*.[1]

"There we found a throng dancing by torch-light to the cymbal and the tambourine.—The women were dressed like Bacchanalians; and the men like the frantic fiends of Pandemonium.[2] The moon, which rose over the trees, was eclipsed by the flaming torches; and the *tout ensemble* inspired the mind with terror and astonishment. We had not been many minutes spectators of this extraordinary scene, when I felt my arm gently pressed. I looked round, and observed the lovely girl who had been our deliverer, with a young French soldier. I instantly knew her countenance, for it was too beautiful to be forgotten: but her dress was wholly changed.— Her arms were naked to the shoulders, her robe flowed loosely, displaying her left leg nearly as high as the knee. Her brows were dressed with roses; her bosom was uncovered.[3]

"'Heavens!' exclaimed I, 'I should not have known you!' She laughed while she suppressed a sigh.—'I am so obliged to follow the example of others,' said she; 'my own safety tell me to make the sacrifice. This is Henri Saint Val, my love,' added she; 'we will go to

---

1   A royal palace that had been transformed and opened to the public in 1784.
    According to one contemporary observer, this "capital of Paris" offered an unparal-
    leled "assemblage of delights," including shops, restaurants, theaters, prostitutes, and
    scientific exhibitions. Quoted in Howard C. Rice, *Thomas Jefferson's Paris* (Princeton:
    Princeton UP, 1976), 14–15.
2   Pandaemonium is the "high capital / Of Satan and his peers" in Milton's *Paradise Lost*
    (1. 756–57); Bacchanalians, participants in any riotous celebration associated with
    Bacchus, the god of wine, were generally represented in scanty attire.
3   Cf. Richard Polwhele's *The Unsex'd Females*, Appendix C, 305.

be marry to-morrow, and I am go to serve with him *en Flanders.*[1] I smiled.

"'Indeed!' said she, 'I speak what is true; I am very much love of him; and I must die if he fall in battle!'—The tone of her voice and the sweet smile she gave her Henri, drew my attention wholly from the bacchanalian dancers. She requested that I would not remain in the garden of the *Palais Royale*, where there were spies of every description lurking under every colonnade to seize on the unwary. We took her advice, and sought a lodging in the Fauxbourg Saint Germain.

"The good genius of Lisette did not continue to protect us;—for on the following day we were arrested, and, under separate guards, conveyed to the prison of the Abbaye.[2]

"There how often did I sigh for the solitudes of Drumbender. How did I wish to encounter all the spectres of the Scottish Castle, rather than await the mandate of a sanguinary judge; for at that period the monster, MARAT, was in the full zenith of his power.[3] The ivy battlements, the mouldering turrets of my family habitation were chearful and exhilarating objects, when Fancy placed them in comparison with the damp walls and triple bars of my subterraneous dungeon. I was now taught to know that all human happiness is felt only by comparison.

"At the expiration of three weeks I found that our travelling companion had, through the intercession of the British Court, been liberated. And on the same morning that this intelligence reached me, I received a note from him, informing me that if I would consent to become his wife, I should also be set at

---

[1] In 1792–93, the French army suffered heavy casualties in their engagements with the Austrian forces in Flanders. The situation was so volatile in the summer of 1792 that Robinson abandoned her plans to travel through Flanders to Spa in Belgium and remained in Calais until September 2, the date of the first of the September Massacres. According to her *Memoirs*, it was only "a few hours [after her departure] when the *arrêt* arrived, by which every British subject throughout France was restrained" (2: 137–39).

[2] A prison attached to the abbey of St. Germain. It was the scene of the first of the September Massacres in 1792. Madame Roland and Charlotte Corday were later imprisoned there.

[3] Jean-Paul Marat: a revolutionary journalist and deputy to the National Convention in Paris. Cf. *A Letter to the Women of England*, 53; and Helen Maria Williams's account of his diabolical character in Appendix F, 318–19.

liberty.—I requested two days to consider, before I gave a decided answer to his proposal.

"Every hour during this tedious interval I heard of public executions. The tocsin sounded night and day. The cannon shook my dungeon with concussions that made me tremble. I heard the hoofs of horses, as the troops passed my prison to attend the restless process of the guillotine.—I accepted the proposal made me by the English traveller;—life was the temptation offered; and I had not fortitude to resist it.

"On the same night we were married *à la Revolution.*——My husband promised to procure my emancipation. We obtained, by the powerful mediator gold, a *suite* of convenient and even comfortable apartments in the upper story of the prison. A week only had passed, when to my unutterable chagrin I was informed, that my husband had set out for England; and that the pretended priest who had united us was nothing more than the *valet de chambre* of the infamous Marat.

"I next inquired after my female friend and *chaperone.* She also had been gone to England several days. I was almost despairing. Five months passed, and I was still in prison; when one day an unknown visitor entered my apartment. He addressed me with politeness; complimented my personal attractions; and offered me my freedom, but on terms that made me shudder. I rejected the proposal.

"My visitor now assumed another aspect; he affected to treat me as an avowed licentious character; abused the prudish cunning of women of my nation; laughed at all laws, moral and divine; assured me that none but the sons of Liberty knew how to live; and declared, that if I would consent to share his destiny, my will should be omnipotent.—Still I disdained to accept my freedom on terms so base, so repugnant to my feelings.

"He now drew a paper from his pocket. It contained a list of thirty signatures. 'These,' said he, 'I have ordered for immediate execution. I have only one to add.'—The monster then commanded me to write my name.—He transcribed it on the list of death. I sunk upon the ground before him.—Neither my horror-stricken countenance nor my situation, for I was then visibly with child, seemed to affect him.—He assumed a demonian smile; and, as he was quitting the apartment, exclaimed: '*Songez Citoyenne; ou Marat, ou la guillotin!*'[1]

"I now discovered that the barbarian inquisitor was the despot Marat; whose death on the following day rescued me from misery or annihilation. But alas! though permitted to depart for England, I was not in a situation to appear before the eyes of an offended family. I dreaded their austere opinions on political events; and I knew that every thing which bore the faintest shadow of democracy was hateful to their feelings. The horrible scenes which I had recently witnessed justified their sentiments, and had I dared to present myself before them, I would have convinced their minds, that though an idolater of Rational Liberty, I most decidedly execrated the cruelty and licentiousness which blacken the page of Time, while History traces the annals of this momentous era. But alas! the impetuosity of political partizans, will not permit them to draw conclusions with candour, or to judge opinions by the fair rule of reason. Every individual who shrinks from oppression, every friend to the superior claims of worth and genius, is, in these suspecting times, condemned without even an examination; though were truth and impartiality to influence their judges, they would be found the first to venerate the sacred rights of social order, and the last to uphold the atrocities of anarchy.

"My family paid little attention to causes, and were only led to draw their conclusions from effects. I had been compelled to form an union for the preservation of existence. But I *had* formed it, and that circumstance was sufficient to stigmatize me in their opinion for ever. I had received many letters from them, demanding to know the name of my husband. Ah! how severe were the conflicts of my heart; I loved the betrayer of my confidence, and though he had exposed me to every insult, to misery and death, I made a vow never to reveal his name, or to subject him to the fury and resentment of my family. This oath I have kept inviolate.

---

[1] "Consider [your options] Citizen: Marat or the guillotine." The following reference to Marat's death (July 13, 1793) creates chronological inconsistencies between Mrs. Sedgley's inset narrative and the main narrative, which opens in April 1792. If one dates the birth of Fanny from Mrs. Sedgley's narrative, it probably would have occurred in November 1793, approximately one year after the date implied by the main narrative.

"Finding myself alone, in a perilous state of health, in a strange country, where massacre and devastation every hour raised their hydra heads above all laws human and sacred, I resolved to depart for my native kingdom; where, though sorrowful, depressed, and persecuted, I still hoped to find protection and repose. I knew that there lived in Britain, women who had feeling, and men, who to the character of the philosopher added that of the philanthropist. In my early youth I had been known to one female, whose illustrious virtues placed her far above even her exalted rank. I knew that from her bosom the benignant graces of sensibility and generosity banished the mean fastidious scorn which, in less enlightened beings, acts as a watch-guard on the feelings, keeping aloof the noblest sentiments of friendship and humanity. This amiable woman was the duchess of Chatsworth;[1] whose virtues will live on the records of a thousand hearts, when fortune, birth, and titles are no more remembered.

"On my journey towards Calais, near a scattered village within two miles of Abbeville,[2] I observed a young woman sitting on a small rude bench at the door of a cottage, situated on the skirts of a thick wood. She was singing a melancholy ditty, but with a tone so touchingly mournful, that it seemed to vibrate on my heart. The day was serene, and it was near the hour of sun-set. I alighted from my cabriolet, and proceeded along a narrow path, just within the wood; by which means I soon came behind the cottage unseen by the melancholy songstress. The sweetness of the air, which she sang with a still sweeter voice, induced me to pause and to listen. My postillion being like myself, inclined to indulge his fancy, stopped his horses at a little distance, while he arranged his pipe and began to smoke it deliberately.

"The words which the young damsel chanted so sweetly were French; I copied them as she twice repeated the verses, and, on my arrival at Abbeville, translated them into English."—Mrs. Sedgley then recited the stanzas:[3]

---

1   See Introduction, 14, n. 1, and Appendix A.
2   A city approximately sixty miles south of Calais.
3   They are a slightly different version of the "Stanzas" Robinson published under her own name in *The Oracle* on June 9, 1794.

Hark! 'tis the merry bells that ring
    On yonder upland sunny green;
Their sounds to mournful mem'ry bring
    The blissful days and hours I've seen!
Their swelling changes die away,
So did my heart's best love decay!

Hark! 'tis the Beetle flitting round,
    O'er yonder hawthorn fresh and sweet;
Once could I mock the drowsy sound—
    With Henry on the greensward seat;
But now, I weep to hear its tone,
For O! my heart's true love is flown!

Hark! 'tis the Raven's dismal croak,
    My boding breast is chill'd with fear!
Yet once, beneath yon spreading oak
    The bird of woe, I smil'd to hear:
For love and fancy cheared the gloom,
Where now the turf is Henry's tomb!

Come, pale-cheek'd vestal of the night,
    And spangle the long grass with dew;
Dress the tall woods with silv'ry light,
    And buds of fragrant flowrets strew,
While Love in secret sorrow hies,
To guard the grave where Henry lies!

There will I lay me down forlorn,
    And close my weeping eyes, and die!
And when the smiling blushing morn
    Shall rush along the eastern sky,
There shall the thronging village see,
To part no more—my love and me!

"The solitary mourner," continued Mrs. Sedgley, "was poor
Lisette! my heart thrilled with pity when I beheld her figure,
which presented the languor of incurable affliction. Too readily

did I conjecture that her misfortune was irremediable; her Henry, the hero of her affections, the cause of her despair, had fallen in battle. I approached her,—my bosom throbbed with all the agonies of sympathy.—She looked at me without the smallest change of countenance.—Her eyes were full of tears.—Her dark hair was fastened up with a band of laurel leaves; she had a black knot of riband on her left side, just upon her heart. The evening being warm, she wore nothing but her corset with a short white petticoat; it is impossible to describe a figure more interesting.

"The chain and locket which I had given to her at Paris were round her neck. As I looked earnestly at them she suddenly arose from her seat, and hid the latter within her corset. I advanced a few paces,—she stopped me with her hand extended, while her eyes looked eagerly towards the door of the cottage. I perceived the impulse of her mind,—she was fearful that I should interrupt the scene of sacred sorrow.—'You cannot enter,' said she; 'Happy is no one in this little hovel.—We are all sorrow, for since my love was die, we have no joy to see the stranger.'

"I begged her to forgive me, and was departing, for my heart was too full to check the tears which rushed into my eyes.

"'You have tears for poor Lisette!' said she, taking my hand, and looking earnestly under my downcast eye-lids. 'You can pity my distress!—You have perhaps know my Henri?' Then taking the locket again from her bosom, she added, 'it is his hair—I did cut it from his forehead so white, after the bullet fatal did lodge in his brave heart. They did bury him in the cimetiere on the side of that green hill;—do you not see it yonder? I have not go home, I live in the little cottage of his mother; for I have promise not to go leave him, never!'

"She spoke with a smile, though her eyes glistened with tears. Her senses were scattered, but not lost: she now knew me; and inquired how I had escaped from Paris. She invited me into the cottage; but I declined entering.—I sat myself down at the door; the little bench was over-hung with roses, and a thick vine covered the whole front of the thatched dwelling. Again she looked towards the hills. 'There,' said she, 'after the battle was all done, there he was buried! you have see him at Paris. He was as beautiful as the sun of the morning! I have love him dearly; I shall forget him never!'

"Night was rapidly advancing, and the postillion reminded me that he could not lose time while I was talking with mad folks. I perceived that his pipe was exhausted, and Lisette shook her head. 'I should be happy,' said she, 'if I was mad; for then I should forget what I now cannot help feel. Helas! he had not know Henri, or he would very much pity me!'

"I entered the cabriolet and she kissed my hand. Her lips were feverish, her face was as pale as death, and her large dark eyes seemed to penetrate my soul.

"We parted, I drove swiftly towards Abbeville.—She strolled towards the hill. I saw her ascend the little beaten path, till the postillion's clacking whip reminded me that I was near the inn.

"I dreamed all night of Lisette and her sorrows: on the following morning I awoke with a violent head-ache, which prevented my quitting my pillow; and before noon I was overwhelmed with a fever. The hostess of the inn proposed my staying till the succeeding day; not thinking it prudent that I should continue my journey under such unfavourable symptoms. I followed her counsel. But four days passed before I was able to leave my chamber. On the evening of the fifth I ordered my cabriolet, and resolved to make one visit more to Lisette, before I recommenced my journey to England.

"The lustre of the setting sun cast a beautiful animation on the calm and soothing hour. Those who have travelled in France will acknowledge that there is something in the summer scenery, the clear bland atmosphere, and the empurpled sky of a glowing evening, which exceeds the powers of a descriptive pen. Every thing looked tranquil; the air scarcely fanned the branches of the trees; and the more gloomy objects, as they grew less distinct by distance, seemed to soothe the mind by a sweet and melancholy sympathy. I sighed for poor Lisette; I lamented the fate of her dear Henry; and I shuddered at the horrors which usurpation diffused under the mask of freedom.

"As I approached the cottage, the road was strewed with flowers, and my heart was beginning to beat, when I saw six young girls, dressed all in white. They were returning from the funeral of Lisette. At a little distance the venerable mother of the rash Henry was kneeling before a cross which stood by the road side.

She was praying fervently, and weeping bitterly. The scene was too afflicting. I hastened back to Abbeville, and on the same evening pursued my *route* towards Calais.

"Calumny's wings are as swift as those of the whirlwind. A report had reached London, and thence been conveyed to Drumbender Castle, that I had been married, *à la revolution*, at Paris, to an English prisoner, and afterwards had been the avowed mistress of the abhorred Marat. The high sentiments of aristocracy which my kindred professed were no less insulted by the former report than their morality was wounded by the latter. I was met at Dover by a courier, with the commands of all my relations never again to disgrace them by either bearing the name or venturing into the presence of my family.

"On my arrival in London I threw myself upon the mercy of my female friend. She denied all knowledge of me. I sought the protection of my destroyer. He was shocked at the immorality of avowing such a marriage, and assured me that he had never pardoned himself for having adopted such a republican custom. He added, that by claiming him as an husband, I should only blazon my own disgrace: but that if I would content myself to relinquish the name of wife, and conceal the transaction wholly from the world, he would ever be my friend and my protector. I had no remedy. I set out for Wales, to conceal my sorrow and my approaching anguish. All parts of the habitable globe were at that moment indifferent to me.

"I had resided at the foot of a bleak and barren mountain near Crickhowel[1] a fortnight, when my female friend came on a visit to a neighbouring mansion, and within a few hours after her arrival she discovered my solitary habitation. I had passed for the widow of an officer, and was kindly received by every family in the vicinity of the mountain: but, alas! the soothing dream of happiness was ended. My real name and situation were whispered about with a malevolent avidity: I was shunned, abhorred, and driven from the sanctuary of compunction to seek a new asylum—among strangers.

---

[1] A small town in Wales, at the foot of the Black Mountains, not far from the estate of Robinson's father-in-law.

"I repaired to Bath, where, through the benevolence of a friend, I obtained a benefit-play. The unknown philanthropist was acquainted with my family, and on condition that I would instantly depart, exerted his interest with the manager in my favour. My real name was concealed; for I had adopted that which I now bear. You must remember me: I spoke to you in the library; I thanked you."

She hesitated.

"Heavens! is it possible?" exclaimed Mrs. Morley. "Did you know the person who obtained the benefit-play for you?"

"I did not. He begged leave to conceal his name, and the profits were conveyed to me through the hands of the manager."

"You quitted Bath on the following day?" said Mrs. Morley.

"I did: but, alas! my misfortunes did not find any alleviation from the benevolence of the unknown friend; for I had not travelled three miles before I was stopped by a highwayman, and robbed of my pocket-book containing the whole sum which I had received from the manager. With a few guineas, which were loose in my pocket, I was therefore obliged to continue my journey, more wretched, more distressed, and more desponding than ever.

"On my return to my Welsh cottage I found it burnt to the ground, through the carelessness of the girl whom I had left to take care of it; and all my property, even my scanty wardrobe, which I had saved amidst the wrecks of fortune, was consumed in the conflagration. The girl, terrified, and conscious of the mischief she had occasioned, fled, and has not since been heard of. Her mother, overwhelmed with grief, consented to be my companion. We proceeded to Derbyshire, and it was under her care that you found me and my dear offspring, the deserted Fanny."

"What was your reason for making Derbyshire the place of your retreat?" said Mrs. Morley.

Mrs. Sedgley blushed, and hesitated. After many unsuccessful efforts, she at last replied, "Alas! I had heard that the object of my affections, the dear, the unkind father of my offspring, was in that part of England; and I had hoped that if it should please heaven to take me from this world of persecution, the unoffending infant, whom I should leave behind me, would be blessed with one friend to save it."

"Is it possible that you could love a monster who had so cruelly deceived you?" said Mrs. Morley.

"Ah!" replied Mrs. Sedgley, "how strangely are we prone to love, where we feel conscious that the affections of our hearts are hopeless! The deserter of me and my sorrows was, to all other beings, the most amiable of mortals. The noblest philanthropy, the tenderest feelings, seemed to characterize his nature. So pure, so amiable was he in the opinion of all mankind, that even had I accused him of dishonour, the story would not have been believed; and I loved him too tenderly to be the destroyer of that reputation, the loss of which I felt but too acutely."

Mrs. Morley perceiving the pain which this conversation gave Mrs. Sedgley, forbore to question her farther on the subject; and a short time after Mrs. Sedgley had finished her pathetic story, the stage-coach stopped to take up two passengers. The remainder of the morning elapsed in melancholy rumination. Mrs. Sedgley was, in the opinion of Mrs. Morley, the victim of lord Francis Sherville, who, it was well known, had been on his continental travels ever since his minority. The female friend she justly concluded to be lady Penelope Pryer; and she forbore to make any further inquiries on a subject which seemed to present conviction so unequivocal.

CHAPTER XXV

The esteem which Mrs. Morley entertained for lord Francis was considerably diminished by the recital of Mrs. Sedgley's story; yet the manner of his absenting himself from her society, the evident emotion which Mrs. Sedgley felt when she was informed that he was the protector of her infant, and his unaccountable seclusion in Derbyshire, convinced Mrs. Morley that she was not mistaken. They proceeded on their journey. The bosom of the amiable mother seemed considerably lightened of its burthen by the confidence she had placed in her old friend, though new companion. One of the passengers whom they had taken up on the first day's journey was a young hero, who had just stepped out of the trammels of Juvenal into the fields of Bellona,[1] equally qualified by the one and by the other; as learned as he was amiable, and as wise as he was valiant!

He had not been in the coach half an hour, which he had passed in silence, (for the son of Mars was bashful in the society of modest women,) when he proposed taking his seat as an outside passenger. The coachman informed him that there was no room excepting on the box. "I like it," said young Caesar. "I am a good whip, and often drive father's nags, four in hand, twelve miles within the hour. All the jockies about our castle say I am the best hand at it of any in our county; and when the old one dies, I mean to have a phaeton and eight, to cut a dash, and to vex my neighbours."[2]

"Very amiable!" said Mrs. Morley.

The coachman begged leave to decline submitting the reins to such desperate hands. "I cannot trust the lives of my passengers, or, what is more, of my horses, to such a harem-scarem," said he.

"Why I trust my own," said young Leadenhead, "and I am heir to four thousand a-year. I question if your passengers or your horses can say as much—Ask 'em."

"You'll upset us," said the coachman, sliding his hand under his hat, and looking doubtfully.

"Well! and if I do, I can afford to pay for all bones broken. You know father is as rich a man as any in the county. You have had many a bumper with me in the butler's room at Plummet Castle! Come, don't be crabbed! I won't hurt any body; and if I do, I shan't mind paying a surgeon." 'Squire Caesar now shaking half a score guineas between his hands so deafened the coachman's ears, that he archly smiling, replied, "If I was but sure, your honour, that you would not upset us, I would indulge you in your frolic."

"Try me: you can but find fault when the thing is done. If I should be laid in the ditch, it will not be the first time; and there is nothing like experience."

---

[1] Juvenal was a Roman satirist featured in many translation exercises assigned to school boys; Bellona was the Roman goddess of war.

[2] A phaeton was a light, open carriage, usually drawn by two horses rather than eight. The vehicle was named after the mythological Phaeton, who was destroyed by a thunderbolt after he overturned the chariot of his father, Helios.

"Perhaps the ladies won't like it," said the coachman, looking towards the inside passengers.

"Who minds women?" interrupted young Leadenhead; "they can but squall, and there is an end of it. I often drive sister Bridget in my tandem, and she's as pleased as Punch.[1] We never go to Plummet Castle but I upset half a dozen country lasses in the course of a summer. My tandem is the terror of the county: but father's money pays for all."

Two guineas slipped into the coachman's hand obtained for the son of Mars, though not of Minerva, that triumphal seat which, like the car of Achilles, was destined to roll over the vanquished.[2] Young Leadenhead was also in one extremity invulnerable, though, like his prototype of the moment, his heel was the part which exposed him to the most imminent danger; for by forcibly striking it on the foot-board as he set off full speed, he startled the horses. They pursued their way without restraint till they passed a flock of geese. The hero dashed through the cackling multitude, annihilating at least a score; while the bearer of the red flag pursued the vehicle with the fury of indignation till they were stopped by a turnpike gate, where a handful of gold again paid for the squire's frolic, and the coach continued its career with unabating velocity.

They now had to pass through a deep brook. The bold charioteer dashed into the stream. "Here we go! sink or swim!"

"Sink!"[3] cried a countryman, who was leaning over a bridge which crossed the swift current. True was the prediction; for young Phaeton being at that moment, by a sudden jolt of the carriage, precipitated into the deepest part of the water, he consequently reached the bottom of the stream, head foremost. The horses, frightened by the splashing of so ponderous a body, continued their course on full speed, till in the village they were stopped without doing farther mischief.

---

1   The self-satisfied, roguish hero of the popular Punch and Judy puppet play.
2   In Roman mythology, Mars was the god of war, and Minerva was the goddess of wisdom. Achilles, the most illustrious Greek warrior in Homer's *The Iliad*, was fatally wounded by an arrow shot into his heel, the weak spot on his otherwise invulnerable body.
3   A question mark follows "Sink" in the original.

While the crowd assembled round the coach, the adventurous son of Mars, with one eye closed by his fall, came crying and swearing that he had been cheated out of his two guineas. "I paid for my seat," said he.

"Then why did you resign it?" inquired Mrs. Morley. "Perhaps you thought, like some politicians, that having bought your seat, you had a right to vacate it at pleasure."

"Better he should do that than drive his employers to their own destruction," said Mrs. Sedgley.

"I don't care what you say," cried the mortified squire: "I'll oblige father to prosecute. He is rich enough to make an example of those who want to trick me out of my guineas. Father has as much money as any man in the county, and father would as soon punish any body that affronts me as he would look at them."

"Who has affronted you?" said Mrs. Morley. "You endangered our lives by your bad coachmanship."

"That's nothing," replied Gregory; "I have been cheated, and I will make father prosecute."

"Cheated! What do you mean by that?" said the coachman. "Will you fight it out? and if I have the best of it, why '*father*' can but prosecute after all."

At this moment the family coach luckily came in sight, and the weeping Hannibal[1] mounting the box, escaped from the honest indignation of his accused adversary, while the lives of the terrified passengers were once more committed to safe hands; which, had they not been contaminated by the poison gold, would not have resigned the reins to so daring an adventurer. Young Leadenhead proceeded to Plummet Castle, while the fair friends pursued their way towards their place of destination. Little more being said by the passengers, who were exhausted by the terrors they had encountered, Mrs. Morley beguiled the time by recording her reflections in the following

---

[1]   Hannibal, a renowned Carthaginian general and sworn enemy of the Romans, reputedly wept when he was recalled from Italy to defend his homeland.

SONNET

O, GOLD! thou pois'nous dross, whose subtle power
Can change men's souls, or captive take the will!
Thou, whose fell potency can save or kill,
Illume or darken life's precarious hour!

Thou tipp'st the leaves of Fancy's fairest flow'r
With glitt'ring tears: it feels the numbing chill
Creep through each fibre slow, while every ill
Of sordid misery blossoms to devour.

The bland and lust'rous morn of mental grace
Thy touch contaminates: thy sev'ring force
Breaks Friendship's charm, bids Honour's wreath decay;
Tears the pure blush of love from Beauty's face;
Arms bold Oppression in her ruthless course,
While the wide groaning world, feels thy destructive sway.[1]

CHAPTER XXVI

Mrs. Morley, on joining the dramatic company, made her *debut* in
the character of Lady Teazle.[2] The task was an arduous one: but the
high spirit which upheld her under the pressure of unmerited
persecutions did not, in this moment of trial, lose any part of its
sustaining quality. She knew that the labour of talents is more
honourable than the independence of indolence: she felt the glow
of innate dignity, and little heeded the tinsel decorations of adventitious fortune. But Mrs. Morley was not aware of the trials she had
to undergo in a profession which has too frequently been subjected
to the petty scorn of upstart insignificance: she did not recollect
that the wealthy fool can always point the shaft of prejudice against

---

[1] This sonnet was published under Robinson's own name in *The Morning Post* on
October 1, 1799.
[2] The leading lady in Richard Brinsley Sheridan's comedy *The School for Scandal* (1777).

the children of Genius and Misfortune; and that the liberal patronage of talents can alone spring from minds through a sympathizing similitude of taste, feeling, education, and refinement: for the proud, the vulgar, and the ostentatious are ever ready to condemn that which, not possessing, they do not comprehend. The success which attended her first essay surpassed even her most sanguine expectations. She was the pupil of Nature; her feelings were spontaneous, her ideas expanded, and her judgment correct. She scorned to avail herself of that factitious mummery, that artificial, disgusting trick, which deludes the senses by exciting laughter at the expence of the understanding. She was lively and unaffected: her smiles were exhilarating; her sighs were pathetic; her voice was either delicately animating or persuasively soothing: she neither giggled convulsively nor wept methodically: she was the thing she seemed, while even the perfection of her art was Nature.

Mrs. Morley's time and her friendship were divided with Mrs. Sedgley, whose dramatic genius taking the tragic walk, strewed no thorns of contention between her and her contemporary. The fair heroines participated both the labour and the popularity of the company; and their mutual sorrows naturally produced that friendship which meliorated the destiny that pursued them.

Mrs. Morley was neither elated nor changed by the fame which rapidly followed her footsteps. She had good sense to consider the possession of the most illustrious distinction, the celebrity of genius, as a gift of Nature which was destined, in a great degree, to compensate for the frowns of Fortune. Just at this period, when Mrs. Morley was in the zenith of her reputation, the manager proposed removing the company to another town in the same county. The names of Denison and Sedgley had been borne on the wings of Fame even to the most remote parts of the kingdom, and every patron of dramatic talents (for patronage and ostentation are frequently synonymous) impatiently awaited their arrival.

The dramatic heroines were both remarkably handsome; they had resided in the metropolis; they were extolled for their exquisite taste in the choice of their habiliments; and they were both supposed to be better born than what low minds imagine the criterion of respectability. Curiosity therefore induced some of the minor families to invite them once, for their own amusement and the gratification of their friends. The invitation to meet the new actresses was whispered as though they were meditating to exhibit something monstrous and extraordinary. The females begged it might not be mentioned beyond the proposed circle, and the males prepared for a great deal of flirtation with '*the ladies*,' by way of anticipating their Green-Room[1] gallantries when they should become more intimately acquainted. They piqued themselves upon their polite condescension, and made no doubt but their easy familiarity would take from them the erroneous imputation of pride and vulgarity.

Expectation was not disappointed by the high report which Fame had made of the twin constellations in the dramatic hemisphere. Mrs. Sedgley was, after her first appearance in The Grecian Daughter, pronounced a juvenile Siddons; while the lively and engaging Martha was greeted, in the sportive walks of Thalia, with boundless adoration. The easy elegance of a Farren, who had frequently trod the same boards with considerable *eclat*, and the genuine playful graces of the queen of smiles—the attractive Jordan, were blended in the person and talents of Mrs. Morley.[2] She was the idol of the day: but she was set up by caprice, and surrounded by all the demons of envy, slander, and malevolence.

"Where did she come from?"

Nobody knew.

Conjecture was busy. The name of Denison, which she still assumed, was highly respectable: but she had no letters of recommendation to the opulent leaders of theatrical patronage; she had no peers to protect her, no women of rank to lead her into the path of popularity; and, above all, she wanted that arrogant

---

[1] A room in the theater where actors and actresses awaited their calls to go on stage and received visitors after a play.

[2] Sarah Siddons, the most acclaimed tragic actress of the day, played the lead role in Arthur Murphy's tragedy *The Grecian Daughter*. Siddons' most famous counterparts in "the sportive walks of Thalia," the muse of comedy, were Julia Farren and Dorothy Jordan. As Robinson invokes these familiar names to define the respective talents of her dramatic heroines, she also posits their friendship as a desirable alternative to the notorious rivalry between Jordan and Siddons. According to Sandra Richards, "their competition gave form to the struggle between comedy and tragedy for dominance with eighteenth-century audiences, waged with all the vehemence of political factionalism." See *The Rise of the English Actress* (New York: St. Martin's, 1993), 59.

effrontery, that unblushing self-conceit, which has in many instances supplied the deficiency of more substantial merit. She stood before the tribunal of the public on the basis of her own talents: but it was undermined by arts which even the most transcendent genius cannot always counteract. Mrs. Morley played several characters with unbounded applause. The modesty of innate worth is not like the obtrusive impertinence of false pretensions. She looked not forward to any thing beyond a decent independence; she sought not to attain that eminence which might teach her to forget those friends who, in her days of humble industry, approved, sanctioned, and esteemed her. She knew that Fortune was a dazzling phantom, a delusive, glittering *ignis fatuus*, [1] which was apt to mislead the weak and giddy brain beyond the bounds of gratitude and reflection. Mrs. Morley's popularity was boundless: but, reader, the approbation of her patrons was wholly confined to the boards of scenic exhibition: the aristocracy of wealth had little to do with the aristocracy of genius; for great and admired talents, where they are entirely separated from the advantages of fortune, oftener prove evils than blessings to their possessors. They excite envy, they awaken jealousy, and they nourish abhorrence; because the master of great riches, amidst the very plenitude of enjoyments, cannot bear to behold the child of Penury and Genius receiving that homage which the liberal heart bestows spontaneously, while he is obliged to purchase those smiles which he knows to be factitious.

Mrs. Morley had to struggle against the all-potent tyrant Prejudice. She had engaged in a profession which vulgar minds, though they are amused by its labours, frequently condemn with unpitying asperity. She was engaging, discreet, sensible, and accomplished: but she was an actress, and therefore deemed an unfit associate for the wives and daughters of the proud, the opulent, and the unenlightened.

Among others, the wealthy tribe of the Leadenheads were most rigidly fastidious in their opinions of social distinctions. Mr.

---

[1] A naturally occurring phosphorescent light seen at night over swampy ground. Because the natural phenomenon often misled weary travelers searching for a human habitation, the term was frequently used to describe any bright, but delusive prospect.

Humphry Leadenhead was the head of his family; and no person had ever been malignant enough to deny that, in every acceptation of the word, he did honour to his name—a name which he had scorned to change, though wealth had accumulated and homage followed his footsteps, for more than twenty years, through all the mazy walks of unremitting industry.

The race of the Leadenheads had gradually risen from obscurity, and they were now of the most weighty consideration in the great scale of worldly importance: but, alas! the swift wing of time had wasted from their memory the means by which they had acquired their consequence. They were too exalted to reflect, too wealthy to be humble. The Miss Leadenheads were, in the vicinity of Plummet Castle, wondered at as beauties of the first order; while young squire Gregory was considered as a prodigy of learning and intrepidity; though his knowledge extended not beyond the game-laws, and his valour had never been evinced in any scene of action excepting that of a cock-fight or a bull-baiting.

At the age of nineteen young Leadenhead had been honoured with a commission in the army, and anticipation already named him as the hero of the family. Mr. Leadenhead senior, though he had attained considerable wealth in a long series of animated traffic, fancied that his consequence was augmented by his son's elevation. At one time the young squire was emulous of a black gown: but reflection suggested to the family that the sable habit might lead to gloomy reflections; and that the basis of their present opulence being of a dark complexion,[1] the lustre of military achievements might be deemed more desirable as trophies to adorn the Leadenhead mausoleum.

Mr. Humphry Leadenhead, like many of his name, was not wholly divested of certain prejudices. Among others, he deemed all human perfections of little importance, when placed in

---

[1] Robinson's contemporaries would have been quick to pick up on her hints that the Leadenhead family owed its wealth to the slave trade, a topic of heated debate in Parliament. Although Robinson was sometimes identified as the ghost writer of anti-abolitionist speeches delivered by her lover Tarleton, an MP representing the port city of Liverpool, a number of her poems support the abolitionist cause. For a more detailed consideration of the issue, see Moira Ferguson's *Subject to Others: British Women Writers and Colonial Slavery, 1670–1834* (New York: Routledge, 1992).

comparison with those of ancestry and fortune. With this opinion, it had been the ambition of his prosperous days to see his sons and daughters mingling the deep tide of commerce with the glittering, shallow stream of titled insignificance. His undeviating counsel to his children was, "Ennoble your family; buy honours, dignities, titles, precedence, and connections; and above all things consult the book of heraldry as the book of fate."

Shortly after Mrs. Morley's arrival, the young squire became enamoured of her attractions. He was her constant attendant, her avowed admirer. Mrs. Morley passed for a widow; and the pride of the Leadenheads was deeply wounded by the apprehension that the heir of the family should degrade himself by an alliance with a strolling actress;[1] while Mrs. Morley looked as far above the pretensions of her suitor, as worth and talents have a right to soar beyond the track of vulgar association.

In order to divert young Leadenhead's attention from the pursuit which occasioned so much family inquietude, a party was proposed to York races. A new landau,[2] which had been purchased in the metropolis the preceding summer, with four horses, contained Humphry and his wife, the young squire, and Miss Bridget; forming a group not unlike the family of the Wrongheads, in their memorable journey to London.[3]

Indeed it had long been the recreation of the Leadenheads to visit the metropolis once a-year, for their edification in the mysteries of politeness; and for the supreme gratification of standing at the windows of an hotel near St. James's, to see the nobility go to and from court on his Majesty's birthday.[4]

---

[1] "Strolling" actresses moved from one provincial theater to another and were generally deemed morally and socially inferior to actresses who had long-term engagements at the major London theaters, Covent Garden and Drury Lane. According to her *Memoirs*, Robinson herself "refused several offers from provincial managers" because she "felt an almost insurmountable aversion to the idea of strolling" (2: 12).

[2] A four-wheeled carriage with front and back seats facing each other and a roof that could be lowered or detached.

[3] The Wrongheads are a ridiculous family in Colley Cibber's comedy *The Provok'd Husband; or, a Journey to London* (1728).

[4] St. James's Palace was the principal London residence of the Royal Family. Robinson's poem "The Birth-Day" (originally published as "St. James's Street, on the Eighteenth of January, 1795") juxtaposes the royal pomp of a birthday celebration for Queen Charlotte with striking images of poverty.

Previous to their departure for York races, the old and unvarying lesson, "Ennoble your family," was again and again repeated. Young Gregory was tolerably well-looking, and not likely to meet with any impediment in the road to preferment from those gothic stumbling-blocks, modesty and self-knowledge. The squire was heir to a splendid fortune; and he had, by many striking examples in his own family occurrences, already discovered that effrontery is the infallible substitute for every deficiency of personal or mental importance.

A waggon load of finery had arrived from the metropolis to adorn the females for this important expedition; all the newest fashions had been purchased; and they fancied, because they wore the habiliments of distinguished women, that they were also of the most illustrious consequence in the broad scale of popularity. Miss Bridget was strictly enjoined not even to look at any persons who had not a title to recommend them; and young Gregory was with most pompous solemnity commanded for once to forget the stable and the butler's pantry, and to assume the manners of a man of consequence. But the most important injunction was, that of never speaking to people of his own rank in life: the sons of industry and commerce were no longer fit companions for the heir of Plummet Castle. He was destined to soar in a more exalted sphere, to forget the beaten track of sordid labour, and to prove that the Leadenheads were of the most weighty importance in the scale of social intercourse. He could buy "*golden* opinions from all sorts of people,"[1] and therefore was qualified to follow the unbridled bent of his own refined and polished inclinations.

On their arrival at York, nearly the whole hotel was engaged for the opulent guests. Five guineas were sent to the bell-ringers to ring the consequence of the wealthy visitors in the ears of an admiring multitude; minute inquiries were made after names of persons of distinction, and cards were prepared to return visits even before they had received a single proof of their being known in the gay and busy circle. Miss Bridget had studied a fashionable demeanor the whole morning, and Gregory had

---

[1]   Cf. Shakespeare's *Macbeth*: "I have bought / Golden opinions from all sorts of people" (1. 7. 32–33).

dressed himself in his new regimentals, when the master of the house informed them that a lady of fashion had been making particular inquiries about them.

Bridget went nearly into hysterics, and Gregory jumped almost out of regimental splendours at this propitious information; while Mrs. Leadenhead desired their host to take their cards to the lady, and to inform her that they should be proud to have the honour of seeing her to dinner.

"The lady did not seem to know you, madam," said the messenger.

"How should she?" cried Gregory. "Every thing must have a beginning. Father did not make his fortune in a day."

"Brother," interrupted Miss Bridget, "what is that to the purpose?"

"It is proper that people should know who we are," said Mrs. Leadenhead, "and Gregory is very right. We did not travel so far from Plummet Castle to be taken for nobody. The Leadenheads are not ashamed of their name."

"They need not, madam," said their host, "for they do it infinite honour."

Gregory giving the host a smart stroke upon the shoulder, cried, "That was civil, and well spoken, and we will drink a bottle together, to become better acquainted. Father's purse-strings are loose, and I'm determined to be jolly."

"Heavens!" exclaimed Miss Bridget, "will you never know your own importance?" Then turning to the master of the hotel, she added, "My brother is a little eccentric in his manners, and sometimes forgets himself."

"Evidently, madam," replied their host. "It is a natural failing."

"Well," cried Mrs. Leadenhead, "you may take our cards; and if her grace or her ladyship chooses to notice the visit, we shall be on the course in our landau and four, and at the ball this evening."

"Yes, take the cards," added Gregory; "a few scraps of paper are no object. We can afford to buy more when they are gone. Besides, we brought six packs for the week's visits. We people of fortune don't value trifles; for who knows, among the nobles we may be acquainted with, but Bridget may light on a husband; or I may get a wife to take back, and make the folks stare at Plummet Castle."

It may not be improper here to inform the reader, that among other singular opinions which were entertained by this eccentric family, they felt an unconquerable predilection for every thing that wore a semblance of nobility. For this reason their houses were all named castles, halls, and places. Plummet-Castle, Golden-Hall, and Leadenhead-Place were the well-known habitations of this illustrious lineage; for to live in a house that was not dubbed with a splendid name would have been, to them, the very acme of degradation.

The secondary mania of the Leadenheads was that of seeing their consequence recorded in the periodical publications of the time. The arrival of a Leadenhead in London or at a fashionable watering-place was duly announced with all pompous panegyric, and Mrs. Leadenhead, in the streets of the metropolis, fancied that she was as well known and as highly respected as in the vicinity of Plummet Castle. Indeed half way, on the score of calculation, she was right in her conjectures.

Three hours were wasted in selecting a dress for Miss Bridget to receive the illustrious visitor. This she thought too fine, that too simple; one was unbecoming; another was ill-made. Gregory, who was present at the debate, advised his sister to find out her grace's or her ladyship's woman, and to bribe her for the sight of one of her lady's new dresses. "You need not grudge the money," said the young 'squire, "for father can afford it."

Miss Bridget thought the plan a good one: but Mrs. Leadenhead objected to the idea of permitting the opulent family of Plummet Castle to demean themselves by copying any body. "I like to be the original," said she, with an air of self-importance.

"And so you are," cried Gregory, "and originals we are all likely to be; for nobody will take the pains to imitate us, unless we learn something of people of fashion. Why there is Bridget, she is no more like a London woman of quality than I am like King Solomon."[1]

"Then I have little resemblance, God knows!" retorted Bridget. "But who made you so clever? You are but just come from school; and I am sure you never learnt any thing there but

---

[1]   King Solomon, son of David in the Old Testament, was a proverbial example of wisdom.

to break windows and to overset whiskies. You were the greatest dunce in the school, and that every body said; so you need not talk about wisdom and self-importance."

"I don't want the first, while father can leave me four thousand a-year," replied Gregory; "and as for the last, there is enough in the family already. The Leadenheads will always make their way, while they can pay for smoothing the path, I'll warrant them. Father's money is the best passport, all the world over."

Miss Bridget now, after making a variety of grimaces at Gregory, which terminated by a smart box on the ear that set him crying, darted out of the room to settle her features into a nobility simper against the important trial of the evening.

At the ball, the indefatigable family became acquainted with lady Penelope Pryer, sir Lionel Beacon, and the all-accomplished Julia Bradford. Mrs. Leadenhead was more consequential than ever; and Bridget was delighted, even to ecstasy, in being at last noticed by a woman of lady Penelope's rank and appearance. She hung upon her arm during the intervals between the dances, admired her dress, imitated her demeanor, curtsied whenever lady Pen nodded to her familiar friends; and declared, that since she left school she had never passed so delightful an evening.

Gregory, amidst the scene of triumph, entertained himself by joking with the fidlers, and playing tricks with the waiters; not without frequent frowns and nods from Mrs. Leadenhead, and more than once a whisper, to recollect the old maxim of ennobling his family.

On the following day the whole party met on the race-course. The Leadenheads had opened their landau, though the weather was intensely cold, in order to display the feathers which towered above the brows of the female part of the family. Notwithstanding the waggon-load of decorations, a taylor had been at work all night to make Miss Bridget a new-fashioned dress similar to one which lady Penelope had worn at the ball on the preceding evening. It was composed of purple sarsnet,[1] in the form of a great coat, and trimmed with silver edging. But what was Bridget's sorrow when she beheld lady Pen on the

---

[1] A soft, finely-woven silk fabric.

race-course in a plain brown habit and a straw hat, without a single plume to dispute the palm of rivalry: she absolutely shed tears; while Gregory consoled her by reminding her that "father could afford to pay for twenty gowns, and that she would do right to have a new one every hour while she staid at the races."

During the second morning of display on the course, Gregory unfortunately drove his tandem over an old woman who was earnestly employed in vociferating the list of horses. He nevertheless continued to gallop round the lines, till the populace, incensed at his unfeeling conduct, pursued and stopped him.

"You have broken an old woman's leg," said a by-stander.

"Well, tell father to pay for it," said Gregory; "he's rich enough to buy twenty old women, and their legs into the bargain."

"It's a pity, then, that he does not purchase a little understanding for his son," said the observer.

"I can do without it," replied Gregory, shewing a handful of guineas.

"I see you can," said the spectator. "Nothing can be more evident; and since you are so able to supply your own deficiency, you may as well do something for the necessities of the old woman."

"I don't like old women," cried Gregory.

"You have no right to kill them, notwithstanding," said the monitor.

At this moment sir Lionel came up to the carriage. The poor woman was brought in the arms of the multitude.

"You'll not win the race, my old one!" cried Gregory, "you are broken down!"

"By running against a post," said the by-stander.

Sir Lionel threw the woman his purse, and ordered her to be taken care of; while the family of the Leadenheads generously subscribed three guineas, to pay the surgeon for setting the limb; wisely remarking, "It was fortunate for her that she happened to meet with an opulent family."

On the following morning Mrs. Leadenhead ordered their wardrobe to be unpacked, and hung round the dressing-room, where herself and her daughter purposed receiving visitors. Miss Bridget was dressed in a white sarsnet powdering-gown, and Mrs. Leadenhead wore a scarlet riding-habit, lined with blue, with blue cuffs and collar. She had heard that it was the Royal Hunt, only reversing the colours; and she therefore, to keep up the contrast, ordered it to be adopted as the *habit de chasse* of Plummet Castle.

She had not been seated in studied negligence many minutes when sir Lionel made his appearance. "By Jupiter!" exclaimed he, "an old clothes shop!" at the same time glancing round at the expensive decorations which were displayed in every direction.

"What, are you going to set up a masquerade warehouse?" continued the sportive baronet. "I propose a masked ball this evening, and shall send the whole county to sport your wardrobe. By all that is comical, this is amazingly astonishing! Why you are a famous family, and worth paying to amuse the populace! But what have you done with your gala suit, Miss Leatherhead? Where is your fine purple and silver? Hang me if I don't believe you borrowed it from old Pen. I told her never to wear it again, for it made her look like a travelling show-woman."

Miss Bridget was near fainting.

"Are you going to be married in that fine white dress?" continued he. "Why you look like Tilburnia, mad in white satin![1] And as for you, my old girl, you want nothing but three horses and a trumpeter to rival the notorious Mrs. Whad-d'ye-call-her, that rides at the amphitheater. Do you mean to sport such famous figures on the course? By Jupiter, you will only frighten the horses!" Mrs. Leadenhead looked aghast, when lady Pen entered the apartment.

"Heavens!" exclaimed her ladyship, "I did not know that they were come!"

"Whom!" said Mrs. Leadenhead, smiling through the flush of indignation.

"The strolling actors! I see their wardrobe is already unpacked, and a very gay one it is. I suppose you are come to admire it?"

Not a syllable was uttered in reply.

"Well! this is charming!" said lady Penelope. "Suppose we bespeak a play—the Provoked Husband, or All the World's a Stage,

---

[1]   Tilburnia, the parodic sentimental heroine of Richard Brinsley Sheridan's farce *The Critic* (1779), enters the last act "stark mad in white satin" after the death of her lover, Don Ferolo Whiskerandos.

or the Devil to Pay, or Every Man in His Humour?[1] It will be delightful!" So saying, lady Pen and sir Lionel departed, leaving the mortified Leadenheads to weep over their insulted magnificence.

CHAPTER XXVII

Miss Bradford had been recently accustomed to fashionable life; and adopted a more subtle line of conduct in the scene of action. She humoured the eccentric opinions of young Gregory; praised his polished manners; commended his familiar and easy conversation; ventured to accompany him on the course in his tandem; and played her cards so skillfully, that she completely won the heart of her companion. He danced with her at the next ball; he betted with her on the race; gave the waiters a guinea to drink her health; he made the fidlers play all the morning in the hall of her hotel; he stole her faded bouquet, and wore it in his helmet; he swore to call his favourite pointer Julia; and declared that a trip to Scotland would to him be the most desirable of all earthly gratifications.[2]

Promptitude and perseverance are said to be the promoters of great and glorious achievements. Four days had scarcely shone on the Leadenheads, since their initiation in the arcanum of fashionable propensities, when an elopement astonished the admiring multitude. Lady Penelope and sir Lionel Beacon, having also set out for London, on the same morning, without even condescending to take leave of their new intimates, Humphrey, and indeed the whole family concluded, for anticipation often keeps pace with desire, that Gregory had carried off a titled prize, in the fair person of lady Pen Pryer. Large sums were sent to the metropolis to

---

[1] To "bespeak" a play is to request or to order a performance. The four possibilities mentioned by Lady Penelope were popular plays written by Colley Cibber, Isaac Jackman, Charles Coffey, and Ben Jonson, respectively.

[2] Elopements to Scotland became a romantic cliché of sorts after the English Parliament passed Lord Hardwicke's Marriage Act in 1753. Under the provisions of this Act, which did not apply in Scotland, a person under the age of twenty-one could not be legally married without the consent of a parent or guardian.

purchase splendid accounts of the family elevation in all the diurnal prints. The marriage of a Leadenhead was a weighty business. The interesting process of the courtship till the hour of decisive triumph, was described in a large type in every paper; while the whole town either read the pompous detail as an amusing farago[1] of folly, or wisely passed it over, as a new instance of that inordinate vanity which, on various occasions, had distinguished the family.—Among other accounts, the following appeared in one of the most popular daily prints:

It is confidently asserted that Gregory Leadenhead esquire, heir to the opulent Humphrey Leadenhead of Plummet Castle, is shortly to be favoured with the fair hand of the right honorable lady Penelope Pryer, daughter of John James Edward, earl of Brentford and Isleworth, knight of the most noble order of the Bath, and nearly related to all the most illustrious families in the three kingdoms! The accomplished bride is endowed with the most superlative mental and personal qualifications! She is said to be mistress of all the living and dead languages! To understand the most profound mysteries of astrology and theology, mythology, philology, etymology, and phisiology! She is well versed in philosophy, psalmography, biography, topography, orthography, and phytography! She is an adept in geometry, electricity, chemistry, trigonometry, phisiognomy, botany, metaphysics, history, algebra, mechanics, optics, astronomy, and the occult sciences!! She is perfect mistress of music, poetry, painting, sculpture, architecture, physic, and anatomy!! She is the first dancer, singer, orator, writer, equestrian, and pedestrian in the known world! And she not only ennobles the Leadenheads, by quartering in the heraldry of four dukes, eight earls, twelve barons, fourteen baronets, and sixty-five members of the British parliament, but by the unexampled accomplishments of her mind and the unequalled brilliancy of her talents!!!!

Grand preparations are now making at Plummet Castle for this joyful occasion; and the whole country in which

---

[1] A jumble or hotchpotch.

this opulent family resides, is invited to partake of an entertainment the most elegant, sumptuous, expensive, tasteful, and profuse that ever was seen in this or any other country.

This splendid eulogium, which cost the family two days of deep and laborious rumination, was the theme of nine days wonder. The Leadenhead family, from the senior 'squire to the meanest stable boy, was frantic with exultation. Letters were dispatched to the metropolis, to hire a splendid mansion in one of the western squares for the ensuing winter. The arms of the new landau were effaced, to make room for the emblazoned quarterings of the exalted alliance. The pages of heraldry were ransacked, to explore every iota of armorial distinction; and the Miss Leadenheads sent off an express to London, for a fresh cargo of fashions, to pay and to receive the wedding visits. Plummet Castle was to be new furnished for the reception of the noble relative; and twenty dozen of cards were ordered to be struck off, with the name of the right honorable lady Penelope Leadenhead, against the visits of condescension to the associates of their almost forgotten rank in society.

These important preparations being fully arranged by letters to agents both in town and country, and the first fluttering emotions of joy having settled into a fixed consciousness of newly created importance, the family once more set out for the castle. White cockades were displayed in the hats of the domestics; in every town and village through which they passed, the bells were taught to tell the glorious tidings.—On their arrival at Plummet Castle, good humour, mirth, and revelry surprised the peasantry; they had never before witnessed such extraordinary condescension; and the illumined eyes of the joyful multitude were only surpassed in brilliancy by the illumined windows of the family mansion.

But direful was the change when the bride returned to share the honours of the day! No title! no rank! plain Mrs. Leadenhead! the thought was insupportable. She had not even to boast an illegitimate alliance with any branches of nobility. She could not even produce a shadow of probability that she had noble blood in her veins; or exult in the patronage of those who credulously believed themselves her relations. Miss Julia Bradford was nobody, and *nobody* was obliged to endure the alliance.

Though the bride was not illustriously born, the Leadenheads had every reason to rejoice in the prospect of increasing honours. What she wanted in quality she made up in quantity;—it could not be said that she brought nothing into the family; she had been indefatigable in the labour of dignifying it to posterity; for on the fourth month after her alliance with young Gregory, she presented him with a lusty boy, whose veins might boast a stream flowing from a source as ancient as the Heptarchy.[1]

This abrupt augmentation of family honours, excited no small surprize in the vicinity of Plummet Castle. For Humphrey Leadenhead had forgotten in his mania for noble patronage, to secure the affections of the virtuously humble. Ostentation had been displayed on birthdays, and days of public rejoicing; yet had the Leadenheads never been born, society would not have been less embellished; and the annihilation of the whole race would not have occasioned one single hour of mourning.

But the unexpected present which the squire had received, did not so completely humble the pride of the family as the unfortunate discovery that Mrs. Denison, the strolling actress, was the sister of the elegant Julia. This was indeed a thunderbolt of destruction to the ambitious hopes of Humphrey Leadenhead; the bastard-bar, which was destined to darken the glow of armorial bearings, they considered as the misfortune of fashionable life; but the vulgar necessities of an itinerant beggar were too degrading not to be felt; though it was the first time that the Leadenhead family had even been known to feel for a person in Mrs. Morley's situation.

Julia and her heroic squire, by mutual consent, signed articles of separation. They returned to London, and the enlightened husband shortly after joined his regiment, then quartered in Dorsetshire. While the disappointed Leadenheads vented their regrets at Plummet Castle, and lamented the hour when they first indulged the hope of ennobling their family.

The misfortune which had humbled the heir of Humphrey, in his *debut* on the theatre of fashion, was not more severe than that which attended Martha on the boards of necessity. The arrogance of appearing in the county where the Leadenheads were

---

[1]   A confederation of seven Anglo-Saxon kingdoms, dating back to the fifth century.

persons of such importance was deemed unpardonable. A combination was formed to punish the offender: gold flew about in every direction; power was exercised in every subordinate circle of society. The young squire treated all the grooms and stable-boys in the county; heading the phalanx himself, into the upper gallery: and Mrs. Morley was received with such marked indignation by the family and their suborned confederates, that her appearance again on the dramatic boards was prevented by the manager.[1] She was therefore discharged from the company, and once more driven to wander over the globe, the victim of persecution. Mrs. Morley, on the day of her dismission from her scenic labour, published in the county paper these stanzas:

> Unhappy is the pilgrim's lot
>   Who wanders o'er the desart heath;
> By friends and by the world forgot—
>   Whose only hope—depends on death!
> Yet, may he smile when memory shews,
> The tort'ring stings, the weary woes,
> Which forc'd his bosom to abide
> The *vulgar scorn* of VULGAR PRIDE.

> Forlorn is he, who on the sand
>   Of some bleak isle his hovel rears;
> Or shipwreck'd on the breezy strand,
>   The billow's deep'ning murmur hears.
> Yet, when his aching eyes survey,
> The white sails gliding far away,
> He feels, he shall no more abide
> The *vulgar scorn* of VULGAR PRIDE.

> Sadly the exil'd traveller strays
>   Benighted in some forest drear;

---

[1]   Young Gregory's tactics here recall those of the female gamesters who sent their servants to disrupt the performance of Robinson's comedy *Nobody* in 1794. According to her *Memoirs*, "several persons in the galleries, whose *liveries* betrayed their *employers*, were heard to declare that they were sent to *do up* Nobody. Even women of distinguished rank hissed through their fans" (2: 140–41).

Where by the paly star-light rays
 He sees no hut, no hovel near.
The fire-eyed wolf, which howls for prey,
Glares hideous in his briery way;
Yet, can he smile! for he has borne
The sneers of PRIDE and VULGAR SCORN.

Of all the ills the feeling mind
 Is destin'd in this world to share;
Of pain and poverty combin'd,
 Of friendship's frown, or love's despair!
Still reason arms the conscious soul,
And bids it ev'ry pang control,—
Save, when the patient heart is tried
By VULGAR SCORN and VULGAR PRIDE.

Go wealth, and in the hermit's cell,
 Behold that peace thou can'st not have;
Go rank, and lift the passing knell
 That warns thee, to oblivion's grave!
Go pow'r, and where the peasant's breast
Enjoys the balm of conscious rest,
Confess, that VIRTUE can deride
The VULGAR SCORN of VULGAR PRIDE!

This effusion of a proudly indignant mind did not produce
the desired effect. The whole family of the Leadenheads read the
stanzas; but they were too refined in their satire for inferior intellects. Humphrey declared they were nonsense. Gregory took
them for Greek. Bridget said they were vulgar, low, and impertinent; and Mrs. Leadenhead pronounced them incomprehensible. Yet the printer of the paper, in which they appeared, was
menaced with a prosecution, because the whole county was
unanimous in the opinion, that the burthen of the song was
peculiarly applicable to the Leadenhead family.[1]

---

[1] *Burthen*, or *burden*, is a literary term for a refrain as well as a more general term for
the primary theme that a song or poem bears.

END OF THE FIRST VOLUME

CHAPTER XXVIII

The unlucky termination of Mrs. Morley's dramatic campaign, and the illiberal treatment which she had experienced from vulgar minds, did not more severely afflict her than the disgrace which had attended her sister's misconduct. Her heart was susceptible, her sentiments were liberal, and her feelings infinitely too acute for the repose of her existence. She was one of those ill-starred mortals, whose bosoms participated in the pains and pleasures of beings, who had the inhumanity to behold her sorrows with the most frigid apathy. She could not see a kindred breast throbbing with anguish, or shrinking from persecution, without heaving a responsive sigh, or bestowing a tear to meliorate its sufferings.

Julia had been from her infancy the favourite of her parents; she wore that external passport to indiscriminating minds, which is so often mistaken for genuine sensibility. She was practised in the languishments of romantic softness; she could adapt her smile or fashion her tear, to touch that chord which vibrates in bosoms unenlightened by the finely organizing hand of nature. Her mind was enfeebled by indulgence, and her temper peevish, because it had no stimulating griefs to rouse its energies, or to teach it, by the realities of woe, to shake off the visions of a capricious imagination.

Mrs. Morley knew that her sister's disposition was but ill suited to bear the persecutions of fortune, or the malignity of a world, which never fails to triumph over the fallen and unhappy. She knew that those, who in her prosperous moments hovered round her, as the insect myriads bask in the beams of summer, would, when the gloomy hour overshadowed her perspective, fly with the swiftness of the storm, or linger in her path, to taunt her with reproaches. She was taught, by the unerring monitor Experience, that fortune bears the talisman of fate; that the magnet which draws the busy phalanx of society together, is formed of gold; and that its only substitute, placed in the grasp of poverty, is a petrifying wand, which freezes all the inroads to the heart.—Yet she would have willingly endured the load of mortification which Julia's misguided conduct had drawn upon herself; because her proud mind would have placed her beyond the reach of calumny or insult. She would, in the consciousness of innate qualities, which depend not on the perishable basis of worldly splendour, have laughed at the low scorn, the vulgar arrogance of less ennobled beings: and even in the meanest habitation of indigence, wounded by ingratitude, assailed by malevolence, chilled by neglect, or irritated by the insolence of taunting pride, she would have been the creature nature made; on which a stamp was set that eclipsed all less adventitious honours.

The secondary cause of Mrs. Morley's inquietude originated in her separation from Mrs. Sedgley. They had built their fabric of esteem on the firm foundation of congenial virtues, cemented by congenial sorrows. The strong power of sympathy had wound a spell about their hearts, which seemed to exclude every sentiment less pure and less exalted. Severe was the pang which was destined to divide them; while each commenced a new and painful journey, either to behold the flowers of fancy prematurely wither; or to know that weeds, thriving as they were destructive, would perpetually annoy them.

Mrs. Sedgley would willingly have quitted the dramatic company, to participate in the precarious fortunes of her friend; but the manager informed her that he would exact the penalty of her engagement, if she presumed to consult her own felicity, in preference to his interest or the good opinion of her patrons.

Early in the morning, Mrs. Morley, after receiving her discharge from the manager, set out in a stage-coach for London. Her heart was full of sorrow: she had passed a night of sleepless meditation. The labyrinths of life were once more to be trodden; the opening path was dark and dreary; she had no hand to guide her through its bewildering mazes. The nerve of feeling was still throbbing with a mixture of disdain and disappointment; she believed herself to be the most ill-fated of the human race; and, as all the joys and sorrows of existence depend, in a great measure, on the force of imagination, she could not have been more wretched had she been really what she fancied.

But her pride was still more powerful than her misfortunes; again the inborn spirit of her soul armed her with courage to resist oppression. She had been deeply wounded, but the blow was given by a vulgar hand; she had been treated with scorn, but it was the low scorn of recreant ignorance; she had been neglected, but there was distinction in the neglect of unenlightened beings. She had been hurled from affluence to indigence, from the sunny smiles of flattering folly, to the stern and darkening frown of unequivocal adversity—that true delineator of mankind, which gives the light and shade of life, drawn by the hand of nature.

On the first day's journey, where the stage-coach rested its passengers to dine, while they were at table a chaise and four stopped to change horses. Mrs. Morley was prompted by curiosity, natural to active minds, and rising hastily, flew towards the window. But as her steps advanced the circulation quickened at her heart.—The traveller was Mr. Morley.

Language cannot describe her distress. The alteration in her looks, for she was become pale and meagre; the shabby appearance of her dress; the deep dejection which marked her features; the mode of her travelling; and the profession, which necessity had compelled her to adopt, without the knowledge of her husband, all conspired to shake her fortitude and to awaken her apprehensions.

For the first time in her life, the littleness of worldly vanity usurped a momentary influence over her feelings. She felt a faint flush of shame diffusing itself on her cheek, while her eyes, bent downwards, contemplated her half-soiled gown, of the coarsest muslin; her once white gloves, which had served for many a scenic exhibition; and her worn out veil, through whose more than woven transparency her tears were visible to every observer.

There, thought she, there sits the uninjured husband, who has driven me from the home which I have not dishonoured. He is prosperous and happy; he revels in the luxury of his heart's utmost wishes. She now observed the postillions just going to mount their horses; her heart beat convulsively; she again looked at herself, then at the chaise. At this moment the landlord, who waited on the passengers, reminded her that the stage would soon set out, and desired her not to keep the dinner on the table. "We have more hungry guests waiting," said he, "while you are amusing yourself with gazing through the windows."

"You are in great haste," said Mrs. Morley.

"Why there is nothing to look at that can concern you," interrupted the surly host.

"Mind your own affairs, and do not be impertinent," replied Mrs. Morley, peevishly.

"Impertinent indeed!" repeated the innkeeper; "I like to see stage-coach travellers giving themselves airs, like people of consequence. I shall remove the dinner, for that is, at least, my business."—He was preparing to fulfil his word, when Mrs. Morley, urged on by irritation and distress, opened the glass door before which she stood, and, without the power to utter a syllable, rushed towards the carriage.

Here the pride of her heart triumphed over its sensibility. The insulting language of an undiscriminating stranger was less supportable than even the resentment of an unfeeling husband. Her power of speech was still denied her; but her eyes, her whole countenance spoke with an eloquence that mocked the force of words; her cheek became more pale; a tear still lingered on it; it was the pure appeal of nature to the heart; and no heart but such a one as Mrs. Morley's could have resisted its persuasion.

Mrs. Morley attempted to articulate, "Do you not know me?" but her lip quivered, and her tone of voice was scarcely audible. A loud laugh from her fellow passengers, who had placed themselves at the window to watch the result of her extraordinary conduct, augmented her distress, while she leant against the wheel of her husband's carriage, overpowered and feeble. Mr. Morley descended; and raising her veil, beheld a countenance that would have softened a soul of adamant. Her eyes were closed, her lip was colourless, her dark brows were convulsed, and the tear still glistened, as if the coldness of her cheek had frozen it.

CHAPTER XXIX

Mr. Morley supported her on his arm and they entered the inn. The landlord bowed them into the best apartment, now smiling and now afraid; rather wishing to place the attention of the post-horse traveller to the account of humanity, than supposing that the stage-coach passenger was of that rank in life which vulgar minds consider as the most respectable.

As soon as Mr. Morley and his wife were left alone, with a tone half severe and half tremulous, he addressed her. "Martha," said he, "how comes it that you are in this altered state, an unprotected wanderer? What has produced this change?"

"Necessity," replied Mrs. Morley.

"Whither are you going?" was the second question.

"Indeed I scarcely know."

"Whence came you?"

She named the place which she had quitted that morning.

"What was your business there?"

Mrs. Morley sighed, and after a few moments of struggling hesitation replied, "To obtain the means of life, without doing any thing dishonourable that may embitter it by remembrance."

"What were the means?"

"The exercise of those talents which heaven sometimes bestows as the substitutes for fortune."

"I do not comprehend you," said Mr. Morley.

"By a profession—a dramatic profession."

"A strolling actress! God forbid!" exclaimed Mr. Morley.

"Even so," replied Martha calmly; "for I felt assured that I might do credit to a pursuit which had not the power, with all its perils, to disgrace me."

Mr. Morley's high-bearing severity was humbled to the very extent of humiliation by this avowal; for with all his vaunted philanthropy, he had yet to learn that genius was the first and noblest gift of the Creator—a gift which does not perish with the frail and mortal compound which, having borne the varying impressions of its destined hour, fades into nothing.

After pacing the room for some minutes, he resumed the conversation. "Why have you disgraced yourself—your family?" said he.

"Rather ask me how, so pressed by poverty, so deserted, so scorned, I have prevented both my own and my family's dishonour."

"So irreligious a profession!" interrupted Mr. Morley.

"Religion and humanity—at least what seemed such—deserted me to perish!" Mr. Morley shuddered.

"But your imprudent conduct," said he, after a short pause, "your rash defiance of my authority, your protection of a bastard———"

"I only snatched it from destruction," replied Mrs. Morley: "it had no friends, no father that would acknowledge it. Its mother had been deceived, and then deserted, by a libertine."

"That was not your business. You could not help it: you were not accessary to the crime, and had therefore no right to share the obloquy attending it."

"If none will feel for those that err, where are we to hope for reformation?" said Mrs. Morley. "Oh! if the first fault were but more frequently forgiven, how few would commit a second! But it is the chilling breath of reproof that chases the blush of honest shame, while it fixes a smile of scorn upon the cheek that braves all the throbbings of compunction."

"You have been imposed on—you have disgraced your feelings by believing the fabricated tale of some hypocritical impostor. You would have had me held forth as an example of credulity, in addition to others which the world has seen; and by persuading me to sanction a supposed child of reputable extraction, had sheltered under my roof the illegitimate offspring of a shameless mother: you would have persuaded me that the blood of a noble parent flowed in its veins, while its vital source in reality sprang from plebeian baseness."

"I never wished to do more than humanity would have sanctioned; and had I done less, I should not have been worthy of your confidence," said Mrs. Morley.

"Where is the child?" inquired her husband.

"I consigned it to the protection of its father," replied Mrs. Morley.

"Of its father!" repeated Mr. Morley, with a penetrating look. "I thought you were a stranger to its origin! Who was its father?"

"A man of rank and fortune," answered Martha, blushing. "But," added she, with a confused tone and manner, "I am not bound to reveal that which you will———"

"What?" interrupted Mr. Morley, sternly.

"You overpower me," said Martha; "you intimidate me by your violence: but you shall never force me to betray a being whom I would ever hold nearest to my heart, even though you menaced to arrest its beating."

"Infamous woman!" exclaimed Mr. Morley; "the infant was your own!"

Mrs. Morley smiled with half-stifled scorn, but made no answer.

"Your smile is but a tacit confirmation of your guilt," said Mr. Morley, now more impetuously vindictive than ever. "Your falsehood in unquestionable. Your low, licentious occupation marks the tenor of your mind. All the claims of honour and religion are violated by your conduct; and your name will be handed down to posterity with disgrace, if it be not consigned to perpetual oblivion."

"I can endure your reproaches, because I feel conscious of not deserving them," replied Mrs. Morley: "but no mortal power shall force me to acknowledge that saving a friendless child from misery or death is infamous or even culpable. Its father was a high-born libertine, a *right honourable* deceiver, who had betrayed its mother under promises the most sacred."

"What is the mother?" interrupted Mr. Morley.

"A woman, and therefore entitled to the protection of the being who deceived her."

"What is her situation—her rank in life?"

"She is also a strolling actress."

"And you defend her! You talk of her virtues—her misfortunes! Ridiculous! Return with me to Morley-house: consent to seclude yourself for ever from the world's reproaches; and evince, by penitence, a just sense of your past folly: I will then conceal your disgrace."

"Rather say my sorrows—those sorrows to which distress and persecution have exposed me," said Mrs. Morley. "It is easy to condemn: but it is the privilege of Fortune's favourites; and the unhappy have no remedy but silent scorn."

"My heart aches when I reflect on your imprudence."

"Your pride shrinks when you recollect my humiliations. Would to heaven, that your conscience were equally susceptible of my wrongs!" replied Martha.

"If you can bear seclusion, my house is open to receive you," cried Mr. Morley.

"I must be received acquitted, or not received at all," replied Martha.

"Then follow your own propensities," cried Mr. Morley; "be wretched by inclination—by choice be degraded! Abjure all the refinements of sensibility, all the moral graces that once adorned you." So saying, he quitted the room; and before Mrs. Morley had power to expostulate on the impetuosity of his conduct the chaise departed from the inn door, leaving her to reflect on the benignity and feeling of a professed philanthropist.

CHAPTER XXX

After heaving a deep sigh, which in some degree unburthened her full heart, she returned to the place where she had left her travelling companions. On her entering the parlour, every countenance evinced the predominating opinion of every mind, and all conspired to betray a secret pleasure at that disappointment which wrung her breast with unutterable anguish.

She now felt herself faint, having tasted nothing since daybreak. The dinner-table had been removed during her interview with Mr. Morley, and the stage-coachman informed the passengers that the horses were ready to depart.

Two females, who had been the morning companions of Mrs. Morley's journey, now consulted each other in an audible whisper. "It is the same," said one; "I now remember having seen her at Bath! She eloped from her husband with a young libertine nobleman, and has ever since been roving about the country with strolling actors. For my part I would rather forfeit my place in the coach, than sit beside a woman of such a description."

"And if you quit the carriage, what will become of me?" cried the other. "It is evident, from her conduct since we stopped to dine, that she is capable of any improper behavior. The man with whom she quitted our society was——"

"My husband, madam," interrupted Mrs. Morley sternly.

"I thought so!" exclaimed the first, who had objected to her society.

"Why, madam, did you think so?" inquired Mrs. Morley.

"By the evident contempt with which he treated you," replied the fastidious traveller. "When a husband abandons his wife, she must expect that the world will shew her little kindness."

"Though while she is countenanced by him, the most licentious profligacy may be passed over in silent toleration," replied Mrs. Morley. "Shame, shame on such distinctions! Shame on that custom which permits an unblushing wife to brave the eye of scorn, because her deviation from propriety is attended with the most culpable hypocrisy, and patiently endured by a dishonoured husband."

"Yours, at least, was not of that description," said the moral-mending traveller.

"No, madam; thank heaven, my husband never was dishonored," replied Mrs. Morley; "though he is disgraced by exposing an unoffending woman to the insolence of vulgar commentators."

The fastidious observer now rung the bell with violence. "Order a chaise for this lady and myself!" said she, pointing to her fellow-traveller. "It is not possible for women of reputation to proceed in the same carriage with strolling actresses." Mrs. Morley smiled. The stage-driver again reminded them that he was waiting, and Mrs. Morley, with one male passenger, took her seat; leaving the over-delicate travellers to reflect at leisure.

The reader has probably, in the journey of existence, remarked that the most scrupulous part of the female sex are generally those who feel the strongest disposition to err. Some, indeed there are who, their vices being varnished over by the golden hand of Prosperity, suddenly assume a vulgar self-importance which, so far from obliterating their faults, draws them more glaringly into notice; and, shame on the false morality of the age! such women, with no *mental* passport to respect, with no claim excepting the ill-acquired wealth which they unblushingly display, receive the countenance even of the most fastidiously virtuous. The stage-coach commentator was a female of this description.

CHAPTER XXXI

It happened that Mrs. Morley's remaining companion was a man "learned in the law," of most conciliating manners, and so indefatigable in the labours of his profession, that he never lost an opportunity of urging a suit. His sagacity was equal to his industry; and at first glance he perceived that Mrs. Morley was a fair subject for his attention.

They had not travelled far when Mr. Snatchem commenced his pleadings with all the mystery of confused and incomprehensible explanation. He assured Mrs. Morley that neither her talents nor her persecutions had escaped his notice; and he declared that though the Leadenheads were a very powerful and numerous family, he should feel the most superlative gratification in opposing the claims of insulted genius to the sordid arrogance of ostentatious insignificance. Mr. Snatchem also informed Mrs. Morley that her opponents were more feared than honoured, respected, or beloved; that there were many worthy and far more popular persons in the county who would rejoice in the humiliation of the parties; and that it would procure him infinite praise as well as pleasure to commence a process, which would at once avenge her wrongs, and expose the malevolence of her enemies.

Mrs. Morley's feelings had been too severely wounded by the Leadenhead cabal[1] not to make her heart throb with delight at the idea of retaliation. The insolent contempt and scorn with which she had been treated; the low and malignant arts that had been practiced to mortify and vex her, the miserable exultation which they displayed when her repose and her fame were made the subjects of their subtle machinations; determined her to lose no opportunity of seeking retribution. Mr. Snatchem was the willing instrument of revenge; and Mrs. Morley, after explaining all her causes of complaint, authorised him to commence a suit without farther consultation.

On Mrs. Morley's arrival in London, she again repaired to her old lodgings in the vicinity of Bloomsbury-square. A faint hope

---

[1] An intrigue, or group of people united by some design.

suggested to her mind the possibility that during her absence lord Francis had not wholly forgotten her: it was probable, she thought, that he had either sent or called to inquire after her; and, at a moment when the heart is heavy with the pressure of sorrow, the smallest proof of kindness comes with redoubled power to solace. Lord Francis was, to all external appearance, too amiable to be known and not esteemed by a woman of Mrs. Morley's judgment and susceptibility: but the pride of her heart was still its impenetrable safeguard against every encroachment of the passions, which might in the smallest degree tend to her degradation.

Her lodgings were vacant, and she engaged them. Weary of a profession which had already presented such distressing vicissitudes, she was again at a loss to determine on any plan for her future support.[1] The busy metropolis, it is true, presented a variety of roads to independence: but a female without protection, or even the power to apply for character to her own relatives—a being, who seemed alone even in the midst of multitudes, had little to hope for from a world selfish and prejudging. She knew that men would seek to betray her; that women, through envy or malignity, would affect to suppose her reprehensible. With these opinions, which were the result of experience and reflection, she resolved to adopt some new mode of obtaining a subsistence; and after various resolutions, rapidly formed and as rapidly relinquished; after weighing and rejecting, musing and trembling, hoping, fearing, and anticipating the chances for and against her in the revolving wheel of fortune, she determined on making the modern experiment, both for the attainment of fame and profit, by writing a Novel.

She was now at a loss what kind of story to delineate. The terrific had been worn to a mere spectre; the lively required either keen satire or genuine wit to make it tolerably palatable; the sentimental would no longer suit the languid nerves of those who were devoted to dissipation; and the pathetic, which described the force of enthusiastic honour and genuine sensibility, was deemed both gothic and unnatural; chivalry was out of fashion; the tales

---

[1]   For a contemporary survey of a genteel woman's employment options, see the excerpts from Priscilla Wakefield's *Reflections on the Present Condition of the Female Sex* in Appendix D, 309–15.

of adventurous knights were considered as ridiculously romantic; and the sober lessons of good sense and morality had long been consigned, exclusively, to the shelves of boarding-school libraries. During six weeks she confined herself to incessant labour, at the end of which time she completed a work of two volumes. The story was melancholy, the portraits drawn from living characters, and the title both interesting and attractive.

Elated with the hope of attaining at least a sprig of that prolific laurel which in these reading days spreads its wide and pliant branches over every species of literature, Mrs. Morley, with her lettered bantling, set out for the mart of mental traffic, yclept the Row of Paternoster.[1] After offering her first-born to a variety of patrons, she was informed that the market was already overstocked, and that the species of composition in which she had indulged her fancy was become a very drug, only palatable to splenetic valetudinarians[2] and boarding-school misses. She sighed as she quitted the renowned emporium of genius, and with a desponding heart directed her footsteps towards the more fashionable vicinity of Pall-Mall and Bond-street.

There she again found obstacles almost insurmountable. The characters were drawn from life, and the booksellers were fearful of prosecutions. After various attempts to dispose of her literary treasure, a dashing publisher, in order to encourage a first attempt, and in compliance with her earnest solicitations, gave her ten pounds for the work; assuring her, at the same time, with mortifying commiseration, that he should lose very considerably by the bargain.

"We have our warehouses full of unsold sentimental novels already," said Mr. Index: "they only sell for waste paper; and you may frequently see 'The Tears of Genius,'[3] 'Moral Tales,' 'Wedded

---

[1] Paternoster Row was the address of many booksellers and publishers, including Longman and Rees, the firm that published *The Natural Daughter*. The word *bantling*, which frequently bore connotations of illegitimate birth, was often used with reference to books as well as children.

[2] Invalids, convalescents, or persons generally in poor health.

[3] Robinson was undoubtedly familiar with two poems entitled "The Tears of Genius." The first, published in 1774 by Samuel Jackson Pratt, was an elegy on the death of Oliver Goldsmith. The second, published by Richard Brinsley Sheridan in 1780, was a monody on the death of David Garrick, Robinson's dramatic mentor. The following titles, including those in the paragraph below, identify popular themes rather than specific novels.

Love,' 'Disinterested Attachment,' 'The Felicities of Friendship,' and 'The Sublime System of Social Sympathy,' lining trunks, or enveloping the merchandize of pastry-cooks and cheese-mongers." Mrs. Morley sighed. Mr. Index continued.

"If you have any talent for satire, you may write a work that would be worth purchasing: or if your fertile pen can make a story out of some recent popular event, such as an highly-fashioned elopement, a deserted, distracted husband, an abandoned wife, an ungrateful runaway daughter, or a son ruined by sharpers; with such a title as 'Noble Daring; or, The Disinterested Lovers;' *Chacun à son Tour*; or, The Modern Husband;' 'Passion in Leading-Strings; or, Love's Captive;' 'Modern Wives and Antique Spouses,' 'Old Dowagers and Schoolboy Lovers,' or any thing from real life of equal celebrity or notoriety, your fortune is made; your works will sell, and you will either be admired or feared by the whole phalanx of fashionable readers; particularly if you have the good luck to be menaced with a prosecution."

"Heaven forbid!" cried Mrs. Morley.

"O! I see you are but a novice in the arcanum of literature," said the bookseller. "You are too timid ever to obtain the laurel of victory: you will never dash into the broad stream of popularity, or bathe in the luxurious sea of satirical celebrity: you will never wield the keen-edged weapon in the field of ridicule, or scatter, amidst the flowers of Parnassus,[1] the seeds of critical contention: you will write with a mere pen!"

"What else should I write with?" said Mrs. Morley.

"A lancet, to be sure. You should cut your subject keenly; make your operations salutary; teach your patients to tremble, while you cure them of their most obstinate and contagious follies. A pen! ridiculous! Who now thinks of writing with a pen, except a few old, hum-drum novelists, who convert sermons into romances, and make the press tremble, while it groans with their ponderous faragoes of moral insipidity. No, no; if you wish for celebrity, write with a lancet; touch your subject lightly, neatly, but effectually; and, above all things, mind the title. Nothing in these times will sell so highly as a title."

---

[1] A mountain in Greece, associated with Apollo and the Muses.

"Indeed!" said Mrs. Morley.

"Most assuredly. A title is the thing above all others. It pleases every order of the high world, and charms into admiration every species of the low: it will cover a multitude of faults: a kind of compendious errata, which sets to rights all the errors of a work, and makes it popular, however incorrect and illiterate it may appear to the eyes of fastidious criticisers. Mind a title. Do not forget that a title is a wonderful harmonizer of things, in all ranks and all opinions of men, both morally and politically." Mrs. Morley smiled.

"How do you mean to make your book sell?" continued Mr. Index. "You should write a Dedication, full of fine words and laboured panegyric. That part of your business should be done skillfully. A feather of the finest dimensions, dipped in honey, will compose an excellent introductory passport. You must be careful to enumerate all the good qualities of your patron, and to skim lightly over all the bad ones. You must profess yourself his obedient and devoted servant; and before you conclude your tribute to his many inestimable virtues, you must not forget to declare that you abhor flattery, and that your mind is as independent as your writings."

While Mrs. Morley was listening to the intelligent Mr. Index, a young woman entered the shop. She came to change a book. "I want another novel," said she, "but I have forgot the name."

"Why you had this not an hour since," said Mr. Index. "How troublesome these women are! They never get through more than the first six pages; they then dip into the middle, and conclude their reading by glancing over the catastrophe. Were it not for the labours of some novel-manufactories, we should never be able to satisfy our female customers." Then turning to the shopman, Mr. Index added, "Send any thing: the lady never looks beyond the table of contents."

"It was something about Virtue Rewarded,"[1] said the girl, recollecting herself.

"O, child! that is a work of such gothic antiquity, that we have not had one copy in our shop these twenty years. Nobody would

---

[1]   *Virtue Rewarded* is the subtitle of Samuel Richardson's popular epistolary novel *Pamela* (1740–42).

think of dosing over such dull lessons. If your mistress wants something to make her melancholy, I recommend 'Delicate Distresses,'[1] 'Victims of Sensibility,' 'The Sorrows of Love,' 'The Deserted Wife'——"

"O dear, sir!" interrupted the girl, "we have enough of those already. My mistress is confined to her bed with a putrid fever, and I believe she has not even money to pay the doctor." Mrs. Morley shuddered.

"Is she very ill?" inquired Mr. Index: "Is her disorder catching?"

"Yes, sir; and she sends back the book you chose for her this morning, because it is full of distresses and misfortunes."

"To infect half the town with her disorder," cried Mr. Index angrily. "I have known no less than four persons destroyed within the last six weeks, merely by the infection which has been conveyed through the medium of novels.[2] Nothing can be more destructive. It is really singular that sick people will read works of genius, while the stalls are groaning with sermons at sixpence a dozen."

"O here is the name of the book," said the girl, taking a paper from the leaves of the returned novel. It was written on the superscription of a torn letter. Mrs. Morley's curiosity was excited by the mournful account which the girl had given of her mistress's situation; therefore, after reading the name, she followed the messenger into the street.

"Is your mistress really ill?"

"I am afraid she is dying ma'am."

"Take her this paper," said Martha, "and tell her that Mrs. Morley will call upon her to-morrow morning. Mind that you do not lose it; it is a five-pound bank-note." The girl took the money, and with joy visible in her countenance hastened to relieve her suffering mistress.

Reader, accuse not Martha of unthinking prodigality. The poor, the afflicted female, whose sorrows pierced her heart, was her sister—the deserted Julia.

---

[1]   Robinson may be referring to Elizabeth Griffith's epistolary novel *Delicate Distress* (1769). Like Robinson, Griffith had a brief stage career before she turned to writing as a livelihood. The other titles identify recurring themes rather than specific novels.

[2]   A comic literalization of the standard complaint that novels were pernicious agents of moral infection.

CHAPTER XXXII

The night passed sleepless. Mrs. Morley's pillow was uneasy, because her mind wandered to that where disease and vexation fevered the brain of her imprudent sister. She rose as soon as the shops were opened, and hastened to Julia's lodgings. As she approached the door her heart beat quickly with a mixture of pity and affection. She longed, yet dreaded to behold the altered face of her proud and unfeeling enemy: but that enemy was overwhelmed with sickness and with sorrow, and Martha almost taught herself to think she was her friend.

Still her bosom throbbed convulsively. There was a sensation of forgiving tenderness; but there was also a strong sense of injury, which struggled for pre-eminence. Nothing could prevent Martha's seeing her sister; yet something told her that there was meanness in the visit. This sister had driven her from her natural home; from the bosom of her mother; from the world, from its society.—But Julia was in distress; she was punished for her unkindness; she wanted that support which the industry and talents of Martha enabled her to bestow.—"I am favoured by Heaven," said she, sighing; "poor Julia is an outcast; she has no friend.

"Yes, yes, Julia! thou hast still one friend," continued Martha, as she knocked at the door of her sister's lodgings.

The master of the house informed her that the lady had departed the preceding night; leaving a letter for Mrs. Morley, which he then delivered.—Martha's hand trembled as she took it.—She thought, she hoped, to have embraced a repentant sister; to have consoled her, and to have lent her aid in shielding her bosom from the world's unkindness. She endeavoured to break the seal, but was prevented by the thought, that, perhaps the contents of the letter might be unpleasing or even painful. Her heart was softened, full, and palpitating. Her tears were ready to rush into her eyes in the street. I shall only expose myself, thought she. I will take the letter to my lodgings.

She hastened along one street, then along another. Every moment acquiring courage, and again losing it, while the letter was still the object of inquietude. At length, unable to bear the anxiety which lay heavy on her mind, she called a hackney-coach, and entering it hastily, bade the coachman drive to Bloomsbury-square. No sooner had he lashed his wretched animals into motion, than Mrs. Morley opened Julia's letter. It contained a request that she would not trouble herself with affairs which did not concern her. For, that Julia had made a vow never again to own a strolling actress as a sister. Mrs. Morley was nearly overwhelmed. The coach arrived at her lodgings, and she passed the remainder of the day in regret that was unutterable.

On the following morning Mrs. Morley set out to make inquiries after little Fanny; and to her inexpressible chagrin, she heard, that lady Louisa Franklin had, only ten days before, departed from the metropolis, taking her infant *protegée* as the companion of her journey. "Poor Fanny!" sighed Mrs. Morley; "she would not have treated me as Julia did; and yet I did not love my sister less. But there is something in kindred blood that freezes, when the blast of poverty blows cold: it is the bright, the summer sun of prosperous fortune, that draws forth smiles and offices of kindness."

Mrs. Morley then made a visit to Crutched-Friars, where she was informed that her mother had removed from London, and afterwards had died of a broken heart, in consequence of Julia's imprudent conduct. By this intelligence Martha's affliction seemed completed. Her mother dead! an orphan's misery was hers; for she had no friend to solace or to protect her. Her unfeeling husband was too proud to recal her wandering footsteps, or even to destroy the poisonous weeds that, growing in her path, menaced her destruction. A wife, a young and lovely woman, exposed to the insidious machinations of man; deserted, driven forth to seek for support, alone and stigmatized!—How many, like Martha, have been hurried on to ruin, by the sharp sting of kindred persecution! How many generous, feeling, noble natures have withered in obscurity and sorrow; while dullness, ignorance, and overweening pride revel in luxury, and set all the claims of modest merit at defiance.

CHAPTER XXXIII

Once more left with no resource but that which would arise from her own talents, Mrs. Morley resolved on making another effort. The wide world was still before her: she had for many months read the book of human nature, and was now tolerably acquainted with the various characters it presented. At first she thought of dipping her pen in the Heliconian fountain;[1] but after sending several poetical pieces to the magazines and newspapers, she found that her thoughts were too refined, her subjects too delicate for the vitiated taste of the present day.—She could not pen the coarse *double entendre* of a modern epigram; nor could she court the patronage of dullness, by offering flattering incense at the shrine of vanity. This mode of obtaining an independence was therefore relinquished.

She then thought of gaining a livelihood by the dull drudgery of diffusing knowledge in a seminary of fashionable education; and therefore offered her services, as the daughter of the late wealthy Mrs. Popkins, in the capacity of a teacher at a boarding school near the metropolis. Her manners and appearance interested the feelings of her employer, and she was engaged at a handsome salary, to instruct the young pupils in English, needle-work, and every other species of minor accomplishments.

Here indeed her patience was put to the trial, by the stupidity of some; the infantine impertinence of others; the budding pride of the high-born; the pert vulgarity of the low; while the dawning consequence of the wealthy, and the confirmed arrogance of the dull-minded presented to her view a little phalanx of future tyrants; coquettes in the bud of beauty; satirists yet poring over the columns of a spelling-book; wits in their slate exercises; with a long list of embryo poetesses, novelists, tragedians, prudes, peeresses, and petticoat philosophers.

---

[1] The Hippocrene, fountain of the Muses on Mount Helicon. The following commentary on the literary marketplace seems rather ironic when one considers all the poems that Robinson herself published in magazines and newspapers and the particular praise she received for composing verses that exuded an air of delicacy and refinement. The irony certainly would not have been lost on readers who found "Martha's" poems from *The Natural Daughter* reprinted in *The Morning Post.*

Several months had passed, and Mrs. Morley, (who still assumed the name of Denison,) by her attention to the duties of her occupation, commanded the esteem of her employer and affection of her pupils, when one evening a chaise and four stopped at the gates, and a young lady was immediately introduced as an inmate. The gentleman who accompanied the new scholar departed: Mrs. Morley received the juvenile charge, and conducted her from the parlour to the school-room. She was near eleven years old, pert, bold, and forward; her tone was arrogant, her demeanour haughty, her brow elevated, and her glances contemptuous; she scarcely condescended to converse with her companions, and passed nearly the remainder of the evening in gloomy silence; making notes on the table of her little brain either to the prejudice or advantage of every one present.

Mrs. Morley's rest was disturbed by unpleasing anticipations; she beheld a new scene of perplexity now opening before her; she was uneasy, vexed, and apprehensive. Gentle reader, she had cause for her inquietude: the pupil whose arrival had been marked with such unfavourable prospects, was the youngest daughter of Mr. Humphrey Leadenhead.

The name of Denison was still fresh in the memory of Miss Sophinisba Leadenhead; but the pleasure which she would have felt in indulging a family propensity, was counteracted by that powerful silencer Family Pride, and she did not acquaint her governess that Mrs. Morley was a wandering comedian; because such information might lead to a discovery that she was also the sister of the imprudent Julia. But though Sophinisba's prudence kept her silent, as far as her tone of voice was within hearing of her governess, she did not fail to communicate the secret to her juvenile companions. The malignant tale was whispered with confidence; and Mrs. Morley's authority decreased in proportion as her character became doubtful. On the school breaking up at the Easter vacation, every heart was throbbing to unravel the important enigma; and the mistress of the seminary on recalling her young family to the labours of education, found the number diminished from fifty to five and thirty. The cause of so extraordinary a desertion was demanded; and her answer was, that persons of fortune and respectability could not suffer the morals of their daughters to be contaminated by the loose opinions and familiar manners of an itinerant actress. Such were the doctrines of ignorance and prejudice; and the reader will judge more correctly on the discernment and rationality of the sentence, when he is informed, that of those fastidious commentators, whose imperious mandate would have consigned a deserving object to shame and to affliction, there was not an individual whose rank in life soared above mediocrity; while those of loftier birth and more enlightened education, respected the merit and applauded the industry which had led Mrs. Morley to adopt a profession, at once honourable to her heart and creditable to her talents.

The consequence of this unfortunate discovery was Mrs. Morley's dismission from the habitation of her employer. Once more destined to seek for support, she returned to London; and again determined on exercising her talents till fortune should present a new prospect of independence. Mrs. Morley, on taking leave of her juvenile pupils, wrote the following stanzas, which she left with her employer; who, while she felt the necessity of parting with her, lamented the severity which occasioned their separation.

As o'er the world, by sorrow prest,
　　I wander, sad and weary;
In hopes to find a place of rest,
　　From scenes forlorn and dreary:
Where'er I go, I'm doom'd to trace,
If fortune smiles, the smiling face:
But if she frowns, I'm sure to see,
On every face, a frown for *me*!

When morning blushes through her tears,
　　And nature flaunts her treasures,
How gaudy every path appears,
　　How rich, in boundless pleasures!
But if the dawn in misty gloom
Still veils the flouret's vivid bloom,
How droops in shade the loftiest tree,
Whose spreading boughs had shelter'd *me*!

Nor truth nor feeling can insure
   The friend that's ever smiling;
Worth cannot worldly mis'ry cure,
   Its darkest hours beguiling;
This heart, which owns the purest flame,
Must patient throb, nor dare to blame,
Since fortune's frown, the fates decree,
Through ev'ry scene shou'd follow *me*!

Thus all things light or dark appear,
   As fortune cheers or saddens;
For time flies slow when grief is near,
   But swift when transport gladdens.
Hope is a transient summer dream,
Where visions gay and flattering seem;
But truth and reason wake to see
Them waste away and fade like *me*!

O! come, capricious Fortune, blind,
   Subdue this bosom's feeling;
Make dim the fire that warms my mind,
   Thence all its fervour stealing;
Teach me the sordid servile art,
To dress in low disguise the heart,
Then every face shall cheerful be,
And wear a gentle smile for *me*![1]

CHAPTER XXXIV

Mrs. Morley, on her return to London, hired a convenient though not splendid lodging at the west end of the town. The change in her situation, from that which her former days had

---

[1]   This poem was published under Robinson's own name in *The Morning Post* on September 9, 1799.

presented, produced little or no effect upon her feelings. Conscious that her present plan of economy originated in a proud spirit, which panted for independence, as well as in a desire to act honourably, she little cared what an interested world thought respecting the apparent decrease of her usual expenses. Mrs. Morley knew that the mind derived no importance from adventitious circumstances; she therefore left it to the dull and the unenlightened to display the only distinctions they possessed, the favours of fortune; while she looked down with a sigh of commiseration on the weary children of folly and dissipation.

From her window she observed the passing throngs, like the gaudy ephemera of a summer noon; the glittering atoms, which dazzle for an hour, and then shrink into nothing. There did she contemplate, with a philosophic smile, the motley idols of capricious fortune: the light gossomary visions of a day, borne on the gale and towering in the warm regions of a prosperous destiny; or shrinking from the cutting blasts of poverty, and creeping to oblivion.[1]

Often did she mark the cold retiring aspect of deserting friendship, the freezing half bend of distant civility, or the familiar nod of low presuming vanity. She saw features fixed in the unmeaning cast of vacancy, while they passed side-glancing at her habitation; and faces aghast with wonder that a female should evince both prudence and resolution, even in the very vortex of vice and prodigality. She obtained little credit from the malevolent observer for that correct demeanor which marked a proud elevation of mind, even amidst the humiliations of fortune; while from the fastidious she scarcely obtained the justice of credibility.

It was then that she *really* knew many of those worldly associates who fly with the warm beams of a summer destiny; many who had obtrusively paid homage to her mind, and obsequiously courted her society, when she was above the necessity of seeking patronage, but who now, grown suddenly fastidious, scarcely

---

[1] This description of Martha closely resembles brief reports about Robinson that appeared in the *Morning Post* in the summer of 1799: "Mrs. Robinson, from her temporary habitation in Piccadilly, looks down upon the *little great*, without envying their less permanent distinctions" (June 1); "Mrs. Robinson, from her Piccadilly window, has an opportunity of drawing characters from *life*; and her pen is equal to the variety of its subjects" (June 7).

condescended to recognize her. Indeed she was evidently changed by the vicissitudes of her destiny! for adversity so alters the features, that even our "nearest friends do not know us;" and that cheek which used to smile, and that lip which was the placid emblem of a contented spirit, were now pale with the incessant ruminations of the brain, and expressive of a scornful pride which, originating in conscious rectitude, disdained to court the ignorant or flatter the unworthy.

Various were the sensations of her mind while she looked down upon the exalted, and pitied the unfeeling; for often did she behold the audacious smile of uplifted vice upon that cheek from which she had chaced the tear, when poverty and shame had bade it appeal to her for pity. Often did she commiserate the ostentation of overbearing vulgarity, when she observed the insolence or the enormity of women, who, setting the grace of decency at defiance, recalled to memory their recent follies; who wasted in prodigality and tasteless shew that wealth, which might have been applied to nobler and to better purposes.

From the window of her new habitation she daily endured the obtrusive glances of all ranks of persons; from the venerable libertine and ennobled shrew, to the juvenile arbitress of fashion, and the titled school-boy, who had escaped from the Gothic walls of Eton College,[1] to become a disciplinarian in the field of military prowess. Often did the smile of contempt involuntarily pass over her lip, when she interpreted the significant looks of those who calculate the mind's value by the outward decorations of life; often did she pity the low scorn of unenlightened natures, when, born to that rank which they dishonoured, women of equivocal virtue considered themselves as Mrs. Morley's superiors; while in reality they were as far below her in the scale of intellect, as they were more elevated on the revolving wheel of fortune.

But the most painful sensation which her heart felt, as she surveyed the passing multitude, was that which was inflicted by forgetfulness: for in the busy scene, it was her lot to contemplate

---

[1] Eton College, a famous prepatory school for boys, was founded in 1440 by Henry VI. Cf. Thomas Gray's "Ode on a Distant Prospect of Eton College" (1742).

beings whom she had in her more prosperous days preserved from abject misery; who now repaid with low malignant triumph that charitable impulse which warmed her heart, when they had flown to her for succour; when, abandoned by the world, exposed to ridicule, branded with shame, and stigmatized for infamy, they had experienced the benevolence of her nature, and blessed that pity which contributed to the preservation of an existence, now marked with the worst badge of human depravity, *Ingratitude*!!

Reader—lest the miscreants should be rescued from oblivion by the pen of recording indignation, their names shall for the present rest in silence. But whenever the vulgar pride of upstart baseness presumes to lift its brow above the multitude, when folly, half hid beneath a cloak of gold, obtrudes itself beyond the barrier of decorum, the pen of just and wholesome reprehension shall never fail to mark them.

During the period that Mrs. Morley resided in this temporary sphere of busy observation, she learned a lesson which the shows and empty splendours of existence never could have taught her. She found that worldly friendships are but the fleeting coruscations[1] which illumine the warm hour of sunny fortune. She proved that to *seem* and not to *be* was the all-powerful clue to private praise and public reputation. She discovered that the attributes of nature have little weight in the vast scale of popular estimation; and she was convinced that vice and folly will ever find their votaries, while they place their deformities beneath the mask of wealth: that it is not the idol to whom the ill-judging and the base pay homage; but to the glittering sanctuary which enshrines it; yes, indiscriminating fortune! pave the dark threshold to the den of infamy with gems and tinsel; deck the surrounding objects in eye-bewildering splendours; let pomp but smooth the level pathway to applause, and the multitude will cheerfully pursue it; while virtue turns away neglected and despised, and genius flies to solitude forgotten!

---

[1] Flashes of light.

CHAPTER XXXV

Mrs. Morley, under all the sufferings of an indignant spirit, resisted the pressure of pecuniary distress, with a degree of fortitude for which a pre-judging world allowed her little credit. But she found that, not only the consolations of life depended on the possession of fortune's favours, but that even the gratifying shew of outward respect faded into a mere shadow, as the storm of adversity thickened round her. She had employed her pen, till her health was visibly declining; she had denied herself the comforts of existence, till existence itself was scarcely to be valued. All that her honourable, her incessant industry could procure, was insufficient for the purposes of attaining a permanent independence; and she was at length so deeply involved, so menaced with destruction, that nothing but an effort of despair could save her. She found by painful experience, that few among the illiterate and vulgar will extend their patronage to mental worth; that the reward which the aristocracy of wealth bestows is very rarely munificent; though self-gratification is purchased at a prodigal expence, and while genius lingers in adversity, licentious pleasure revels in all the boundless luxuries of fortune.

At this moment of trial, an evil genius prompted the selfish mind of a wealthy libertine, and Mrs. Morley's humble situation again exposed her to the insults of the vulgar. Two thousand pounds for present exigencies, and three hundred pounds per annum, were proffered as the price of her degradation; by one, who not many weeks before, had refused to aid her literary toils by the subscription of a single guinea!

Mrs. Morley's indignation was strong, but her necessities were powerful. She shuddered at the idea of a sordid sacrifice; but she had been convinced that worldly importance depends on wealth and not on virtue. The trial was a severe one; she was trembling, fearful, perplexed, distressed, and wounded by the insults of unfeeling persecutors. The man of wealth was selfish, ignorant, and ostentatious: she was oppressed and humbled.

During this epoch of anxiety, a masquerade was given at

Ranelagh.[1] Mrs. Morley had received a ticket, and promised to accept the protection of her avowed seducer. She had never witnessed an entertainment of that species which now tempted her curiosity, and relying on the fortitude of her own heart, she consented to encounter a new scene of trial.

As soon as she entered the Rotunda her subtle protector began to unfold his purpose. He pointed out to her observation the most exalted women of libertine notoriety. She saw them caressed, followed, and protected, even by the most fastidious. She was astonished.

The next objects of her attention were the avowed mistresses of distinguished characters: they also received the smiles, the homage of the crowd. Their features displayed contented, nay even happy minds; for they, feeling their equality, in moral claims, to their high-titled contemporaries, knew no cause to blush, no fear of reprehension.—She reflected—she was not alarmed.

Again she gazed around her. She discovered many noble vestals, whose looks and conversation belied the timid graces of their youth. And while the "loud laugh bespoke the vacant mind,"[2] she heard the buzzing swarms of thronging insects mingling in tones of unbounded admiration!—She hesitated— she was but half decided.

The hours flew swiftly, for they were winged by dissipation, in the form of love. Her companion urged his precepts by the pernicious doctrines of example. He assured her that, having already "sacrificed her reputation———"

She started.

He repeated the words; he told her that the world would give her little praise for prudence, after the purity of her fame had been so confessedly contaminated. "Your propriety," said he, with an insulting smile, "will only be considered as a proof of your insignificance; and the over scrupulous delicacy of your mind will merely draw on you the imputation of false pride." While

---

[1] Pleasure gardens opened to the public in 1742. The large Rotunda at Ranelagh was a fashionable venue for concerts and masked balls. Robinson mentions several of her many visits to Ranelagh in her *Memoirs*, 1: 95, 160–61, 165.

[2] Cf. Oliver Goldsmith's poem "The Deserted Village," line 122: "And the loud laugh that spoke the vacant mind."

he spoke lord Francis Sherville passed them; on his arm leant lady Penelope Pryer. Mrs. Morley's heart beat high; her whole frame trembled. She was decided.

The tempter who for that night assumed the name of guardian, observed the emotions struggling in her bosom. "I know you love lord Francis," said he; "but he is an universal idolator."

"I fear he is!" sighed Mrs. Morley.

"You ill bestow your affections on such an avowed inconstant," added her companion. "For he is not only a bankrupt in character, but in fortune."

"O Heavens!" exclaimed Mrs. Morley; "what do you tell me? I conjure you to have a care; the poverty of lord Francis may, to my mind, convey an interest, a sympathy, that would prove fatal." Again lord Francis passed them, alone; Mrs. Morley's voice arrested his attention. He turned short, and followed her. He was unmasked. She quitted the Rotunda to avoid him; he pursued, and in the first anti-room, while her companion went in search of his carriage, lord Francis addressed her.

"Hear me but a moment," said he, with agitation. "The person under whose protection I now find you, is unworthy of such an honour. He has already boasted of his triumph, publicly boasted; and, though you are by the world considered as his mistress, I still believe he is a slanderer."

"You astonish me!" replied Mrs. Morley. "How shall I prove my innocence?"

"By accepting my protection. By this instant making your escape from the danger that awaits you; you may rely upon my honour, for you have proved it." While lord Francis was speaking, he led Mrs. Morley imperceptibly across the portico: they entered his carriage, and proceeded towards London.

CHAPTER XXXVI

As they were passing through Grosvenor place, the coach axletree breaking, Mrs. Morley was once more alarmed by a new species of dilemma. With lord Francis's aid she was extricated from the carriage, and was proceeding on foot along the pavement, when her enraged and deserted lover overtook them.

By one blow he levelled lord Francis to the ground. Mrs. Morley shrieked and endeavoured to separate them; but the undaunted champion of her honour, snatching a cane from the hand of his servant, began to inflict such corporeal punishment on his assailant, as taught him to repent of his rash and ill-judging violence. The contest was, during several minutes, a severe one; for the athletic arm of lord Francis met no trifling opposition from the pugilistic skill of his enraged antagonist.

Mrs. Morley, terrified beyond the powers of recollection, concealing her face with her mask, ran swiftly along the pavement. It was just day-break, and she reached Hyde Park Corner before she had courage to look back for her encountering knight errants, when she found herself detained by the strong grasp of a new companion. Her consternation was infinite. He held her hand with a determined firmness, and, being also masked, she had every thing to apprehend from the violence of his manner.

An empty coach passing at this moment, Mrs. Morley, with astonishment, heard her companion stop it. "Resist not," said the stranger; "for you must go with me." She knew the voice, and trembled.

"You are at last detected, madam. Your paramour's high rank shall not shield him from the rigour of the law," said Mr. Morley. "I have been a watchful spectator of all that has passed during the night. I have never for a moment ceased to follow you. I now find that you are no less criminal than capricious; and I command, at least, a temporary penance for your folly, while you bear that name which your conduct has so branded with dishonour." Mrs. Morley, finding that all remonstrance would be useless, consented to enter the carriage, and Mr. Morley ordered the coachman to proceed towards an hotel in Pall Mall.[1]

Mr. Morley immediately retired to his chamber, after having locked Martha in an inner apartment. There she was left to rumi-

---

[1] A wide, fashionable street known for its exclusive shops and elegant houses. The most impressive was Carlton House, the palatial residence of the Prince of Wales.

nate on all that had passed; and though she had every prospect of enduring the tyranny of a jealous husband, she blessed that good genius, which had rescued her from her libertine lover.

On the following morning an interview, as solemn as it was definitive, look place between Martha and Mr. Morley. Weary of the vicissitudes which she had encountered, and happy to adopt any plan that might at least procure her safety from promiscuous insult, she consented to await the decision of Mr. Morley's judgment, and the full explanation of her, seemingly imprudent, conduct.

A few hours confinement in her chamber had tranquillized her spirit, and she began to think even the authority of a wedded ruler far preferable to the miseries of perpetual adversity.

Two days had passed since Mrs. Morley had placed herself under the protection of her husband, when the servant of the hotel informed her that Mr. Morley had at dawn-light departed for Derbyshire, accompanied by a young lady. Her surprize was only to be equalled by her chagrin; but on inquiry she found that all demands at the hotel were settled; and that a letter had been left for her, inclosing a bank note of thirty pounds, with the following lines:

I have investigated your conduct, and I find that it has been less culpable than report had made it. Still the disgrace which you have brought upon my name, by the profession you have chosen, and the strong symptoms of guilt which attended the birth of your darling Fanny, prevent the possibility of our ever re-uniting. Had there been sufficient proofs of your criminality a divorce might have set us both at liberty; but, under the stigma of a doubtful reputation, I cannot, without dishonouring my family, and injuring my moral character, receive you.

Mrs. Morley read this brief farewell with calmness and resignation. And as she again entered her humble habitation, sighed an adieu, to every hope of happiness. She would have returned Mr. Morley the thirty pounds which he left her; but she was involved in many pecuniary embarrassments, and necessity is often the propelling power which makes worth and genius endure the insolence of pride, the vaunted display of vulgar ostentation, and the regret of owing a short hour of repose to the ignorant and unworthy.

CHAPTER XXXVII

A few weeks after Mrs. Morley's return to her old lodging she received a letter from the attorney who had undertaken her suit against the Leadenhead family, informing her that she had lost her cause; and requesting the immediate payment of fifty pounds, the costs of her unsuccessful prosecution. Her amazement was infinite, and her distress was equal to her surprize, for by this intelligence her prospects now became more gloomy than ever.

How to extricate herself from the sharp fangs of legal persecution, she knew not; though she knew by fatal experience that oppression never fails to follow the oppressed. She had seen but too many instances, where the enlightened and feeling mind was exposed to the low machinations of empty pride and tyrannical presumption; and her heart shuddered when reflection told her, that she must once more seek for patronage where the sweetly soothing task would be contaminated by the littleness of ostentation.

To her pen she flew for that passport, which was the only one she could obtain, to those who by rank and fortune were far removed from the sorrows which annoyed her. Twelve days of intense application produced a small collection of odes, which she neatly copied, and resolved on dedicating, by permission, to a personage of high distinction.

She had often heard the marquis of Downlands spoken of as the very Maecenas[1] of modern times. She therefore doubted not

---

[1]   A Roman statesman famous for his patronage of Virgil, Horace, and other promising young authors. In the following sentence, Robinson lists examples of neglected men of genius in Restoration and eighteenth-century England. Thomas Chatterton, dubbed "the marvelous boy" by Wordsworth, committed suicide at the age of seventeen. William Collins, author of odes and other poems, went insane. Thomas Otway, best known for his tragedy *Venice Preserved*, died in poverty. Richard Savage, a playwright and poet, died in debtor's prison.

that he would readily patronize the efforts of a female pen, particularly when he was informed that the writer was at that moment placed in the most distressing predicament, unhappy, persecuted, and unprotected. She wrote to this patron of the Muses, this guardian of unfriended genius, this modern Maecenas, this Atlas of British literature! but, though he had probably heard that a Chatterton had been spurned by unfeeling greatness; that an Otway had perished in misery; that the inspired mind of a Collins had been bowed to despondency by neglect; that a Savage had been urged on to crimes by the effects of indigence and the frowns of the exalted, her letter remained unanswered, her application unregarded, while the laws not only of philanthropy, but of *bienseance*,[1] were violated by his silence.

She then addressed herself to a baronet, whose wealth had raised his name above the vulgar, but whose heart had not taught him to feel for the sorrows of those whom nature had ennobled. The sufferings of a woman of talents did not impress his mind with any thing like sympathy; he felt no inclination to dignify his character by an act of generous patronage; or to bestow any portion of that wealth on an enlightened female, which he did not scruple publicly to lavish on the most ignorant, profligate, and mercenary of the sex.

Mrs. Morley's third trial of British liberality was made in the feelings of a wealthy Asiatic; a collection of odes excited little interest in a bosom which was proof against all the inspirations of genius and philanthropy. He therefore begged leave to decline patronizing her works; at the same time sending her a guinea by a domestic, with a verbal message, that if she was in distress she was welcome to it as a present. Resentment roused her throbbing heart, and she returned the insulting tribute, with all the pride of scorn and indignation, accompanied by a letter, which *repaid* the obligation.

Her next application was made to a venerable dowager of high rank. The word, Dedication, flattered her self-love, and Mrs. Morley was appointed to wait on her ladyship on the following day, and to bring the odes, for the approbation of her patroness. With a beating heart she approached the threshold of that temple

---

[1] Etiquette.

where worth and talents were destined to pay homage to dulness and ostentation.

The porter who opened the door with surly importance demanded her business. Mrs. Morley blushed and hesitated. "If you are come with a begging letter," said the pride-pampered Cerberus,[1] "you make take my answer; my lady never opens them, excepting when they come from her ladyship's own relations."

"You mistake my errand," cried Mrs. Morley sternly; "I am not a beggar. I have business of importance with lady Eldercourt."

"Some favor to ask, I dare say," replied the porter; "for I never saw you before; what is your name?"

"Morley."

"No such person on my lady's visiting list. Perhaps you are a trades-woman. You have no chance of seeing my lady; she never talks to people of business."

"I came by appointment," said Mrs. Morley. "Lady Eldercourt will know my business when my name is announced."

"Indeed! I much doubt it," answered the saucy varlet: "but you may go to the housekeeper's room, and she will inquire more about the matter." A liveried coxcomb who had witnessed this conversation, and whose obtrusive looks had distressed Mrs. Morley while she was speaking, now offered to conduct her to the housekeeper's apartment; at the same time with a supercilious sneer assuring her that he was excessively delighted in having an opportunity of obliging so pretty a woman.

Mrs. Morley, on entering the room, observed a lusty, vulgar-looking female seated at a breakfast-table. Without rising from her chair, she inquired, "What is your business with me, child?"

"I came to wait on lady Eldercourt, respecting a small collection of poems."

"O, child!" exclaimed the woman, "you have certainly mistaken the house. My lady never reads! And as to authors, she cannot endure them.—Who could lead you into such an error? If you had but told the porter your business, he would not have given me the trouble of answering you."

---

[1] In Roman mythology, the three-headed dog that guarded the entrance to the under-world.

"But lady Eldercourt appointed me to wait on her this morning."

"No matter for that," replied the woman, at the same time looking Mrs. Morley into confusion. "My lady appoints a dozen of people every forenoon, but never sees one of them. That toil generally falls to my share; and, God knows, I have enough to do with our troublesome visitors."

"I wish to dedicate some Odes to her ladyship; for I have been informed that she is the patroness of the Muses."

"Of whom?" inquired the housekeeper earnestly.

"The Muses."

"They are not on our visiting list: I cannot say that ever I heard of them. Are they noble?"

"Of the most exalted nobility!" said Mrs. Morley smiling. "They are nine lovely sisters."

"And patronized by my lady? Impossible!" interrupted the housekeeper. "Her ladyship has too many poor relations of her own to throw away her money upon strangers."

"Indeed!" said Mrs. Morley.

"Aye, aye, child! great people have their plagues as well as little ones. And though my lady is as good as most folks, where she takes a liking, she is no better born than myself, who am but her housekeeper."

"I know nothing of lady Eldercourt's family," said Mrs. Morley: "but I have always heard that she is spoken highly of by the *literati*." [1]

"Aye, that is the Italian singer, I suppose, who is such a favorite with my lady. She makes nothing of giving him fifties and hundreds, though many of her own relations are starving." Mrs. Morley smiled.

"But high folks are apt to forget themselves as well as low ones," continued the housekeeper. "They think that nobody knows them in their new character. They imagine that what is done in the drawing-room is not noticed in the servants'-hall: but they are mightily mistaken. We know the birth and parentage of all our visitors, from the right honorable bar-maid, the strolling actress, and the milliner, down to the French opera-dancer and

---

[1] Elite members of literary society.

the thief-taker's daughter; and this I will say, that none of our ladies or duchesses born, are near so proud, or give themselves half so many airs, as these second-hand nobility. But we know them, notwithstanding they think to the contrary."

By this time the housekeeper had finished her fifth cup of tea, and Mrs. Morley's patience was almost exhausted, when Lady Eldercourt's *femme de chambre* entered the room.

"I believe," said she, looking consequentially at Mrs. Morley, "you are the young woman whom my lady expects about some books or verses."

"My name is Morley."

"The same," replied the lady of the bedchamber. "We shall be at leisure in about twenty minutes, and then we will give you an audience. My lady is at present engaged with a poor clergyman, who has brought some sermons to make her melancholy; for I am sure there is nothing in this world she dislikes so much, except poetry."

Mrs. Morley blushed.

"But my lady is very good-natured; for she knows that people come with their books as a genteel sort of begging, and she generally pays them handsomely for their trouble. Would you like some refreshment—a cold pheasant or a glass of frontiniac?[1] Pray make no ceremony: most likely you are hungry." Mrs. Morley thanked the lady in waiting, but declined her offer; patiently looking on while she made her second morning meal on the articles she had mentioned, though her own fast was that day unbroken.

CHAPTER XXXVIII

Mrs. Morley now followed the attendant of the bed-chamber to lady Eldercourt's dressing-room, where she found her new patroness recently risen, and sitting at her toilette. Lady Eldercourt was neither lovely nor juvenile: but a flattering delu-

---

[1]   Frontignac, or frontignan, is a muscat wine made at Frontignan, France.

sion, which is often the replenishing glow of life's waning lustre, frequently told her she was both. Proud she certainly was: but her understanding was circumscribed and her education limited. Lady Eldercourt, with high rank and high opinions, at least as far as they towered above the less fortunate, was not born noble; neither did she, by acting nobly, supply the deficiency which Fortune had, till her youth was past, forgotten to remedy. This introductory preamble to the toilette of lady Eldercourt will inform the reader what kind of personage Mrs. Morley had to encounter: for though she was of human kind, her conduct was not at all times such as did honour to humanity.

When Mrs. Morley approached her ladyship she was busily employed in settling her features into a dignified solemnity. The looking-glass presented them before she was conscious of the reflection it conveyed; while Mrs. Morley sighed, and anticipated a new scene of probation.

"Madam," said the poetess, "I have the honour to wait on you, by your ladyship's commands, to read some poetical trifles which I shall be proud to dedicate to your ladyship."

"Very well, child; I shall be glad to hear them," cried lady Eldercourt. "I have half an hour's leisure, and you may begin to read them as soon as you please." Mrs. Morley unfolded the odes; lady Eldercourt, for the first time, glanced at her.

"How long have you wrote verses, child?" inquired her ladyship.

"I have always been an admirer of the Muses."

"They will scarcely repay you for your trouble, child. People of fashion have little time to read. You had better think of some other occupation." Mrs. Morley blushed, and began to repent of having made the visit.

"Have you nothing but poetry to depend on?" continued lady Eldercourt. "Writing is very well as an amusement, but it very rarely pays the expences attending it. 'Tis an idle trade, child. However, let me hear your verses. I hope they are intelligible; for really some of our modern poetry is a mere jargon of words, without either sense or sound to make them palatable."

"Your ladyship is a competent judge, I dare say," cried Mrs. Morley, confused and trembling.

"I never read; I only draw my conclusions from report. My

femme de chambre is an excellent critic, and she tells me that most living poets are mere pretenders to the art." The lady of the bed-chamber grew consequential, and glanced at Mrs. Morley, over her shoulder, with the importance of a modern censor. She sighed, and again looked at her odes.

"I hope they are not of a melancholy cast," said lady Eldercourt; "for I am nervous, and cannot bear pathetic subjects."

"No, my lady; they are rather allegorical than serious."

"I trust that they are not political. Much poison may be concealed beneath the flowers of poesy." Mrs. Morley half smiled.

"Now, child, you may begin. Of course you read well?" The odes were again unfolded.

"You may take a seat, child: I suppose you are tired.—Now first let me hear the Dedication."

"Madam! the Dedication!"

"The Dedication. That, I understand, is the object of your visit to me, child. I shall be glad to hear how you introduce yourself."

"The Dedication is not yet written: I did not know whether it was your ladyship's intention to honour my odes with your patronage."

"Then what brought you here, child?"

"The wish to read my efforts, and the hope of obtaining your ladyship's approbation."

By this time lady Eldercourt had nearly completed her morning toilette, and a loud knocking at the street door interrupted the conversation. "You must retire, child," said her ladyship; "I hear company. You must wait till I am again at leisure." Mrs. Morley returned to the housekeeper's room, accompanied by lady Eldercourt's woman.

As soon as they had taken their seats, (for the arbitress of the decorative department condescendingly requested that Mrs. Morley would waive all ceremony,) she was again addressed. "Have you been an authoress long? What books have you written?"

"A novel, and several poetical pieces."

"I don't dislike novels: though I have a tolerable library of my own; for a vast number of writers solicit my lady's patronage, and they generally send me a set of their works bound with elegance, as a passport to her favour."

Mrs. Morley understood the meaning of this information, and smiled.

"Indeed," added the enlightened censor, "I am little indebted to their attentions; for if they omit paying me proper respect, I always obtain their books free of obligations."

"I do not comprehend you," said Mrs. Morley.

"Why," replied the woman, "I always read works that are sent for my lady's inspection, and those that I abuse are consigned to my shelves; while their authors are compelled to endure an equal share of oblivion."

"Has lady Eldercourt so implicit a reliance on your judgment?"

"She has little confidence in her own," replied the critic; "and therefore it is easy to control her opinions. Besides, I am her privy counsellor, her secretary, and her *confidante*. I have had a tolerable education, and every body knows that my poor lady was not so fortunate as to be born in the highest circles."

"Your lady is nevertheless fond of books," said Mrs. Morley.

"If they are elegantly bound. The outside of most things is the best badge of importance with weak minds."

"Lady Eldercourt is considered as a woman of taste," said Mrs. Morley.

"That reputation she owes to me, and I liberally transfer the praise of it to her milliner. I find my advantage in my generosity: I have always the first fashions sent me, gratis."

"Indeed!" said Mrs. Morley. "You are fortunate!"

"It is lady Eldercourt that is indebted to Fortune, in having such a friend," said the preceptress. "Her ladyship was much neglected in her youth, and is terribly unpolished. I write all her letters, and she passes for a second *Sevigny*."[1]

"Astonishing!" exclaimed Mrs. Morley.

"Not at all," interrupted the female secretary: "women of fashion seldom write elegantly. They have other things to do of more importance in the world of discernment, and they easily get authors to scribble for them; for the poverty of real genius is almost proverbial."

---

[1] See *A Letter to the Women of England*, 45, n. 2.

Mrs. Morley sighed deeply.

"We see authors waiting every day in our hall, without a dinner," added the *femme de chambre*, "while my lady is giving audience to French dancers, Italian musicians, fancy-dress-makers, and professors of animal magnetism. My lady has resided in a warm climate, and her nervous system has been nearly annihilated." She was proceeding, when a message again summoned Mrs. Morley to the presence of her patroness.

On entering the drawing-room, she saw several persons of both sexes. "Now, child," said lady Eldercourt, with a tone of self-importance, "you may read your verses as soon as you please. Here are several excellent judges, and some successful authors." Mrs. Morley's courage began to fail, and she felt her face redden deeply, while the inquisitive eyes of all present were fixed upon her. The odes were again unrolled; her hand trembled: she attempted to read; her voice faltered, and she could not articulate a single syllable.

"Well, child, when do you mean to begin?" said lady Eldercourt, with a tone of austerity. "Time is precious, and I am in haste." At this moment a new trio augmented the circle. Mrs. Morley stood like a culprit at the bar of condemnation; her heart throbbed with alarm, while her cheek glowed with resentment.

"Heavens! what is to be done now?" cried a flippant girl of fashion, as she entered the room and flew towards the looking-glass.

"Only a poetess going to read her verses," replied a male sprig of nobility.

"I dare swear we shall be wonderfully entertained!"

"From lips like those what precepts fail to move?"[1]

"I do not question it," interrupted a venerable dowager; "for I suppose she is one of the Julias or Sapphos of the present day.[2] I never read their productions without being amused beyond measure—Poor things!"

---

[1]   An inexact quotation of Pope's "Eloisa to Abelard," line 67: "From lips like those what precept fail'd to move?"

[2]   "Julia" and "Sappho" were among the many poetic pseudonyms used by Robinson herself.

"Pray, ma'am, do you write in the newspapers?" said the young lady who introduced the conversation: "Are you Anna Matilda, or Della Crusca, or Laura Maria?[1] Comical creatures! they have made me shed many a tear, though I never more than half understood them."

"I never wrote under either of those signatures," said Mrs. Morley.

"Well, now, child, begin," interrupted lady Eldercourt: "It is of little importance under what signature you write, if you do but write well. Of that we shall soon judge. Read with an audible voice, and we will all give you our candid opinion." Mrs. Morley opened the first Ode

TO THE BLUE-BELL.

BLUE-BELL! how gaily art thou drest!
   How neat and trim art thou, sweet flower!
How silky is thy azure vest!
   How fresh, to flaunt at morning's hour!
Could'st thou but think, I well might say,
Thou art as proud in rich array
As lady, blithesome, young, and vain,
Prank'd up with folly and disdain,
     Vaunting her power—
          Sweet flower!

BLUE-BELL! O, could'st thou but behold
   Beside thee, where a rival reigns,
All deck'd in robe of glossy gold,
   With speckled crown of ruby stains—

---

[1] Poetic pseudonyms used by Hannah Cowley, Robert Merry, and Mary Robinson, respectively. By the mid 1790s the popularity of the so-called Della Cruscan School of poetry was on the wane, and Robinson here seems to be dissociating her heroine from a poetic style ridiculed for its emotional and stylistic extravagance. Robinson herself, however, did not renounce her poetic identity as "Laura Maria." As *The Morning Post* reported on August 7, 1799, "Mrs. Robinson has resumed her signature of Laura Maria; a name by which her muse first obtained its increasing celebrity, and which will frequently appear in the poetry department of this paper."

Could'st thou but see this COWSLIP gay,
Thou would'st with envy faint, and say,
"Hence from my sight, plebeian vain!
Nor hope, on this my green domain,
   For equal power,
       Bold flower!"

Poor rivals! could ye but look round,
  On yonder hillock ye would see
The NETTLE, with its fangs to wound—
  The HEMLOCK, fraught with destiny!
On them the sun its morning beam
Pours in as rich, as bright a stream,
As on the fairest rose that rears
Its blushing brow midst Nature's tears,
   Chilling its power,
       Faint flower!

Then why dispute this wide domain,
  Since NATURE knows no partial care?
The nipping blast, the pelting rain,
  Both will with equal ruin share:
Then what is vain DISTINCTION, say,
But the short blaze of summer's day?
And what is pomp, or beauty's boast?
An empty shadow, seen and lost!
   Such is thy power,
       Vain flower![1]

An awful silence followed during several moments, when a
nobleman, of polished and amiable manners, with a consoling
smile commended Mrs. Morley's poetical talents in the highest
terms of liberal panegyric. But he was interrupted by lady
Eldercourt, who exclaimed, "Heavens! my lord! can your lordship
disgrace your judgment by praising such impertinent opinions?

---

[1]   This poem was published under Robinson's own name in *The Morning Post* on April
5, 1799.

For my part, I wonder how the woman could presume to read such audacious verses in the presence of people of rank and title! But you are a poet, my lord, and consequently an enthusiast."

"Pardon me, lady Eldercourt," replied the liberal nobleman: "you judge too hastily. The lines are truly poetical, and the moral lesson which they teach is excellent."

"Who will condescend to be taught by an obscure scribbler?" interrupted the patroness of literature. "I thought the woman wanted protection: but I find that she wishes rather to admonish than to be sanctioned. I could have pitied her obscurity, but I cannot pardon her presumption."

"Obscure she cannot be," said the nobleman, "while she has such talents to support her." Mrs. Morley, unconscious of meriting such praise, was overwhelmed with gratitude and confusion. She was retiring, when the young female auditor whispered to lady Eldercourt, "I have seen her before—she is a strolling actress!"

"Impossible!" exclaimed one.

"I thought she was something of the kind," said another.

"Let us desire her to act a scene," cried a third, "Something in tragedy, to make us laugh."

"It is evident she has been used to appear in public," remarked a fourth.

"By her uncommon boldness," whispered a fifth.

Again Mrs. Morley, nearly overcome by confusion, retreated towards the door, when lady Eldercourt rang the bell. A servant entered the room: "Here," said her ladyship, "get change for this bank-note; I want to give this young woman five guineas."

Mrs. Morley's pulse beat high: her proud heart throbbed with indignation. She sunk upon the carpet, and fainted.

The whole party retired, excepting the noble poet, who, with the aid of lady Eldercourt's *femme de chambre*, restored Mrs. Morley, and in his own carriage conducted her safely to her lodgings.

CHAPTER XXXIX

Reader, if you have had patience and curiosity sufficient to accompany the persecuted Martha through her varying scenes of unmerited suffering, you will be able to form some idea of the perplexities, pains, and humiliations which the children of Genius are destined to encounter: you will perceive, that of all the occupations which industry can pursue, those of literary toil are the most fatiguing. That which seems to the vacant eye a mere playful amusement, is in reality an Herculean labour; and to compose a tolerable work is so difficult a task, that the fastidiously severe should make the trial before they presume to condemn even the humblest effort of imagination.

Mrs. Morley was completely discomfited by the cold reception she had experienced at the countess of Eldercourt's. She forgot the motive which had procured for her the display of protection, and her self-love had taught her to place the prospect to the account of her own merit, which merely originated in the vanity of her patroness.

Reduced once more to seek a livelihood, by this unexpected dilemma, Mrs. Morley applied to her city friend, the benevolent Mr. Dodson, with whom, during the vicissitudes of fortune, she had kept up a regular correspondence.

Again his philanthropic heart was open to her solicitation. With his assistance she obtained a new asylum, as companion to the daughter of an eminent banker. The young lady was heiress to a splendid fortune, of a delicate constitution, and by her physicians ordered to the Spa of Germany.[1] Mrs. Morley accepted the situation, and Mr. Dodson promised without delay to investigate and arrange the lawyer's demand, and to take every opportunity of succouring the misguided Julia.

Mrs. Morley found her new patroness amiable and interesting, but unfortunately under the stern authority of an insolent stepmother. Mrs. Gerard had been the favourite of her husband's affections during his first wife's days: she had long set decency and

---

[1] Spa, now a part of Belgium, was the most popular health resort on the Continent.

morality at defiance by publicly taking that place and usurping that name which belonged to a more worthy object. She had been, a few days before, made an honest woman: but unfortunately the accommodating powers of a priest did not extend to the capability of making her a good one. She was envious, haughty, obtrusive, ill-natured, vain, and ostentatious: so elated by the new rank which she held in society, that by her presuming arrogance she perpetually reminded the world of that from which she had been recently removed. Her extravagance was only to be equalled by her vanity; and her tyranny, which was unblushingly exercised over her wedded benefactor, plainly evinced that she had neither gratitude nor decency; while he was an object of universal pity and contempt, and his wife an example that the little mind cannot rise upon the wings of Time, even though his feet are placed on the swift wheel of Fortune.

Mrs. Gerard was uniformly severe on all who did not pay obsequious homage to her newly-acquired dignities. But unfortunately the world cannot forget what has once been the theme of public notoriety. Mrs. Gerard's conduct had been the subject of universal reprobation; and the grave which hid the remains of her predecessor did not, at the same time, consign her follies to oblivion. Had she chosen the still paths of life, Time might have softened the stern frown of reflecting indignation; but Mrs. Gerard braved the broad eye of day, and vainly hoped that the lustre of her new-born honours would so dazzle the eye of observation, that in their full splendour her faults would be invisible. She was proud and imperious; and if the severity of her mind knew any discrimination, it was that of feeling a decided and more than common hatred towards the withering but accomplished Sophia.

Mrs. Gerard had long witnessed Sophia's power over the mind of her father, and her deep regret for the loss of her heart-broken mother. Mr. Gerard had married this second wife from a point of interest as well as honour; having bestowed on her a large portion of his fortune, and entered into engagements to forfeit a considerable sum in case he did not make her his legal associate, as soon as his first alliance should be dissolved by inevitable destiny. The only obstacle, therefore, to her power over the actions and fortune of her husband was his fondness for Sophia, who was doubly hateful to Mrs. Gerard—first, because she was expected to share an equal portion of her father's property; and secondly, because she was a living memento of his folly; being extremely pretty, and a very striking resemblance of her mother.

Mrs. Morley hoped, in her new state of probation, to enjoy some share of domestic felicity: but her hopes had ever been delusive, and her prospects visionary. On her presenting herself before the step-mother of her lovely pupil, a mutual consternation at the same moment evinced effects of a different nature, though equally distressing to both parties; for in the person of Mrs. Gerard she instantly recognized the fastidious traveller, whose scrupulous delicacy could not permit a strolling actress to become her associate even for a few hours, though she had been the object, for many years, of an illicit attachment.

Mrs. Gerard exerted her utmost art to prevent Mrs. Morley's becoming an inmate of her house: but Mr. Dodson's power being likewise infinite, with all her supposed imperfections on her head, she was established as governess and companion to the amiable Sophia. The refinement of this young person's mind had long excluded her from the society of her high-bearing step-mother; and as the pupil and preceptress were equally the reverse of their domineering duenna,[1] the separation was only productive of augmented felicity: for while Mrs. Gerard was daily occupied in searching for society, in obtruding her gaudy vulgarity on those who received her more to wonder than to admire—who were either influenced by her husband or intimidated by her effrontery, Mrs. Morley and Sophia enjoyed the sober pleasures of congenial sorrows, even amidst the toils of mental cultivation.

CHAPTER XL

Mrs. Morley had only passed a few months in Mr. Gerard's family when, after a short illness, he expired, leaving, excepting a small

---

[1] An elderly woman serving as governess or chaperone.

annuity to Mrs. Gerard, his whole fortune to Sophia during her life; and at her decease, if she should die unmarried, to the heirs or relatives of his second union. Mrs. Gerard was disappointed almost beyond her patience at what she thought a proof of unjust and barbarous neglect: but being shrewd, though illiterate, being taught in the school of interested duplicity, having long fawned where she could not love, and flattered where she did not esteem, she employed all her machinations to counteract the purpose of her ungrateful husband.

During this interval Mr. Dodson had completely investigated the lawyer's bill of costs, and to his utter astonishment discovered that the cause had never been brought into a court of justice. He had threatened to expose and to punish the impostor; who, fearful of the consequences which would attend his trial, quitted his native county, and sought concealment in the bustle of the metropolis—the only safe retreat for villainy and deception

Mrs. Gerard, who was indefatigable in her project of revenge, was a distant relation of the despicable Snatchem. She consulted him on the possibility of defeating her late husband's purpose, and a plan was shortly after concerted for their mutual advantage; upon condition that if he succeeded, the hand of Mrs. Gerard would be the reward of his iniquity.

CHAPTER XLI

Every thing was prepared for Miss Gerard's journey to Spa, when one evening, returning from the family seat in Essex, with no companion but Mrs. Morley, the chaise was suddenly overtaken by four men with crape on their faces, who, uttering the most horrid imprecations, commanded them to stop. Sophia was near fainting with terror, when one of the villains demanded which was Miss Gerard. The dusk of twilight prevented their seeing into the carriage; and Mrs. Morley, instantly suspecting some plot for the destruction of her friend, readily answered that she was the person.

By this time Sophia had fainted. Mrs. Morley, whose resolution was equal to her friendship, was ordered to quit the carriage. She obeyed, and in a moment was placed on a pillion[1] behind a ruffian, whose horse stood by the road side; a cord was fastened round her waist, and held by her conductor, who set out full speed on the road leading from London.

As no attempt had been made upon property, Mrs. Morley naturally concluded that the person of Miss Gerard was the object of the outrage; and that as soon as the villains should discover their mistake she would be again set at liberty.

They continued galloping some time, when the rider suddenly stopped at a large old-fashioned house near the termination of a narrow lane. They alighted. Mrs. Morley was led into the hall, and, without a syllable being uttered, consigned to the care of an elderly gentlewoman. Lights being brought, the female quitted the room; and a young man, whose dress bespoke something above the middle classes of society, approached Mrs. Morley.

Her terror now became scarcely supportable. Her companion perceived the fluttering agitation of her bosom, and taking her hand, endeavoured to console her. She withdrew it hastily. He smiled, and attempted to salute her. She rose to quit the room: he prevented her departure. She shrieked, and in a moment two stout fellows entered with a waistcoat of coercion. Mrs. Morley now discovered that she was in a private mad-house.

The louder she shrieked, the more she was insulted. Her arms were confined; her distress was taunted by menaces and grimaces. She was compelled to swallow the most nauseous medicines, and informed that unless she remained tranquil, a more rigid process would be deemed absolutely necessary. The night passed tediously. Mrs. Morley requested that she might be permitted, on the following morning, to have a book for her amusement. After a long consultation with the physician of the household, it was agreed that a book might be read, without any peril to the patient.

A novel was presented. It was the sixth edition of her own work, for which the purchaser had paid her ten pounds. Her chagrin was considerably augmented, and she threw the book

---

[1]   A pad behind the saddle.

on the ground in an agony of vexation.[1] Another consultation was held, and Mrs. Morley was pronounced to be in the most decided state of raving insanity.

She was hurried into a strong room, where the physician of the household endeavoured to soothe her by insulting familiarities. She shrieked: she was menaced, taunted, and commanded to be silent. She requested to have the book which had so strongly influenced her feelings. "It is mine," said she; "I wrote it."

"Poor thing!" sighed one of the keepers, "she thinks that she can make books. She is not the only crazy woman who fancies herself an authoress. I have seen many since I first took up my business."

"I tell you that I composed every line of it," said Mrs. Morley.

"Very well," cried the compassionate attendant; "then compose your mind; that will do you more good than all the novels in the world."

"Six editions for ten pounds!" said Mrs. Morley, raising her eyes towards heaven.

"We don't sell books, God bless you, my dear ma'am!" said the nurse; "we only comfort the afflicted."

"Perish such comfort!" exclaimed Mrs. Morley. "You shall answer for this outrage, if there be justice or humanity in Britain."

The doctor now again commanded her to be silent. "You will disturb the whole family!" said he. "The house is full of persons of distinction who are placed here by their relations to be happy and unmolested."

"To be driven frantic," cried Mrs. Morley. "You take them under your protection to taunt them into madness!"

The doctor now whispered to one of his keepers that the business would not do. "This woman is in her senses, and will ruin our house if ever she should obtain her liberty. Perhaps she has friends."

"I have an husband," interrupted Mrs. Morley; "and though he is unkind and cruel, he will avenge this outrage."

"A husband! O, then she is mad indeed!" said the doctor. "She

---

[1] Robinson is probably alluding to the popularity of her first novel, *Vancenza; or the Dangers of Credulity*. In a letter to John Taylor, Robinson complained, "My mental labours have failed through the dishonest conduct of my publishers. My works have sold handsomely but the profits have been theirs." Quoted in Bass, *The Green Dragoon*, 344.

is not married: she is heiress to a large fortune, single, and in the way of her family."

She was now bled, blistered, menaced, and tortured, till the irritation of her mind produced all the symptoms of a delirious fever. In this situation she remained two days; and her returning senses only discovered to her that her head had been shaved, and her limbs bruised even to the privation of the powers of motion.

She had been confined near a fortnight, when it was discovered, at midnight, that the house had taken fire. The flames raged furiously; and as there was no engine within three miles of the scene of horror, the destruction of the whole fabric was deemed inevitable. Mrs. Morley had been confined in her chamber: but the peril of her situation gave her new strength, and she forced the door just as the conflagration had reached the stair-case. All the rest of the family had escaped, excepting a female, whose piercing shrieks met Mrs. Morley's ear while she was descending amidst the smoke which filled the passage. She had passed the door where the prisoner was left to perish: she forced the lock, and seizing the terrified woman, dragged her from the scene of desolation.

As soon as they reached the garden, Mrs. Morley knelt by the side of her companion, who was lying senseless on the ground. The strong glare of light presented her features: they were pale and ghastly: but though emaciated, grief-worn, and haggard with the terrors of destruction, they were the features of her mother!

This moment of exquisite delight seemed to compensate for all her former sufferings. She threw her lacerated arms about her parent's neck, bathed her with tears, kissed her pale withered cheek, and would have recalled to her memory her deserted daughter; but sorrow and compunction had taken possession of her heart, and reason was no longer capable of that delight which her neglected child experienced. She was reclined upon the ground, supporting her mother's head upon her bosom, and uttering the language of despair, prompted by filial, fond affection, when a traveller, who had seen the conflagration at some distance, stopped his carriage.

The shrieks of women, in such a scene of peril, awakened all the feelings of the traveller's soul. He flew to their assistance; and

Mrs. Morley, on raising her eyes with the wildness of distraction, beheld lord Francis Sherville.

But the change in Mrs. Morley's appearance presented her to his gaze as an entire stranger. He assisted her in raising her mother from the ground, and in a few moments they conveyed her to his carriage. The stupor of despair prevented Mrs. Morley's uttering another syllable till they reached London.

CHAPTER XLII

By the time that they arrived in Harley-street it was day-break; and lord Francis, at the first glimpse of light, recognized the pallid countenance and emaciated form of his adored Martha. It is impossible to describe the contending emotions of sorrow, astonishment, and pity which struggled in his breast while he contemplated the object of his affections, so exhausted, so changed, so afflicted. A thousand dreadful ideas possessed his mind; while he naturally concluded that the loss of reason had been the origin of her confinement and its consequent sufferings. He knew not how to address her. His countenance was the expressive index of his heart, where all the virtues, all the sorrows of Mrs. Morley had been indelibly recorded.

As they approached the door, lord Francis, fixing his eyes on the wan countenance of an object at all times dear to him, but rendered more interesting than ever by her misfortunes, with a soothing voice inquired whether she knew him.

She smiled, while she sorrowfully answered, "Yes. Can I ever forget you? Can I cease to remember the protector of poor Fanny?"

Lord Francis, considering her reply as the effect of a lucid interval, took her hand, and pressed it on his heart. "Oh! suffering angel!" said he, while tears rushed into his eyes, "why, why art thou thus exposed to persecution? Why do I behold such worth, such sensibility, the sport of sorrow, while the world is over-run with ignorance and vice? Yet let me hope that you will receive the consolations of a friend, who loves you."

"Alas!" cried Mrs. Morley, with a voice scarcely articulate, "I never shall again be happy! But of all existing beings, from *you* I cannot receive consolation."

"Why?" inquired lord Francis tenderly.

"Look here!" said Mrs. Morley, bursting into tears, and turning towards her mother; "look at this victim of compunction, and shudder while you behold a mortal deprived of reason, because she had driven from her bosom an unoffending object!" Her tears prevented her proceeding. She threw her arms about her mother: "O God!" continued she, after a short pause, "restore this dear, repentant sufferer! Spare her, if only for a few short years, that I may prove my duty, my affection!"

Lord Francis, on the carriage stopping at his door, conducted Mrs. Morley and her mother to the drawing-room, where he ordered his housekeeper to wait on them, and to shew them every possible attention. After taking some refreshment they retired to a chamber, where Mrs. Morley passed the following hour in kneeling by her mother's bed and watching her.

As soon as the maniac's exhausted spirit sunk to rest, Martha endeavoured to close her eyes, but in vain. The agitations of the last twelve hours, the sight of a dear mother whom she had lamented as in her grave, and whom she found deprived of reason, the kindness of lord Francis, and the terrors which she had encountered at the moment when she snatched a parent from the most agonizing death, filled her mind with such pleasing, painful ruminations, that sleep was a stranger to her pillow. The repose which her mother experienced, however, compensated for her own feverish inquietude; and while she passed the succeeding noon in watching, she indulged the delusive hope that the sleep of a disordered brain might soothe it into sanity.

Several days elapsed, and Mrs. Morley heard no more of lord Francis, excepting by his almost hourly inquiries after hers and her mother's health. All the zeal of attentions springing from the soul, all the apparent solicitude of a feeling bosom, were exemplified by the constant attendance of physicians and the family. Mrs. Morley in vain endeavoured to recal the wandering senses of her unhappy mother. She was assailed by the tormentor, Conscience; and all the sophistry of the most persuasive tongue could not produce one lucid moment, to convince the wretched parent that she was blessed with the attentions of her deserted daughter; till one day, while she was kneeling before her, and bathing her hands with tears, on a sudden her mother shrieked, "My child! my dear dead Martha! An angel come to save me!" The tone of voice, and the distracted look which accompanied these words, nearly annihilated Mrs. Morley; while with a tremulous voice she replied, "Not dead, but kneeling before you, and imploring you to bless her!"

Her mother now fixed her eyes intently on her: "No, no," said she; "I killed my poor Martha—my best child—I would not own her! She is in heaven, and I shall never see her more!" The faint recollection of her past severity seemed to augment her affliction, and a paroxysm followed which menaced the most fatal consequences.

During the time that the unhappy maniac had been at lord Francis Sherville's, her state of health had precluded the possibility of her being removed with safety. The violent emotions which followed her momentary recollection of Mrs. Morley had scarcely subsided when her wandering fancy again presented the original cause of her derangement. "My poor Martha!" exclaimed the desponding mother: "From her infancy she was never treated kindly: her father did not love her! But they are now together, never again to be separated—all are alike in heaven!" She then inquired after her ungrateful Julia. "She placed me in a prison, to be tortured, to be murdered!" said she. "I held her fast, but she threw me from her arms! I shall never trouble her again!"

The tone of voice and look which accompanied these words convinced Mrs. Morley that the powers of recollection were not wholly annihilated. The mental faculties were shaken, but not overturned. She knew her neglected daughter; she remembered the unfeeling Julia. The breaking heart yet throbbed in unison with the disordered brain, and the sorrows of the former were by memory imprinted on the latter. Hers was the most agonizing species of insanity; for reason had just left sufficient powers of reflection to remind her, by incessant pangs, of the origin of her calamity.

Mrs. Morley, since the hour that she heard of Julia's separation from her husband, had never failed to trace her through all the labyrinths of her destiny. She had from time to time secretly bestowed on her such small sums as her industry provided, with the hope that, by screening her from the misery of pecuniary temptation, she should also shield her from the shame of public degradation: but Julia's mind required not the all-powerful plea of poverty, the stimulating demon Want, to propel her steps where profligate debasement assumed the mask of pleasure: she had not been driven to indiscretion by those taunting mischiefs, pride and adversity: affluence had been her companion from her earliest days; a parent's house, a parent's bosom, were her safeguards. She had still that house, that friend to solace her: she was not driven to wander on the mazy paths of perilous attraction unshielded, and oppressed by a prejudging world.

Mrs. Morley, dreading the fatal termination of her mother's illness, dispatched a letter to her sister, informing her of what had passed, and requesting to see her without delay in Harley-street. She informed her that their parent was in a situation hopeless, and that perhaps a few days would close her scene of mortal misery. In less than an hour the servant returned with an answer, that since Mrs. Morley had thought fit to remove her mother from that house of security in which Julia had placed her—

"Julia!" exclaimed Mrs. Morley, (for she could not proceed,) "did Julia place her parent, her doating parent, in such an habitation?" After a pause, which was marked by a shuddering of horror, she continued to read the letter. It added, that Julia should "take care to prevent any artifice being practised which might operate to her prejudice; for that the will of her mother was in her possession, which was signed when she was in her senses."— She reminded Martha also, "that the deed of a maniac would not prove valid;" and concluded her infernal epistle by informing Mrs. Morley, that she could not think of visiting any part of her family under the roof of such a person as lord Francis Sherville.

Martha was almost frantic. She knelt before her dying mother, and in mute despair beheld her altered features. They were already fixed in death; her eyes had lost their lustre, her lip was parched and colourless; and in a few moments her last sigh proclaimed the termination of every earthly suffering. Mrs. Morley's shrieks brought lord Francis to the chamber. He bore her from the scene of unutterable anguish; and by every gentle, kind attention, restored her nearly palsied senses.

On the following day lord Francis entreated that Mrs. Morley would indulge him in the task of solacing her grief, by reading to her, and by his conversation. It was at this interesting moment that he confessed a cherished and undeviating passion; that he had seen Mrs. Morley at Bath previous to her marriage, and had disclosed his intentions of making her the offer of his hand in confidence to lady Penelope Pryer, who dissuaded him from his purpose by an assurance that she was engaged to Mr. Morley. Still he could not conquer the affection of his heart; and having been informed by Julia that Mr. Morley had departed for the continent shortly after their marriage, he resolved on secluding himself in the neighbourhood of the family mansion, with the hope of finding a favourable opportunity of speaking to her.

Mrs. Morley recollected the story of Mrs. Sedgley, and shuddered.

Lady Penelope was still the confidante of his proceedings, and by her concerted plan with sir Lionel, lord Francis was introduced at Morley-house. Julia readily became a confederate in the mischief, because she had her designs also: but they were on the heart of Mr. Morley; which circumstances propelled lady Pen to take an active part in the confederacy; for she hoped that, by promoting an attachment between Julia and Mr. Morley, she should wholly destroy any remaining partiality which might be entertained for her by sir Lionel Beacon.

CHAPTER XLIII

Lord Francis having candidly avowed the whole series of machinations, with noble and ingenuous pride confessed himself her lover: but at the same time he conjured her to believe that his sense of her virtues would ever shield her from a dishonourable motive. "Your distresses," said he, "your sensibility, awaken all the purer feelings of my soul. But destiny having placed you under my protection, you shall find it a safe and sacred shelter from every species of persecution. Yet as calumny is lynx-eyed, and as I value your reputation far more than I should enjoy the triumphs of a boyish vanity, I will not remain under the roof while you condescend to acknowledge it as your asylum. This night I will find a lodging where I shall remain as long as you will honour my home by calling it your own."

The generosity of lord Francis's conduct penetrated Mrs. Morley's heart, and almost staggered her belief respecting the authenticity of Mrs. Sedgley's story: she could scarcely suppose it possible that a soul so nobly philanthropic would have debased itself by an action so unworthy; and yet the circumstances which had transpired were so strongly calculated to corroborate his guilt, that even the humanity of his behaviour towards her, by appearing like assumed virtue, tended only to brand him with hypocrisy.

"Ah, my lord!" said Mrs. Morley with a sigh, "had you been always thus kind, thus generous——" she hesitated.

"Go on," cried lord Francis: "I entreat you, if you think that I have ever deviated from feeling or humanity, I conjure you to accuse me."

"My lord, I have no right."

"You have a right," interrupted lord Francis. "You command my affections, and I only wish to prove them worthy of your acceptance."

"Not exclusively," said Mrs. Morley: "there is another object to whom you owe at least some share of tenderness."

"Another object!" repeated lord Francis, changing colour.

"A suffering, amiable woman! an involuntary offender! a widowed wife! a deserted mother!" Lord Francis started, and turned pale.

"I comprehend you," said he, with a tremulous voice: "but I can never see her more."

"Oh, do not utter so barbarous a sentence!" interrupted Martha, taking his hand, and holding it between hers. "Let me be the mediator; let me plead for the unhappy wanderer!" Lord Francis held his handkerchief before his eyes; but the convulsive movement of his lip discovered his emotion.

"You relent—you feel! You are again the angel that I thought you!" said Mrs. Morley.

"I cannot—indeed, Mrs. Morley, I cannot listen to you," said Lord Francis: "My mind has long been struggling betwixt pride and pity."

"Think how amiable the object is for whom I am pleading!"

"I know it all—I know her worth, her claims on my affection; yet——"

"Ah! why will you suffer an intervening thought to sever you from such a being!" interrupted Mrs. Morley.

"I will not! I cannot hear you," replied lord Francis. "I could not bear the thought of a reconciliation! My soul shudders! A revolutionary marriage, followed by debasement which places her beneath the most abject infamy!"

"She is innocent—indeed she is innocent!"

"Impossible!" cried lord Francis. "Proofs are too strong against her. The mistress of a sanguinary monster! Name her no more!"

"Think how severely she had suffered; and if your heart be not dead to every feeling of humanity, let me awaken all its sensibility for the unhappy, the deserted parent of the infant Fanny—the innocent that never has offended."

Lord Francis was overwhelmed. He tore himself from Mrs. Morley's hold, and darted out of the apartment.

This conversation convinced Mrs. Morley that she had not been mistaken respecting the origin of her little *protegée*. The warm affection which she felt for Mrs. Sedgley only tended to excite emotions of resentment towards lord Francis; yet so magically was her heart interested in his favour, that the conflict betwixt admiration and abhorrence was painfully perplexing. At all events she resolved on seeing the unkind lord Francis no more; she therefore wrote a short letter, thanking him for his generous attentions to her and to her mother, and on the same night quitted Harley-street; once more requesting an asylum under the hospitable roof of her city protector, the liberal Mr. Dodson.

CHAPTER XLIV

With the aid of Mr. Dodson Martha arranged the last solemn and sacred offices of filial duty. The body was removed with funeral pomp to the family seat in Kent, where only a few weeks before Mr. Popkins had also paid the great debt of nature. Martha attended the gloomy cavalcade: but what was her surprize, when on arriving at the park-lodge she was refused admittance, by order of her unnatural sister, who had taken possession of the house according to the will of her departed mother.

Mrs. Morley returned to London, and immediately set out in search of her friend Miss Gerard.

On inquiry she found that she had departed for Spa, after eluding the vigilance of her fiend-like step-mother, by the aid of Mr. Dodson. She also heard, that various advertisements, offering a large reward, had been in the several diurnal prints, for the discovery of Mrs. Morley's retreat. She consulted her humane monitor Mr. Dodson, who advised her to follow Sophia to Germany; and liberally provided her with money, for the expences of her journey. On investigating the last will of her deceased mother, she found that twenty thousand pounds had been left to Julia; and only ten guineas to her, to buy decent and necessary mourning. She endeavoured to obtain an interview with her sister previous to her departure for the continent; but she was informed that, in consequence of her mother's legacy, the Leadenhead family had proposed terms of reconciliation, provided Julia never degraded the consequence of the name, by acknowledging the vagabond Mrs. Morley.

The reader will perhaps be anxious to know, during this lapse of time, what became of Mr. Morley. He had secluded himself entirely at the family mansion; regularly attending the duties of religion, and uniformly preaching the importance of piety and benevolence. The sanctity of his manners bespoke the most unexampled virtues. He was the sternly reproving moralist; the village censor; the promulgator of Christian charity; and the unequalled example of candour, honour, and humanity. The labour of his life was that of obtaining a reputation, which might, when the grave closed upon his efforts, ensure the applause and admiration of posterity. The past conduct of his wife had been hostile to all his professed ideas of propriety: she had avowed her opinions without reserve: she had been neglectful of sacred duties; familiar with the humbler orders of society; enthusiastically attached to unexalted merit; and uniformly eager to exercise her will, even in defiance of an husband's authority. All and each of these propensities were by Mr. Morley deemed inimical to social and domestic happiness. He married Martha with the hope of controlling all her actions: he did not reflect that the ingenuous and liberal mind intuitively resists oppression; nor that the husband who would wisely govern, must hold the rein with a yielding, gentle hand, or he will find the effort both painful and destructive.

Mrs. Morley, with one female servant, arrived at Spa without any marvelous adventure. They had travelled without ostentation, and they had consequently been neither cheated nor molested. On stopping near the barrier they inquired after an English lady of the name of Gerard, and were informed that only a few days before her corpse had set out for England. Mrs. Morley's grief was sincere, as her chagrin was poignant. Alone, in a strange country, with only one companion and that a foreigner, she was perplexed almost to desperation.

The carriage arrived at a spacious hotel, and the travellers descended: it was late in the evening; and mademoiselle Josephene, her *companion du voyage*, requested permission to retire to rest, being fatigued with her long journey. Mrs. Morley readily acquiesced in her wish; and, after a short supper, hastened also to her chamber.

She slept but little; her ruminations were of the most sombre cast, and her regret was no less sincere than natural. It was sunrise before she had even slumbered; when, weary with incessant thought, she fell into a deep sleep, which lasted till near noon. On inquiring after her *femme de chambre*, she was informed that mademoiselle had quitted Spa the preceding evening, taking with her the whole of their luggage, not even leaving Mrs. Morley a single change of habiliments.

This event seemed the climax of her vexations; and she was standing near the balcony of her apartment when a beautiful and elegant female, in company with two others, passed the window.

She instantly, by her natural and unaffected manners, knew her to be an Englishwoman; and on inquiry she found that it was the amiable and accomplished Georgina, duchess of Chatsworth.

Mrs. Morley's heart bounded with ecstasy; for what heart that feels the pressure of sorrow does not bound at the name of this enchanting woman? Who that has seen her smile, that has heard her voice, can forbear to own the magic of their power, where they soothe the unhappy, or delight the discerning?

A short note was dispatched, merely saying, that an Englishwoman was unprotected and unhappy. The duchess was not slow in answering such an intimation; for before the messenger could deliver her words, she entered Mrs. Morley's apartment.

Mrs. Morley approached her, not with the mean obsequious bend of servile adulation; but if she inclined her form as the duchess put forth her hand to raise her, it was because she felt that species of adoration which warms the Persian's bosom, when he beholds the rising-sun, the source of all his zeal and all his blessings.

CHAPTER XLV

The duchess requested that Mrs. Morley would return with her to the hotel de ———, where she immediately presented her the choice of whatever habiliments her wardrobe afforded. It was near the hour of dinner, and Mrs. Morley was requested to remain with the duchess. There was a prepossessing diffidence in Martha's manner, which was at the same time blended with an easy modest grace, that never failed to interest the feeling bosom. It cannot therefore astonish the reader that she made a forcible impression on that of the duchess of Chatsworth.

The hour of dinner approached, and Mrs. Morley's spirits were considerably revived by the kindness of her liberal protectress, when the servant announced lady Penelope Pryer.

Mrs. Morley's cheek was blanched by this unexpected event. It seemed as though lady Pen was created to diffuse a perpetual cloud over all her prospects: every corner of the globe appeared to present this evil genius; and every hour convinced her mind, that she was born to be the victim of prejudice.

But the duchess of Chatsworth was not a being created in the common mould; she could hear and she could feel for the child of persecution: Mrs. Morley's manners and her artless story were sure passports to a soul, sustained, inspired, and softened by the fine-wrought energies of virtue and benevolence: she knew that woman was an ill-fated being; that the world was ever ready to condemn, though tardy to investigate; she could discriminate betwixt the erring and the vicious; she could by soothing the compunctuous pangs of a too credulous bosom, reconcile it to that hope, that conscious pride, which would in future be its best and strongest safeguard.

Lady Penelope, during dinner, directed many sidelong glances at the dejected Mrs. Morley; but she studiously avoided making any kind of acknowledgment that she had ever before seen her; until she had satisfied her curiosity, how such a woman could become the associate of the duchess of Chatsworth. But the reader must be informed, that lady Louisa Franklin and lord Francis Sherville were the particular friends of her grace; and that part of Mrs. Morley's story, which appertained to little Fanny, was not wholly enigmatical to the duchess of Chatsworth.

The curious lady Pen waited with painful impatience for an opportunity to hear and to be heard fully on the subject of Mrs. Morley's extraordinary visit. She could not conceive how the duchess of Chatsworth, a woman of the most exemplary conduct, could receive a doubtful character, foster a stranger in a foreign country, and become the avowed patroness of one, who had nothing but talents to support her. Lady Penelope was astonished at such mistaken liberality; and thought it a duty incumbent on her to open the eyes of the duchess, with an idea that she should at the same time close her heart against a defenceless and innocent sufferer.

Mrs. Morley's situation, during dinner, was perplexing and painful. Every word that she addressed to the duchess was listened to with more than common avidity by the ambiguous lady Pen. Every time that her grace evinced the attentions of politeness and hospitality, her ladyship smiled with a sarcastic meaning, which humbled the pride, though it did not diminish the merit of Mrs. Morley. At last the *dessert* was placed upon the table, and the bosom of lady Pen, which was bursting to find vent for its sensations, began to heave with more freedom, because it anticipated the speedy humiliation of her victim.

Mrs. Morley was nothing loath, in affording lady Penelope an opportunity to unburthen the load which evidently oppressed her. She therefore, soon after dinner, quitted the room, and strolling towards the fountain *de la Pouhan*, began to ruminate on the perplexity of her situation. She had not wandered long, when she perceived a chaise driving furiously through the street; being an English carriage, it attracted her attention; she observed it stop at an hotel; when, in a moment, lord Francis and sir Lionel Beacon descended from it. Mrs. Morley would have escaped unseen, but she had not the good fortune to elude the eyes of the baronet. Lord Francis entered the hotel, and sir Lionel hastened down the street in pursuit of Mrs. Morley.

She returned as fast as her fears would carry her, towards her lodgings; and trembling, flew with the most extreme perturbation to her own apartment. The sight of lord Francis had powerfully affected her, and she burst into a flood of tears which came to her relief just at the moment that sir Lionel entered the room.

"This is astonishingly amazing," said the baronet, laughing: "I thought lord Francis had some motive for flying to Spa, beyond that of visiting a sick sister: though he kept up the joke famously, and never even mentioned your being here, during the journey."

"He could not speak of that which he did not know," said Mrs. Morley; "but in order to defeat even the tongue of calumny, I shall instantly depart—"

"And take me with you," interrupted the baronet.

"Pardon me, sir Lionel, I should thereby set calumny at work upon her favorite topic."

"It would be famous notwithstanding," replied the baronet, "and would certainly make old Pen amazingly wretched."

"I cannot enter into the modern system of tormenting my own sex," replied Mrs. Morley: "I cannot destroy my own reputation, merely for the pleasure of levelling that of another."

"Astonishingly foolish indeed!" said the baronet. "Pen has had her share of amusement; and she should give precedence to those who have more pretensions to celebrity."

"Notoriety would be the more appropriate term," said Mrs. Morley.

"Oh! that she will claim unrivalled to the close of the century," said sir Lionel; "and they will probably end together; no less distinguished for their series of eventful changes. Pen, like the *anno Domini*,[1] has had her days, and will soon be forgotten. Her old friends already begin to forsake her."

"She has one at least that is indulgent," said Mrs. Morley; "and he is certainly the oldest."

"Who the devil is he?" cried the baronet; "I should like to know, for the curiosity of the thing."

"Time," replied Mrs. Morley.

"I find him my greatest torment," said sir Lionel; "for he is ever before me, and I do not know how to employ him."

"And yet Time is always moving," said Mrs. Morley.

"And always tedious," sighed the baronet. "Nobody knows how to make him gay but old Pen Pryer."

"In return for which he will, when she steals to the grave, consign her to oblivion," cried Mrs. Morley. As she spoke the door flew open, and lady Penelope rushed into the apartment.

"Monstrous effrontery!" exclaimed her ladyship. Mrs. Morley, with a glance of ineffable contempt, quitted the room, and hastened to find the duchess of Chatsworth.

She found her exactly what she had left her; kind, liberal, and unprejudiced. She received Mrs. Morley with the same undescribable and fascinating affability, and with the most graced sincerity unfolded all the mystery of lady Penelope's evident inquietude. Mrs. Morley again assured the duchess of her innocence, and only requested her aid which might enable her, without delay, to set out for England.

---

[1] The Latin phrase meaning "in the year of our lord," was also used colloquially as a term for old age.

CHAPTER XLVI

Martha's bosom was somewhat relieved from its load of anxiety by the duchess's kindness; yet, had she not known that lord Francis was at Spa, she had commenced her journey with more heartfelt satisfaction. The place which contains the object dearest to our affections seems always more delightful than any other; and England had already lost more than half its attractions, by the discovery of the preceding evening. Yet it would have been frenzy not to depart. Every pang of disappointed hope menaced her in a foreign country, with such an enemy as lady Penelope Pryer. The carriage waited at her door more than an hour, when, with a constrained resolution, she entered it, and with a faltering voice bid the postillions proceed towards Liege.[1]

Mrs. Morley had delayed setting out till the sun was more than half way in its diurnal progress. In addition to this circumstance her limited finances only allowed her a pair of horses, which, fastened to a heavy German carriage, moved as slow as though she had been attending a funeral procession. The evening began to close before she had half accomplished her day's route, and at the still gloomy hour of twilight she found herself in a solitary wood, with no guide or companion but a German postillion, who, studying his own convenience more than her safety, jogged on, either singing or smoking, as his fancy dictated.

Night rapidly advanced, and Mrs. Morley's terrors augmented with the deepening gloom that every moment shut in the prospect. She had passed the wood, and was now crossing a wide and barren plain, which presented neither tree nor hovel, to diversify the blank space of darkness, till the full moon rose majestically, crimson, and emerging from black clouds, and only rendering the scene more melancholy, by presenting its barren wild expanse; while the wind whistled shrilly, and the weary horses proceeded more tardily than ever.

They had not proceeded half a league, when the postillion suddenly stopped, and informed her that he could go no farther.

---

[1]   A town approximately seventeen miles northwest of Spa.

He added, that the road at about a mile's distance was inundated by a deep flood, so as to render it impassable; that she had her choice either to remain till morning in her carriage, or to pass the night in a small post-house on the heath. Mrs. Morley in vain endeavoured to persuade her guide to pursue his journey. His horses were weary; the waters were dangerous to pass; the night was cold; his hands were nearly frozen; and his pipe extinguished: such persuasive and cogent reasons decided Mrs. Morley's conduct, and she consented to remain that night at the post-house.

On entering a dirty room she found the whole family singing after supper. The appearance of such a traveller caused no small commotion; and in a few minutes she was ushered into a gloomy chamber, where a tolerable repast was served; and she once more, by a clear coal-fire, considered herself in perfect safety.

Mrs. Morley now began to reproach herself for her reluctance to leave lord Francis; his kindness towards her had been unbounded, but the story of Mrs. Sedgley rushed into her mind, and while her heart throbbed with gratitude, it also shuddered at the idea of his past conduct: on reflection she beheld lord Francis as the betrayer of her friend, as the deserter of the unborn Fanny; and at the same moment she loved and hated, revered and detested the man, whom she considered as the most fascinating and most dangerous of human beings.

However such a character might seem the reverse of that which lord Francis's conduct towards Mrs. Morley had exemplified, she had just cause for her conclusions. The handkerchief, with the coronet and initial of his name; his evident distress on finding the infant; his change of countenance when he first saw it; his inquiries respecting the mother; his knowledge of her hand-writing; his consequent determination to adopt it as his own; and her last conversation with him in Harley-street; all confirmed her suspicions too strongly, to leave even a shadow of skepticism.

Mrs. Morley was little inclined to sleep; and the family in the room beneath her chamber continued singing till near midnight. Her soul was deeply troubled by a variety of hopes and fears respecting her future destiny; till she opened her window, when the bleak plain, presenting to her view a clear moon-light giving a solemnity to the solitary expanse, inspired her mind with a

pensive melancholy that seemed to harmonize every perturbed
sensation. The wind blew keen, and the air was chilling; she again
closed the window, and once more trimming her woodfire,
sought the soft solace of the muse, while the pale moon-beams
aided the feeble lamp which shed its light upon her table. After
a pause of a few minutes, alternately looking towards the lonely
plain and on the paper before her, she hastily wrote as follows:

'Tis night, and o'er the barren plain
　The weary wand'rer bends his way;
　While on his path the silv'ry ray
Soothes him with hope that he shall see
The cloudy shadows quickly flee,
　And morn return again.

The blast blows nipping on his breast,
　Swift flies the wild and foamy stream;
　Yet hope presents a feeble gleam,
That ere day rises he shall close
His weary lids in soft repose,
　And find a bed of rest.

The moon is dim, by clouds o'ercast,
　Loud roars the torrent down the vale;
　The wand'rer's cheek is cold and pale;
He hears the owl with boding cry
Across the dreary desert fly;
　He starts, and stops, aghast!

And now in haste, with dumb despair,
　O'er bush and brier he bends his way;
　No cottage taper's length'ning ray
Gleams faint across the barren heath;
He trembles, sighs, and thinks of death—
　And breathes a timid prayer.

And now the dawn is rising fast,
　Soft flies the fresh and cheering gale;

The purpling clouds on light wings fail,
The dew begems the fragrant heath,
No more he starts or thinks of death,
    Or sighs for sorrows past.

So through life's journey we descry
    Man gay or sad; he weeps or smiles,
    As care annoys or hope beguiles;
Then, blest are those who wisely say—
    "We will enjoy the *present* day,
    "To-morrow we may DIE!"[1]

CHAPTER XLVII

As she concluded the last stanza she heard a loud knocking at the
door of the post-house, and a voice calling at the same time for
assistance. She opened her window and inquired the meaning of
so unseasonable a visit. The messenger was a peasant-youth, who
informed her, that a carriage had been overturned by the rapid-
ity of the flood, which every moment swelled higher in the valley,
and that the travellers were in danger of speedy destruction.

Mrs. Morley rushed from her chamber; and, with the whole
family, flew to the scene of menaced desolation. A female had,
with the aid of the postillion, reached the outside of the carriage,
and was sitting on the hind wheel, while the roaring torrent
foamed on every side round her perilous situation. The moonlight presented her figure, but her shrieks were lost in the terrific
din of the impetuous stream. Mrs. Morley was almost subdued
by terror, when the peasant-boy proposed wading chin-deep
through the water, to assist the traveller. The postillion endeavoured to prevent his attempting so dangerous an enterprize, with
a muttered remark, that they were aristocrats, and consequently

---

[1] This poem was published in *The Morning Post* on September 6, 1799, as "Stanzas, from
Mrs. Robinson's *Natural Daughter*."

not worth preserving. The inhumanity of this observation only served to stimulate the noble-minded peasant, who instantly entered the water, and proceeded towards the carriage.

The spectators who stood as if petrified with astonishment at the philanthropy of the heroic boy, encouraged him with acclamations of applause, though no one attempted to follow his example. He reached the carriage, and in a moment was observed returning towards the margin of the stream; leaving the female in the same fearful situation as when he had first seen her. He approached the bank; Mrs. Morley stretched forth her hands to receive a bundle which he presented. She snatched it eagerly; it was an infant.

On taking it to her bosom she felt its little arms thrown round her neck, clasping her with all its strength and trembling with terror. The valiant boy again rushed into the torrent, followed by a traveller who had the moment before arrived at the scene of disaster. Mrs. Morley, not doubting but that success would attend their enterprize, flew to the post-house with her little treasure. She uncovered the infant, which was wrapped in a satin cloak, and found it as beautiful, as from its dress it was evidently high-born. She pressed it again and again to her beating heart; and was absorbed in caressing it, when lord Francis Sherville entered the room, bearing lady Louisa in his arms, whom he had rescued from destruction. The joy on all sides was only to be equalled by the consternation; when lady Louisa embracing Mrs. Morley, exclaimed, "O, my amiable, my long lost friend! the infant you have saved, is little Fanny!"

Mrs. Morley's sensations may be imagined, but cannot be described. Lady Louisa was in a state of health that rendered her unequal to the fatigue and terror she had experienced, and she shortly after retired to rest, Mrs. Morley willingly taking charge of Fanny.

At breakfast, on the following morning, lord Francis informed the friends, that through the busy information of lady Pen Pryer, he had discovered Mrs. Morley's being driven from Spa by the persecutions of sir Lionel; and fortunate was the moment when he, in the pursuit of the amiable fugitive, found a lost and suffering sister.

"We will return together," said lord Francis; "Mrs. Morley will not refuse to be the companion of my drooping Louisa; where, where can minds be more congenially united?"

"You shall not leave me, my friend," said lady Louisa; taking her hand and faintly smiling.

"I *will* not," replied Mrs. Morley.

Lord Francis immediately ordered horses to his carriage, and they all set out for Spa, delighted with their unexpected meeting. They travelled slowly, lady Louisa's ill-state of health rendering her scarcely able to bear the fatigue of a carriage; and it was some time after sun-set that they arrived.

On the following morning they all hastened to visit the duchess of Chatsworth, who informed them that lady Penelope and sir Lionel had departed on the preceding evening. The duchess was also on the point of setting out for England; and lady Louisa having consulted her physicians, was ordered back to her own country; where her native air and the Bristol waters were recommended as the most promising restoratives.[1]

CHAPTER XLVIII

One evening, previous to their departure, lord Francis accompanied lady Louisa and Mrs. Morley to the public rooms; where persons of all ranks and all nations indiscriminately assembled. Several gaming-tables were open in various parts of the saloon; and gold seemed a mere drug, which every one was eager to obtain, and as eager to get rid of.

Lord Francis, though not by habit a professed gamester, had not resolution to resist the temptations around him. He took his seat at a faro table,[2] lost a few guineas, became irritated by his ill-

---

[1] Receiving the same advice from her physician in the spring of 1800, Robinson wrote a letter asking "a *noble* debtor" for financial assistance: "Without your aid I cannot make trial of the Bristol waters, the *only* remedy that presents to me any hope of preserving my existence." According to her *Memoirs*, "no answer was returned" (2: 152–54).

[2] Faro was an enormously popular betting game. According to Rosamond Bayne-Powell, the game, originally spelled "pharo," took its name from the Egyptian king depicted on one of the cards. See *Eighteenth-Century London Life* (New York: E.P. Dutton, 1938), 46–47.

fortune, redoubled his stake, and in less than half an hour rose a loser of four thousand pounds. But what was his surprize when he was informed that the faro bank was supplied by an Englishman, and that a credulous and unsuspecting woman was the dupe of his illegal occupation.

Lord Francis remained two days at Spa wholly for the purpose of investigating this business. Report affirmed that the gamester had won no less than ten thousand pounds, in the course of a few months, in his honourable undertaking; though his creditors in England were left to lament their confidence in one whom public fame and public chronicles had denominated a man of private worth and professional reputation.

On the third day lord Francis made a visit to the lady, who was supposed to be the confidential friend of the adventurer. He found her in sorrow for his departure, but wholly a stranger to his recent good fortune; for the liberal gamester had allowed her no participation in the smiles of the capricious goddess; though he had left her a plentiful share of debts, which had been contracted for their mutual support; and which, by her mistaken credulity, during a long tried and generous friendship, she was totally unable to discharge.

Lord Francis, his sister, Mrs. Morley, and little Fanny, now set out for England. Lady Louisa's spirits were considerably exhilarated by the attentions of her brother, and by the hope that, in case of her death, her infant *protegée* would find a feeling and affectionate protector.

On their arrival in London Mrs. Morley's first inquiries were after her sister Julia; but she could obtain no intelligence what was become of her. The Leadenheads had failed in their wish for a reconciliation, and the young squire now wore the badge of military prowess, with an *eclat* that did honour to his family. He had twice marched from Norwich to Canterbury, and from Canterbury to Dover; and his feats of valour had even rivalled those of a sir John Falstaff, or a major Sturgeon.[1]

---

[1] Major Sturgeon, in Samuel Foote's comedy *The Mayor of Garratt* (1763), is a fishmonger commissioned to serve as an officer in the Middlesex militia. Like Shakespeare's Falstaff, he is associated with bumbling bravado rather than with genuine feats of valor.

Finding every inquiry after Julia ineffectual, Mrs. Morley set out for Bristol with lady Louisa Franklin and little Fanny. Lord Francis having business of importance to transact in London, made his excuses and promised to follow them. Mrs. Morley's assiduities continued to solace her sick friend, till hope at length began to brighten in her eyes, and smile upon her cheek, in defiance of the canker-worm which preyed upon her heart. Lady Louisa loved sir Lionel Beacon; she knew that beneath a volatile and dissipated exterior, many virtues were concealed, which only wanted energy to draw them into action. Sir Lionel had been spoilt in his education; but the graces of his person had been the origin of all his eccentricity. He was like a beautiful casket, which every eye admired; but which contained a jewel that would, if carefully polished, convert admiration into idolatry. Even his language and his manners were prompted by the capricious Sylph, which holds the rein of fashion: for there were moments when his conversation was rational and his demeanour grave. He could be what he pleased; and he could please whenever he chose to be what nature made him. The society of a lady Penelope Pryer was not calculated to steal the thorns from this fascinating bud of fashion. That task remained for the more omnipotent powers of lady Louisa Franklin.

On their arrival at Bath, in their *route* towards Bristol, they found the duchess of Chatsworth the object of universal idolatry: all ranks, all ages, from the lisping infant to the feeble veteran, blessed her: Mrs. Morley again experienced the most liberal attention, and received a request to accompany lady Louisa on a visit to the family castle. It was situated in Derbyshire, and a promise was made that as soon as lady Louisa should be sufficiently recovered she would, accompanied by her friend, accept the invitation. After two days they proceeded to Bristol. Lady Louisa, on her arrival, immediately drank of that salubrious spring which has been known to counteract even the ravages of mental pain; and in the course of three weeks she began to display a renovation of health which gladdened every beholder.

During this interval lord Francis had been indefatigable in his attentions towards Mrs. Morley. She had by her unassuming virtues so entirely taken possession of his heart, that her dominion was indubitably visible: while she, with an unconsciousness originating in the diffidence of her nature, considered his zeal as the effect of gratitude for her unceasing devotions to his amiable and suffering sister.

Lady Louisa's health continued to improve daily, and having left off drinking the waters, her physician advised change of air to complete her recovery. It was now that Mrs. Morley reminded her of her engagement in Derbyshire, and every arrangement was speedily made for their journey; all parties being equally impatient to enjoy the society of the lovely duchess.

On the evening preceding that which was fixed on for their departure, lady Louisa proposed going to the theatre. The play was a comedy; and they engaged a stage box for the accommodation of their party. On the curtain drawing up, the first female that entered was Mrs. Sedgley. Mrs. Morley's heart bounded with joy at the sight of her old companion in misfortune; but lady Louisa complained of sudden indisposition; requested lord Francis to call up her carriage, and with feeble steps, leaning at the same time on Mrs. Morley's arm for support, quitted the theater.

"Oh, my friend!" said lady Louisa, as soon as she was seated in the carriage, "the Mrs. Sedgley whom we just now saw upon the stage, in the character of lady Townley,[1] is———" She could say no more.

Mrs. Morley had not power to speak, and they returned home without any farther conversation; a thousand conjectures haunted Martha's brain, and interrupted her slumbers. She hoped, feared, pitied, and admired, as her thoughts wandered alternately to little Fanny, lord Francis, Mrs. Sedgley, and lady Louisa.

CHAPTER XLIX

On the following morning lord Francis rose early, and requested a private interview with Mrs. Morley. Guessing the origin of

---

[1] Lady Townley is a character in George Etherege's comedy *The Man of Mode* (1676). Robinson, however, may be referring to Lady Townly, the leading lady in Colley Cibber's *The Provoked Husband*. At the end of the play, she renounces the pleasures of the town and proclaims that "Married Happiness is never found from Home."

such a message, she readily acquiesced, and as it was her hour of walking before breakfast, they proceeded towards the hot-wells, at the foot of the precipice, together.

"I am always intruding on your goodness," said lord Francis, "but I know by experience that it is inexhaustible. I have now a task to impose which will, however, require no apology. The sensations of your own heart will repay you for the trouble." Mrs. Morley thanked lord Francis for his good opinion, and he proceeded, not without evident embarrassment.

"The person whom you saw last night, though perhaps in her present situation not recognized by you, is the mother of little Fanny. Long, too long, has she been lost to the world; it shall be your office to restore her."

"Oh heavens!" cried Mrs. Morley, while tears of sensibility, trembling with the trill of joy, glistened in her eyes.

"Yes, amiable philanthropist, from your lips she shall receive the pledge of my future kindness; from your hands this earnest of my returning affection." Lord Francis took from his pocket-book a bank note of one hundred pounds; "take it to the unfortunate Mrs. Sedgley."

"Not from me, my lord, not from my hand must she receive this generous proof of your relenting kindness; your voice will soothe her sorrows; your arm will shield her from the world's unkindness; your protection will defeat the power of envious persecution."

"I cannot see her," replied lord Francis; "I should not be able to support the trial."

"And will you never see her?" said Mrs. Morley earnestly; "can you forget that you once loved her tenderly?"

"A time may come," hesitated lord Francis.

"That time may be too late; think what a weary period a few hours of solicitude presents. Consult your own feelings, and by them judge what the unhappy Mrs. Sedgley suffers." Mrs. Morley's words visibly affected lord Francis, and they were walking slowly by the river side, where they perceived, standing on the woody point of the opposite precipice, a woman.

She seemed impatient; now descending by the narrow path of the declivity; now darting amidst the overhanging trees, which blackened the stupendous altitude of ridgy rocks, and cast a deep shadow on the slow gliding water. They watched her with fearful agitation. The deep river parted them from the object of their solicitude; and the thin vapours of morning rendered her indistinctly visible. Her dress was white, which, contrasted with the dark woods behind her, first rendered her an object of attention. They hastened to the ferry at a small distance, with the hope of crossing the river and snatching the rash woman from destruction; but on traversing the opposite bank, they saw no more of her. Horror and despair filled the bosom of Mrs. Morley and lord Francis; they concluded that the victim had perished; and, with the most deeply impressive sorrow, returned to their lodgings.

Mrs. Morley, with much eloquence, at length persuaded lord Francis to accompany her to Bristol in search of Mrs. Sedgley. On their arrival at her lodgings, they were informed that before sun-rise she had departed.

On the evening of the following day they set out for Derbyshire. On Mrs. Morley's passing within a few miles of Morley-house, she found that her husband had been for some time gradually wasting in health and strength, and that little hope was entertained of his recovery. The exquisite sensibility of Martha's heart was roused at hearing this intelligence. "Perhaps," said she sighing, "time and reflection have taught him to think kindly of me. Religion and philanthropy are the antidotes of prejudice and revenge; Mr. Morley must not die in ignorance of my wrongs, nor unsatisfied of my innocence."

Lady Louisa, who felt the force of Mrs. Morley's appeal to sympathy, instantly offered to become the mediator. The proposal was accepted, and Martha's hope of an honourable acquittal triumphed over the affections of her heart. She loved lord Francis, but Mr. Morley was her husband; her dying husband, perhaps the victim of mistaken opinions, or, what was still more painful, of compunctious sorrows.

They stopped at an inn two miles from Morley-house. Lord Francis and Martha alighted, while lady Louisa proceeded in her carriage towards the family mansion. She was scarcely out of sight when Mr. Morley passed the window at which his wife and lord Francis were standing. He stopped his horse, and entered the inn. Mrs. Morley's heart beat high with agitation. She flew to meet him; she would have thrown herself into his arms; but a repulsive effort flung her from him, and she fell; the blow completely stunned her.

Lord Francis, hearing her fall, rushed from the apartment where Mrs. Morley had left him, and hastened to her assistance. Mr. Morley was wild and frantic. His face was pale and ghastly; the spirit of implacable revenge raged in his veins, and as lord Francis attempted to raise Mrs. Morley from the ground, a blow was aimed at him; it met his breast. Lord Francis flew to his pistols, which he had brought from the carriage, and they instantly retired to a field near the road side; where, each being deaf to reason, madly incensed, and furiously impetuous, they measured distance, and at the same moment fired. Mr. Morley's shoulder received the ball of his antagonist, and he was, shortly after, conveyed to Morley-house in a state of excruciating torture.

On Mrs. Morley's recovering from the insensibility which was occasioned by the concussion of her fall, she perceived lord Francis pale and bloody. Her fears interpreted the dreadful symptoms, and she was nearly frantic; with the wildness of despair she hastened to Morley-house. On her attempting to cross the lawn she was stopped by Mrs. Grimwood, who informed her that she could not enter.

"Who shall prevent me?" inquired Mrs. Morley. "Is it not my husband's house, my natural home; my rightful, merited asylum?"

"This house," said Mrs. Grimwood, "has a new mistress!"

"Heavenly powers!" exclaimed Mrs. Morley, "the pious, the fastidious Mr. Morley! can he avowedly protect a mistress?"

"It is even so," said Mrs. Grimwood, "but neither my master's piety nor his morality can be called in question; for the person I allude to is your sister."

"Julia! is it possible? then I will desist," cried Mrs. Morley; "I will not debase my proudly throbbing breast by resenting such ingratitude. The cold return of scorn shall be their punishment." Mrs. Morley now hastened back to the inn, where she found lady Louisa and her brother waiting impatiently for her return. The ball was extracted the same evening, and lord Francis being assured by the surgeon that Mr. Morley was not in the smallest danger, the party once more set forward to the duchess of Chatsworth's.

CHAPTER L

It is proper that the inquisitive reader should know how Julia came to be the reigning sovereign of Morley-house. Shortly after Mrs. Morley's departure for the continent, her husband received a letter from Julia, informing him that Martha had set out for Spa with lord Francis Sherville, while she was disconsolate for the loss of her mother, and left wholly unprotected to combat her affliction. Mr. Morley, who had always evinced a partiality for Julia, now invited her to pass her days of mourning at the manor house; where her merits and her sensibility would be properly appreciated. Julia had wasted many months in unbounded dissipation; she had indulged the capricious feelings of her heart, even at the expence of every moral virtue. Weary of the swift routine of folly and of vice, and stung by the remembrance of her past duplicity, she resolved on laying siege to the heart of Mr. Morley, for three reasons: first, because he was rich and had no heir; secondly, because he was declining rapidly to the grave; and thirdly, because being a near relation, the purity of her character would not be violated by her claiming his avowed protection.

Julia seemed all softness and complacency. She never omitted the duties of devotion. At church she was piously humble; at home dignified and sentimental; she was an admirer of hereditary distinctions; she never conversed familiarly with her inferiors; and, above all, she pitied with energetic sorrow, the unmerited neglect which Mr. Morley had experienced from her ill-fated sister.

With this powerful artillery of arts the subtle Julia soon undermined the affections of Mr. Morley; and, at the period of her sister's return, she was in full possession of that dominion which Martha's noble and ingenuous nature could not accomplish.

CHAPTER LI

Shortly after their arrival at the duchess of Chatsworth's, a party was made to Buxton. The name of Mrs. Morley would have terrified the whole phalanx of fastidious water-drinkers, had she appeared among them under any protection less powerful than that of the duchess. But the lustre of her virtue shed light on every lesser constellation; and the dark shades which prejudice had thrown on Mrs. Morley's character, were wholly done away amidst the splendours of her patroness.

The only personages who rigidly resisted the claims of persecuted merit, were those that composed the Leadenhead family. They could not condescend to notice a woman who had been an actress, and who had separated herself from her husband; though the exercise of her talents had been the effect of necessity, exciting her to a laudable and honourable species of obtaining independence; and though her husband's unkindness and neglect had driven her from her natural home, to seek for support from an unfeeling world.

The Leadenheads, notwithstanding their high sense of family dignity, could stoop as low as lesser persons, where they hoped to obtain a smile or a nod from the titled or the exalted. It was only the needy child of genius who had no tribute to hope for from the petrifying hand of avaricious pride; yet if the most contaminated stream of noble blood deigned to mingle with their dull source of circulation, their hearts beat gratefully, and their veins confessed a prouder glow of self-importance.

Young Leadenhead, finding that all hopes failed of reconciliation with his frail wife's splendid fortune, instituted a suit in Doctor's Commons[1] to set aside the marriage, both parties being under age, and the gentle bride having presented him an heir at least some months before he could have been the natural father. This circumstance being fully proved, success did not fail to attend the legal experiment; and young Leadenhead, once more unencumbered by domestic adornments, as well as by domestic

---

[1] A London court that heard suits for divorce.

virtues, set out on a new matrimonial pursuit, with that confidence which had ever been the prominent characteristic of his family.

Truth was not a perfection much in practice beneath the lofty battlements of Plummet Castle; which might well have been adopted by a modern author of fanciful exhibitions, and justly would it have been denominated the Castle of Romance. Humphrey had so accustomed himself to the sallies of his imagination, that every thing except the labours of a gloomy traffic, appeared to him chimerical. Those he found substantial blessings, yet nature had so closed the avenues of feeling in his bosom, that he was the only person who had cause to rejoice in their reality.

While the Leadenheads were society-hunting at Buxton, the young and enlightened heir of the family was in full chase of another matrimonial alliance. Gregory was not without some pretensions to personal merit. He was what the generality of observers would denominate handsome; if a countenance which presented the blank page of uncultivated intellects can entitle human features to that appellation. In conversation he was as uninformed as the toil-worn Ethiop, whose labours give the stamp of worth to the base dross, which nature scorns to mark as her own sterling treasure. He was a man of letters, it is true; but they were only to his groom or to his father's game-keeper. He wrote many languages, but they were unintelligible even to the most learned. With these and many minor requisites young Leadenhead set out once more, on a laudable embassy to the court of fashion; his credentials written in characters of gold; the most attractive characters to sordid and uncultivated minds; and the object of his important mission was that of ennobling his family.

CHAPER LII

Mrs. Sedgley, during her sojourn at Bristol, inhabited a small cottage near the hanging woods on the summit of those cliffs which tower above the slow-winding Avon, opposite the wells. The sight of lord

Francis had nearly driven her to despair; and at the moment when Mrs. Morley discovered her on the tremendous precipice, she was waiting for a boat which she had engaged, in consequence of having seen them the preceding evening, and which was to convey her secretly across the channel to Chepstow.[1]

On landing at the place of her destination she wrote a letter to lord Francis, explaining the agonies of her mind, and expressing her deep regret for the evident distress which her presence had occasioned lady Louisa to suffer. This letter never reached the hands of lord Francis till six weeks after it was written. He was at Buxton when he received it.

Shortly after the whole party set out for London. Mrs. Morley was still the inseparable friend of lady Louisa Franklin, and the exclusive object of lord Francis's tenderest affections. Every day augmented her power over his mind, and every hour convinced her that he was the most amiable of mortals.

Mrs. Sedgley's retirement was tranquil, and congenial to her feelings. A pleasant lodging in a farm house (with an annuity of two hundred pounds from the duchess of Chatsworth, who had once known, and never ceased to love her) presented more serene repose to her aching heart than that heart had ever enjoyed in the turmoil of life, or the glittering paths of ever-varying fashion. Her days passed peacefully, and her nights were undisturbed by feverish dreams. She knew that her little Fanny was safe under the protection of lady Louisa and lord Francis, and she had too sensibly experienced the low, fastidious prejudices of an unpitying world, to wish for any further intercourse with its society.

A correspondence was constantly kept up between Mrs. Morley and the world-weary recluse; but with strict injunctions from the latter never to reveal the place of her retirement.

Six months passed, and nothing material occurred in the progress of our history. Little Fanny became a lovely girl, and the darling of her protector's family. Her infantile graces promised all that affection could anticipate, and her sweetness of temper repaid the assiduities which were hourly fostering them to perfection.

---

[1] A port on the Wye River, across the Bristol Channel. The preceding sentence describes a scenic view of St. Vincent's Rocks.

Mrs. Sedgley's health appearing to decay, a change of climate was judged absolutely necessary for the preservation of her existence; she therefore purposed, without delay, setting out for Switzerland. Six months' retirement from the world had left her no relish for its enjoyments. She loathed the din of cities, and with a silent, calm delight looked forward to the mountain solitudes, where she should become the associate of unsophisticated beings, the student of NATURE's school, the inhabitant of those solitudes made sacred by her own philosopher.[1]

On her *route* towards Dover she passed through the metropolis. Her friendship for Martha made her wish for an interview previous to her quitting England: but she had a still more powerful incitement—the maternal longings of a heart, softened by solitude, and throbbing with regret for what she now considered as her past unkindness. The path which leads towards the grave is strewed with thorns, where the compunctious spirit is doomed to measure it. It is in its gloomy, awful mazes, that Reason searches with a discriminating eye, and Memory re-contemplates the gaudy scenes where Folly danced on roses, while Pleasure dashed the cup of life with poisons, whose dregs were destined for the freezing lips of Death.

Mrs. Sedgley had deserted her unhappy offspring—had left it to the mercy of a hard-judging world: she had given it to a stranger's bosom, without even a name; and though that Power, which shields the innocent and fosters the forsaken, had warmed the heart of Martha with the glow of genuine pity, her deed was no less criminal. She reflected—she was wretched.

On the night of her arrival in London she repaired to Harley-street. The family being at the Opera, Mrs. Sedgley inquired for the nurse who had the care of Fanny. By informing her that she was a distant relation of the infant's mother, and on the eve of setting out for the continent, she obtained a sight of her long-lost infant. The sorrows which she had been doomed to suffer were less agonizing than this moment of excessive sensibility. She pressed the unacknowledged innocent to her bosom: she blessed it, for the first time, with a mother's kisses: she wished now,

---

[1]   Rousseau [M.R.'s note].

ardently wished, to steal that precious treasure which fear and a false pride had once induced her to abandon.

She longed to embrace lord Francis: but the recollection of his past unkindness checked the warm impulse of affection; and while her bosom throbbed with tenderness, it glowed with indignation.

Still, in the delirium of parental joy, she hung over her unconscious offspring. She raised her from the pillow where she was sleeping. The infant shrieked, and struggled to get from her. "Well may'st thou shun me!" exclaimed the agonized mother: "Well may those eyes behold me with abhorrence—those tears reproach me! Forgive me, innocent, deserted angel! forgive that wretch whose false delicacy could master her maternal fondness—who could expose thy helpless infancy to the perils of a world, whose scorn her timid sensibility had not courage to encounter!"

At this moment the nurse quitted the apartment. Fanny, soothed by her mother's softness of voice, smiled as she stretched forth her arms to fold them round Mrs. Sedgley's neck. The sensation which this involuntary movement conveyed was such as she had never before experienced. She snatched her hitherto-deserted offspring to her heart, and wrapping it in her cloak, rushed out of the nursery. In a few moments she reached the street, and on the same night set off for Dover.

Mrs. Sedgley, previous to her embarkation for the continent, wrote an affectionate letter to lady Louisa Franklin, thanking her and lord Francis for their care of her deserted child, and avowing her resolution to pass the remainder of her days in Switzerland, far from the pride of her oppressors and the scorn of an ill-judging world.

CHAPTER LIII

The divorce which had separated Julia from her husband had so completely blazoned the infamy of her conduct, that Mr. Morley deemed his reputation in some danger, by affording her any longer an asylum at Morley-house: she had therefore retired to Bath, where, having established a faro-table in partnership with an Irish adventurer, her fortune was soon nearly squandered, and her beauty faded in a perpetual series of profligate dissipation. Once more propelled by necessity, Julia set out for the metropolis, resolved, like Milwood,[1] to be rich whatever peril she might encounter in the labour of becoming so. Two thousand pounds, the remnant of her fortune, were laid out in the purchase of a carriage, and the furniture of a house in the vicinity of Mary-le-bone. Julia was still pretty; her face, at least, presented novelty; and for a time she was considered as an acquisition to the world of senseless gallantry.

Among the most zealous of her admirers was a foreign nobleman, whose rank gave consequence to the object of his devotions, but whose necessity was the source of his convenient idolatry. Julia now resumed the name of her family, and the dashing Mrs. Bradford was an object of universal envy. Her curricle was the best appointed of any in Hyde Park; her dress at the Opera, for elegance and splendour, exceeded that of any titled *demirep*[2] in the whole courtly circle; her *faro*-bank was resorted to by all the adventurous minors of nobility; and her table was surrounded by divorced women of quality, military school-boys, dotards of distinction, needy dependents, and gamesters of the most unequivocal reputation.

During one of the nocturnal revels, a constant attendant at her faro-bank, a man of *ton* whose rank was sufficient to silence the tongue of busy animadversion, and whose approved courage was the shield which covered the very blackest vices, introduced a friend to Mrs. Bradford—a friend whom she had seen before, but whose inebriety at that moment absorbed the powers of mutual recollection. The scheme was shortly understood by the sir Clement Cotterel of the scene, and Mrs. Bradford readily agreed to share the advantages of the night with her fashionable *croupier*.[3]

---

[1] Cf. *A Letter to the Women of England*, 77, n. 1.
[2] A woman of dubious reputation.
[3] One who collects and pays bets at a gambling table. Sir Clement Cotterel was master of ceremonies at court.

The newly-initialed gamester was seated at the vortex of destruction; the hostess of the hell kept wisely in the background; and the noon-day sun shed its bright beams on the sleeping heir of the Leadenhead family; while his divorced wife shared the sum of three thousand guineas with her thrice-renowned and thrice-infamous confederate.

Here the matter did not terminate. Young Leadenhead had been entrusted with the sum he had lost for the purchase of a commission. He represented the transaction as illegal: Mrs. Bradford's house was indicted, and the fair hostess sent to do penance in the gloomy cells of solitary confinement.

This unlucky event being announced in the public papers, it was soon conveyed by a variety of channels, to the ear of Mrs. Morley. Mrs. Bradford's situation was the theme of wonder and of pity. She had violated the laws; she deserved the punishment which a less popular person would inevitably have suffered. But Mrs. Bradford was a woman of *haut ton*, and at least a dozen right honourables exerted all their interest to rescue her from her disgraceful predicament. They did not exert themselves in vain; for at the expiration of four days the fair transgressor was liberated, while the adventurous Gregory Leadenhead was content to bear his loss, with a penitent promise to lose no time in ennobling his family.

Lady Louisa Franklin having recovered her health, and with it her personal attractions, sir Lionel Beacon once more confessed himself her zealous admirer. The young baronet had revelled in the plentitude of fashionable pleasure, and satiety had already succeeded the fatigues of dissipation. In addition to the many causes for disgust which every hour presented, sir Lionel had detected his enchanting lady Pen in a *tête-a-tête* party with the younger Leadenhead; and the baronet being more pleased than mortified in finding an opportunity to shake off his long-worn chains, took leave of the right honourable coquette just at the period when lady Louisa returned to London.

For the first moment in his life he felt a serious passion. Lady Louisa's bosom owned a powerful pleader in behalf of her truant favourite; and in a few days, with the consent of lord Francis, they were married.

CHAPTER LIV

Julia, whose credit in the fashionable world had suffered considerably by the adventure at her *faro*-table, departed, with her Gallic lover, for the land of liberty;[1] while Mrs. Morley remained the domesticated friend of the lovely lady Louisa. Felicity now seemed to strew with roses her journey of existence, and every day looked brighter than the former. This scene of rational delight had continued four months, when Mrs. Morley received a letter from Derbyshire, informing her that her husband's health required his speedy departure for Italy; and at the same time requesting to see her previous to his commencing the journey.

The summons of a dying, though undeserving husband, was not to be resisted by a being, generous, noble, and forgiving, like the ill-treated Martha. She had never, in the smallest instance, violated the proprieties of wedded life; she had never been guilty of any action that might, even by the most fastidious, be deemed derogatory to the delicacy of the female character, or the honour of her husband. Prejudice had been her destruction—prejudice, originating in the malevolence of those who envied her felicity.

She informed lady Louisa of the letter which she had received, and requested her counsel, or rather her approbation, of a step which she deemed indispensible. She informed lord Francis of her resolution once more to see Mr. Morley; and, before he closed his eyes for ever, to convince him of her innocence. She took her leave of these friends of her bosom, and on the day after she received the summons she commenced her journey.

On her arrival at Morley-house she found her husband in a state of health which evidently declared his approaching dissolution. His days had been shortened by that stern reprover Conscience; his strength was wasted by nights of feverish rumination, and days of immitigable sorrow. There are mental miseries which reason and reflection cannot meliorate. The consciousness of having injured the innocent and the defenceless is the never-failing source of this heart-corroding evil: this ill, which neither

---

[1] France.

time, nor fortune, nor the swift *routine* of earthly changes, can obliterate or cure. This misery was Mr. Morley's.

As Martha approached him, his pale cheek became suddenly flushed with a sensation of agonizing regret, which all his affected stoicism could not suppress. He met her on the lawn, and taking her hand, led her into the house. He trembled: she was firmly serene. The feelings of their minds, at that trying moment, were wholly dissimilar: he was the voluntary aggressor—she the injured sufferer: he was perturbed, perplexed, and agitated—she was tranquil, collected, and self-acquitted.

They entered the parlour. His looks were languid and his manners confused. Mrs. Morley longed to reassure him with a smile or word of forgiving kindness, but she knew that his proud spirit hated to be obliged; and she was not without apprehensions that any conciliatory advance on her side might, by giving him fresh confidence, turn the compunction of his heart into a new source of tyranny.

She conjectured rightly. Mr. Morley was a being of that order which, to be vanquished, must be little feared. He was struggling with a mental monitor, who, by convincing him of his error, so greatly humbled his self-love, that his pride was ever ready to become the centinel upon his heart, and to banish thence those feelings which would have honoured its sensibility. He dreaded the just resentment of an injured woman, and the conviction that he ought to be ashamed of his past conduct, made him so. His contrition was therefore involuntary.

After a silence of several minutes, during which Mr. Morley endeavoured to suppress the conflicts of pride and justice, he addressed his wife: "Martha," said he, "behold the victim of a reproving conscience! Behold a being, grief-worn and subdued! The grave will shortly open to receive me. I should expire resigned and tranquil could I but know that you are——"

At this moment Martha's soul spoke in the eloquent tear which rushed from her pitying heart. Her husband saw it fall. The word with which he meant to conclude was, *happy*: but encouraged by her visible tenderness and returning solicitude, he substituted that of *innocent*. Mrs. Morley started.

"Forgive my unkindness," said her husband, pressing her hand to

his quivering lips. "I am proud and delicate of my honour——"
Here he paused—"an husband's honor: prove but your innocence——"

"How shall I prove it? Conscious of no offence, I have not even
thought of a defence that might acquit me," said Mrs. Morley.

"Declare whether or not you are the mother of little Frances."

"Heavens, what a question!" exclaimed Martha, with a smile
of innocence. She then related the circumstances of her first
discovering the infant and its mother at the cottage: but her
regard for lord Francis, and the respectful affection which she
bore towards his family, prevented her making any discovery of
his being the suspected father.

"Would to heaven I could find its mother!" said Mr. Morley,
as Martha concluded her story. "Do you suppose she is still alive?"

"I hope so," replied Mrs. Morley.

"Do you think so?"

"She lived a few weeks since."

"She must be found," said Mr. Morley: "her concurring testimony would acquit you."

"Am I still suspected?" interrupted Martha, with a blush of
indignant sensibility.

"Not suspected—no, not indeed suspected, Martha," replied
her husband, hesitating and confused: "but I would have your
fame as spotless as your mind; I would see you blameless, exonerated from every shadow of imputation."

"What is there to tarnish my reputation?"

"The profession which you for a time adopted."

"None but the prejudiced and narrow-minded will consider
me culpable from the exercise of my talents."

"True: but the pride of my family will be humbled. You know,
Martha, that religion is the—"

"Talk not of religion," interrupted Mrs. Morley, "after what
you have done!"

"What have I done?" inquired her husband, growing still
more pale and agitated.

"Deserted and exposed to scorn, an innocent wife!"

"Wife!" repeated Mr. Morley: "Yes, Martha," said he, recovering
himself, "you are my wife. I have been to blame. But your sorrows

were not wholly of my creating: your sister——"

"Julia?" cried Mrs. Morley.

"Yes, Julia: she was the serpent whose subtle poison contaminated your repose: she first told me——"

"What?"

"That you were infamous!"

"O God! is it possible?" cried Mrs. Morley: "my sister!"

"That sister was your rival. The child she bore was mine! She was the soft, seducing fiend that tempted me to the destruction of your happiness; and I should even to this hour have been the dupe of her artifice, had I not suspected that, to augment her catalogue of crimes, she neglected and destroyed it."

Mrs. Morley fell into her husband's arms, overpowered with horror.

"Martha, exert your fortitude," cried Mr. Morley. "Remember, you have yet an awful task to perform: you have yet to close the eyes of a repentant sufferer!"

"O, heaven forbid!" cried Mrs. Morley, throwing her arms round the drooping form of her subdued and dying husband. "I forgive you all! I can forgive and pity even your unjust suspicions! Revive, live, and be happy!"

"That is impossible," replied her husband. "I have a load of sorrow on my heart that weighs it down to despondency.—But we must find the mother of your fugitive."

"She resides in Switzerland," said Mrs. Morley: "she has long been weary of the world, and now, I trust, enjoys that calm felicity which its busy scenes denied her. I know her place of residence; for I have never, during all the changes of her destiny, amidst the anguish of fond regret, or the perpetual pressure of unmerited vicissitudes, forgotten her."

"Tell me her name," said Mr. Morley, eagerly.

"I must first obtain her leave," replied Martha. "The confidence of sorrow is too sacred to be violated for any interested motives. She has already been compelled to bear insult, neglect, and scorn; shall I, who am her friend, the dearest friend she has, betray her? Shall I drag forth her treasured silent griefs to public view, and expose her poverty to the unpitying eye of vulgar observation?"

"Your own reputation is at stake," said Mr. Morley.

"And so is hers."

"Think of the disgrace that you will suffer."

"That disgrace I bear," said Mrs. Morley; "and having, by an adverse destiny, so long endured it, I have been taught to know its pain too well to inflict it on another."

"An husband claims this confidence."

"And a dear suffering friend deserves it," said Mrs. Morley.

"Remember, Martha, I can command a fortune that will ensure you every pleasure, every means of gratifying the utmost wishes of your heart," said Mr. Morley: "you will act wisely in satisfying my mind on this important subject."

"You would but ill bestow your wealth on a being who could break a promise made so solemnly to such a woman. The sufferings of superior natures bear a charm that twines about the heart; for grief and persecution fall most heavily on that bosom whose fibres are softened by early habits of tenderness and sensibility."

"You acknowledge some *distinctions* in society, then?" said Mr. Morley, with an approving smile.

"I respect superior talents, when they are converted to laudable uses by the polish of education," replied Martha; "and humanity tells us to soothe the unhappy."

"True, Martha—true, my love!" interrupted Mr. Morley, taking her hand, and again pressing it to his lips.

"Besides," continued Martha, "the mother of poor Frances had no friend to solace her afflictions. Destined to endure a melancholy exile, she mourns the falsehood of an ungrateful husband."

"Husband!" repeated Mr. Morley. "Is she then married?"

"Married and deserted," replied Martha: "left to encounter the scorn of a taunting and pitiless world, yet blest with a mind so rich and so enlightened, that even its severest scorn cannot subdue her fortitude."

"Left by an ungrateful husband! married, and then deserted!" again repeated Mr. Morley.

"Does her deceiver live? Of what rank is he? This is not a moment to dissemble. The happiness of an amiable woman, (for as such you report the mother of Fanny), the future welfare of the infant, my peace of mind, and your own honour, demand an unequivocal explanation."

"The father of poor Fanny is a man of the most exalted rank."

"Indeed!"

"Most certainly," answered Martha: "a man who, to all outward seeming, is the most honourable, the most liberal of mortals."

"You know him, Martha? It is in vain that you would endeavour to deceive me," said Mr. Morley, with increased agitation.

"I do know him; and I should, but for his conduct respecting the mother of Fanny, idolize his name."

"Perdition seize him!" exclaimed Mr. Morley, starting from his seat, and becoming pale with anger. Then suddenly turning hastily towards his wife, he continued, "Is it well, madam—is it decent to avow your fondness even in the presence of an injured husband? But lord Francis Sherville, though placed on the highest eminence of fortune, is not above the penalty of his dishonour. His crimes appear with tenfold enormity, because they are placed on an altitude which renders them more conspicuous than those of common beings. Born to embellish society, to exhibit an example to those of an humbler destiny, his birth, his education, his noble, liberal mind, on which you so love to expatiate, should teach him to soar above the vices of vulgar individuals."

Mrs. Morley's eyes were bent upon the ground. She sighed: but she felt the truth of her husband's reasoning; and even her partiality for lord Francis could not urge a plea in extenuation of his conduct. Mr. Morley, after a short pause, again addressed her.

"You do not answer me! Are then even the vices of lord Francis exempt from your abhorrence? Cannot your fond, your fatal enthralment yield to the conviction of his unworthiness?"

"Lord Francis is but a mortal," said Mrs. Morley, with a still deeper sigh; "and heaven can bear witness that my regret has been severe as his folly has been reprehensible."

"Folly!" repeated Mr. Morley. "What a softening impulse is that of love, when it possesses the weak heart of woman! So, then, the atrocities of lord Francis Sherville are denominated follies! In men less idolized they would be deemed rank vices, contaminating poisons, which should be exterminated, lest they infect the very source of moral virtue. Lord Francis Sherville is exempt from blame, because he is gifted by Nature with the privilege to err."

"Pardon me," interrupted Martha: "I never even attempted to

excuse lord Francis: his conduct has been cruel, but the pride of his family and his high birth were the destroyers of his honour."

"You confess, then, that lord Francis *is* the father of your infant?"

"He is the father of poor Fanny," replied Martha.

"And the mother," said Mr. Morley——

"Still loves him, still adores him," answered Martha. "All the combining powers of reason and reflection cannot subdue the fatal dominion which he had obtained over her feelings."

"Insulting woman!" exclaimed Mr. Morley. "You love lord Francis—you adore him! Your cunning cannot hide the secret you would wish to cherish. Lord Francis is a villain! I know the cause of his infernal conduct: to me he shall answer for it; by me he shall, with all his rank and all his virtues, be taught the lesson of retribution." Mrs. Morley's colour changed from red to pale; her features were fixed by the melancholy reverie which possessed her mind. Mr. Morley became more agitated by Martha's silence, because it evinced the secret sorrow of her heart; and after pacing about the room for several minutes, he suddenly quitted it, leaving her to indulge her perplexing ruminations.

Mr. Morley's mind was no less unquiet than Martha's. He felt the strongest conviction that lord Francis had seduced his wife, from a motive of which the reader will be shortly acquainted. Every event respecting the birth of Fanny tended to confirm his opinion; and while he anxiously awaited the proofs of her innocence, he was more than half convinced of her guilt, by that prejudging, dangerous suspicion which, having conjured up a phantom to torment him, hourly cherished all the agonies which jealousy and conscious dissimulation kept alive within his bosom.

The peevish inquietude of Mr. Morley's mind did not either soften or diminish by the augmentation of corporeal suffering. His decaying health only tended to increase the irritability of his nature; and having, by habit, learnt to think himself deceived, he had wholly relinquished the sustaining charms of confidence and affection. He was watchful rather to detect his wife's falsehood than to be convinced of her innocence. He was more disposed to believe her guilty than to confess, by the rectitude of her conduct, that he had been the dupe of his own credulity.

Mrs. Morley, with the serenity of conscious truth, watched the varying emotions of her husband's mind, and resolved on awaiting placidly for the moment which was to decide her destiny. Every arrangement was made for their departure from England, and Martha looked forward impatiently to that period which she felt confidently assured would exonerate her from every imputation.

CHAPTER LV

On the morning previous to their departure from Derbyshire Mr. Morley appeared more calm and composed than he had been during many preceding days. His mind seemed settled into a pensive resignation, and while he looked with earnest and impressive sadness on the placid countenance of an ill-treated wife, sometimes a sudden flush, or tear of self-reproof, would betray such feelings as nearly taught her to pardon even his suspicions.

"Is every thing ready for our long journey?" inquired Martha, as she took her seat at the breakfast-table.

"Every thing," sighed Mr. Morley.

"I am impatient to depart," cried Martha; "for your health and peace of mind require much care, much kind attention."

"My peace of mind! Ah! Martha, that will never be restored! I have a thorn too deeply planted in my heart ever to be extracted."

"I trust that you deceive yourself," said Martha.

"Was not the father of Fanny a villain?" interrupted Mr. Morley. Martha made no reply.

"Is not the woman whom he deceived to blame for screening him from the obloquy he merits?"

"There is something in the present instance due to feelings, more sacred and more delicate than those of resentment."

"Why?" inquired Mr. Morley hastily.

"Because he is her husband."

"Then you confess that *husbands* have a claim to some respect?"

"I never yet denied it. Religion as well as moral virtue should be the safeguard of an husband's honour."

"Dearest Martha!" cried Mr. Morley, taking her hand as he interrupted her; "had your sentiments been always such—your conduct ever thus—we had been happy."

Little more passed till they set out for London, where Mr. Morley proposed remaining a fortnight or three weeks for the advantage of the best medical advice previous to his continental journey.

On their arrival in the metropolis a splendid house was hired in Albemarle-street. Mr. Morley had provided an handsome retinue for his foreign expedition, and Martha once more appeared in all the elegancies of life which her husband's fortune could procure.

Now came her hour of triumph; now the self-interested, basely-thinking herd of worldly sycophants sought her with eagerness, and smiled upon her with unbounded admiration. Her husband's sanction obliterated the tarnish which her reputation had received, and her door was thronged with long-deserting friends, who, in return for their past kindness, were refused admittance.

From her window (how striking was the contrast of a few short weeks!) she saw the servile bow and the soft smile of pliant condescension. She marked the change; she shuddered at the baseness of the human mind; she felt the just scorn of an exalted soul, and repaid the worthless tribe with silent indignation.

Among others who called at Mrs. Morley's door was lord Francis Sherville. The name of such an inquirer filled her mind with undescribable agitation. She had promised to discover the father, and to elucidate the mystery of Fanny's birth; she had determined to sacrifice the hopes of lord Francis, in justice to Mrs. Sedgley's wrongs and her own reputation; she feared that the sight of him might induce her to swerve from her purpose, and she sighed deeply even at the moment that she felt the necessity of exposing his baseness. In lord Francis Sherville she fancied she contemplated the most extraordinary of characters; the most noble, and at the same time the most cruel nature; the most generous and the most interesting of mortals; the preserver of Fanny—the destroyer of Mrs. Sedgley. How obvious were the fine distinctions betwixt vice and virtue! how laudable were the father's feelings! how barbarous the husband's falsehood!

The struggle which her mind experienced, where the love of

justice and the sentiment of affection contended equally for pre-eminence, may easily be imagined; yet she fancied that it would be nobler to avow, with that ingenuousness which had ever been the prominent characteristic of her soul, the determination she had formed, than basely to harbour the littleness of resentment, and inflict a punishment without acquainting the offender with his crime. While her mind was ruminating on these circumstances, the subject of them a second time requested earnestly to be admitted. Mr. Morley was absent from home, and Mrs. Morley consented to see lord Francis.

The meeting was embarrassed on both sides. Lord Francis perceived a cold repulsive spell, which Martha had suffered to command her affections; and though she sighed as he approached her, it was rather the sigh of regret for past hopes than of the consciousness of present happiness.

Lord Francis experienced the very acme of chagrin. He hesitated—he was fearful of inquiring the cause, while he felt the full force of her evident displeasure.

After many attempts to speak, he requested to know by what means he had forfeited Mrs. Morley's good opinion. "What has been my fault? How have I sinned against you?" said lord Francis.

"Your fault you know: your sins are yet within the reach of pardon," replied Mrs. Morley. "I first valued your esteem, because I thought your mind as perfect as your manners were attaching."

"And how have I forfeited your kindness? Who can accuse me of any action which merits your reproof?"

"Mrs. Sedgley———"

Lord Francis shrunk, and seemed to shudder. "Mrs. Sedgley has forfeited all claims to my protection," said he: "she has disgraced the name she bears."

"The name which she *ought* to bear, you would say, lord Francis; and till she be permitted to resume it, I cannot own it as the name of my friend."

Lord Francis sighed deeply.

"Will my reconciliation to Mrs. Sedgley ensure me your esteem? Will it reinstate me in your good opinion?"

After a pause of some moments, during which Mrs. Morley felt more than she dared acknowledge, while she hoped yet dreaded to behold lord Francis and Mrs. Sedgley re-united, she replied, "Unquestionably."

"Then (for I am no stranger to your intended journey) you shall see us completely reconciled. You shall behold me while I press her to my heart, while I forgive her indiscretions, and avow myself her dearest friend, her tenderest——"

Mrs. Morley's cheek became as pale as ashes: she was near sinking to the ground. All her affection for lord Francis returned. They began to master the heroic sentiment which friendship for Mrs. Sedgley had prompted: she recollected the declining state of Mr. Morley's health—the more than probable chance of her being the wife of lord Francis. The agitation of her heart warmed and awakened all its sensibility. She rose to quit the room.

Lord Francis was no novice in the intricacies of the passions. He had studied the female heart: he had been accustomed to subdue it. He was convinced that Martha loved him; and he conjured her to promise, that when he had proved his regard for Mrs. Sedgley, his reward should be equal to his affection.

Mrs. Morley trembled. Lord Francis caught her hand, and pressed it to his lips. At that moment Mr. Morley entered the room. Lord Francis retired in the utmost agitation; and Martha, unable to support the fluttering perturbation of her heart, sunk at the feet of her astonished husband.

Mr. Morley's mind was sternly fortified for the elucidation of a mystery which he had long dreaded, and was now determined to explore. He was sullenly silent. Not a syllable of reproach passed his lips from the period of lord Francis's visit till the following day, when they set out for Paris on their route to Switzerland. His resolution was strengthened by the hope of a speedy termination of every thing like doubt respecting his wife's infidelity; and he determined that his vengeance should be as complete as his wrongs were unequivocal.

Lord Francis, immediately on his quitting Mrs. Morley, departed for the continent, for the purpose of effecting a complete reconciliation with the deserted Mrs. Sedgley.

CHAPTER LVI

On their arrival at the hotel *de la Libertè*, near the barrier of Paris, they found themselves surrounded with guards, and the objects of suspicion. Every eye viewed them with inquisitive and menacing contempt; while the anxiety which Mrs. Morley's ingenuous nature could not conceal, only tended to augment the dangers of their situation. They had been twelve hours in Paris, when they were seized and conveyed to the prison of the *Abbaye*, where every horror and every insult convinced them, that their peril was no less imminent than certain.

They had been four days in this state of misery and suspense, when Mrs. Morley was summoned to attend the ruler of her destiny. With a palpitating bosom she reached the hotel, guarded by two soldiers. It was spacious and splendid. She ascended the stairs to the first suite of apartments; she entered a saloon magnificently furnished; and she beheld a barbarous, an unrelenting judge, the abandoned Julia. Mrs. Morley shrieked and fainted.

On recovering from the effect of her surprize and sudden agitation, she looked around in vain for her sister. The unnatural fiend had departed, leaving her to the mercy of two insulting ruffians; while she with eager haste repaired to the *Abbaye* in search of Mr. Morley.

His liberation was offered, on condition that she should be the companion of his journey. "I have long loved you," said Julia, "and rather than see you re-united to my sister, I will see you perish. Your life is in my hands. My lover is your judge; and he is all powerful, the daring Robespierre."

Mr. Morley was almost petrified with horror! but he disdained to accept his liberty on such terms; death had long menaced the termination of his compunctious torments, and he had little mercy to expect, from the capricious passions of an unfeeling woman. He answered her with scorn and with reproaches; she aimed a dagger at his breast; he warded off the blow: she shrieked; accused him of the premeditated deed; and ordered him to a more close confinement. He smiled, and followed the jailor to his dungeon.

During three weeks Mr. Morley and his distracted wife were

lodged in separate subterraneous cells; no sun beamed on their aching eyelids; no refreshing breeze visited their despairing bosoms; when at dawn-light their dungeons were thrown open, and they were conducted forth to witness the last scene of their persecutor's misery; on a scaffold, pale, ghastly, lacerated, trembling at his approaching destiny, and shuddering while he anticipated the just vengeance of an offended Creator, they beheld the homicide Robespierre.[1]

Mrs. Morley, whose sublimity of soul neither insult nor oppression could contaminate, flew to the hotel where she had last seen her abandoned sister. She found the gates all open; the populace had plundered the apartments; she entered the saloon, beyond the anti-chamber; the floor was deluged with blood! murder had been permitted to blur the face of noon-day, and the abode of guilty luxury now presented the mere wreck of desolation. Every wretch, whose heart had palpitated under the tyranny of the remorseless despot, now dealt its groans and exercised its vengeance, on even those objects which, only by being inanimate, had escaped his cruelty.

Martha was stricken with terrors that nearly annihilated her; she had never witnessed such a scene, and imagination had not power to paint it. As soon as the first spell of horror began to subside, she rushed through the apartments wild and astonished; the hangings which were of velvet were torn from the walls and trampled by the multitude; the costly plates of looking-glass were shattered in every direction; the inlaid cabinets defaced and thrown upon the ground; the splendid lustres torn from their suspending chains, and strewed about in glittering fragments. She entered the chamber of the exterminated monster: the bed on which he had slumbered, but not reposed; the pillow on which he had, for many preceding months, pressed his guilt-fevered brain, now supported the head of the lifeless, self-murdered Julia. Her blackening form declared the potency of that poison, which freed her soul from mortal, conscious misery, to endure——Here let her memory rest.

---

[1]   Robespierre, chief architect of the Reign of Terror, was executed on July 28, 1794. For Helen Maria Williams's account of events following his death, see Appendix F, 322–23. See also Wordsworth's joyful response to news of Robespierre's death in *The Prelude* (1805), 10. 529–52.

CHAPTER LVII

After paying a large bribe for the interment of Julia's corpse, on the same evening Mr. Morley and his wife pursued their *route* towards Switzerland. Martha was too deeply impressed with the horrors of the past twelve hours, to feel the joy of being once more restored to liberty. The sorrow which sunk deep into her mind, took from it every sense of anticipated pleasure; and, in the agitations of regret, the anguish of a still vivid recollection, even her friend Mrs. Sedgley was forgotten.

On Mrs. Morley's arrival at Lausanne, she requested permission to visit Mrs. Sedgley alone, in order to apprize her of the motive which prompted her journey. Mr. Morley readily consented, and waited impatiently for the interview. The pride of his heart was interested in this meeting because he supposed that it was destined to exculpate his name from dishonour, by sanctioning his long cherished revenge. The idea of Martha's having deceived him, and of her being the parent of the little fugitive, still so powerfully possessed his mind, that all other ruminations were wholly absorbed by the strong ruling power of self-love, acting upon feelings with which the reader is already acquainted.

The spot which Mrs. Sedgley had chosen as the abode of her unrepining sorrows, was beautifully romantic. It was situated on the borders of a lake, adorned with vineyards, and sheltered by the mountains, at once grand and stupendous. Neatness and simplicity were the substitutes for less enervating luxuries; while the charm of solitude was rendered doubly pleasing, by the disgust scarcely yet obliterated from the mind of the recluse. Sweet were the noiseless labyrinths, which wound along the acclivity; and impressive was the Alpine solitude which enabled her to look down upon the din of life, without one sigh to interrupt its silence.

As Mrs. Morley approached the threshold, the setting-sun shone on the yellow front of the rustic habitation. The whiteness of the high-towering peaks which formed a spiral ampitheatre, mingled with the scattered clouds half reddened or empurpled by the reflecting horizon; while the thin mists of evening rose in grey flakes from the still water, refreshing the scorched and interwoven vineyard over which they floated.

On the step of the cottage-door was seated little Fanny. Mrs. Morley ran towards her, and pressing her to her bosom, bestowed on her a thousand kisses. Mrs. Sedgley was absent; she had wandered up the mountain to the cell of an hermit, in whose solitary abode she found both wisdom and philosophy. A little girl, the single inmate of Mrs. Sedgley's habitation, pointed out the path, and Martha with the smiling Fanny hastened towards the hermitage.

The ascent was steep, and the evening sultry. The light breezes which rose from the valley scarcely ruffled the dry foliage of the surrounding plantations. The dusk of twilight thickened, and the last crimson glow of light receded from the horizon. Mrs. Morley was weary, for she had borne Fanny in her arms; and she seated herself on the steps of a rude cross, which the hermit had placed on a jutting part of the precipice. Here again she kissed and pressed her little companion to her bosom. "My Fanny, my own darling Fanny," exclaimed Martha; "what have I not suffered for thy sake? what have I not borne, rather than betray the parent who deserted thee?"

As she spoke she heard a rustling among the trees, and in a moment Mr. Morley darted forth like one that was deprived of reason. He had followed Martha; he had heard her expressions of fondness, her kisses, her sighs, as she addressed her innocent companion. His countenance was wild and furious.

"You have deceived me, vile and abandoned woman!" exclaimed Mr. Morley, grasping one arm, while with the other she shielded Fanny from his resentment. "Mrs. Sedgley is not the mother of this infant; confess that she is not; own that you have practised on my weak credulity; avow your infamy, and shew yourself the wretch you really are."

Mrs. Morley was amazed and terrified. The countenance of her husband bespoke the horrible purposes which wrung his brain; his eyes rolled wildly, now glancing towards heaven, then bending gloomily on the deep and darkening valley. The infant, as if actuated by an instinctive terror, looked fearfully at Martha, while her little arms were closely interwoven round her neck. She kissed it, and bursting into tears, reproached Mr. Morley for his unfeeling rage; every caress which she bestowed augmented his distraction. They stood upon the jutting point of the precipice; the hour was awfully still; not a breath of wind was heard; the gloom every moment deepened, and the trembling child crept close into the bosom which shielded it; accustomed to see no woman but Mrs. Sedgley, it knew no accent but that of nature; and with a trembling voice it addressed Mrs. Morley by the name of *mother*.

"Accursed bastard!" exclaimed the frantic Morley, "she *is* thy mother!" while with one convulsive hand pressing his brain, the other grasped the arm of his wife, who shrieked with agony. The sound of her voice echoed down the mountain, and, in a moment, lord Francis Sherville presented himself before them.

"Oh! shield your helpless innocent from destruction," exclaimed Mrs. Morley, while she held forth the trembling Fanny. Mr. Morley, maddened with jealous rage, rushed forward, and before lord Francis could interpose, tearing the child from Martha's arms, sprang towards the edge of the acclivity.

Lord Francis was terror-struck; but he had still power to hold the arm of Morley, while Martha fell at his feet and in the agony of fear and tenderness conjured him to be merciful. "For its mother's sake, O, spare it!" cried she, clasping his knees and bathing them with tears.

"Infamous woman!" exclaimed Morley, "let loose your arms. I will not be defrauded of my vengeance."

"Then let it fall on me—"

"On *me*," cried Lord Francis, interrupting Mrs. Morley, "*I* claim the infant."

"Then claim it in hell!" vociferated the frantic husband, at the same moment struggling to obtain the infant and looking with the wildness of a maniac towards the deep and darkened valley. Lord Francis held his arms; the infant shrieked repeatedly.

"Rend it to atoms!" cried Morley; "for alive you never shall again behold it!"

"Monster of cruelty!" exclaimed Martha, "would you be a murderer?"

They now heard footsteps proceeding down the flinty pathway; they called for help, and Mrs. Sedgley flew towards them. As soon as she perceived the frenzied group she exclaimed, "My child! my infant! oh Morley, Morley! thou inhuman *father!*"

Mr. Morley heard the fiat of his destiny! He heard it pronounced by lady Susan Sherville; the sister of the noble, the liberal lord Francis. The deserted mother of his *own* unknown offspring.

Lady Susan was conveyed by her brother and Mrs. Morley, to the hermit's cell. They had witnessed the just vengeance of insulted Heaven! They had seen the libertine who, under the mask of sanctity, had violated all the laws of honour and religion, who had assumed through life the name of a philanthropist merely as a safeguard from suspicion, perish! The scene was awfully impressive. It was the stern judgment of an offended GOD, exemplified amidst the grandest works of nature! Darkness no longer veiled the hour. The moon ascended majestically solemn above the white Alpine summits. The wind rose suddenly; and the shrill gust howled over the hermit's rushy hovel. The venerable recluse attended the silent group to lady Susan's cottage. Often did they listen, as they descended the narrow path, to hear whether a groan met their ears, when silence marked an interval between the gusts of wind, till they arrived at the vineyard, which spread its brown amphitheatre along the circling border of the lake.

The hermit listened, and ejaculated, "Father of mercies! Awful in judgment! Omnipotent in power! thy will be done!"

He was prompted by an awful signal! The agonized sigh of a deep-wounded spirit, preparing to take its flight to worlds unknown. On the margin of the lake, writhing with agonies, both mental and corporeal, lay the expiring Morley. The mangled body was conveyed to lady Susan's cottage. The hermit passed his night in prayer. Lady Susan and Mrs. Morley wasted theirs in tears.

The sufferer was still sensible. He clasped his injured wife to his convulsed and bleeding bosom. He implored lady Susan's forgiveness. He shuddered when he beheld her generous brother.

In the delirium of fever which preceded his dissolution, he talked wildly of Julia and her murdered infant. Confessed that to screen his name from obloquy, *he* had supplied the means for its destruction; and fearful that at some unguarded moment she might reveal the secret, owned that he had, by his information, occasioned the disgrace which had compelled her to quit England.

The fever every moment augmented; his limbs were fractured; his whole body bruised and lacerated; he dictated a short deed, by which he divided his fortune between Martha and little Fanny; and, as the bright dawn broke over the top of the mountains, closed his darkened eyes, in *death*.

CHAPTER LVIII

After the first concussion of horror had subsided, and the brain began to feel the returning powers of reflection, lady Susan informed Mrs. Morley of her motive for first leaving Fanny under her protection. "I had in vain endeavoured to soften the indignation of my family; I had firmly and inviolably kept my resolution, not to disclose the name or condition of my betrayer. For, alas! though rendered the most wretched of the human race, I still loved him too tenderly to expose him to the resentment of my brother, whose high-souled sensibility would have produced a rencontre which must have terminated fatally. I knew that your nature was tender, as it was exalted; and I consigned my offspring to your bosom, beneath the roof of its unnatural father.

"On the day of my departure, from the village, I stopped the chaise when I reached the summit of a neighbouring hill, and for the last time contemplated the wretched dwelling where my child first saw the light. I also faintly distinguished the front of Morley-house, where I hoped that she was destined to find a safe asylum. Oh God! how did my heart palpitate, how did my tears flow when I reflected, that perhaps I should embrace my child no more. But the pride of shame was more powerful than the tenderness of maternal sorrow. I closed my eyes and fled."

"I conjure you to think of it no more," said Mrs. Morley. "I trust that my guilty husband's last hour of suffering has expiated his crimes, and that his fate will afford a lesson to the vicious; your patience, an example to the persecuted; and my sorrows, a proof of the danger which always awaits a precipitate marriage."

As soon as lady Susan had made arrangements for her journey, she set out with her brother, Mrs. Morley, and little Fanny for England; where, as speedily as the decencies of life would permit, lord Francis solicited and received the hand of Mrs. Morley; who bestowed it on one condition only, which was, that of lady Susan's accepting her share of Mr. Morley's fortune.

If the reader amidst these busy changes should desire to know what became of lady Penelope Pryer, it will be sufficient eulogium on her merit to say, that by her alliance with the junior Leadenhead, she has at this hour the honour of ENNOBLING HIS FAMILY.

THE END

Appendix A: Robinson's Tributes to the Duchess of Devonshire

[The following tributes to Georgiana, Duchess of Devonshire (1757–1806), offer sketches of the woman who was the model for the Duchess of Chatsworth in *The Natural Daughter*. As Robinson's particular praise for Georgiana's sympathetic heart and "polished" mind suggest, these tributes cannot be fully appreciated apart from the larger eighteenth-century discourses exalting sensibility and the intellectual abilities of women. The first selection, taken from Robinson's posthumously published *Memoirs*, looks back to 1775, when she was living with her husband in King's Bench Prison. Although it is difficult to know just how consistent Georgiana's patronage was over the next twenty-five years, *The Morning Post* reported on December 26, 1799, that she was still "the zealous patroness of Mrs. Robinson."]

1. Robinson's Account of Her First Meeting with the Duchess. From *The Memoirs of Mrs. Robinson* (1801), 1: 171–75.

At this period, I was informed that the Duchess of Devonshire was the admirer and patroness of literature; with a mixture of timidity and hope I sent Her Grace a neatly bound volume of my Poems, accompanied by a short letter apologizing for their defects, and pleading my age as the only excuse for their inaccuracy. My brother, who was a charming youth, was the bearer of my first literary offering at the shrine of nobility. The Duchess admitted him; and with the most generous and amiable sensibility inquired some particulars respecting my situation, with a request that on the following day I would make her a visit.—

I knew not what to do. Her liberality claimed my compliance; yet, as I had never, during my husband's long captivity, quitted him for half an hour, I felt a sort of reluctance that pained the romantic firmness of my mind, while I meditated what I considered as a breach of my domestic attachment. However, at the particular and earnest request of Mr. Robinson, I consented; and accordingly accepted the Duchess's invitation.

During my seclusion from the world I had adapted my dress to my situation. Neatness was at all times my pride; but now plainness was the conformity to necessity: simple habiliments became the abode of adversity; and the plain brown satin gown which I wore on my first visit to the Duchess of Devonshire, appeared to me as strange as a birth-day court-suit[1] to a newly-married citizen's daughter.

To describe the Duchess's look and manner when she entered the back drawing-room of Devonshire-house, would be impracticable; mildness and sensibility beamed in her eyes, and irradiated her countenance. She expressed her surprise at seeing so young a person, who had already experienced such vicissitude of fortune; she lamented that my destiny was so little proportioned to what she was pleased to term my desert, and with a tear of gentle sympathy requested that I would accept a proof of her good wishes. I had not words to express my feelings, and was departing, when the Duchess requested me to call on her very often, and to bring my little daughter with me.

I made frequent visits to the amiable Duchess, and was at all times received with the warmest proofs of friendship. My little girl, to whom I was still a nurse, generally accompanied me, and always experienced the kindest caresses from my admired patroness, my liberal and affectionate friend. Frequently the Duchess inquired most minutely into the story of my sorrows, and as often gave me tears of the most spontaneous sympathy. But, such was my destiny, that while I cultivated the esteem of this best of women, by a conduct which was above the reach of reprobation, my husband, even though I was the partner of his captivity, the devoted slave to his necessities, indulged in the lowest and most degrading intrigues; frequently, during my short absence with the Duchess, for I never quitted the prison but to obey her summons, he was known to admit the most abandoned of their sex; women whose low licentious lives were such as to render them the shame and outcasts of society.

2. "Sonnet Inscribed to Her Grace the Duchess of Devonshire." From Robinson's *Poems* (1791).

'Tis not thy flowing hair of orient gold,
  Nor those bright eyes, like sapphire gems that glow;

---

[1] On royal birthdays, courtly celebrants wore elaborate attire, such as that described in Robinson's poem "The Birth-Day."

Nor cheek of blushing rose, nor breast of snow,
The varying passions of the heart could hold:

Those locks, too soon, shall own a silv'ry ray,
  Those radient orbs their magic fires forego;
Insatiate TIME shall steal those tints away,
  Warp thy fine form, and bend thy beauties low:

But the rare wonders of thy polish'd MIND
  Shall mock the empty menace of decay;
The GEM, that in thy SPOTLESS BREAST enshrin'd,
  Glows with the light of intellectual ray;
Shall, like the Brilliant, scorn each borrow'd aid,
  And deck'd with native lustre NEVER FADE!

3. "On the Duchess of Devonshire." Published under the signature of "Oberon" in *The Oracle*, April 4, 1799.

The Nightingale, with mourning lay,
  Amid the twilight's purpling glow,
May sweetly hymn the loss of day,
  While Echo chaunts her melting woe!
But what can soothe the wounded breast,
  And ev'ry aching sense beguile,
Ah! What can charm the soul to rest,
  Like DEVON's voice, or DEVON's smile!

The modest Orb, with trembling light,
  Beams through the soft and fresh'ning show'r;
And, stealing o'er the realm of Night,
  Gives lustre to the silent hour!
But what can chear the fainting heart,
  When gloomy Sorrow frowns severe;
Ah! what can Sympathy impart
  Like DEVON's sigh, or DEVON's tear!

Though Nature's proudest toils combin'd
  To give her form unequall'd grace!
And though the feelings of her mind
  With fine expression mark her face;

Yet, as the *Casket* charms the view,
    But till the treasur'd *Gem* is seen,
Her MIND demands the tribute due,
    Which else, her BEAUTY's claim had been.

If there be magic in her Tear,
    And if her Smile can bliss impart,
Her Sigh is still to feeling dear,
    And well her Voice can soothe the Heart!
Then where shall wond'ring Fancy dwell,
    Nor own exclusive pow'r the while?
O! say, which holds the strongest spell,
    Her VOICE, her SIGH, her TEAR, or SMILE.

Appendix B: Excerpts from The Morning Post

[*The Morning Post* is an invaluable source of information about the cultural contexts of Robinson's works. The following excerpts, which appeared during Robinson's tenure as poetry editor for the newspaper, constitute part of the dynamic, ever-expanding context that shaped the reception history of *A Letter to the Women of England*. Although there is no solid evidence, the puff for Robinson's epistolary novel *The False Friend* (1798) seems calculated to generate collateral interest in *A Letter to the Women of England* and perhaps even to hint at Robinson's authorship.]

1. A Puff for Robinson's *The False Friend* (March 28, 1799).

Mrs. Robinson's *"False Friend"* now excites universal attention. The *language* of the work being extolled to the very extent of panegyric, we select the following extract for the gratification of our readers:— "What a machine is the human mind! How easily is the system of uniformity destroyed; and what a useless chaos does it become, the moment that reason ceases to guide the springs of action. What a creature is *woman*! How wildly inconsistent! How daring, yet how timid! We are at once the most ambitious tyrants, and the most abject slaves. We think that our dominion is secure at the very moment when we are under the control of our imperious rulers. How slender is the thread which holds our captives! how rashly do we strain it! how easily is it broken! How completely are we the dupes of our affections; and how justly does the tyrant who controls us laugh at our vaunted power over the sensations of his mind! That woman mistakes her influence, if she supposes that it originates in the gratitude or honour of her lover. Man is only constant, while he feels the flame of affection burn vividly within his bosom: he is not the creature of our dominion, but of his own passions. He will love, as long as he is pleased; and he will please, as long as he can love. Sentiment forms no part of his attachment; all the claims of esteem, generosity, and friendship sink subdued before the ruling power of self gratification. The moment that the spell which chains the senses is broken, the phantom *Love* takes flight, leaving no substitutes but regret and indignation. These are the despots who hold us in a state of bondage! who call themselves idolators, till the caprice of their natures prove their apostacy. Created to protect us, they expose us to every danger; endowed with the strength to sustain our erring judgment, they are ever eager to mislead us. Formed to fascinate our senses, they govern them at pleasure. We boast a resisting power, formed on the basis of stern and frigid virtue; we are philosophers in precept,—but how often are we women in example! We vaunt our mental energy; man appears to bend beneath conviction; he knows that by his humility he obtains confidence; he seems the pupil of our laws, at the same moment that he acts in open violation of the justice we would exercise. O man! thou pleasing, subtle, fawning, conquering foe! thou yielding tyrant! thou imperious slave! What language can describe thee? What mortal delineate thee as thou art? except the being who has been by turns thy idol and thy victim!"

2. An Account of Charles-Guillaume Theremin's Pamphlet *De la condition des femmes dans les Républiques* (August 30, 1799).

A very curious Work has been published at Paris on the *condition of Women under Republican Governments*. The Author's object is to make it felt that women are at present not in their proper places, or rather that they have, as they are treated now, no place at all in the social order; he argues that it is the duty of the Republic to draw them from the nullity in which they are plunged by the laws of all nations, and that they ought to enjoy a much happier and more honourable lot. He allows them no share in the Sovereignty because the will of the family, which is one and the same, is represented by the voice of the father or the husband; but he wishes that they should be rendered capable of receiving certain delegations from the sovereign authority. Why, for example, should they not discharge to their own sex the functions that relate to public Instruction? Why, above all, should not the exercise of the national benevolence and a share in the administration of charitable establishments be entrusted to them? There are other missions in which they might appear with advantage.

"Governments," says the Author, in another part of his work, "which think they did every thing in providing for the wants of men, have, in extraordinary circumstances, done but half their work; they have still to provide for the wants of those women who are not married, and whose support is not derived from men.—The Establishment of St. Cyr, which was founded at the close of a long

War, and which provided not only for the instruction but the maintenance and future establishment of a number of young females, was
by no means an absurd institution.[1] Retrench the aristocratic part
of it, establish and endow, in a given number of Departments, a St.
Cyr, and you will see morals, talents, and beauty—the honour, the
glory, and the charm of France."

The Author thinks it improper that women should not be admitted into learned Societies, when, by their acquirements, they are fit
to have a seat in them; he is also properly indignant that the criminal laws suppose them to have so perfect a knowledge of good and
evil, and the provisions of law, that they punish them like men when
they violate the laws, and yet they are treated as children, under
guardianship, in matters of civil law.

3. A Puff for Robinson's *Thoughts on the Condition of Women* (August 31, 1799).

The work On the Condition of Women, which now makes so
much noise in Paris, is little more than a translation of a pamphlet
published last February by Mrs. Robinson, under the fictitious
signature of Anne Frances Randall. The Pamphlet was called A
Letter to the Women of England, and a large impression was sold
by Messrs. Longman and Rees, Paternoster Row. Mrs. Robinson's
publication on The Condition of Women, is already advertised, a
second edition. The sale will, probably, be extensive; particularly
among the sex which it vindicates.

---

[1]   St. Cyr was a boarding school established by Madame Maintenon for the daughters
of impoverished aristocrats.

Appendix C: Richard Polwhele, from The Unsex'd Females: A Poem, Addressed to the Author of The Pursuits of Literature *(1798)*

[In a note to his satiric poem *The Pursuits of Literature* (1794–97), T.J. Mathias observed, "Our unsex'd female writers now instruct, or confuse, us and themselves, in the labyrinth of politics, or turn us wild with Gallic frenzy." Polwhele's expansion upon this theme in *The Unsex'd Females*, exemplifies the virulent rhetoric that stigmatized Robinson and other women writers who threatened traditional social and sexual hierarchies. Not surprisingly, the ultra-conservative *Anti-Jacobin Review*, commended Polwhele for "employing his poetical talents ... in vindication of all that is dear to us as Britons and as Christians." The following excerpt from Polwhele's poem includes only a few of the copious notes that accompany the original.]

Thou, who with all the poet's genuine rage,
Thy "fine eye rolling" o'er "this aweful age,"[1]
Where polish'd life unfolds its various views,
Hast mark'd the magic influence of the muse;
Sever'd, with nice precision, from her beam
Of genial power, her false or feeble gleam;
Expos'd the Sciolist's vain-glorious claim,
And boldly thwarted Innovation's aim,
Where witlings wildly think, or madly dare,
With Honor, Virtue, Truth, announcing war;
Survey with me, what ne'er our fathers saw,
A female band despising NATURE's law,[2]
As "proud defiance"[3] flashes from their arms,

---

[1] Polwhele is quoting from Mathias's *Pursuits of Literature*.

[2] Nature is the grand basis of all laws human and divine; and the woman, who has no regard to nature, either in the decoration of her person, or the culture of her mind, will soon "walk after the flesh; in the lust of uncleanness, and despise government" [R.P's note].

[3] Cf. Alexander Pope's "The Temple of Fame," ll. 342–43: "A troop came next, who Crowns and Armour wore, / And proud Defiance in their Looks they bore."

And vengeance smothers all their softer charms.
I shudder at the new unpictur'd scene,
Where unsex'd woman vaunts the imperious mien;
Where girls, affecting to dismiss the heart,
Invoke the Proteus of petrific art;
With equal ease, in body or in mind,
To Gallic freaks or Gallic faith resign'd,
The crane-like neck, as Fashion bids, lay bare,
Or frizzle, bold in front, their borrow'd hair;
Scarce by a gossamery film carest,
Sport,[1] in full view, the meretricious breast;[2]
Loose the chaste cincture, where the graces shone,
And languish'd all the Loves, the ambrosial zone;
As lordly domes inspire dramatic rage,
Court prurient Fancy to the private stage;
With bliss botanic as their bosoms heave,
Still pluck forbidden fruit, with mother Eve,
For puberty in sighing florets pant,
Or point the prostitution of a plant;
Dissect its organ of unhallow'd lust,
And fondly gaze the titillating dust;
And liberty's sublimer views expand,
And o'er the wreck of kingdoms[3] sternly stand;
And, frantic, midst the democratic storm,
Pursue, Philosophy! thy phantom-form.[4]
    Far other is the female shape and mind,
By modest luxury heighten'd and refin'd,
Those limbs, that figure, tho' by Fashion grac'd,

---

[1] To "sport a face," is a cant phrase in one of our Universities, by which is meant an
impudent obtrusion of a man's person in company. It is not inapplicable, perhaps, to
the open bosom—a fashion which we have never invited or sanctioned [R.P.'s note].

[2] The fashions of France, which have been always imitated by the English, were, heretofore, unexceptionable in a moral point of view; since, however ridiculous or absurd,
they were innocent. But they have now their source among prostitutes—among
women of the most abandoned character [R.P.'s note].

[3] The female advocates of Democracy in this country, though they have had no opportunity of imitating the French ladies, in their atrocious acts of cruelty; have yet
assumed a stern serenity in the contemplation of those savage excesses [R.P.'s note].

[4] Philosophism, the false image of philosophy, ... a phantom which heretofore appeared
not in open day, though it now attempts the loftiest flights in the face of the sun
[R.P.'s note].

By Beauty polish'd, and adorn'd by Taste;
That soul, whose harmony perennial flows,
In Music trembles, and in Color glows;
Which bids sweet Poesy reclaim the praise
With faery light to gild fastidious days,
From sullen clouds relieve domestic care,
And melt in smiles the withering frown of war.
Ah! once the female Muse, to NATURE true,
The unvalued store from FANCY, FEELING drew;
Won, from the grasp of woe, the roseate hours,
Cheer'd life's dim vale, and strew'd the grave with flowers.

But lo! where, pale amidst the wild, she draws
Each precept cold from sceptic Reason's vase;
Pours with rash arm the turbid stream along,
And in the foaming torrent whelms the throng.

Alas! her pride sophistic flings a gloom,
To chase, sweet Innocence! thy vernal bloom,
Of each light joy to damp the genial glow,
And with new terrors clothe the groupe of woe,
Quench the pure daystar in oblivion deep,
And Death! restore thy "long, unbroken sleep."[1]

See Wollstonecraft, whom no decorum checks,
Arise, the intrepid champion of her sex;
O'er humbled man assert the sovereign claim,
And slight the timid blush of virgin fame.

"Go, go (she cries) ye tribes of melting maids,
Go, screen your softness in sequester'd shades;
With plaintive whispers woo the unconscious grove,
And feebly perish, as depis'd ye love.
What tho' the fine Romances of Rousseau
Bid the frame flutter, and the bosom glow;
Tho' the rapt Bard, your empire fond to own,
Fall prostrate and adore your living throne,
The living throne his hands presum'd to rear,
Its seat a simper, and its base a tear;

---

[1] Cf. Polwhele's "The Epitaph on Bion from Moschus," ll. 119–22: "But we, the great, the valiant, and the wise / When once the seal of death hath clos'd our eyes, / Lost in the hollow tomb obscure and deep, / Slumber, to wake no more, one long unbroken sleep."

Soon shall the sex disdain the illusive sway,
And wield the sceptre in yon blaze of day;
Ere long, each little artifice discard,
No more by weakness winning fond regard;
Nor eyes, that sparkle from their blushes, roll,
Nor catch the languors of the sick'ning soul,
Nor the quick flutter, nor the coy reserve,
But nobly boast the firm gymnastic nerve;
Nor more affect with Delicacy's fan
To hide the emotion from congenial man;
To the bold heights where glory beams, aspire,
Blend mental energy with Passion's fire,
Surpass their rivals in the powers of mind
And vindicate *the Rights of womankind*."

  She spoke: and veteran BARBAULD[1] caught the strain,
And deem'd her songs of Love, her Lyrics vain;

---

[1] Here, and at the conclusion of the Poem, I have formed a groupe of female Writers;
whose productions have been appreciated by the public as works of learning or
genius—though not praised with that extravagance of panegyric, which was once a
customary tribute to the literary compositions of women. In this country, a female
author was formerly esteemed a Phenomenon in Literature: and she was sure of a
favourable reception among the critics, in consideration of her sex. This species of
gallantry, however, conveyed no compliment to her understanding. It implied such
an inferiority of woman in the scale of intellect as was justly humiliating: and critical forbearance was mortifying to female vanity. At the present day, indeed, our literary women are so numerous, that their judges, waving all complimentary civilities,
decide upon their merits with the same rigid impartiality as it seems right to exercise towards the men. The tribunal of criticism is no longer charmed into compla-
cence by the blushes of modest apprehension. It no longer imagines the pleading eye
of feminine diffidence that speaks a consciousness of comparative imbecillity, or a
fearfulness of having offended by intrusion. Experience hath drawn aside the flimsy
veil of affected timidity, that only served to hide the smile of complacency; the glow
of self-gratulation. Yet, alas! The crimsoning blush of modesty, will be always more
attractive, than the sparkle of confident intelligence ... [R.P.'s note]. Like
Wollstonecraft, Anna Letitia Aikin Barbauld (1743–1825) asserted her capacity for
rational thought and boldly entered into the political discourse of her day. After voic-
ing opposition to the slave trade in her "Epistle to Mr. Wilberforce" (1791), Barbauld
launched more far-reaching attacks on British policies in her prose pamphlet *Sins of
Government, Sins of the Nation* (1793) and in her later poem "Eighteen Hundred and
Eleven" (1812). As her posthumously published poem "The Rights of Woman" indicates, however, Barbauld was hardly a disciple of Wollstonecraft.

And ROBINSON[1] to Gaul her Fancy gave,
And trac'd the picture of a Deist's grave!
And charming SMITH[2] resign'd her power to please,
Poetic feeling and poetic ease;
And HELEN, fir'd by Freedom, bade adieu
To all the broken visions of Peru....[3]

[The poem continues with attacks on other women writers and more detailed criticism of Wollstonecraft.]

---

[1] In Mrs. Robinson's Poetry, there is a peculiar delicacy: but her Novels, as literary compositions, have no great claim to approbation—. As containing the doctrines of Philosophism, they merit the severest censure. Would that, for the sake of herself and her beautiful daughter (whose personal charms are only equalled by the elegance of her mind) would, that, for the sake of public morality, Mrs. Robinson were persuaded to dismiss the gloomy phantom of annihilation; to think seriously of a future retribution; and to communicate to the world, a recantation of errors that originated in levity, and have been nursed by pleasure! I have seen her, "glittering like the morning-star, full of life, and splendor and joy!" Such, and more glorious, may I meet her again, when the just "shall shine forth as the brightness of the firmament, and as the stars for ever and ever!" [R.P.'s note]. Polwhele is quoting from Edmund Burke's description of Marie Antoinette in *Reflections on the Revolution in France* and from Daniel 12:3: "And they that be wise shall shine as the brightness of the firmament; and they that turn many to righteousness as the stars for ever and ever."

[2] Like Mary Robinson, Charlotte Turner Smith (1749–1806) embarked upon a writing career after spending time in King's Bench Prison with a profligate husband. Although Smith's first volume, *Elegiac Sonnets and Other Poems* (1784), established her reputation as a poet, she also published ten novels, including *The Young Philosopher* (1798), a novel that Polwhele and others identified with a rampant "Gallic mania."

[3] Miss Helen Williams is, doubtless, a true poet. But is it not extraordinary, that such a genius, a female and so young, should have become a politician—that the fair Helen, whose notes of love have charmed the moonlight vallies, should stand forward, an intemperate advocate for Gallic licentiousness—that such a woman should import with her, a blast more pestilential than that of Avernus, though she has so often delighted us with melodies, soft as the sighs of the Zephyr, delicious as the airs of Paradise? [R.P.'s note]. Polwhele suggests that Williams became a politician when she started publishing her *Letters from France* (see Appendix F). Polwhele's distinction between Williams, the poet, and Williams, the politician, however, effaces the political implications of her earlier work *Peru, A Poem in Six Cantos* (1784).

Appendix D: Priscilla Wakefield, from Reflections on the Present Condition of the Female Sex; With Suggestions for Its Improvement *(1798)*

[Priscilla Bell Wakefield, a well-known philanthropist of Quaker descent, wrote a number of educational books for children as well as *Reflections on the Present Condition of the Female Sex.* The following excerpts, which focus on the plight of genteel women, help to clarify the social and economic realities confronting Robinson and her fictional heroine Martha Morley.]

From Chapter 3: "The necessity of Women being educated for the exercise of lucrative employments shewn, and the absurdity of a Woman honourably earning a support, being excluded from Society, exposed."

....There is scarcely a more helpless object in the wide circle of misery which the vicissitudes of civilized society display, than a woman genteelly educated, whether single or married, who is deprived, by any unfortunate accident, of the protection and support of male relations; unaccustomed to struggle with difficulty, unacquainted with any resource to supply an independent maintenance, she is reduced to the depths of wretchedness, and not unfrequently, if she be young and handsome, is driven by despair to those paths which lead to infamy. Is it not time to find a remedy for such evils, when the contention of nations has produced the most affecting transitions in private life, and transferred the affluent and the noble to the humiliating extremes of want and obscurity? When our streets teem with multitudes of unhappy women, many of whom might have been rescued from their present degradation, or who would perhaps never have fallen into it, had they been instructed in the exercise of some art or profession, which would have enabled them to procure for themselves a respectable support by their own industry.

This reasonable precaution against the accidents of life is resisted by prejudice, which rises like an insurmountable barrier against a woman, of any degree above the vulgar, employing her time and her abilities, towards the maintenance of herself and her family: degradation of rank immediately follows the virtuous attempt, as it did formerly, among the younger branches of the noble families in France. But the nature of truth is immutable, however it may be obscured by error: that which is a moral excellence in one rational being, deserves the same estimation in another; therefore, if it be really honourable in a man, to exert the utmost of his abilities, whether mental or corporal, in the acquisition of a competent support for himself, and for those who have a natural claim upon his protection; it must be equally so in a woman, nay, perhaps still more incumbent, as in many cases, there is nothing so inimical to the preservation of her virtue as a state of poverty, which leaves her dependant upon the generosity of others, to supply those accommodations, which use has rendered necessary to her comfort.

There appears then no moral impediment to prevent women from the application of their talents to purposes of utility; on the contrary, an improvement in public manners must infallibly result from it; as their influence over the other sex is universally acknowledged, it may be boldly asserted, that a conversion of their time from trifling and unproductive employments, to those that are both useful and profitable, would operate as a check upon luxury, dissipation, and prodigality, and retard the progress of that general dissoluteness, the offspring of idleness, which is deprecated by all political writers, as the sure forerunner of national decay....

Chapter 6: "Lucrative Employments for the first and second classes suggested ... With Strictures on a Theatrical Life."

Transitions in private life from affluence to poverty, like the sable pageantry of death, from their frequency, produce no lasting impressions upon the beholders. Unexpected misfortunes befal an acquaintance, who has been caressed in the days of prosperity: the change is lamented, and she is consoled by the visits of her friends, in the first moments of affliction: she sinks gradually into wretchedness; she becomes obscure, and is forgotten. The case would be different, could avocations be suggested, which would enable these, who suffer such a reverse of fortune, to maintain a decent appearance, and procure them a degree of respect. It is far from my present design, to point out all the various pursuits which may consistently engage the talents, or employ the industry of women, whose refinement of manners unfit them for any occupation of a sordid menial kind; such an undertaking would require an extensive acquaintance with the distinct branches of the fine arts, which adorn, and of the numerous manufactures which enrich, this country. But a few remarks upon the nature of those employments, which are best adapted to the higher classes of the sex, when reduced to necessitous circumstances, may, perhaps, afford useful hints to those, who are languishing under the pressure of misfortune, and induce abler pens to treat a subject hitherto greatly neglected.

Numerous difficulties arise in the choice of occupations for the purpose. They must be such as are neither laborious nor servile, and they must of course be productive, without requiring a capital.

For these reasons, pursuits which require the exercise of intellectual, rather than bodily powers, are generally the most eligible.

Literature affords a respectable and pleasing employment, for those who possess talents, and an adequate degree of mental cultivation. For although the emolument is precarious, and seldom equal to a maintenance, yet if the attempt be tolerably successful, it may yield a comfortable assistance in narrow circumstances, and beguile many hours, which might otherwise be passed in solitude or unavailing regret. The fine arts offer a mode of subsistence, congenial to the delicacy of the most refined minds, and they are peculiarly adapted by their elegance, to the gratification of taste. The perfection of every species of painting is attainable by women, from the representation of historic facts, to the minute execution of the miniature portrait, if they will bestow sufficient time and application for the acquisition of the principles of the art, in the study of those models, which have been the means of transmitting the names and character of so many men, to the admiration of posterity. The successful exercise of this imitative art requires invention, taste and judgment: in the two first, the sex are allowed to excel, and the last may be obtained by a perseverance in examining, comparing, and reflecting upon the works of those masters, who have copied nature in her most graceful forms.

Compared with the numbers of the other sex, it does not appear that many females, either in ancient or modern times, have rendered themselves celebrated in this line of excellence; but the cause of this disproportion may surely, with greater probability, be attributed to its having been attempted by so few women, than to incapacity; among the very small number of female artists, who have practised painting as a profession, there have not been wanting some instances of rare merit. But it is to the genial influence of education only, that society must stand indebted for the frequent recurrence of such examples: rare, indeed, is that genius which overcomes all obstacles; too often do the powers of the mind, like the undiscovered diamond in the mine, lie dormant, if they be not called forth by a propitious combination of circumstances. As it is not customary for girls to study the art of painting, with a view to adopt it as a profession, it is impossible to ascertain the extent of their capacity for the pencil; but certainly there appears no natural deficiency, either mental or corporeal, to prevent them from becoming proficients in that art, were the bent of their education favourable to the attempt. It must be allowed, that within the last twenty years, it has been a general fashion for young ladies to learn to draw, and that it is not unusual to see performances executed in such a manner as to excite a reasonable expectation that their powers, if properly cultivated, would produce testimonials of no inferior ability. But as the view of the generality is only elegant amusement, they do not endeavour to attain any degree of excellence, beyond that of copying prints or drawings; original design is too arduous, and it is conceived that the qualifications it requires, would engross too large a portion of time. They neither read those books which treat of the subject in a scientific manner; they do not associate with those persons, whose conversation is adapted to form their taste, nor have they an opportunity of imbibing the enthusiasm, which is produced by the contemplation of the precious models of antiquity. No surprise can therefore be excited, that those fruits are not visible, which are the effects of such necessary preparation.

But as neither exalted genius, nor the means of cultivating that portion of it which nature has bestowed, to the utmost extent, are likely to be very generally possessed; it is fortunate for those who are less liberally endowed, that there are many profitable, though inferior branches of design, or of arts connected with it. The drapery and landscape both of portraits and historical pieces, are often entrusted to the pupils of the master, and constitute a branch of the art, for which women might be allowed to be candidates. The elegant as well as the humorous designs which embellish the windows of print-sellers, &c. also sketches for the frontispieces of books, and other ornaments of the same kind, must employ many artists, nor does it appear that any good reason for consigning them to one sex has been assigned.

Colouring of prints is a lucrative employment; there was a few years ago in London, a French woman, who had a peculiar method of applying water colours to prints, by which she might have gained a very liberal income, had her industry and morals been equal to her ingenuity. Designs for needle-work, and ornamental works of all kinds, are now mostly performed by men, and those who have a good taste, obtain a great deal of money by them; but surely this employment is one, among many, which has been improperly assumed by the other sex, and should be appropriated to women. The delicate touches of miniature painting, and painting in enamel, with devices for rings and lockets in hair-work, are more characteristic of female talents than of masculine powers. The delineation of animals or plants for books of natural history, and colouring of maps or globes may be followed with some advantage. Patterns for calico-printers and paper-stainers are lower departments of the same art, which might surely be allowed as sources of subsistence to one sex with equal propriety as to the other.

Engraving, though it differ from painting in the execution, may be said to have the same origin, both being regulated by similar principles, as far as relates to design and shadow; therefore, if the faculties of women are capable of directing the pencil, there can be no apprehension that they are not also equal to guide the graver with the same success.

Statuary and modelling are arts with which I am too little acquainted to hazard any opinion concerning, but the productions of the honourable Mrs. Damer,[1] and a few others, authorize an assurance, that women have only to apply their talents to them in order to excel. If the resistance of marble and hard substances be too powerful for them to subdue, wax and other materials of a softer nature, will easily yield to their impressions. The necessity of vigour and perseverance in cultivating natural talents, is equally great in attaining perfection of any kind. The same remarks which have been made upon that subject, with respect to painting, are equally applicable to music. Composition affords an ample support to many professors, and depends rather upon a fine taste, and a theoretic knowledge of the powers of harmony, more than upon a deep understanding or philosophical research. The names of celebrated female composers are probably still more rare than those of female

---

[1]   See *A Letter to the Women of England*, p. 84, n. 2, above.

painters; for the scarcity of the latter we have already endeavoured to account, and similar reasons may be assigned for the former.

The stage is a profession, to which many women of refined manners, and a literary turn of mind have had recourse. Since it has been customary for females to assume dramatic characters, there appears to have been full as great a proportion of women, who have attained celebrity, among those who have devoted themselves to a theatrical life, as of the other sex; a fact which argues that there is no inequality of genius, in the sexes, for the imitative arts; the observation may operate as a stimulant to women to those pursuits which are less objectionable than the stage; which is not mentioned for the purpose of recommending it, but of proving that the abilities of the female sex are equal to nobler labours than are usually undertaken by women. The profession of an actress is indeed most unsuitable to the sex in every point of view, whether it be considered with respect to the courage requisite to face an audience, or the variety of situations incident to it, which expose moral virtue to the most severe trials. Let the daughters of a happier destiny, whilst they lament the evils to which some of their sex are exposed, remember those unpropitious circumstances, that have cast them into a line of life, in which it is scarcely possible to preserve that purity of sentiment and conduct, which characterizes female excellence. When their errors are discussed, let the harsh voice of censure be restrained, by the reflection, that she who has made the greatest advances towards perfection, might have fallen, had she been surrounded by the same influences.

That species of agriculture which depends upon skill in the management of the nursery ground, in rearing the various kinds of shrubs and flowers, for the supply of gentlemen's gardens and pleasure grounds, would supply an elegant means of support to those women who are able to raise a capital for carrying on a work of that magnitude. Ornamental gardening, and the laying out of pleasure grounds and parks, with the improvement of natural landscape, one of the refinements of modern times, may likewise afford an eligible maintenance to some of those females, who in the days of their prosperity, displayed their taste in the embellishment of the own domains.

The presiding over seminaries for female education, is likewise a suitable employment for those, whose minds have been enlarged by liberal cultivation, whilst the under parts of that profession may be more suitably filled by persons whose early views have been contracted within narrower limits. After all that can be suggested by general remarks, the different circumstances of individuals must decide the profession most convenient to them. But it is a consolatory reflection, that amidst the daily vicissitudes of human life, from which no rank is exempt, there are resources, from which aid may be drawn, without derogating from the true dignity of a rational being.

Appendix E: Mary Robinson, from

The Progress of Liberty (1801)

[*The Progress of Liberty. A Poem in Two Books* was first published in volume four of Robinson's *Memoirs*. The following excerpt, describing the Reign of Terror, offers an excellent poetic gloss on the revolutionary episodes in *The Natural Daughter*.]

Now Anarchy roam'd wide a monster fierce,
Of sullen Discontent, and Rancour born,
And nurs'd with blood! Breaking the sacred bonds
Of social order, trampling to the dust,
Destructions requisite of worth and laws,
And dealing desolation all around!
Veil'd by its growing wing, the dawning hour,
Which welcom'd LIBERTY, and spread around
A pure effulgence, suddenly grew dark,
And storms impending blacken'd the broad sun.
The highmost hills re-echoed with the shouts
Of yell'd destruction; while the concave vast
Of heav'n shook horrible! ....
.... Liberty,
Thou rational delight! Thou good
Ordain'd to bless mankind, how was thy name
Profan'd by cruelty! How dimly gleam'd
Thy Heav'n-illumin'd orbs, beneath a front
Blood-stain'd and ghastly! How was thy domain
By slaughter desolated, while around,
A dread depopulation swept the path
Which Anarchy had trodden. Where were then
Thy fields prolific, and thy hamlets gay,
Thy mountain revelries, and peaceful glens,
The boast of a brave peasantry? Each hour
Mark'd on the page of Time some guilty deed,
The rav'nous hords wolf-like were gorg'd with blood.
While two arch demons, the fierce phalanx led

Lawless and cruel![1] Daring homicides,
Apostates to their God! How many fell
Beneath the arm, in usurpation strong,
Yet recreant in oppression!
                                   On the plain
The mangled carcase black'ned; rivers bore
Their murder'd victims down the blushing wave
Of blank oblivion. O'er the flinty way
The mutilated limb and streaming heart
Met the full eye of Pity. Beauty's breast,
Polluted by the touch of sensual rage,
Quiver'd beneath the fell assassin's sword;—
While outrag'd Nature stamp'd the hellish deed
On Retribution's tablet. Ev'ry street
Presented the wide scaffold, crimson-stain'd,
And menacing destruction. Palaces
Were now the haunts of ruthless revellers,
Of vices abject, dark conspiracies—
While uncurb'd rapine, and blaspheming rage,
Rov'd with licentious frenzy. Sacred shrines
And temples consecrate, were public marts
Of profligate debasement. Not the wise,
The virtuous, or the brave, THEN held the scale
Of even Justice; Freedom's sons inspir'd,
In vain rear'd high their banners 'mid the scene
Of madd'ning slaughter. For a time their zeal
Was mock'd with barb'rous rage; their great design
By frenzy violated, or constrain'd
By spells infernal. Then, O Liberty!
Thy frantic mien, and Heav'n-imploring eye,
Turn'd from the dreadful throng to trace new paths,
And seek, in distant climes, new scenes of woe.

---

[1] Marat and Robespierre [M.R.'s note].

Appendix F: Helen Maria Williams, from Letters from France (1795–96)

[Publishing eight volumes of *Letters from France* between 1790 and 1796, Helen Maria Williams was one of the most enthusiastic and influential English commentators on the French Revolution. During her extended sojourn in France, Williams developed close ties with many of the moderate Girondin leaders who were executed after the Jacobin party won control of the National Convention, suspended the Constitution, and instituted a number of ruthless policies to squelch opposition. The following excerpts from Williams's *Letters* describe events that provide the historical basis for Robinson's sensational plot in *The Natural Daughter*.]

From Letter V, Volume One: The Deaths of Jean-Paul Marat and Charlotte Corday (July 13 and July 17, 1793)

In the first dawn of the conspiracy Marat became a principal instrument in the hands of the traitors,[1] who found him well fitted for their purposes; and being saved from the punishment which usually follows personal insult by the contempt which the deformity and diminutiveness of his person excited, he became the habitual retailer of all the falsehoods and calumnies which were invented by his party against every man of influence or reputation. He was the Thersites of the convention, whom no one would deign to chastise; for his extravagance made his employers often disclaim him as a fool, while the general sentiment he excited was the sort of antipathy we feel for a loathsome reptile.[2] His political sentiments often varied; for he sometimes exhorted the choice of a chief, and sometimes made declamations in favour of a

---

1 From Williams's perspective, Robespierre and other influential members of the Jacobin party were "traitors" because they forestalled implementation of the Constitution and "boldly proclaimed a new-invented species of tyranny under the denomination of revolutionary government." See *Letters Containing a Sketch of the Politics of France*, 1: 114.

2 Thersites, in *The Iliad*, is a malevolent and misshapen officer in the Greek army. In Shakespeare's *Troilus and Cressida*, he is aptly described as "a slave whose gall coins slanders like a mint" (1. 3. 193).

limited monarchy; but what rendered him useful to the conspirators was his readiness to publish every slander which they framed, and to exhort to every horror which they meditated.—His rage for denunciation was so great that he became the dupe of the idle; and his daily paper contains the names of great criminals who existed only in the imagination of those who imposed on his credulous malignity.[1]

After this first preacher of blood had performed the part allotted to him in the plan of evil, he was confined to his chamber by a lingering disease to which he was subject, and of which he would probably soon have died. But he was assassinated in his bath by a young woman who had travelled with this intention from Caen in Normandy. Charlotte Anne Marie Corday was a native of St. Saturnin in the department of the Orne. She appears to have lived in a state of literary retirement with her father, and by the study of antient and modern historians to have imbibed a strong attachment to liberty. She had been accustomed to assimilate certain periods of antient history with the events that were passing before her, and was probably excited by the examples of antiquity to the commission of a deed, which she believed with fond enthusiasm would deliver and save her country.[2]

Being at Caen when the citizens of the department were enrolling themselves to march to the relief of the convention,[3] the animation with which she saw them devoting their lives to their country, led her to execute, without delay, the project she had formed. Under pretence of going home, she came to Paris, and the third day after her arrival obtained admission to Marat. She had invented a story to deceive him; and when he promised her that all the promoters of the insurrection in the departments should be sent to the guillotine, she drew out a knife which she had purchased for the occasion, and plunged it into his breast.

She was immediately apprehended, and conducted to the Abbaye prison, from which she was transferred to the Conciergerie, and brought before the revolutionary tribunal.

---

[1]   Marat's newspaper, *L'Ami du Peuple*, was an extremely influential organ of Jacobin propaganda.

[2]   Corday's initial plan to stab Marat on the floor of the National Convention had a particularly telling precedent in Marcus Brutus's plot to assassinate Julius Caesar. The story was included in Plutarch's *Lives*, one of Corday's favorite books.

[3]   After the Jacobins took control of the National Convention in June of 1793, a small group of the ousted Girondins escaped from Paris and went to Caen, where they recruited volunteers to mount a reprisal.

She acknowledged the deed, and justified it by asserting that it was a duty she owed her country and mankind to rid the world of a monster whose sanguinary doctrines were framed to involve the country in anarchy and civil war, and asserted her right to put Marat to death as a convict already condemned by the public opinion. She trusted that her example would inspire the people with that energy which had been at all times the distinguished characteristic of republicans; and which she defined to be that devotedness to our country which renders life of little comparative estimation.

Her deportment during the trial was modest and dignified. There was so engaging a softness in her countenance, that it was difficult to conceive how she could have armed herself with sufficient intrepidity to execute the deed. Her answers to the interrogatories of the court were full of point and energy. She sometimes surprised the audience by her wit, and excited their admiration by her eloquence. Her face sometimes beamed with sublimity, and was sometimes covered with smiles....

[I]t is difficult to conceive the kind of heroism which she displayed in the way to execution. The women who were called furies of the guillotine, and who had assembled to insult her on leaving the prison, were awed into silence by her demeanour, while some of the spectators uncovered their heads before her, and others gave loud tokens of applause. There was such an air of chastened exultation thrown over her countenance, that she inspired sentiments of love rather than sensations of pity. She ascended the scaffold with undaunted firmness, and, knowing that she had only to die, was resolved to die with dignity. She had learned from her jailor the mode of punishment, but she was not instructed in the detail; and when the executioner attempted to tie her feet to the plank, she resisted, from an apprehension that he had been ordered to insult her; but on his explaining himself she submitted with a smile. When he took off her handkerchief,[1] the moment before she bent under the fatal stroke, she blushed deeply; and her head, which was held up to the multitude the moment after, exhibited the last impression of offended modesty.

---

[1] A scarf that crossed over the low-cut front bodice of a dress.

From Letter I, Volume One: The Arrest and Imprisonment of Foreigners in Paris (August, 1793)

Not long after the reign of Robespierre began, all passports to leave the country were refused, and the arrestation of the English residing in France was decreed by the national convention; but the very next day the decree was repealed on the representations of some French merchants, who shewed its impolicy. We therefore concluded that we had no such measures to fear in future; and we heard from what we believed to be good authority, that if any decree passed with respect to the English, it would be that of their being ordered to leave the republic. The political clouds in the mean time gathered thick around the hemisphere: we heard rumours of severity and terror, which seemed like those hollow noises that roll in the dark gulph of the volcano, and portend its dangerous eruptions: but no one could calculate how far the threatened mischief would extend, and how wide a waste of ruin would desolate the land. Already considerable numbers were imprisoned as suspected— *suspected!* that indefinite word, which was tortured into every meaning of injustice and oppression, and became what the French call the *mot de ralliement*, the initiative term of captivity and death.[1]

One evening [October 11, 1793] when Bernardin St. Pierre, the author of the charming little novel of Paul and Virginia, was drinking tea with me, ... I was suddenly called away ... by the appearance of a friend, who rushed into the room, and with great agitation told us that a decree had just passed in the national convention, ordering all the English in France to be put into arrestation in the space of four-and-twenty hours, and their property to be confiscated. We passed the night without sleep, and the following day in anxiety and perturbation not to be described, expecting every moment the commissaries of the revolutionary committee and their guards, to put in force the mandates of the convention. As the day advanced, our terror increased: in the evening we received information that most of our English acquaintances were conducted to prison. At length night came; and no commissaries appearing, we began to flatter ourselves that, being a family of women, it was intended that we should be

---

[1] The infamous Law of Suspects was passed by the National Convention on September 17, 1793.

spared; for the time was only now arrived when neither sex nor age gave any claim to compassion. Overcome with fatigue and emotion, we went to bed with some faint hopes of exemption from the general calamity of our countrymen. These hopes were however but of short duration. At two in the morning we were awakened by a loud knocking at the gate of the hotel, which we well knew to be the fatal signal of our approaching captivity; and a few minutes after, the bell of our apartments was rung with violence. My sister and myself hurried on our clothes and went with trembling steps to the anti-chamber, when we found two commissaries of the revolutionary committee of our section, accompanied by a guard, two of whom were placed at the outer door with their swords drawn, while the rest entered the room. One of these constituted authorities held a paper in his hand, which was a copy of the decree of the convention, and which he offered to read to us; but we declined hearing it, and told him we were ready to obey the law. Seeing us pale and trembling, he and his colleague endeavoured to comfort us; they begged us to compose ourselves; they repeated that our arrestation was only part of a general political measure, and that innocence had nothing to fear.—Alas! innocence was no longer any plea for safety.

From Letter VII, Volume Three: The Release of Prisoners after the Execution of Robespierre

Soon after the execution of Robespierre [July 28, 1794], the committee of general safety appointed a deputation of its members to visit the prisons, and speak the words of comfort to the prisoners; to hear from their own lips the motives of their captivity, and to change the bloody rolls of proscription into registers of promised freedom. In the mean time orders for liberty arrived in glad succession; and the prisons of Paris, so lately the abodes of hopeless misery, now exhibited scenes which an angel of mercy might have contemplated with pleasure.

The first persons released from the Luxembourg were mons. and madame Bitauby, two days after the fall of Robespierre. When they departed, the prisoners, to the amount of nine hundred persons, formed a lane to see them pass; they embraced them, they bathed them with tears, they overwhelmed them with benedictions, they hailed with transport the moment which gave themselves the earnest of returning freedom: but the soul has emotions for which the lips have no utterance, and the feelings of such moments may be imagined, but cannot be defined.

Crowds of people were constantly assembled at the gates of the prisons, to enjoy the luxury of seeing the prisoners snatched from their living tombs, and restored to freedom: that very people, who had beheld in stupid silence the daily work of death, now melted in tears over the sufferers, and filled the air with acclamations at their release....

Upon the fall of Robespierre, the terrible spell which bound the land of France was broken; the shrieking whirlwinds, the black precipices, the bottomless gulphs, suddenly vanished; and reviving nature covered the wastes with flowers, and the rocks with verdure.

All the fountains of public prosperity and public happiness were indeed poisoned by that malignant genius, and therefore the streams have since occasionally run bitter; but the waters are regaining their purity, are returning to their natural channels, and are no longer disturbed and sullied in their course.

Appendix G: Contemporary Reviews of
A Letter to the Women of England

[For the most part, reviews of Robinson's *Letter to the Women of England* say less about the work itself than the anxieties of her conservative male contemporaries. With the exception of the favorable notice in *The New Annual Register*, the following reviews put up a united front against a woman writer who encroaches upon the traditionally masculine fields of political and philosophical discourse. Not surprisingly, the most extreme response comes from the *Anti-Jacobin* critic who not only demonizes the "legion of Wollstonecrafts" but also assumes the role of exorcist "to cast them out."]

1. From *The Anti-Jacobin Review and Magazine* 3 (1799): 144–45.

[The review opens with quotations from Robinson's *Letter*.]

...Whilst we thank our fair letter-writer for "assertions incontrovertible," expressed in "the most undecorated language," we cannot but congratulate her countrywomen who are ambitious of being entitled philosophers, on her discovery of a new mode of acquiring so honourable a distinction.—Among other novelties in this epistle, is the attempt to prove "the barbarity of custom's law, in restraining to man the privilege of vindicating his honor in a duel." [The reviewer summarizes the story of the woman who shot her lover in a duel.]

"An ignominious death," or "confinement for life as a maniac" which, "in Britain would probably" be the recompence of so heroic an action, seems scarcely to repress the ardour of our fair authoress, in recommending the example before us to the imitation of the British females.

The character of Miss Anne Frances Randall, as well as her epistolary production, (both argumentative and historical,) is, by this time, we presume, sufficiently developed to our readers. Lest, however, they shall still consider her as coming in "a questionable shape," and hesitate in determining, whether she bring with her, "Airs from Heaven, or blasts from Hell," we shall call upon the lady to produce her credentials, which will remove all doubts upon the subject.[1] "The writer of this letter," says she, "though avowedly of the school of Wollstonecraft, disdains the drudgery of servile imitation. The same subject may be argued in a variety of ways; and, though this letter *may* not display the philosophical reasoning with which 'the Rights of Women' abounded, it is not less suited to the purpose. For it requires 'A LEGION OF WOLLSTONECRAFTS to *undermine the poisons* of prejudice and malevolence.'"

Miss Anne Frances Randall, then, belongs to the "legion of Wollstonecrafts," whose office is to "undermine poison." Though we are not "profound scholars"[2] enough to comprehend the art of "undermining a poison," either literal or metaphorical, yet we know what it is to diffuse the poison of corruption through the mass of society. This, we conceive, is the peculiar office of "the *legion* of Wollstonecrafts." It is *our* province, and our duty, to meet this legion; ("*for they are many!*") and, since "*no man can bind them, no, not, with chains,*" to endeavour to "cast them out!"[3]

2. From *The British Critic* 14 (1799): 682.

This is a lively Essay, by a hopeful pupil of the school of Mrs. Wollstonecraft. It displays a very credible share of reading, and a much larger share of spirit; but it is so desultory, that to give an analysis of it, if it were worth while, would be impracticable. We agree with Mrs. Randall, in wishing that greater care were taken to furnish the minds of our fair country-women with solid and useful knowledge, than with superficial and trifling accomplishments; but even in that case, whether their "interference in theological and political opinions" would conduce much to the speedy adjustment of them, we must be so ungallant as to question. At any rate, we cannot admit, that "the evils of bigotry and religious imposition" arose from the want of that

---

[1]   Cf. Hamlet's address to the ghost of his father: "Be thou a spirit of health, or goblin damn'd / Bring with thee airs from heaven, or blasts from hell, / Be thy intents wicked, or charitable, / Thou com'st in such a questionable shape / That I will speak to thee" (1. 4. 40–44).

[2]   The phrase comes from Robinson's postscript, quoted in a footnote.

[3]   Cf. Mark 5:1–3: In Mark's narrative, Jesus encounters "a man with an unclean spirit, Who had his dwelling among the tombs; and no man could bind him, no, not with chains." After commanding the spirit to leave the man, Jesus asks, "What is thy name?" and the spirit replies, "My name is Legion: for we are many."

interference. P. 57. In a note, at p. 2. We are threatened with a *legion of Wollstonecrafts,* "to *undermine* the *poisons* of prejudice and malevolence." Probably such a body would prefer storming to mining.

3. From *The Gentleman's Magazine* 69 (1799): 311.

In the general confusion of ideas, religious, moral, and political, we are not surprized to find claims set up for the female sex, unsupported we must not say by *prescription*, but we are justified in saying by *reason*. Mrs. R. avows herself of the school of Wolstencroft [sic]; and that is enough for all who have any regard to decency, order, or prudence, to avoid her company. She has travelled for her improvement; and what are the blessed fruits of her travels? Let the motley list of heroines subjoined to this letter, and the anecdotes of female characters of all descriptions, interspersed in it, speak for themselves.

4. From *The New Annual Register* (1799) 3: 275.

"The Letter to the Women of England, on the Injustice of mental Subordination, with Anecdotes, by Anne Frances Randall," is a lively and spirited piece of declamation, in support of the rights of woman, as laid down in the code of Mrs. Wollstonecraft. Her list of distinguished female writers certainly reflects much honour on the sex, and affords convincing proof of the considerable extent to which their powers can be carried, when proper care has been taken to instruct them in solid and useful knowledge, instead of superficial and trifling accomplishments. How far it contributes to the decision of the question respecting the equality of the sexes, we leave her readers to determine.

Appendix H: Contemporary Reviews of The Natural Daughter

[William S. Ward's *Literary Reviews in British Periodicals, 1798–1820* (1972) lists six reviews of *The Natural Daughter*, all of which are reproduced in part or in their entirety below. As the disparity between the articles in the liberal *Monthly Review* and the staunchly conservative *British Critic* suggests, the reviews were not entirely disinterested aesthetic judgments. More often than not, genre expectations were inextricably bound up with gender expectations. One might, in fact, construe the reiterated praise for Robinson's poetry as a coercive gesture, reinscribing a feminine ideal of beautiful, but largely ineffectual, expressiveness.[1]]

1. From *The British Critic* 16 (1800): 320–21.

It is frequently the task of the modern critic to labour through volumes, of which the best report that can be made is, that they contain no harm, and may be read with no other ill consequence than a waste of time. But even this "sad civility" must be refused "The Natural Daughter." The heroine, a decidedly flippant female, apparently of the Wollstonecraft school, is the daughter of a rich citizen, who, during a visit to Bath, attracts a gentleman of the name of Morley, and becomes his wife. Soon after this marriage, Morley has occasion to quit his home; and Mrs. Morley, in his absence, adopts an infant, whom chance has thrown in her way, and from this adoption the whole embarrassment of the story arises. Many circumstances contribute to excite a suspicion that this child is her own; instead of explaining them, she departs with the supposed father of the child, and after a variety of adventures becomes a widow, and is united to the object of her attachment. This is all in the usual course of novel reading; but it is the tendency of these volumes which we

---

[1]   Richard Polwhele makes such gestures throughout *The Unsex'd Females* as he praises the lyric strains of Robinson, Charlotte Smith, Helen Maria Williams, and other women writers. For a pertinent discussion of the gender issues underlying critical distinctions between lyric and narrative genres, see Mary A. Fevret, "Telling Tales About Genre: Poetry in the Romantic Novel," *Studies in the Novel* 26 (1994): 153–72.

find ourselves obliged to disapprove. A heroine, whose "impenetrable safeguard" is pride; who is said to be "invulnerable" from pride only; who quits her home with a man of gallantry, lives at a lodging, and receives his visits; who, under circumstances of great pecuniary distress, goes to a masquerade with a libertine avowedly endeavouring to seduce her; and, after she has given her hand to one man, her heart to another, debates seriously whether she shall bestow her person on a third; ought not, in our opinion, to be held up as one "who had never in the smallest instance violated the proprieties of wedded life; who had never been guilty of any action that might, even by the most fastidious, be deemed derogatory to the delicacy of the female character, or the honour of her husband."

Through the whole work, during all the vicissitudes of its heroine, we meet with no sentiment of religion, nor any moral derived from it; and the character of Morley appears to have been conceived purposely to show that an attention to religious duties, a regard for the subordinations of society, and a regular and decent conduct, are to be considered only as a mask for consummate vice. In a novel of this description, we are not sorry to find the style without those attractions which may give it currency. It is inflated, and abounding in phrases which might be called the technicals of literary discontent: "the petrifying hand of avaritious pride—" "pre-judging world"—"unfeeling world"— "unpitying world"—"ill-judging, illiberal world" with divers other words of like qualifications. Then the inhabitants of these worlds are as unmercifully epitheted as the worlds themselves: "vulgar minds"— "unenlightened minds"—"bosoms unenlightened by the finely organized hand of Nature"—"recreant ignorance"—"vulgar arrogance of less ennobled beings"—"aristocracy of wealth," &c. &c. &c. It is needless to add to such examples; we will only observe, that the appellation of "daring" cannot be applied to Robespierre; and that, it is of little use to lament or censure the French revolution, if the morals and manners which tended to produce it, are inculcated and held up for imitation.

2. From *The Critical Review* 28 (1800): 477.

From a perusal of the first pages of this novel we were led to expect a production superior to the general trash of the circulating library: we have, however, been completely disappointed; nor can the interspersion of a few pieces of elegant poetry, in these two volumes, protect them from the unqualified censure which the absurd improbability of the incidents related in them, and the plotless insipidity of the story demand. The characters of Martha and Mrs. Morley, on their introduction to the notice of the reader, give promise of interesting, if not of original delineation; but the promise is not fulfilled; and we are sorry to remark, that, in the present instance, Mrs. Robinson has produced a novel which is not likely to obtain a high rank even among the common-place effusions that periodically regale the not very fastidious appetites of subscription readers.

3. From *The European Magazine* 37 (1800): 138–39.

Can such things be
Without our special wonder![1]

Indeed, fair Lady, they cannot! and sorry we are to find a genius, capable of soaring to the sublimest subjects in Poetry, and whose former productions, even in the Novel line, communicated innocent amusement and salutary instruction to youthful readers of both sexes, descend to the adoption of that vitiated taste for the marvellous and improbable, which are unfortunately revived in this country by the author of The Monk and The Castle Spectre.[2] In the present performance, every characteristic of a moral Novel is wanting. The title is a misprision of treason against common sense; for every page of the work demonstrates that it ought to have been The *Unnatural* Wife, Daughter, and Sister; and as to the natural daughter, she is only an infant fly in the cobweb texture of the wonderful and woeful story; of which the following is the outline:....

We regret that the author will not confine her labours to poetry, in which she superiorly excels, and has given fresh proofs of in this Novel, where the reader will find an ode to Pity, on the death of a soldier slain in battle; another on the flower called the Blue Bell; and two more on different subjects. We must likewise inform the curious, that memoirs of herself, in some trying situations, are introduced into these volumes, under the fictitious character of Mrs. Sedgley.

---

[1] The reviewer is quoting the epigraph on Robinson's title page, taken from Shakespeare's *Macbeth*, 3. 4. 109–11. Macbeth poses the question after seeing the ghost of Banquo.

[2] The gothic novel *Ambrosio, or The Monk* (1796) and the play *The Castle Spectre* (1798) were enormously popular works by Matthew Gregory Lewis, or "Monk" Lewis, as he was often called.

4. From *The Monthly Magazine* 9 (1800): 640.

"The Natural Daughter, with portraits of the Leadenhead Family," by Mrs. Robinson, we cannot speak of in terms of high commendation; it is interspersed, however, with some pieces of truly elegant poetry.

5. From *The Monthly Review* 32 (1800): 93–94.

Fancy has been little restrained in the composition of this novel, and the satirical talent of the writer has not lain dormant. The story may be said to possess more of entertainment than of probability; a predominance which will more readily find favour with the generality of readers, (and, critics as we are, we cannot in conscience much blame their tastes,) than if it had been reversed. *Marat* and *Robespierre* are made to appear; and in affairs, we were going to say, of gallantry,— so unrestrained is the acceptation of the word! The Leadenhead family we did not deem the most diverting part of the company introduced. Sir Lionel Beacon afforded us more amusement.

    Mrs. R. has occasionally interspersed small pieces of poetry; which have feeling and imagination, and form by no means the least commendable part of the work.... We give the following stanza from the description of a poor soldier:

[The review prints the last stanza of the poem on pp. 103-04, above.]

6. From *The New London Review* 2 (1799): 285–86.

This novel has less of the sombre cast than some of Mrs. R.'s former productions. The characters are numerous and well sustained; the incidents for the most part natural, and always either diverting or interesting. The Bradford family is skilfully pourtrayed; and the adventures of Martha, under her wedded name of Morley, lay strong hold on the reader's mind; though we cannot help sometimes thinking that the situations into which she is thrown are rather too frequently varied to satisfy the mind of their natural occurrence or probability. When incidents are too much sought after and crowded, they occupy room that would be more satisfactorily employed (at least in the opinions of readers whose applause could be gratifying to such a mind as Mrs. Robinson's) in the delineation of character and manners. We make this remark the more freely because we think the sketching of mental portraits is our fair author's forte; and we wish her, considering that as an honourable pre-eminence, to leave the meaner task of multiplying incidents to those who have no other talents.

Select Bibliography

Primary Sources

Ballard, George. *Memoirs of Several Ladies of Great Britain: Who Have Been Celebrated for Their Writings or Skill in the Learned Languages, Arts and Sciences.* 1752. Ed. Ruth Perry. Detroit: Wayne State UP, 1985.

Duncombe, John. *The Feminad, A Poem.* 1754. Introd. Jocelyn Harris. Los Angeles: William Andrews Clark Memorial Library, U of California, 1981.

Edgeworth, Maria. *Letters for Literary Ladies.* 1795. Introd. Gina Luria. New York: Garland, 1974.

Godwin, William. *Memoirs of the Author of A Vindication of the Rights of Woman.* 1798. Eds. Pamela Clemit and Gina Luria Walker. Peterborough: Broadview, 2001.

Hays, Mary. *Appeal to the Men of Great Britain in Behalf of Women.* London: J. Johnson, 1798.

Macaulay, Catharine. *Letters on Education.* 1790. New York: Woodstock Books, 1994.

Montagu, Mary Wortley. *The Complete Letters of Lady Mary Wortley Montagu.* 3 vols. Ed. Robert Halsband. Oxford: Clarendon, 1965–67.

Radcliffe, Mary Anne. *The Female Advocate; Or an Attempt to Recover the Rights of Woman from Male Usurpation.* London: Vernor and Hood, 1799.

Robinson, Mary. *The Memoirs of the Late Mrs. Robinson, Written by Herself. With Some Posthumous Pieces.* 4 vols. London: R. Phillips, 1801.

Scott, Mary. *The Female Advocate: A Poem Occasioned by Reading Mr. Duncombe's Feminead.* 1774. Introd. Gae Holladay. Los Angeles: William Andrews Clark Memorial Library, U of California, 1984.

"Sophia." *Woman Not Inferior to Man: Or, a Short and Modest Vindication of the Natural Right of the Fair-Sex to a Perfect Equality of Power, Dignity, and Esteem, with the Men.* London: John Hawkins, 1739.

Wakefield, Priscilla. *Reflections on the Present Condition of the Female Sex.* 1798. Introd. Gina Luria. New York: Garland, 1974.

Williams, Helen Maria. *Letters from France.* 5th ed. 2 vols. Introd. Janet M. Todd. Delmar, NY: Scholar's Facsimiles and Reprints, 1975.

Wollstonecraft, Mary. *The Works of Mary Wollstonecraft.* 7 vols. Eds. Janet M. Todd and Marilyn Butler. Washington Square, NY: New York UP, 1989.

Secondary Sources

Adams, M. Ray. *Studies in the Literary Backgrounds of English Radicalism.* London: Franklin and Marshall, 1947.

Arnold, Ellen. "Genre, Gender, and Cross-Dressing in Mary Robinson's *Walsingham*." *Postscript* 16 (1999): 57–68.

Bass, Robert D. *The Green Dragoon: The Lives of Banastre Tarleton and Mary Robinson.* 1957. Columbia, SC: Sandlapper, 1973.

Black, Jeremy. *The British Abroad: The Grand Tour in the Eighteenth Century.* New York: St. Martin's, 1992.

Bolton, Betsy. "Romancing the Stone: 'Perdita' Robinson in Wordsworth's London." *ELH* 64 (1997): 727–59.

Brown, Alice. *The Eighteenth-Century Feminist Mind.* Detroit: Wayne State UP, 1987.

Craciun, Adriana. "The New Cordays: Helen Craik and British Representations of Charlotte Corday, 1793–1800." *Rebellious Hearts: British Women Writers and the French Revolution.* Eds. Adriana Craciun and Kari E. Lokke. Albany: State U of New York P, 2001. 193–232.

———. "Violence Against Difference: Mary Wollstonecraft and Mary Robinson." *Bucknell Review* 42 (1998): 111–41.

Cullens, Chris. "Mrs. Robinson and the Masquerade of Womanliness." *Body and Text in the Eighteenth Century.* Eds. Veronica Kelly and Dorothea von Mücke. Stanford: Stanford UP, 1994. 266–89.

Curran, Stuart. "Mary Robinson's *Lyrical Tales* in Context." *Re-Visioning Romanticism: British Women Writers, 1776–1837.* Eds. Carol Shiner Wilson and Joel Haefner. Philadelphia: U of Pennsylvania P, 1994. 17–35.

Daly, Mary. *Gyn/Ecology: The Metaethics of Radical Feminism.* Boston: Beacon, 1978.

Dolan, Brian. *Ladies of the Grand Tour: British Women in Pursuit of Enlightenment and Adventure in Eighteenth-Century Europe.* London: HarperCollins, 2001.

Favret, Mary. "Telling Tales About Genre: Poetry in the Romantic Novel." *Studies in the Novel* 26 (1994): 153–72.

Fergus, Jan and Janice Farrar Thaddeus. "Women, Publishers, and Money, 1790–1820." *Studies in Eighteenth-Century Culture* 17 (1987): 191–207.

Ferguson, Moira. *Subject to Others: British Women Writers and Colonial Slavery, 1670–1834.* New York: Routledge, 1992.

Ford, Susan Allen. "'A Name More Dear': Daughters, Fathers, and Desire in *A Simple Story*, *The False Friend*, and *Mathilda*." *Re-Visioning Romanticism: British Women Writers, 1776–1837.* Eds. Carol

Shiner Wilson and Joel Haefner. Philadelphia: U of Pennsylvania P, 1994. 51–71.

Foreman, Amanda. *Georgiana, Duchess of Devonshire*. New York: Random House, 1998.

Hembry, Phyllis. *The English Spa, 1560–1815: A Social History*. London: Athlone, 1990.

Highfill, Philip H. et al. *A Biographical Dictionary of Actors, Actresses, Musicians, Dancers, Managers and Other Stage Personnel in London, 1660–1800*. 16 vols. Carbondale: Southern Illinois UP, 1973–93.

Hunt, Lynn. *The Family Romance of the French Revolution*. Berkeley: U of California P, 1992.

Ingamells, John. *Mrs. Robinson and Her Portraits*. London: Trustees of the Wallace Collection, 1978.

Jensen, Katharine. *Writing Love: Letters, Women, and the Novel in France, 1605–1776*. Carbondale: Southern Illinois UP, 1995.

Jones, Vivien. "Women Writing Revolution: Narratives of History and Sexuality in Wollstonecraft and Williams." *Beyond Romanticism: New Approaches to Texts and Contexts, 1780–1832*. Eds. Stephen Copley and John Whale. London: Routledge, 1992. 178–99.

——, ed. *Women in the Eighteenth Century: Constructions of Femininity*. London and New York: Routledge, 1990.

Kelly Gary. *English Fiction of the Romantic Period, 1789–1830*. London and New York: Longman, 1989.

——. *Women, Writing, and Revolution, 1790–1827*. Oxford: Clarendon, 1993.

Kennedy, Deborah. "Benevolent Historian: Helen Maria Williams and Her British Readers." *Rebellious Hearts: British Women Writers and the French Revolution*. Eds. Adriana Craciun and Kari E. Lokke. Albany: State U of New York P, 2001. 317–36.

Labbe, Jacqueline M. "Selling One's Sorrows: Charlotte Smith, Mary Robinson, and the Marketing of Poetry." *Wordsworth Circle* 25 (1994): 68–71.

Ledbetter, Kathryn. "A Woman of Undoubted Genius: Mary Robinson and S.T. Coleridge." *Postscript* 11 (1994): 43–49.

Lee, Debbie. "*The Wild Wreath*: Cultivating a Poetic Circle for Mary Robinson." *Studies in the Literary Imagination* 30 (1997): 23–34.

Levy, Martin J. "Coleridge, Mary Robinson and *Kubla Khan*." *Charles Lamb Bulletin* 77 (1992): 156–66.

——, ed. *Perdita: The Memoirs of Mrs. Robinson*. London: Peter Owen, 1994.

Luther, Susan. "A Stranger Minstrel: Coleridge's Mrs. Robinson." *Studies in Romanticism* 33 (1994): 391–409.

Maclean, Marie. *The Name of the Mother: Writing Illegitimacy*. London: Routledge, 1994.

McGann, Jerome J. *The Poetics of Sensibility: A Revolution in Literary Style*. Oxford: Clarendon, 1996.

Mellor, Anne K. "British Romanticism, Gender, and Three Women Artists." *The Consumption of Culture, 1600–1800: Image, Object, Text*. Eds. Ann Bermingham and John Brewer. New York: Routledge, 1995. 121–42.

———. "English Women Writers and the French Revolution." *Rebel Daughters: Women and the French Revolution*. Eds. Sara Melzer and Leslie Rabine. Oxford: Oxford UP, 1992. 255–72.

———. "Making an Exhibition of Her Self: Mary 'Perdita' Robinson and the Nineteenth-Century Scripts of Female Sexuality." *Nineteenth-Century Contexts* 22 (2000): 271–304.

Miskolcze, Robin L. "Snapshots of Contradiction in Mary Robinson's *Poetical Works*." *Papers on Language and Literature* 31 (1995): 206–19.

Pascoe, Judith. "Mary Robinson and the Literary Marketplace." *Romantic Women Writers: Voices and Countervoices*. Eds. Paula R. Feldman and Theresa M. Kelley. Hanover, NH: UP of New England, 1995. 252–68.

———. *Romantic Theatricality: Gender, Poetry, and Spectatorship*. Ithaca: Cornell UP, 1997.

———. "The Spectacular Flaneuse: Mary Robinson and the City of London." *The Wordsworth Circle* 23 (1992): 165–71.

———, ed. *Mary Robinson: Selected Poems*. Peterborough: Broadview, 2000.

Perry, Gill. "'The British Sappho': Borrowed Identities and the Representation of Women Artists in Late Eighteenth-Century British Art." *Oxford Art Journal* 18 (1995): 44–57.

Peterson, Linda H. "Becoming an Author: Mary Robinson's *Memoirs* and the Origins of the Woman Artist's Autobiography." *Re-Visioning Romanticism: British Women Writers, 1776–1837*. Eds. Carol Shiner Wilson and Joel Haefner. Philadelphia: U of Pennsylvania P, 1994. 36–50.

Richards, Sandra. *The Rise of the English Actress*. New York: St. Martin's, 1993.

Robinson, Daniel. "From 'Mingled Measure' to 'Ecstatic Measures': Mary Robinson's Poetic Reading of 'Kubla Khan.'" *The Wordsworth Circle* 26 (1995): 4–7.

———. "Reviving the Sonnet: Women Romantic Poets and the Sonnet Claim." *European Romantic Review* 6 (1995): 98–127.

Rogers, Katharine M. *Feminism in Eighteenth-Century England*. Urbana: U of Illinois P, 1982.

Saglia, Diego. "The Dangers of Over-Refinement: The Language of Luxury in Romantic Poetry by Women." *Studies in Romanticism* 38 (1999): 641–72.

Setzer, Sharon M. "The Dying Game: Crossdressing in Mary Robinson's *Walsingham*." *Nineteenth-Century Contexts* 22 (2000): 305–28.

———. "Mary Robinson's Sylphid Self: The End of Feminine Self-Fashioning." *Philological Quarterly* 75 (1996): 501–20.

———. "Romancing the Reign of Terror: Sexual Politics in Mary Robinson's *Natural Daughter*." *Criticism* (1997): 531–55.

Shaffer, Julie. "Cross-Dressing and the Nature of Gender in Mary Robinson's *Walsingham*." *Presenting Gender: Changing Sex in Early-Modern Europe*. Ed. Chris Mounsey. Lewisburg, PA: Bucknell UP, 2001. 136–67.

———. "Illegitimate Female Sexualities in Romantic-Era Women-Penned Novels in Corvey." *Corvey Journal* 5 (1993): 44–52.

Todd, Janet. *Sensibility: An Introduction*. London: Methuen, 1986.

———. *The Sign of Angellica: Women, Writing, and Fiction, 1660–1800*. New York: Columbia UP, 1989,

Turner, Cheryl. *Living by the Pen: Women Writers in the Eighteenth Century*. London and New York: Routledge, 1992.

Ty, Eleanor. *Empowering the Feminine: The Narratives of Mary Robinson, Jane West, and Amelia Opie, 1796–1812*. Toronto: U of Toronto P, 1998.

———. "Engendering a Female Subject: Mary Robinson's (Re)Presentations of the Self." *English Studies in Canada* 21 (1995): 407–31.

Vargo, Lisa. The Claims of 'Real life and Manners': Coleridge and Mary Robinson." *Wordsworth Circle* 26 (1995): 134–37.